The Mad Patagonian

Part One
An Echo of Paradise

Javier Pedro Zabala

Translated from The Spanish
and with an Introduction

by

Tomás García Guerrero

Peter Damian Bellis
Editor, English language edition

River Boat Books
St. Paul, MN

The Mad Patagonian: Part One: An Echo of Paradise
Original "First Edition" Copyright © 2015 under the pseudonyms Javier Pedro Zabala and Tomás García Guerrero. "Second Edition" Copyright © 2021 Peter Damian Bellis

All rights reserved.

Printed in the United States of America.

Published by River Boat Books. St. Paul, MN.
First edition of *The Mad Patagonian* - published in a single volume printed on June 26, 2018.

Second Edition of *The Mad Patagonian* published in three volumes. First printing of second edition August 18, 2021.

Volume One:
Part One: An Echo of Paradise
ISBN: 978-1-955823-00-5

Cover Illustration: Adaptation of "The Fair" by Maruja Mallo, 1927. Used under the "Fair Use" provision of aplicable copyright law.

All of the photographs used in "The Translator's Introductory Remarks" are in the Pubic Domain.

Javier Pedro Zabala's *The Mad Patagonian* is a literary supernova. From absolute silence, both the author and his 1,200-page book appeared suddenly and completely. Fans of William T. Vollmann, Roberto Bolaño, Julio Cortázar, and Alain Robbe-Grillet will find it a novel take on recognizable topics and themes. The cumulative effect of this polyphonic novel is akin to a kaleidoscope, each fragmented and embedded narrative falling over each other in an ever-expanding and ever-evolving narrative.
5 Stars
– Jacob Singer, Book Review Editor, *Entropy*

The Mad Patagonian was for me like capturing lightning in a bottle. It is a book that I'd want on whatever desert island I would be shipwrecked on, and to my mind easily comparable in range, multi-dimensionality and execution to my two favorite epics of Latin American fiction — Bolaño's *2666* and Mario Vargas Llosa's *Conversation in the Cathedral*. IMO it is a flat-out masterpiece and I would encourage anyone at all interested in reading great literature to go out and get him/herself a copy.
5 Stars
– Larry Riley, Early Reviewers, *Library Thing*

The Mad Patagonian is borderless unlike Vargas Llosa's masterpiece, *Conversations in the Cathedral*, which is self-contained; and at the same time it is more contained than Bolaño's false epic, *2666*. In this respect it is similar to Cervantes' *Don Quixote*, and also Gabriel García Márquez' *One Hundred Years of Solitude*. One could also say that in his use of language, Zabala also seems a worthy heir to James Joyce, writing each passage according to the dictates of the content.

Of course one other Spanish language comparison is to Borges, for the book's wealth of intricate, labyrinthine arcania—it is brimming with such...to the point that the reader no longer cares in the least what is true and what is not. We do know that there were Merovingian Kings, but was Diego Penalosa governor of Cuba in 1746? There are dozens of such details, all of which are available in the sweep of the language, none of which require a pause—though during my second read, which may not occur this year, I intend to do a great deal more digging, as the book is an extremely learned text that wears its genius lightly.

5 Stars

– Rick Harsch, author of *The Driftless Trilogy*

It's probably fair to say that Javier Pedro Zabala is the greatest Latin American writer you've never heard of, and his magnum opus *The Mad Patagonian* is the greatest novel in Spanish of the 21st century that you've never read. Zabala is acutely aware of the limitations of language, as aware as no other writer of his generation, except perhaps David Foster Wallace. He knows that language describes what is not as much as it describes what is: gun delineates a specific object as much as it rules out the possibility that the object is not something else, like nun or gum. Zabala knows that when a writer writes something as apparently innocuous as a description of the night, he is also drawing a line through other possibilities: *Outside the moon has set.* can also just as well refuse to be: *Outside the moon is glowing in the night sky.* or even *Outside it is twilight and the birds have stopped calling to each other.* Zabala gives us all three descriptions, as if asking us to choose, or to understand them as a radically telescoped sequence, or to consider their possibilities as palimpsest.

At 1,200 plus pages, the book is a daunting read. However Zabala's imagination is a fount of fecundity; a multitudinous world envelopes the reader, crowded with vivid characters and events, a great deal of salt, genuine feeling, irony and humour, and a kind of unstoppable energy. Mahler said of the symphony that it should embrace the world, and the really great novels of the 20th/21st centuries: *Gravity's Rainbow, Infinite Jest, Underworld, 2666,* seem to have also embraced this view. Zabala's novel should rightfully take its place alongside them.

5 Stars

— Tom Murr, Book Critic, *The Lectern*

Is this book for you? At over half a million words, it's likely to keep you busy for a while. Luckily, the beginning is rhythmic and fast-paced. The layered complexities and dense historical detail comes later, once you get to know some key players, are acclimatized to the atmosphere, and once you revel with these frolicsome rogues for a while. In terms of difficulty, it is about as challenging as *Cloud Atlas*, but more than twice as long, with similarly strung together novellas, all differing in form and content and characters. It also brings to mind *The Adventures and Misadventures of Maqroll* for this reason, but *The Mad Patagonian*, in the end, is its own chimerical self.

As detailed in the fabulous introduction, there are many affinities between this book and Bolaño's work, and it is a safe bet that if you enjoyed *2666*, you'll find joy in this expansive new offering. Due to the shifting perspective and kaleidoscopic contexts inherent in the novel, I would call the introduction required reading, if not part of the novel – a tenth layer hidden in plain sight – and it may benefit your reading experience to peruse the articles on the publisher's website after you have completed the last page, to better untangle the history of the book, its themes and integral motifs.

The novel explores, among a vast quantity of other themes, the pursuit of paradise, the possibility of salvation, redemption, and oblivion, and multigenerational connections, vendettas and familial gravitas and the inheritance of culture. Coherence and the malleability of history is one of its main preoccupations, leading to diverging interpretations and recursive speculation by the various narrators, protagonists and bit players.

    Boiling it all down would never give you, the potential reader, an accurate portrait of this voluminous literary undertaking. But the key components, or driving forces of much of the chronicle are the following: impermanence, inner peace versus outer peace, the political nature of writing and the responsibility of the writer to embody the revolutionary spirit, the 'fragile mirror of our misplaced aspirations,' rebirth and renewal of the human spirit beneath the tyranny of history and cultural expectations, disappearance and the anonymity of the struggling artist, solitude versus the sacred ties of family, God's creation and man's relationship to Him, the question of whether He needs us or we need Him, a journey through the mythic realms of the past, existentialist crises and the idealist delusions of youth, the power of the imagination, the abyss of the self, the personal interpretations and quest for a satisfactory paradise, paranoia in government and relationships, the destructive and instinctual power of sexuality, religious atonement, dissolution and corruption, the transitory nature of art, the function of UFOs, inescapable uncertainty, despair and ephemeral beauty – but the more I seek to summarize, the more essential content falls by the wayside. A proper study of this book's inner recesses would necessitate a professional thesis.

    5 Stars

        – L.S. Popovich, Book Critic, *Speculative Fiction and Art*

    The Mad Patagonian is a modern (Modernist!) masterpiece of Latin-American magical realism that goes beyond what you would normally expect of a magical realist novel. The story jumps back and forth in time over the course of nine "Books." Eventually you realize that the stories in these books are all interconnected. You read the central story of one character, who becomes an incidental minor character in the next or turns out to be the child featured in the next...or the great grandmother. You see a new perspective from book to book; so for example in one story you thought a certain character was a violent criminal but then in the next story it turns out he was merely hapless and harmless. The complex intertwining of the Books within the book provides the foundation for one of the primary themes of the novel, which is the value of storytelling and the struggle to coherently construct a story with meaning... given the inherent madness of the world. How can one make sense of this "mad" world? You dig and you can always dig deeper and never understand anything. In some ways, *The Mad Patagonain* is presenting a case that is the opposite of Proust's deep dive into the detailed thoughts and psyche of a man and his experiences. The authorial layering of diverse voices, contexts and time periods in the novel suggests that no matter where you focus, there is always something you are missing, something you can't address or comprehend. No matter how much detail you strive to lay down in your story, the incomprehensible remains.

    I should also point out that this work by no means consistently falls into the genre of magical realism (sometimes it feels like a noir pot-boiler or a Joycean short story), but there are frequent mystical occurrences and coincidences that occur, that would qualify that technique as an aspect of it. There are likely as many different intentions behind the use of magical realism as there are authors who have adopted this technique, but in this case it struck me as another exploration of storytelling. The "magic" represents an author's manipulation of occurrences and characters toward some purpose. The magic is imagination, the art of writing, it's the struggle to control the work and give it intention and meaning. This kind of manipulation extends even to the structure of the novel. There are even some scenes that are theatrical, as if they came from a play by Luigi Pirendello (who was a Modernist playwright whose characters often "come to life" with a mind of their own). One of these characters, a character named Turridu, who is actually a character in a puppet show featured halfway thorugh Book Five, comments on this very notion of trying to give intentionality and meaning to a work of art when he says "We are like so many puppets hung on the wall, waiting for someone to come and move us or make us talk."

Of course, I've merely scratched the surface of the literary value of this book. The craft of the writing itself is also something to admire, and it is a book that should appeal to both realists and experimentalists. *The Mad Patagonian* deserves significant attention.

5 Stars

> – David Katzman, author of *A Greater Monster*, awarded the Gold Medal as an "Outstanding Book of the Year" as part of the 2012 Independent Publisher Book Awards

You have wakened not out of sleep, but into a prior dream, and that dream lies within another, and so on, to infinity, which is the number of the grains of sand. The path that you are to take is endless, and you will die before you have truly awakened.
—Jorge Luis Borges

I know who I am and who I may be, if I choose.
— Miguel de Cervantes Saavedra

When life seems lunatic, who knows where madness lies? Perhaps to be too practical is madness. To surrender dreams — this may be madness. Too much sanity may be madness — and maddest of all, to see life as it is and not as it should be.
— Miguel de Cervantes Saavedra

A Note from the Publisher

It is with great sadness that I must announce the passing of Tomás García Guerrero, the translator of Zabala's masterpiece, The Mad Patagonian. Mr. Guerrero was born in San Pedrito, Mexico in 1937. He earned his Doctorate in Linguistics from UNAM in 1962 and taught at various institutions throughout Mexico. He retired in 1998 from the University of Tamaulipas, Mexico and moved to Toledo, Ohio to live with his daughter. This was his first translation. He died on January 9, 2016 of complications from pneumonia.

I cannot adequately put into words my gratitude to Mr. Guerrero for the time and effort he put into this English edition. I am certain that he felt about this book as a father might feel about a child. I possess a similar feeling, though in my case the word stepchild would be more accurate. But I would be remiss if I did not say that Mr. Guerrero's sudden absence robbed us of an essential voice during the latter stages of the editorial process. This is not to excuse any defects that may exist in the manuscript. It is to suggest instead that I alone, as the editor and publisher of the English edition of The Mad Patagonian, am responsible for any narrative or linguistic shortcomings of the book in its current form, shortcomings that are in all probability a result of my inadequate knowledge of the Spanish language in general, or of the remarkable history and culture of Spain, Cuba and the Americas in particular.

Peter Damian Bellis
Editor & Publisher
River Boat Books

Escoraz Family descended from Andres and Ana

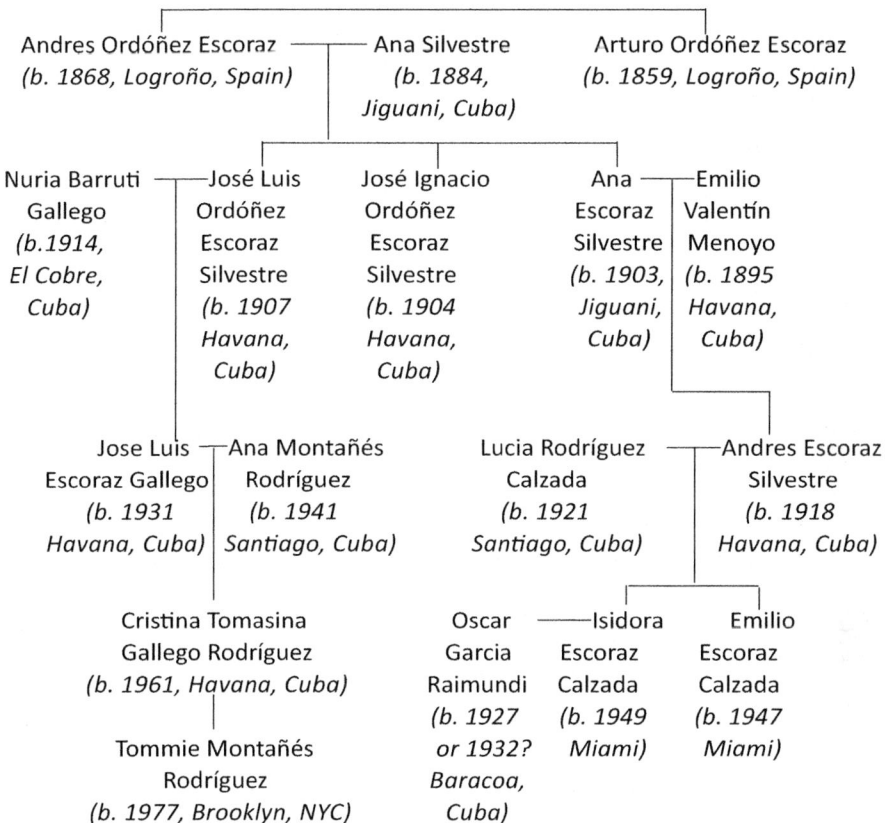

Escoraz Family descended from Arturo and Verona

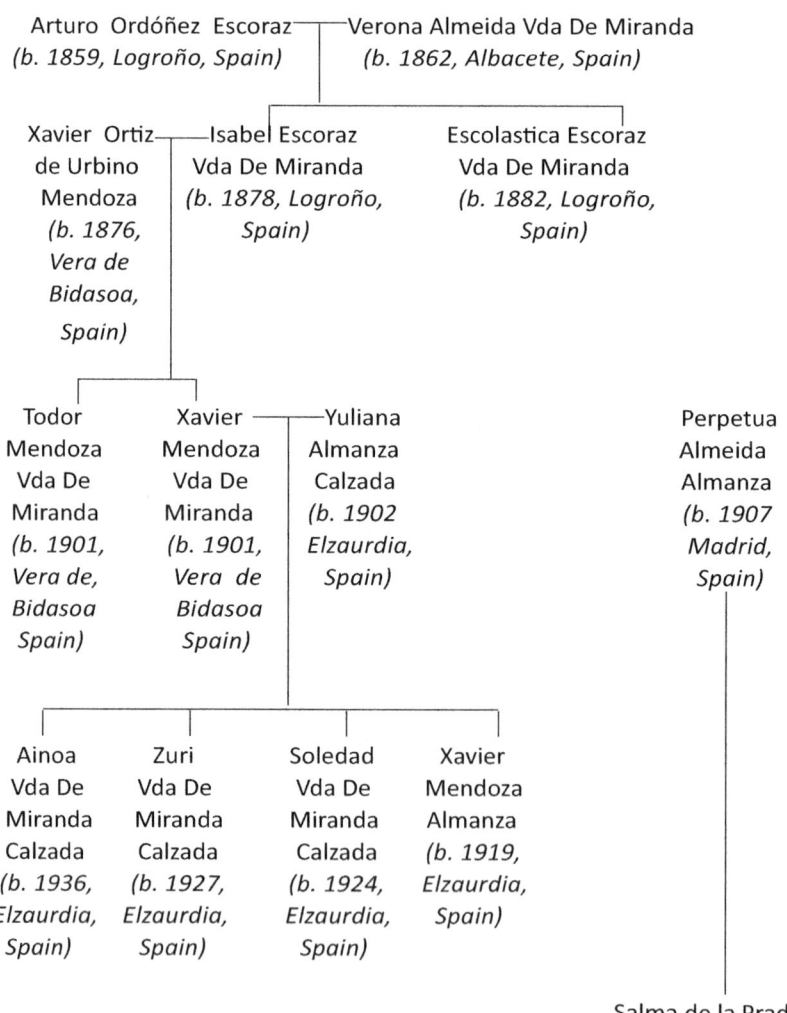

The Translator's Introductory Remarks - xv–lxxi

PART ONE
an echo of paradise

Book One
the house at the beach - 79
Book Two
the heart and soul of Calle Ocho - 163
Book Three
the sex queen of the Moulin Rouge - 251

PART TWO
into the abyss and back again

Book Four
the abduction of
Escolástica Escoraz Vda De Miranda - 401
Book Five
in the shadow of Hotel Milagro - 611
Book Six
the glory days of La Campana - 913

PART THREE
an elegy for a dream once dreamt

Book Seven
the diary of Emilio Escoraz Calzada - 1143
Book Eight
a cry against the twilight - 1267
Book Nine
the clouds, the sea, oblivion - 1349

Afterword - 1391
The Lost Poets of World War One - 1407

The Translator's Introductory Remarks

Cuban writer Javier Pedro Zabala and Chilean writer Roberto Bolaño first crossed paths in Mexico City in the mid-seventies. Their very first meeting, recounted at some length in Zabala's diary, occurred in April of 1975. The meeting did not take place in Librería Gandhi or any other bookstore. It did not take place in that mysterious Mexican hangout known as Café La Habana, although that venue would have been appropriate on many levels, certainly because it was the haunt of writers and artists for generations, but also because it is supposedly the spot where Fidel Castro and Che Guevara drew up their plans for overthrowing the Batista regime and taking control of Cuba. No, the first meeting between Zabala and Bolaño was not imbued with such a heavy-handed sense of history and timing. Instead, the two writers, both young men who had not yet made a dent in the literary world, met by accident in a greasy spoon of a café called El Abrevadero on Calle de Tacuba, a few blocks east of the Palace of Fine Arts. It is now a McDonald's, but back then it was the kind of place where you could get a beer at any hour of the day or night. Bolaño was capping a thirty-six-hour stint of walking and writing by eating a large, overcooked breakfast before he went to bed. He was sitting alone, with his back to the window. 'He was a brightly shining shadow sitting in a pool of dark sunlight,' Zabala later wrote. Zabala was with a young woman, Blanca Barutti, a recent graduate of the Facultad de Medicina UNAM, who would later become Zabala's wife. She was originally from Santiago, Cuba, from the wealthy Vista Alegre neighborhood, but her family had left when Castro came to power. She was extraordinarily beautiful and was often mistaken for a movie star. She also had a reputation for a razor-sharp wit. Both qualities caught Bolaño's attention.

In his diary, which Zabala kept with religious diligence, he recorded that he and Bolaño soon struck up an uneasy conversation, precipitated by the presence of Blanca.

We spent half an hour sparring politely, an imaginary war between two young lions pacing back and forth in the same cage. Blanca was the prize. And then we forgot all about Blanca and talked about everything except the preposterous art of writing. Bolaño said Mexican politics was disheartening. Echeverría had only made things worse. Then he said Echeverría was why he had left Mexico in '72 and spent some time with leftist guerrillas in El Salvador. He said he had been a counter-revolutionary, a spy. He said he had then gone back to Chile to give his heart and soul to Allende's noble struggle to build a socialist state, but then Pinochet seized control. Pinochet is worse than Echeverría, he said. Didn't you know that Echeverría supported Allende? I asked him. How can you be against Echeverría and Pinochet both? But he seemed not to hear me. Of course I was only half serious. I mean who was I to comment on the labyrinthine complexities of Latin American politics? But I thought Bolaño was full of shit, to be frank. He sounded like a counterfeit Trotskyist who knew nothing about the deprivations and personal sacrifice that go along with revolution. Besides, he was too skinny for even the most resolute revolutionary. He seemed more like a refugee. Then he said when he had gone back to Chile the police picked him up because of his odd-sounding accent and tossed him in jail. Everyone around him was smeared with blood. Everyone was suffering from contagious amnesia. He said he spent nine days in a rat-infested swamp of a prison cell, waiting to be tortured like the other prisoners, before a guard he knew from high school recognized him, so they released him. It was at that point I knew he was a writer more than anything else, and I said so, and he laughed. He told me about a new poetry movement he had founded that would pick up the torch lit by Rimbaud. We ordered some beers. Then he said the oddest thing. He said he hoped one day to win the Casa de las Américas Award for a book of poetry. I think he said this to see if I was paying attention. Or maybe to irritate me. Or maybe he was back to flirting with Blanca and wanted to impress her. I looked at him over my glass of beer. What was the use of a literary award to a poet like

Rimbaud, who abandoned poetry for a mercantile career in Africa? I asked him. He put his finger to his mouth to shush me, as if we were both collaborators on the verge of discovery, and then he started laughing and disappeared into his own beer, the morning light refracting through the dirty glass containing his amber colored ambrosia, producing a soft golden halo effect above his head.

Zabala later told his daughter, Cecilia, that he and Bolaño got along well enough. They met now and then over the course of the summer of 1975 and talked about poetry and what it meant to be a writer and whether or not you could call yourself a writer if you didn't write a single word. They talked about their disappointment with establishment writers like Octavio Paz and Juan Rulfo (though Zabala confesses at one point in his diary that their reasons were childish and more a reflection of their own as yet untested literary ambitions than anything else). They were both moved by the surrealistic impulses of Alfonso Reyes. They didn't bother to discuss Carlos Fuentes, except Zabala said he had enjoyed *La muerte de Artemio Cruz* immensely. They agreed about Cuban writer Norberto Fuentes. They disagreed about Gabriel García Marquez. On the whole they liked Mario Vargas Llosa's books. They could not praise enough the literary efforts of Miguel Ángel Asturias and Rómulo Gallegos and, of course, Borges. They tossed around the names of all sorts of eccentric poets. They joked about Carlos Pellicer, who looked like a butcher or a tenor in a barbershop quartet, according to Bolaño. They agreed it was easy to masturbate after reading the erotic poetry of Pierre Louÿs and next to impossible to masturbate after reading the sublime poetry of Sor Juana Inés de la Cruz. Zabala dismissed Luis Cernuda outright. He thought Cernuda would have been nothing at all if he hadn't flung open the doors of his homosexuality for the whole outraged world to see. Bolaño disagreed. Bolaño asked if Zabala had read the Chilean poet Carlos de Rokha and Zabala said he hadn't heard of him and Bolaño said he wasn't surprised because even the Chileans he grew up with hadn't heard of de Rokha. Zabala asked Bolaño if he had read the Mexican poet Sageuo Ruedas but Bolaño had not. Then Zabala asked if Bolaño had heard of the Peruvian activist and poet Eduardo de Jesús Montoyo, who ran in the same circle as the writer José Carlos Mariátegui before they had a falling out, but Bolaño said that except for Adán and Vallejo and Emilio Westphalen, and also Jorge Pimentel, the founder of Movimiento Hora Zero, who had discovered a way to evoke the natural beauty of everyday Peruvian life in his poetry, like in a ballad, and Tulio Moro and Juan Ramírez Ruis, who followed Pimentel down Quilca street, and then there was César Moro, whose real name was Alfredo Quíspez Asín but he thought he would have better success if he hid his true identity so he used the name of a character by the writer Ramón Gómez de la Serna, but aside from all that the only thing he really knew about Peru was they made pretty good Pisco Sours there, but not as good as in Chile. They both respected the lyrical beauty of Emilio Ballagas. They talked intense trash about all sorts of sycophants and university snobs, the vultures waiting in the wings. 'Our opinions contained a great deal of adolescent posturing even though we were both in our twenties,' Zabala later wrote, 'but we had one hell of a time getting drunk.'

By 1976 Bolaño was fully immersed in the world of his infrarealist poetry movement. Zabala was not interested in becoming an infrarealist. He later confessed to his daughter that he thought the whole idea was just a thin disguise for

Roberto Bolaño, Javier Zabala, and Bruno Montané, Mexico City, 1975.

surrealism, which had been around since the twenties. He didn't understand how you could create a movement that already existed. Eventually, the two men parted company. Bolaño published his first book of poetry, *Reinventar el amor*, and after that he fled to France, and then Africa, before settling in Spain. Zabala and Blanca left for Cuba. Bolaño was twenty-three. Zabala was twenty-six. They communicated sporadically with each other over the next thirteen years, always by letter, never by telephone. They did not see each other again until 1989.

To say Javier Pedro Zabala was a Cuban writer is to raise a series of questions about who he truly was and how he came to be that way. Zabala was unknown as a writer during his lifetime. He did not seek out other writers, although he did endeavor to maintain his strange, intermittent, secretive, somewhat conspiratorial relationship with Bolaño; but he did not cultivate a writer's persona; he did not live what we normally conceive as a writer's life, except for the fact that he was constantly writing. In truth, he was a private, as opposed to public, writer. He abandoned all of the pretensions that usually accompany literary pursuits. And though he stopped writing for a time when his wife disappeared in 1996, by 1998 he was back at his typewriter. He died at the age of fifty-two, two months after he had completed his novel, without fanfare, unnoticed by anyone save his daughter, in a tiny cinder block house with a tin roof and a view of the Caribbean Sea in La Boca, Cuba, a small seaside village in Sancti Spíritus province. Zabala lived in La Boca for the last twenty-six years of his life. His daughter was born there. But he himself had not been born in Cuba, nor were his parents Cuban. Thus, we are left with a series of questions regarding his personal identity, which is a by-product of his personal choices as much as his ethnic origins, but we are also forced to grapple with some more problematic questions, at least from a purely academic perspective, about his cultural and spiritual identity as well.

Zabala was in fact a product of the multicultural forces that have been shaping the Americas for over five-hundred years. His father, Miguel Octavio Cercas, was born in 1923 in Matamoros, a border town in northeastern Mexico. His mother, Anabelle Elizabeth Zabala (whose surname he ultimately kept) was from Miami, Florida. She herself was half-Spanish (Basque) and half-German, 'an enigmatic mixture of cold fire and sizzling ice,' according to Zabala. Anabelle Zabala's father, Alberto Diaz Zabala, had emigrated from San Sebastián, Spain in 1922. Her mother, Lucy Elizabeth Wilshusen, had emigrated from Bremervörde, Germany in 1926. They met in New York City in 1927, married, and moved to Florida. So what, then, is Zabala? What is his heritage? Is he Spanish? German? Mexican? American? And what is the relationship between his heritage and his writing? Given the complexities of his family tree, it is tempting to suggest that writing *The Mad Patagonian* was for Zabala a lifelong endeavor to weave a single tapestry from these many disparate threads, a tapestry that would express with unequivocal clarity who he was. But is this a fair assessment? What I think we can say is that the tension between competing cultures was a constant reminder for Zabala that he was always on the outside looking in. He was an exile not just in Miami; he was an exile wherever he went. Even as a small child he found himself wondering if he would ever find a home, a place to rest, to call his own. In a diary entry dated June 6, 1988 he writes:

> *I was a misfit from day one, an outcast, a fallen angel, neither Mexican nor American, neither Spanish nor German. I was the small, starving refugee kid, an exile, always hungry, at least in my imagination, standing outside a gleaming golden bakery or a deli or a diner, staring blankly at the bubble of happy, blank faces on the other side of the plate glass window, the people laughing with joyful, unconcerned, uncomprehending laughter, at least this is how I heard it in my mind, and as this laughter was swirling through my consciousness, a tiny part of me like a wandering hermit crab, a most insignificant part, was wondering when it would be my turn. But I was oblivious to the commotion my lingering presence outside these bakeries or delis or diners might cause until a waiter or a cashier or some other working class stiff would rush out the door to shoo me away. In those moments I had no home, no refuge. Where could*

I go? It seemed to me I could go nowhere. Every place would be the same. Every person I met would view me with either suspicion or pity. I don't know which I hated more. I guess it was pity because by the time I turned fourteen, I actively cultivated suspicion.

One could argue that Zabala's flights of extreme childhood despair were in all likelihood a creation of an older Zabala looking back. This is not to say that he did not feel like an outcast or an exile while growing up. It is only to suggest that a thoughtful understanding of what it meant to be an exile came later. Moreover, Zabala's somewhat malleable sense of his own identity, at least in terms of how his adult self remembered his youthful self, was probably shaped more by growing up in a working-class household than it was by his parents' ethnic origins. From the little biographical information available on Zabala, it would seem that his family life was fairly typical of immigrant working class families living in southern Florida in the fifties. Zabala's parents met in April 1949 in Galveston, Texas, where they were married on May 27, 1949 by a Justice of the Peace. Miguel wanted to move to Mexico, perhaps even Mexico City. Anabelle wanted to go back to Miami. After a four-day honeymoon on Padre Island, she convinced him that moving to Mexico would be a mistake. There was more opportunity living in the United States, she told him. Miguel reluctantly agreed, so they headed east. Zabala was born nine months later on February 6, 1950. His sister, Julia, was born in 1951, and his brother, Emidio, was born in 1953. From 1950 to 1964 the family lived in a modest five-room bungalow with a front porch and a cedar porch swing

Javier Zabala and his father in Allapattah, Florida in 1957.

in Allapattah, a small neighborhood northwest of downtown Miami. They rarely strayed outside the social and economic boundaries of their tiny world. Once a year they made the three-week journey to Matamoros to visit relatives, but that was it for traveling. Zabala's father worked as an auto mechanic and his mother worked in a bakery. Neither were big readers. In fact there wasn't a single book in the house, a material absence which Zabala later recalled with some measure of pride. What they gave him instead of books was the gift of an unrestrained passion for living that did not need the inducements of material comfort. This is what shaped his attitude not only towards his life, but invariably towards his inexorable need to write. In a diary entry dated June 14, 1992 he wrote:

> What others might see as disadvantages have always been my advantages. We grew up without money, without any apparent opportunity. We lived as all the working poor have always lived. There wasn't a single book anywhere in our house. My mother occasionally bought a copy of the magazine Vanidades. My father read the newspaper, but only the Sunday edition. We listened to the radio, but we owned no television. And our car was an old 1932 Studebaker, a Commander 8 that my father was always repairing. But none of this mattered. My parents always said life was short so I should find my happiness wherever I could, whenever I happened to stumble upon it, because it would most certainly vanish before the sun rose the next morning. Life was a gift that should not be taken for granted, they said. It was the experience that counted. So they encouraged me to do whatever I wanted, regardless of books or opportunities or any of the bourgeois accoutrements that most Americans take for granted. That is how I was able to proclaim myself a writer before I had written even a single word.

In 1964, the year Zabala turned fourteen, he experienced for himself the ephemeral nature of happiness. His father, who had become increasingly homesick for Mexico, decided in March to return to Matamoros. His mother did not try to dissuade him. Zabala was devastated by having to choose which parent to live with, and though he ultimately decided to go with his father ('my mother had Julia and Emidio for comfort, but who did my father have?' he wrote), the decision seemed to confirm what would become a central theme of his book, namely: how do we gain some measure of peace when nothing is permanent, not even love. In an entry dated October 11, 1995 he writes:

> At the time I was struck by the impermanence of life, of all experience, even with something so elemental as human emotion. If love did not exist beyond this tiny existential dot we call a moment, then what was the point in cultivating the emotion? What was the point in cultivating any emotion? Of course I was not so philosophical in my musings at the tender age of fourteen. And I failed to consider that if love did not truly exist, then neither did hatred. If joy did not exist, then neither, ultimately, did frustration, and so on and so forth. All of humanity's dualities could be disposed of with a single stroke of an imaginary pen. I did not begin to think so deeply about such matters until much, much later. But the seed was sown the day my father and I left for Mexico.

During the journey from Miami to Matamoros, Zabala and his father stopped for a single night on Padre Island. For Zabala's father it was perhaps a fitting place to say goodbye to the memory of his wife. But for Zabala it marks the first time he began to think about writing as a way of exploring his own identity. They arrived early in the afternoon on Saturday, March 14. Zabala's father was finding temporary solace in a bottle of tequila, so Zabala went for a walk along the beach. He came to the beachfront of a very fancy hotel with a few guests hiding from the sun beneath heavy canvas umbrellas. It was only March, so the temperature was still comfortable, but the sun was very bright off the water. Zabala writes about that day in an entry dated November 14, 1995:

> I was staring at a long line of blue umbrellas like so many teardrops glistening in the sun. It was so bright I almost couldn't see a thing. Then I was distracted by

the sounds of a young woman screaming. She was forty yards or so offshore and she was thrashing about and her voice was vibrating at a very high pitch. She seemed to be tangled up in the sea, maybe a patch of seaweed or some abandoned fishing line, but I could not tell. She was clearly in a panic, and then suddenly it was much more than a panic. The sound of her voice became hundreds of tiny daggers of sound clawing at the air, thousands of daggers. Then a young man rushed into the waves and swam out a little ways towards her, but before he got very far she had stopped screaming. The next thing I remember was a white wooden boat pushing across the waves with four lifeguards with red flotation buoys, and then the boat finally reached the woman and the lifeguards dragged her into the boat and brought her back. They laid her out in the sand and the young man collapsed on top of her, and from what he was saying it was crystal clear that they had just been married, that this was their honeymoon, but nobody moved to comfort him. Nobody said a word. But what would they have said? There was nothing to say. So the lifeguards watched over the young man for a while, and then a small brown jeep came and two of the lifeguards loaded up the woman's lifeless body and helped the young man into the back seat and then they drove up towards the Red Cross station. I didn't ask anyone what had happened to the young woman, but somebody else went over to the other two lifeguards who had stayed behind. They were pulling the long wooden boat up away from the tide, which was rolling in. They said the woman had got tangled up in a patch of Portuguese Man-O-War. They had stung her pretty badly. It was rare to die from the venom, but it did happen. Besides, she must have been stung fifty times. Then the lifeguards went away, and so did everyone else, and I was staring at the spot in the sand where they had laid the woman's body. I could still see the indentation like a passing thought. I was affected by the woman's death in ways that I could not then describe, but strangely I was not sad. I remember staring at the soft mark where she had been, a blank stare, and then I was staring out at the sea. I could see tiny blue umbrellas floating in the water, like the umbrellas on the beach only much smaller, a tiny flotilla of teardrops, and then I realized they were not teardrops or tiny umbrellas, they were dozens and dozens of Portuguese Man-O-War. The tide was bringing them in. In fact the beach was already littered with their flimsy, insubstantial, but obviously deadly bodies. It was a surreal moment, but it was also very beautiful, and I remember wondering how was it that I could see this beauty in the face of the tragic death of this young woman on her honeymoon. I wondered what was wrong with me. But there was no denying how powerfully beautiful the whole moment was. Yes, it was a beauty shaped by the suddenness of the woman's death, but it was also shaped by love and the blue umbrellas and the blue umbrella-like Portuguese Man-O-War, and yes, there was a great sadness there that would linger until the end of time, but it was a surface sadness, an echo of the happiness the young woman had possessed during her lifetime, like the echo of a church bell. I had somehow gone beneath the waves of this sadness to the beauty that existed at a greater depth, a beauty that existed outside of time, outside of this imperfect realm we call the world, so it would always exist. How was this possible? I wondered.

That was the moment when I first knew I would be a writer. That I was already a writer. I also knew that I would spend the rest of my life exploring that strange aberration in my consciousness, my way of seeing the world, that allowed me to glimpse such beauty even in death.

Zabala lived in Mexico from 1964 thru the end of 1976. He lived for a time with his father in a small house in Matamoros, working alongside him in a small auto body shop on Galeana Street. He became interested in American movies, particularly hard-boiled detective movies. Anything film noir. His favorite actor was Humphrey Bogart. But he also admired Peter Lorre. But Zabala would not stay in Matamoros long. Though he had dropped out of high school, he suddenly became an avid reader of borrowed books. He does not share with us why he began to read, only that from

Javier Zabala in Matamoros, Mexico, 1965.

that point forward he was consumed with reading. And because of the books he read, he began to look at the world through newborn eyes. He began to believe he had some control over the direction his life would take, that he had some say in what he might do, that he could in fact shape his own future. He also became politically aware, even angry, though it should be added that his anger at this point was probably modulated as much by a youthful desire to rebel against authority as by an awareness of the very real injustices committed by those in power against those without power in Mexico and elsewhere.

In October 1968, however, Zabala found for the first time a very real cause to anchor his anger. On the 2nd of October, the Mexican army, armed to the hilt with machine guns and tanks and orders to do whatever was necessary to keep the peace, fired randomly into a crowd of twenty-thousand students and other civilians, men, women, and even small children, who had gathered peacefully in the Plaza de las Tres Culturas in Mexico City to protest against the Gustavo Díaz Ordaz government, a protest defined in part by a call for democracy with the goal of forcing the government to honor the constitutional guarantees that already existed in the Mexican constitution. By some estimates as many as nine-hundred protestors were killed. Maybe more. No one knows the exact number. It was a tragedy. It became known as the Tlatelolco massacre, a sad, bloody monument in the history of Mexico to rival the Aztec massacre of the Spanish conquistadors and their Indian collaborators at Zultapec in

1520. Two weeks after Tlatelolco, this crime of the century, Zabala decided to move to the capital. He talks about why in his diary:

> *I couldn't explain to my father why I wanted to move to Mexico City in '68. But I was really troubled by the Tlatelolco massacre. I was overwhelmed by the sadness of La Noche Triste (the sad night), which hung over the entire country like a lingering cloud. There was no escaping it. But I felt I had to do something, so that's what I did. I guess I just had to be there. It was not a political statement at all. It was like an act of faith. Like leaping from a burning building. It was something a writer would do, and I knew at that point that everything I would ever do would be something a writer would do. The only thing I didn't know was what kind of a writer I was going to be. I knew that some writers wrote about politics, but I didn't want to be labeled a political writer. As I said, I wasn't making a political statement by moving to Mexico City. I didn't know a thing about politics. It was only years later that I realized that writing is by its very nature a political act.*

Upon arriving in Mexico City, Zabala had to struggle just to survive. He moved in with an uncle, Humberto Pedro Melina y Cercas. Pedro for short. Pedro worked for a Pontiac car dealership downtown. He had worked there for twenty years so he was able to get Zabala a job in the dealership's garage working on smaller cars, mostly Volkswagen Beetles. Only the more experienced mechanics were allowed to work on Pontiacs. But Zabala didn't mind. He had steady work. He had time to himself to think. And he began to understand the kind of writer he wanted to be. In an entry dated February 22, 1999 Zabala writes:

> *I spent my first three months in Mexico City just getting acclimated to the routine of working in the garage during the day and drinking with my friends during the evenings. Sure, we talked politics over a few beers, but so did everybody else. It's funny looking back on it now. I started telling people I was a writer, but I couldn't even*

tell a story. Thank God for my uncle. My uncle didn't teach me a thing about working on cars when I worked at the Pontiac dealership. I learned about cars from my father, not my uncle. But my uncle taught me the principle rules of storytelling, even though he probably didn't realize he was teaching me a thing. Every day during the lunch break the men would gather around a small picnic table next to an old electric fan in the back of the garage and tell stories. My uncle was the best of the lot. He was a great storyteller. Even though he told the same story over and over again, you could not help but listen. He liked to talk about driving in La Carrera Panamericana, the mythic two-thousand-mile road rally from Ciudad Juárez in the north to Ciudad Cuauhtémoc on the border with Guatemala. My uncle said he drove in the very first race in 1950. He said at that time the owner of the Pontiac dealership, Antonio Cornejo, was also the man in charge of the race. Cornejo put up a car for my uncle to drive. My uncle said over a thousand cars started the

Humberto Pedro Melina y Cercas and a friend standing in front of car #113, which 'Pedro' drove in La Carrera Panamericana in 1950.
(Photograph taken in Ciudad Juárez the day before the race.)

race, but only a handful finished. He said the road went through some of the most treacherous mountain terrain in Mexico. Hundreds of people died because they were terrible drivers or their cars were no good to begin with, so the slightest difficulty or chance encounter sent them spinning over the edge of a cliff in a freefall that ended in a fireball. He also said it was a race without any rules. Except there was one rule. If you stopped your car for any reason you were disqualified. I don't know if I believed him or not. Every time he told the story the details would change. Sometimes he was describing a moment when he was in a duel with another car for space on a narrow winding portion of the road, and the other car shoved him and he almost went over the edge, which was a five-hundred-foot drop and certain death, but then he regained control and shoved the other car the other way and it went careening into the mountain side and burst into flames, an incredible explosion, and my uncle said there was no hope for that driver, but he didn't know for sure because he lost sight of him going around a curve. At other times he recounted how he stopped to help a young woman who had been driving with her husband as if they were heading to a Sunday picnic in the country, but they had gone into a ditch because the husband had been eating an egg sandwich that his wife had prepared for him with great joy that morning and so he had lost sight of the road, this is how my uncle would tell the story, and so this husband was now bleeding, an artery in his leg had been severed, and the moment my uncle stopped his car and stepped out onto the pavement to help, he was disqualified by two race officials who materialized quite suddenly out of thin air, as if they had been suddenly beamed to earth from a distant star or an alien spaceship, waving their flags and shouting with energetic, rapid-fire mania about the one rule, or perhaps they had been driving a small white Fiat and had just happened by at precisely that moment, who could truly say, but if my uncle hadn't stopped when he did, the woman's husband would have surely died. My uncle never said if he finished the race. Not in any of the versions he told. But always he was caught up in *the midst of a life or death struggle, which is why you could not pull yourself away from his tall tale. You were always on the edge of your seat. The lives of the people he encountered on that treacherous road in that terrifying race mattered more in those moments listening to his deep soothing voice than anyone you actually knew. No matter how far-fetched the narrative, no matter how far removed from verifiable fact, the stories my uncle told rang out with the truth, in so far as any human experience can be called true. I learned the art of storytelling from my uncle.*

In the spring of 1970, Zabala was supposedly recruited by members of the Liga Obrero Estudiantil, a radicalized student group that had appeared among a sea of political student groups at UNAM in the mid-sixties. This was a turbulent period for Zabala, as it was for everyone living in Mexico at the time. On the one hand, there was a sense of growing social unrest spurred by rumors of secret goon squad violence. On the other hand, there was the ever-present problem of the Mexican government capitulating without a second thought to the economic interests of the United States at the expense of Mexico's poor and working classes. The impoverished outnumbered the privileged fifty to one, a ratio that had not changed in any substantive way since the Mexican Revolution, and was not likely to change in the foreseeable future. In the face of such overwhelming disparity, Zabala saw no ethical alternative but to stand shoulder to shoulder with the powerless against those pulling the strings. He believed that change was possible, if only everyone worked together. So he joined the Liga Obrero Estudiantil, and then later he joined the Mexican Communist Party (PCM).

In an entry dated September 17, 1992 he writes about his optimistic state of mind:

We were hippies, of course. We had long hair. Many of us wore beards. We rarely bathed. We were almost always broke. And we were no different than anyone else. We were no different than the thousands of Mexican students who had been savagely eliminated by the army back in '68. We were no different than the Mexican police who had been trained to steal children and old women out of their beds in the middle of the night and murder them in secret. We were no different than the farmers and the factory workers and the bus drivers and the nurses and the auto mechanics and the grocers who bled away their lives for a few pesos. We were no different than the lawyers and the businessmen and the teachers and the doctors and the priests and the musicians and the television personalities and the writers and the ambassadors who turned a blind eye to whatever the government was doing or wanted to do. We were no better or worse than anyone else, anywhere in Mexico. We were all of us shadowy, imperfect reflections of each other. And all we wanted was a fair shake. We didn't even want a better life. We just wanted what was fair. That's why we stood up to the government. What other choice did we truly have? If we wanted to change things we had no other choice. We did what we had to do. We wanted these old politicians who had grown fat on the misery of an entire country to remember the ideals of their own youth. We wanted them to look into the fragile mirror of our young lives and see their own misplaced aspirations. This is what we hoped.

Zabala writes with great passion, great conviction, and in reading his diary, one wonders why he did not make a name for himself as a leader within the student community at UNAM, and then later within the crumbling mosaic of Mexican politics. He certainly had an intuitive grasp of the competing tensions that were pulling Mexican society apart. And he was more than able to capture this tension in eloquent, even poetic, yet absolutely precise language. So why is he unknown in Mexican intellectual circles?

Perhaps the answer lies in the simple fact that he was too good of a thinker and a writer to have gone unnoticed. Thus, one must conclude that either he did not share his thoughts with those around him, which given the collaborative nature of political activism in those days seems unlikely; or we must conclude that he did not actually participate in the protests and the demonstrations that he details with great compassion and ideological insight. In other words, Zabala filled his diary with compelling fictions about his life, fictions that expressed, perhaps, what he wished he had done or was capable of doing. When it comes right down to it, he had already begun to work on his craft.

    Zabala claims in his diary that in July of 1970 he participated in a student march expressing solidarity with the workers of a local textile company. He claims that in August of 1970 he began accompanying PCM organizers in secret to various rural communities all over Mexico in support of thousands of unarmed peasants in their struggle to acquire land. He claims that in April of 1971 he drafted a UNAM petition for the amnesty of University professors who had been imprisoned for their political views by the government in '68. And he claims that he helped organize a mass demonstration in Mexico City of nearly ten thousand students who gathered near Santo Tomás, mainly on the Ribera de San Cosme, on June 10, 1971, to express their solidarity with the students of the Autonomous University of Nuevo León in Monterrey. At that time the students in Monterrey were engaged in a battle of wills with the Governor of Nuevo León, Eduardo Elizondo. Zabala also claims that he narrowly avoided becoming a casualty the afternoon of the demonstration as hundreds of men armed with cudgels and clubs and dressed in unassuming plain clothes descended upon the students, attacking them with ferocious, unrestrained zeal in what later became known as the Corpus Christi Massacre. What is more, Zabala claims all of this without batting an equivocal eye, in spite of the fact that he was never a student at UNAM, or at any university for that matter. In fact there is some evidence to suggest that Zabala did not even move to Mexico City until 1974, the year he met Blanca.

    Is it possible that Zabala was involved in various student protests? Certainly. But whether he was or wasn't is irrelevant as far as his growth as a writer is concerned. What is clear from his diary, whether or not the details he records are accurate, is that Zabala's writing is infused with an indomitable revolutionary spirit. Zabala uses words to change reality. He even composed a variation of a popular but rather abusive anthem the students sang at every political rally during the summer of 1968:

Death to the monkey, Díaz Ordaz!
Come out on the balcony, with your big ass snout!
Come out on the balcony, monkey with a big ass snout!
Black monkey, to the fucking wall!
Black monkey, come out on the balcony!
Díaz Ordaz, motherfucker! motherfucker! motherfucker!

Contrary to his claim that he 'did not want a better life' quoted earlier, Zabala did want a better life, but not just for himself and those around him. He wanted a better life for everyone. Ironically, it was this desire, which possessed for Zabala the quality of an unspoken faith, which allowed him to live in a world torn apart by violence. In his diary he writes:
The world is constantly being destroyed by angry, purpose-driven men with guns. But that is only half of the picture, for with each act of unmitigated violence there is an equally powerful counter-insurgency of renewal and rebirth. It is part of the unseen machinery behind creation. It has been this way since the beginning of time.

One might be tempted to label Zabala an idealist, or perhaps a religious anti-intellectual, and certainly his position is a bit of an anachronism by postmodern standards, but these labels would be unfair as well as inaccurate. Zabala's brand of idealism was born of practical interactions with the oppressive tyrannies of modern life and so mirrors the pragmatic idealism of earlier political revolutionaries like Trotsky, whose books Zabala knew intimately, and Julio Antonio Mella, a journalist and the founder of the Communist Party of Cuba in the 1920s, who, according to Cecilia, was one of Zabala's ideological heroes. (Julio Mella had written numerous articles for such leftist publications as *El Libertador* and *Tren Blindado* when he lived in Mexico City, articles espousing equality for all men.) For Zabala, both Trotsky and Mella were symbols of the need to keep the struggle for absolute equality alive no matter the personal cost. Both Trotsky and Mella believed that when the world finally achieved equality for everyone, then everything else would be possible. The world would become a paradise. Zabala took their belief and transformed it into a personal quest to discover if happiness was even possible in a world in which the notion of absolute equality for everyone had been replaced by the notion of absolute liberty for some, which meant that everyone on the planet was unintentionally driving with ruthless efficiency towards unhappiness. This is the terrain Zabala is exploring in his book, *The Mad Patagonian*.

In 1974, Zabala met Blanca Barutti, and his charismatic revolutionary idealism and his evolving identity as a writer were reshaped by Blanca's intense sense of purpose. Blanca was a few years older than Zabala and her heritage was as varied as his. She was of Spanish, Italian, and German descent. Her father, Bruno Barutti, was born in 1920 in Villafranca Piemonte, a small Italian town in the province of Turin, but the family left Italy for Cuba in November 1922 one month after the Fascist blackshirts under Mussolini's direction stormed into the city of Rome. So Bruno Barutti grew up in Santiago, Cuba and then became a civil engineer, working on various municipal construction projects within a ten-block radius of Parque Céspedes, including the City Hall project on Francisco Vicente Aguilera from 1948 until the building was completed in 1950. Blanca's mother, Emily Duarte de Hernani y Arredondo, came from a well-to-do family that had emigrated from Barcelona in the latter half of the 19th century.

One year after Castro came to power, the Barutti family again took the path of exile and moved to Mexico City. They moved into an Art Nouveau style house in Colonia Condesa on a shady, tree-lined street a few blocks from Parque España. Bruno Barutti was seemingly unemployed for several years after moving to Mexico City, but in 1967 he took a position with a civil engineering firm named Ingenieros Civiles y Asociados, which was the lead engineering firm in the construction of the Mexico City Metro. He worked at Ingenieros Civiles y Asociados until he retired for health reasons in 1983.

From the day Blanca was born (July 5, 1947), her parents began grooming her for medical school, so it was no shock when she entered the Facultad de Medicina UNAM in 1970. She was an exemplary student, graduating with distinction in 1973. She met Zabala during her internship (1974) at the Hospital General de México. Supposedly he came into the emergency room with a variety of lacerations and bruises and a broken nose. Blanca was working with the attending physician.

Zabala never fully explained to her how he had acquired his injuries. But according to Cecilia in an interview in April 2015, her mother knew instantly that he had received them fighting for the cause of equality:

> My mother said she first saw Papi at 11 o'clock on September 2, 1974. He was covered in dried blood and possessed a ruthlessly happy smile. Mother said he was also carrying a copy of Madera, one of the dozens of leftist, revolutionary publications circulating around Mexico City at that time. She took him for a passionate but inexperienced revolutionary, partly because of his bearded demeanor, but also because the attending physician, who openly expressed his sympathies for every student cause that made it into the papers and was himself a member of the PCM, seemed to know my father. The next day the attending physician approached my mother with a wink and a smile. He told her there had been a protest or a riot by some student groups during Echeverría's State of the Nation address. The protesters had been clubbed into silence. Some of them had sustained severe injuries, but thankfully, no one had been killed. From that point on, my mother was convinced that my father belonged to one of the groups that had been protesting. My father came back to the hospital one week later and asked my mother to dinner. She said she could not help herself. She had fallen madly in love with him that very first night because of the revolutionary ardor you could see burning in his eyes, and his unrestrained, revolutionary laughter that shook free the very dust from the ceiling. That was how my mother described it. They went to dinner the next evening.

So is Cecilia's somewhat romanticized story accurate? There is no record of the student protest she describes, but that in itself is not unusual, particularly since there were no deaths. The magazine Zabala carried into the emergency room, *Madera*, was in fact a leftist publication printed by Liga Comunista 23 de Septiembre (LC23S), a Marxist-Leninist group quite active in Mexico City during the seventies and eighties. It is certainly conceivable that Zabala provided articles and commentary for the magazine, perhaps under an assumed name. It is also worth noting that the LC23S had ties with the Liga Obrero Estudiantil, which Zabala had supposedly joined in 1970. But whether or not Zabala was affiliated with the LC23S is unimportant. What is important is the story establishes the degree to which Zabala's revolutionary idealism was visible to others, in this case Blanca. It also provides a subtext for understanding the relationship between Zabala and Blanca, why they fell in love with such apparent intensity, why they moved to Cuba, and why Zabala remained in Cuba after Blanca's disappearance. Cecilia comments on their love story:

My father had great passion, but he was undisciplined. He needed my mother's sense of direction, her firm belief in working to fulfill some unwritten destiny, and her unwavering, even ruthless commitment to achieving her goal. She always kept her eyes on her goal. But my mother would never have understood her destiny without my father. His passion helped her see precisely where she needed to go and what she needed to do. They were married almost one year after they first met on the 23rd of August, 1975, in a quiet civil ceremony. My mother made my father shave his beard and get a haircut for the occasion. She said her parents didn't trust him, but they trusted her. After a short honeymoon in the sleepy seaside village of Puerto Morelos, which looked out on the Caribbean Sea, they moved into a little apartment on Calle Soledad in the center of historic Mexico City. Their street was a street filled with vendors. They lived directly above a grocer who opened his stall at seven every morning except Sundays. It was my father's idea, of course. They were one block from the crumbling, antiquated glory (my father's words) of the Church of Santa Cruz y La Soledad. They were a short ten-minute walk from the Candelaria metro station. My mother said that every moment of every day you could feel the surging, seething, irrepressible lifeblood of Mexico City like an ocean swirling around you, carrying you forward with its unrepentant kinetic energy, there was no escaping it, she said, and no use trying, and then one day she realized she did not wish to escape 'this bubbling ocean of humanity,' as she put it. She realized that her value as a doctor would rise or fall in direct proportion to her commitment to easing the suffering of everyday people like the people that moved through the streets of Mexico City. I think my father knew my mother would come to this conclusion. I think he was teaching her, guiding her along the path to herself. My parents lived in their apartment on Soledad for one year so that my mother could finish her post-graduate internship at the General Hospital of Mexico. Then on the 22nd of October 1976, they left for Cuba. My mother decided that the people she felt the greatest connection to lived in Cuba. They were everyday people like the people swirling up and down Calle Soledad, but they were her people. The Cuban people were her first vocation. That is why my parents left for Cuba. But my mother would never have even thought of going to Cuba if my father had not first opened her eyes to the misery and despair of the disenfranchised in Mexico. My father had no choice but to go with her. He would have been lost without her, and he knew this. But then he did not care where he was so long as he was with her. He would have followed her to the moon and back.

Blanca and Javier on their honeymoon
(Puerto Morelos, Mexico in August 1975)

The Translator's Introductory Remarks

In November of 1976, Javier Pedro Zabala and Blanca Barutti moved into a tiny house in the small seaside community of La Boca, Cuba in Sancti Spíritus province. Blanca began working at the medical clinic in Trinidad, seven kilometers to the east. Zabala worked in the sugar cane fields as a cutter during *La Gran Zafra* (the Great Sugar Cane Harvest) that first year and every year after that until 1994. At first he worked in the fields because that is what he thought any good revolutionary and leftist writer would do, and indeed, many leftist writers and thinkers from other countries came to Cuba each year during the *zafra* to help the Cubans bring in Castro's symbolic if not altogether impossible ten million tons of sugar cane. But even as he grew older and became disillusioned with Castro's failed economic policies and the growing poverty of the country, Zabala continued to work in the fields because he 'enjoyed the pure simple escapism of physical exertion. It is not clear from Zabala's diary what he did when he was not working in the cane fields. But his daughter said that sometimes her father worked as a fisherman, sometimes he drove a truck, sometimes he drove one of those bright red tractors from Belarus, and on those days he was smiling from ear to ear, sometimes he did various odd jobs in the medical clinic in Trinidad, and during the last six years of his life he became a farmer and joined a small agricultural cooperative that grew vegetables, mainly beans and cassava, on a nine-acre plot in the Viñales Valley, a fertile but infamous valley that had once been home to over seventy cane sugar mills and fifty-thousand slaves.

It is perhaps one of the peculiarities of living in Cuba under Castro that Zabala could commit to living a full, robust life, even as he was aware of the irony of that life. He realized that Cuba's socialist experiment was a severe caricature of Trotsky's vision of Communism, even during his early years in La Boca, when the euphoria of a young newlywed couple moving to Cuba to make a difference was still palpable. And yet as late as 1994, he was also, somehow, still committed to the idealistic vision of absolute equality for everyone that lay at the foundation of the political thinking of both Trotsky and Mella. In an entry dated March 11, 1994, he saw better days ahead.

> *Our diseased, corrupt, parody of a state is a natural outgrowth of our dependence, both political and economic, upon the Soviet Union, which was itself an absurdist parody of Communism even as early as 1926, as Trotsky points out in The Revolution Betrayed. The death of the Soviet Union was inevitable. Why did we not see this? And what of Cuba? What did we really expect from Castro? But all that is past us. Now that the Soviets are no longer pulling the strings, I see a day when the people will once again reassert their right to govern their own lives. Castro will have no choice but to let them.*

That Zabala could maintain the integrity of his convictions living in a country whose leadership was constantly caught unprepared for the consequences of its own policy choices, to steal a line from Trotsky, is a testament to his creative, intellectual, and artistic temperament. But it is also worth remembering that Zabala had made a conscious choice to reject the materialism of the world at large. He lived the life of a modern ascetic. And he would have lived this life if he had lived in Cuba or New York City or Rome. Geography would have made no difference. His philosophy was an integral part of his make-up. As his daughter, Cecilia, said: "My father lived his life with one foot planted in the physical realities of this world, though barely, and the other foot firmly planted in the spiritual idealism of the next."

It was Zabala's ability to inhabit these two worlds simultaneously that allowed him to live in a state of balance in Castro's Cuba. It was this same ability, I might add, that allowed him to write his magnum opus.

The Mad Patagonian was the only book Zabala finished writing. He spent his entire adult life working on the manuscript, drafting lengthy sections in longhand before transferring them to a more permanent state using an old 1940s Corona typewriter. He wrote most of the book in the small cinder block house in La Boca. He sat by a window with a view of the Caribbean Sea and wrote every day from four in the afternoon until one or two in the morning. Some evenings were more productive than others. Zabala writes:

> *Sometimes, not often, and always very late at night, I come to the conclusion that my only friend is the sound of the sea, the waves rolling in, breaking against the rocks, but even this friend exists only in my mind, for it is dark and I cannot see a thing that is out there. It is only in these moments, when I realize there is only an impenetrable darkness beyond my field of vision, a darkness, moreover, which extends to the edges of the universe, that I understand how completely and totally alone I am and must be. It is only in these moments that I can truly write.*

Many writers have had similar epiphanies, but few have embraced the writer's need for absolute isolation the way Zabala did. Even when he was not writing he had cut himself off from the world. As already noted, with the strange exception of Bolaño, Zabala did not know or communicate with any other writer in Cuba or anywhere else. But what is more astonishing is that none of Zabala's friends, neighbors or co-workers knew he was writing. Certainly his wife, Blanca, knew, and also his daughter, but no one else. To one living in the contemporary world where there is no privacy whatsoever, no matter where you live, and especially in a country like Cuba, where everyone is looking over everyone else's conspiratorial shoulder, it seems inconceivable that Zabala could shut himself away so completely. And yet this is what he did. It is a remarkable accomplishment, almost as remarkable as the book he wrote.

According to Cecilia, Zabala began working on his manuscript in the summer of 1983, but even as late as 1987 he himself wasn't sure what he was doing. He had no clear understanding of what he was trying to write. Indeed, in a letter he sent to Bolaño in August 1987 he confessed that he could not very well be a writer since he had not written anything worthy of publication, to which Bolaño replied:

> *Fear not, my friend, you have simply joined the ranks of those sublime writers who exist in every age who write with exemplary clarity without putting pen to paper.*

Better that than to be a hack who has written too many words without expressing a single intelligible thought.

By mid-January 1988, however, Zabala had decided he was writing a grand, multi-generational epic with the majestic, historic sweep of Tolstoy. His book would follow the fortunes of Escolástica and Isabel Vda De Miranda, two sisters from Logroño, Spain, and their descendants. The younger sister, Escolástica, would emigrate from Spain to Cuba with her uncle in 1899 in search of the paradise of new beginnings. Her descendants would eventually make their way from Santiago, Cuba to Havana to Miami. The older sister, Isabel, would marry into a family from Vera de Bidasoa, Spain and move to the mountains and later fight against the Fascists. Her grandchildren would immigrate to the United States in 1939 and also eventually settle in Miami. Neither branch would know of the other. But the book soon became much more complex in conception than a realistic family saga. Zabala decided he would explore his own complex psychological and cultural heritage through the lives of this fictional family from Spain. In so doing, he hoped the book would provide an alternative view of reality that would stand against what he saw as the resounding failure of religion and traditional philosophy to provide a useful psychological framework for assigning value and hence meaning to the living of one's own life.

In this narrow sense, Zabala was an existentialist. But he himself would not have claimed this label. Indeed, his views are modulated by a subtle yet persistent faith in the existence of God, a faith which he could never quite shed. He firmly believed that if there were no conscious entities to recognize and validate creation, then creation itself would have no value. Thus, all value emanated from humanity's ability to apprehend the universe. But he also maintained a fundamental belief that God was part of the creation equation. 'God needed to create mankind to appreciate His handiwork,' he once wrote, 'otherwise there would be no meaning behind creation. But without God, mankind would serve no purpose. God needs mankind as much as mankind needs God. You cannot have one without the other.' Thus, *The Mad Patagonian* is also an implicit criticism of the existentialists for their inability to strike a balance between 'meaningful human activity in the temporal realm' (the world that we see with our eyes) and 'purposeful human activity in the mythic realm' (the world that we see with our hearts). In short, though certainly with a self-deprecating, tongue-in-cheek sense of the absurdity of life in general, Zabala wanted *The Mad Patagonian* to be all things to all readers.

Zabala decided that the book would be divided into nine separate but interconnected novellas of varying lengths. The stories begun in the earlier novellas would not be concluded until the later sections. Zabala described the first novella as a fictional rendering of his adolescent American self. (Its gently ironic tone and youthful idiomatic perspective are perhaps an echo of Salinger, but stylistically it is a curious blend of Hemingway, André Breton, and Enrique Vila-Matas.) The first novella would introduce the leitmotif of the eternal quest for true love, and then open up into the second novella (a literary nod to Henry Miller, Julio Cortázar, Alfonso Reyes, and again, Vila-Matas), which Zabala described as the beginning of his search for his Spanish roots. The second novella would open up into the third, the third into the fourth, and so on. The ninth novella would circle back to the narrative begun in the first novella. Zabala described this last section as an existential, quasi-objective rendering of reality from the perspective of an individual who must eventually, inevitably, choose between the world as it is and the world as it should be.

The guiding principle of the book is the idea that nothing is what it appears to be. Thus, the arc of the story through the nine novellas works its way backwards through time and history from Jacksonville, Florida and Miami and a quasi-familiar American landscape to the historical melting pot of Logroño, Spain in the 1890s and the mythic stories of Escolástica and Isabel Escoraz Vda De Miranda. From Spain we head to Santiago, Cuba, circa 1900-1907, a tumultuous period in Cuban history when forgotten poets lingered in the shadows before descending into oblivion, the determined followers of José Martí were still seeking liberty and equality for every Cuban citizen, and *brujería* magic was a force to be reckoned with. From Santiago we then travel to a film nourish 1950s Havana, with swanky, exclusive nightclubs overflowing with the sounds of sultry danzón singers; and corrupt government officials and remorseless gangsters who read Pirandello find themselves in a battle to the death with anarchists from Germany, who believe they are working for a sinister, alien (as in outer space) race intent on subjugating the Earth; and then we find ourselves in a contemporary parallel universe America (with one Kafkaesque detour thru parts of France, Germany, and the city of Prague) where an aging Basque immigrant who fought Franco, a World War One tank commander, Latin-American revolutionaries, CIA operatives, FBI agents, ex-poets, ex-priests, atheists, an internationally acclaimed porn star, an expert on Nazi mysticism and the occult, a modern-day saint, a Hollywood movie director who was nominated for an Academy Award, and a hairdresser from Buenos Aires who once cut the hair of Jorge Borges in a hotel room in New York City, all take their turn on center stage, and the hope of finding paradise takes on profoundly spiritual dimensions.

Zabala wanted to blur the lines between history and fiction, and between religion and science, and so create a mythic realm where 'God is granted the power to create, but creation itself is only visible through the prism of the human imagination.' But he soon realized that his epic tale was in fact taking him into the abyss, but he saw the abyss as a temporary construct of delusional thinking that one needed to confront before one could find true happiness. He believed, like Dante, that if you wanted to reach paradise, you first had to go through Hell. But he also felt that Dante's pre-existential view of human freedom, a view that firmly placed on human shoulders the responsibility for one's actions, was limited by Dante's reliance on the framework of Catholic orthodoxy, which Zabala viewed as a form of Fascism. So *The Mad Patagonian* goes far beyond the scope of a generational epic and becomes in the final analysis a psychological, even surreal exploration of the mythic power of the imagination, of human consciousness itself, to lift us out of the darkness that threatens to swallow the universe at any given moment, and that in fact does so from time to time. In this respect, Zabala's notion of both our relation to the abyss and our responsibility when we recognize the abyss is closer to Camus than to Kafka, and closer still to Michel Foucault, (or at least an interpretation of Foucault by various contemporary philosophers) who suggested that 'an interrogation of the limit (the abyss) and of transgression' (moving beyond this limit in the hope of recovering the 'sacred,' as Bataille defined it, from the grave of Nietzsche's dead god) would result in 'a return of the self' (a self free from the limits superimposed on the self not only by society, but by the self itself, so to transgress these limits would be the ultimate paradise, if you will, though Foucault would not have used the word, except, perhaps, to describe the nostalgic symbolism of an Oriental garden).

Thus, Zabala takes us on a journey into his own troubled psyche, which is also a journey into Hell, or at least a symbolic representation of Hell that our collective unconscious would recognize. But he does not leave us there. (It is this aspect of *The Mad Patagonian* that provides a stark counterpoint to the darker vision of much of Roberto Bolaño's work and is, perhaps, an effort on the part of Zabala to engage Bolaño in a metaliterary conversation about the nature of the world and our role in that world. Moreover, the subtextual interplay between these two competing visions is perhaps crucial to understanding Zabala's novel.) In an entry in his diary dated August 24, 1998, Zabala wrote about the journey through Hell:

Hell is that place where consciousness vies with itself for supremacy over creation. It is a place created by the mind to keep us trapped within the spatial and temporal boundaries superimposed on the mind by the mind itself. But it is an illusion. It is a labyrinth with darkly gleaming mirrors at every turn. And once we recognize this truth, we are free to continue our journey towards paradise. In fact we are more than free to continue. We have an ethical responsibility to do so, not just for ourselves, but so others might follow. Hell is but the midpoint of our journey.

But if Hell for Zabala was a product of our mind, then paradise was a product of what Zabala thought of as the antimind, what the Buddhists would call the place of no-mind. Zabala believed that paradise was beyond our comprehension because it existed outside of time and space. He also believed that we could and in fact should claim paradise as our birthright. His beliefs were a reflection of his understanding of the transcendence of the human soul, not as the result of religious conviction, nor as the result of glimpsing the horror of the abyss and retreating to the relative safety and hypocritical respectability of a normative or intellectually pacifying notion of what it means to be human, as Nietzsche seems to have accused most philosophers of doing. For Zabala, a belief in both the transcendence of the human soul and paradise is also a belief in humanity's ability to explore without limits the breadth and depth of human experience and so free us from the 'dark, firm net of custom and habit' (Foucault). Thus, the paradise which the characters in *The Mad Patagonian* hope for, that they are chasing after, the paradise they imagine at the beginning of their separate journeys, is not the paradise they eventually discover because the very act of searching for paradise, however tentatively, changes its composition.

So what then is going on in *The Mad Patagonian*? The journeys that Zabala's characters are taking in search of a real paradise are also for Zabala symbolic representations of the journeys we all are in the process of taking. What his characters must learn, we also must learn. The choices they are faced with mirror our own. Thus, one can read *The Mad Patagonian* as a critique of human evil, but also, more importantly, as a testament to the enduring strength and beauty of the human spirit as humanity itself is consumed by the eternal struggle to reach the shores of paradise. Moreover, Zabala is quite clear in his assertion that not only are we responsible for whether or not we eventually reach these shores (Dante's notion of responsibility), but that ultimately paradise would not exist except that we as creative agents are mysteriously and unconsciously involved in its creation. Unfortunately, Zabala's explanation of how we are mysteriously and unconsciously involved in creating paradise is not so clear. God may be the ultimate source of the creative power of the universe, a belief that Zabala can never quite bring himself to reject, and we may be the unconscious translators of that power into something real, something visible, so we can think of ourselves as co-creators, but Zabala only alludes to the mechanics of this process in cryptic terms. Indeed, one gets the impression from reading both Zabala's diary and his novel that for him God both exists and does not exist, so the question of whether or not paradise actually exists is part of an ongoing debate that can only be determined on a case-by-case basis. Zabala gets tangled up in the labyrinth of his own metaphysical thinking.

To be fair, we must keep in mind that Zabala is not a philosopher. He is not writing a philosophical treatise. He is not engaged in an intellectual debate, except, perhaps, with himself. *The Mad Patagonian* is, after all, a work of fiction. The philosophical foundation of the novel is not so much a solid foundation as it is a sandy beach in constant flux and serves only as a backdrop (a temporary, ever-changing, shifting-sands backdrop) to illuminate the struggles of his characters. In the end, Zabala provides no definitive answer to the philosophical questions he raises, and so to use his diary as a means for interpreting his novel is to perhaps misjudge his intent. He is a poet more than a philosopher, and uses the language of metaphor to express what cannot be rendered in precise, analytical prose. Yes, there is plenty of room in the novel for broad-stroke philosophical interpretations. One can also zoom in on seemingly trivial details and debate their quasi-philosophical implications. For example, what is one to make of the fact that the word 'time' makes 517 appearances in the first five novellas of *The Mad Patagonian*, which on both a psychological and a symbolic level represent the descent into Hell, but the word disappears completely in the last four novellas, which are focused on the ascent towards paradise? The novel is riddled with such riddles, large and small. Indeed, there are so many veiled ironic references to one philosophical position or another that one begins to suspect that Zabala is simply having some fun. (And who does not like to poke fun at philosophy now and then?) But Zabala's focus is not on critiquing the philosophers of any particular age or expressing some particular philosophical message. As any good novelist would, he focuses squarely on the lives of his characters and on the choices they face as they attempt to discover their truest selves in a world where many lose their way. And because Zabala's characters never quite succumb to the darkness of their world, there is always the possibility that they may indeed find happiness, and if not happiness, at least some measure of contentment. Who could reasonably ask for anything more?

Zabala and Bolaño saw each other for the second and last time in November 1989 in Caracas, Venezuela. Zabala had accompanied Blanca, who had been part of a team of doctors from Cuba sent to help the Venezuelans with an outbreak of Dengue fever. They had arrived in September and took up residence in one of the dormitories on the campus of the University of Caracas. Zabala saw very little of Blanca during the four months they were in Venezuela. He took the time to write and read and explore the city. He was particularly interested in the almost mythic blindness of the politicians to the continual economic hardships of the people of Caracas. As he wrote in his dairy in an entry dated January 6, 1990:

I went up into the barrios, those ramshackle shanty towns encroaching on the city limits, neighborhoods without a proper sewer system or even the possibility of electricity. I spoke with survivors of the Caracazo, men and women who had taken to the streets in late February and early March 1989 to protest the neoliberal economic policies of Pérez. Buses were burned. Traffic ground to a halt. And then the people from the barrios began looting and burning stores. A grocery store with a bright blue exterior went up in flames. So did a pasta factory. Some people were carrying cans of evaporated milk and chocolate bars and packages of spaghetti back to their families. In other areas, the looting became more intense. Radios, color television sets, even refrigerators were carted away. The police went up into the barrios and began firing at shadows. Bodies began tumbling down steps. Then the army came in with tanks and machine guns and canisters of tear gas and the will to attack indiscriminately. More tumbling bodies. As many as three thousand civilians were murdered over the ten days of the massacre and the dead bodies were loaded into trucks by shadowy, faceless men and driven to abandoned construction sites along the edge of this ever-expanding city on the edge of paradise. The faceless men tossed the bodies into great, gaping ditches as if no one had died, as if they were simply tossing stones to the ground, as the poet Neruda once wrote, and then the bodies were covered over quickly with lime and dirt. It was an act of erasure. The government did not want anyone to know how many people had died, so the dead were simply erased. But you could still feel their unmentionable deaths lingering over the city like a hemorrhagic haze. I have not felt so closely connected to such an unspeakable, horrific atrocity since '68. It was just as we felt in Mexico City. The same overwhelming, unending, suffocating sadness. Before the February massacre in Caracas, the poor of the barrios had covered the walls of their shanty towns with graffiti that said 'El pueblo está bravo ('the people are angry') or 'Se han burlado de nosotros' ('an end to deception') or El pueblo tiene hambre' ('the people are hungry'). Afterwards the graffiti simply said: 'We are the children of '89.' They will be calling themselves the children of '89 for the rest of their lives. What was Pérez thinking? So many dead, so many orphaned children, so many Venezuelans struggling to stay afloat in an ocean of poverty superimposed from above, and all so the Americans can buy Venezuelan goods at dirt cheap prices as part of a deal with the World Bank.

At the time, Zabala told his wife that the real plague in Caracas was not Dengue fever. The real plague was the propagation of a privileged class at the expense of everyone else. It didn't matter if you were neoliberal or anti-neoliberal. It didn't matter if you were left or right. As soon as you found yourself in a position of power, you worked as hard as you could to become a class unto yourself. Zabala felt quite strongly about the nature of this evil. 'It is like the Nazis all over again,' he wrote, 'though on a smaller scale. But small scales can quickly become large scales, so there is really no substantive difference.'
But Zabala did not spend all of his time in Caracas contemplating the injustice and violence perpetrated on the Venezuelan people by their government. In his diary he notes that he visited the National Pantheon and knelt before the tomb of Rufino Blanco-Fombona, who was nominated for the Nobel prize in literature but never won. He also visited the tombs of Renato Beluche, a sailor and pirate who was Simón Bolívar's favorite admiral, and Rómulo Gallegos, a better writer perhaps than Blanco-Fombona, and also the first

Venezuelan elected president without a controversy, who was also nominated for the Nobel prize in literature, and also never won.

On another day Zabala sat in a pew near the back of the Caracas Cathedral and later wrote that 'the gleaming white and golden brilliance of the interior of this baroque enclave left me dazzled and virtually blind.' He visited the Bellas Artes and split his time between the Latin American collection and the Egyptian collection. Later, by accident, he found himself in Parque Carabobo and stumbled upon a statue of Pedro Camejo, a slave, 'The First Black,' who fought first for the royal army against the rebels but then later switched sides in the Venezuelan War of Independence (1811-1823) and fought at the Battle of Carabobo against Calixto García de Luna e Izquierdo (who, according to Zabala, also switched sides, 'but only after the war had ended, which is why the new government put him in prison, where he languished for almost ten years before he was mysteriously set free, at which point he left his wife and young son and Venezuela altogether and went to Cuba to prove himself against the Spanish').

Zabala also writes that in the first week of October he met a burn victim at the Carabobo metro station, a man who had been a bus driver and had suffered first degree burns on his arms and legs and third degree burns on his neck and face. This chance meeting made quite an impression on Zabala. The man's injuries had happened during the Caracazo. He told Zabala that his bus had been overwhelmed by a maniac crowd and set on fire and he had stupidly (his word) rushed into the flames to do something, put the fire out, save his lunch, he didn't remember, and had caught fire himself. He had lost his job as a bus driver because most people couldn't stomach the reality of a burn victim driving their bus. Zabala noted that the ex-bus driver's skin on the left side of his face all the way down the left side of his neck was leathery and black, almost a charcoal color. It looked like he was suffering from some malignant form of cancer or leprosy. Zabala went back to the Carabobo station several times to talk with the man, but never saw him again. Zabala also notes in his diary that he spent many lonely hours wandering along Avenida Lincoln during the afternoon in search of tiny cafes where he could smoke and drink coffee and watch the people flow back and forth. On a bright sunny day sitting outside a small café near the Sabana Grande metro station he wrote:

Caracas is a violent, dangerous, bustling modern city; it is a city of swirling ghosts and lost bullets; it is a city of enormous privilege standing on the shoulders of an incomprehensible poverty; it is a city of Americanized bureaucrats and drug addicts and leftist insurgents; it is a city suffocating beneath the ever-expanding black cloud of big oil; it is a city of operettas on every street corner and prostitutes lurking in the shadows of every hotel; it is an eternal city of vagabond poets and unrepentant, self-absorbed dictators who arrive with scorn, proclaiming the void and annihilating the competition; it is a city of pirates and writers and visiting bullfighters and international race car drivers who are kidnapped and held for a king's ransom and ambassadors who have outlived their usefulness, all of them now dancing the Joropo by candlelight; it is a city where the flames of the revolution burn brightly each and every night, only to be snuffed out at dawn; it is a city that wakes every morning to the pestilent stench of diesel fumes and ancient church bells tolling for the newly dead; it is a city of fornicating and thievery and angry laughter and Indian families living in makeshift homes made from cardboard boxes and plywood crates and children carrying guns and swift farewells; it is a smoldering powder keg ready to combust; it is an urban jungle where the scent of wild violets and orange blossoms from centuries ago has been replaced by the smells of rotting corpses drifting up through the Metro vents; and the smell of almond trees and the murmur of the ocean's millenary waves have been replaced by the Parisian perfumes of high-priced models and the tinkling of their laughter as they run in and out of shops along Avenida Lincoln looking to buy handbags and shoes; a city where everything is ultimately fatal and vultures pick at the skeletal remains of revolutionaries from a century ago; but all this makes it a writer's paradise.

Zabala was quite taken with Caracas, so it is no wonder that he also wrote Bolaño, the only other writer he knew, and invited him to come to Caracas and share in his discoveries. Bolaño wrote back that he would, and on Wednesday, November 22, 1989, at some point in the evening, they met in the once elegant lobby of Hotel El Conde, an iconic hotel in the historic section of downtown Caracas one block west of Plaza Bolívar. Zabala recorded his thoughts of Bolaño's visit in an entry in his diary dated November 26, 1989:

Bolaño left yesterday. I am only now just recovering. We spent sixty-some hours in a raging, drunken brawl with every preconceived notion about life we have ever held, all in a mad effort to see what would remain standing after we were finished. It was a dismantling of reality of the first order, and then a reassembling of that reality. It was a philosophical maelstrom, but it was also a poetic, anti-poetic, revolutionary, idealistic, paranoid, adolescent, obsessive, religious, atheistic, sexual, anti-sexual, bluesy, jazzy jam session. We crammed in every duality we could think of. And it began the moment Bolaño walked into the lobby of the hotel. I cannot think of a better venue from where to embark on a journey such as we took than Hotel El Conde. It is a modern hotel of iron and concrete, a fairly recent addition (1948) to a city that seems determined to replace the decaying, baroque elegance of the past with the ultra-modernity of the future, and yet the hotel itself is an odd portal that gives us a glimpse of the very past the city wishes to escape. When you first walk into the lobby you are instantly confronted with a few iconic pieces of artwork depicting the stylized faces of dead Venezuelan heroes, and you are almost overwhelmed by the musty odor like incense of the heavy blue drapes that admit into the lobby only surreptitious flashes of sunlight or starlight like vagabond ghosts that have wandered down from the mountains. It is a place where history is constantly whispering even though the architecture is barely forty years old. But a hell of a lot has happened within these walls in those forty years. Politicians and poet ambassadors and bullfighters and rising journalists have slept with society divas in the rooms above the lobby. Decadent drug lords have held court downstairs. International porn stars have tiptoed down the hallways late at night seeking out ritual comfort in one room or another. Murders have been committed here, carnival atrocities. New revolutions have been planned but then the plans have been shelved on the advice of foreign agents. The great writer Rómulo Gallegos himself lived in this hotel for a few months after he was elected President in February 1948 until he was thrown out of the country in November of that same year. It is said you could hear him typing away late at night, supposedly working on new sections of his great novel, Doña Bárbara. Was he ever finished with that book? Is he still hoping to add a chapter or two even in death? How amazing to think that he had only been in San Fernando de Apure for a single week doing research, and to read Doña Bárbara you would have thought he had been born there! The people who actually live in San Fernando say as much. Or perhaps Gallegos was working on something else when he called Hotel El Conde his home. Some say you can still hear him typing away madly. At any rate, this is where we had decided to meet. Hotel El Conde became our jumping off point, our crossroads between the past and the future. Of course the moment Bolaño walked into the lobby he breathed in the intoxicating, beguiling, surreal atmosphere of this hotel caught between two worlds. I was sitting in one of two red leather chairs near the hotel entrance, with a potted fern on one side. But he stopped as soon as he saw me and raised his hand as if to ask for silence. It was a bit dramatic. He just stood there for a while, his face submerged in the glare of a well-placed floor lamp, listening to some unseen music, and for a moment it was almost as if he had vanished. All I could see where he stood was the pulsating aura of the lamp light, as if he had been absorbed into the light itself, beamed up into oblivion by an alien spacecraft. Then he stepped out of the glare and sat down, smiling, a ludicrous smile, and asked me if I thought all that much about immortality, and I laughed and said what does it matter, madness is madness is madness, and sadness too, and he started laughing and said yes, yes, we are all children of Caliban, and I remember how astonished I was that he said that because I was thinking exactly the same thing, and then he asked me if I could feel the unappeased literary genius of Gallegos swirling about the lobby like smoke seeking escape, and I said I could, I said I had suggested Hotel El Conde for precisely that reason, and then we were both laughing hysterically. I think Bolaño and I were cut from the same cloth, though perhaps from opposite ends of the ragged bolt. We would agree and disagree in the same breath. I don't know how long we stayed at the hotel. We did not stay long. The hotel has a small, dingy bar, again a vision of faded, surreal elegance, where we downed a few beers, and then we hit the streets, which is to say we roamed all over the city that first night, searching out hidden bars and cafés tucked away in the crevices of Venezuelan culture, riding the gleaming silver bullet trains of the Metro in search of the burn victim I had discovered back in October, but the further we traveled by train, the further my burn victim retreated into the majesty of my own myth-making. We lingered over midnight snacks and pre-dawn breakfasts and pestilent, sun-blazing, late afternoon lunches, or maybe we ate nothing at all, maybe we only drank, and it is impossible to calculate how much we drank, beer, tequila, wine, whiskey, rum, all sorts of mixed drinks, even Kahlúa and cream, which I absolutely detest, but I drank it anyway. I don't know what we were thinking. I guess we were thinking we were back in Mexico City in 1975. But what does that even mean? What does it mean to think back on a Mexico that existed fourteen years ago, a Mexico that no longer exists? Time lifts us with ancient cymbals, as the poet Gerbasi says, but not quite in the way he imagined it. The distant thunderstorms no longer agonize me. I am no longer stuffed with ashes. The hard geometries of my youth have swiftly bled away. So who cares what we were doing or why oh so many years ago? No one can tell your political sympathies by looking at your bones. The time of our youth was past. We had both moved on. And now we were drinking to the memory of that youth, or to something else. It did not matter. It was an endless night of drinking. The drinking is what mattered. That fact is indisputable. And we talked while we drank. We talked the way I had always imagined writers would talk. That fact is also indisputable. We spoke of the slippery nature of reality, the interconnectedness of things, the intertextuality of all history. We talked at length about Paul Kammerer, who said that history was the serial repetition of a singular event, an idea which he quite properly called seriality, but which Jung later stole and called synchronicity and now nobody knows about Paul Kammerer. We talked about the impossibility of defeating the Fascism of time, especially since we were armed only with the arrows of mortal ambition, which are easily turned aside. We wondered if in fact any writer could truly achieve immortality since the fate of all books, with no exceptions, is that sooner or later they are used for kindling. This is a practical reality. I remember that I talked about my Big Spanish book and Bolaño talked about his German book, which was almost finished, except for the polishing. It was a book which he said wasn't really about Germany, it was more about the intellectual games we all play trying to justify the violence of existence, or the nature of existence in a violent world, or something like that. Germany was just a front, Bolaño said, and he was laughing subversively as he spoke so I knew he was being ironic, but it was more than ironic, there was a smaller seriousness embedded in his irony, but that seriousness was also folded over into irony, with an even smaller seriousness embedded in that, and so on, like a series of opposing mirrors stretching with exquisite precision towards infinity. You never knew how far Bolaño would go when he was being ironic. I told him I would need to read the book to see what he was getting at. Then he talked about an idea he had for another book, a book that would be an encyclopedia of right-wing writers living in Latin America, and he was almost laughing as he talked about this book, but not quite, it was more like he was posing for the future. He said none of the writers would be real writers, they wouldn't actually exist in the world, he *would make it all up, but he was convinced that people reading the book would think the writers were real. And then he did burst out laughing. Actually, it seemed pretty funny when he was talking about it, and Bolaño's laughter was certainly infectious, and it did break the monotony of sitting in a foul-smelling Metro station with the fluorescent lights flickering and buzzing at three in the morning, waiting for the train to Pérez Bonalde, though why we going to Pérez Bonalde I am not quite sure, but I seem to remember that we had heard a lot of gunfire at one point during the afternoon, I don't know where the hell we were, some café or bar or restaurant in Catia, just off Calle El Cristo, or maybe it was closer to Parque del Oeste, I don't really remember, but the gunfire sounded pretty close wherever we were, and there was a lot of it, and Bolaño was convinced there was another riot going on and people were dying right and left, but then the gunfire stopped and the owner of the café came over and smiled with great enthusiasm, a gleaming, hopeful smile like a burning sun that most certainly masked the invincible melancholy of a defeated people, and he said they were working on some of the transformers down at the electricity company, which was only a few blocks away, that was why we had heard all those popping sounds, it sounded like that sometimes, so there was no need to worry, and then he brought us another round of beers, perhaps to disguise the fact that his explanation seemed unconvincing, because the very air of Caracas is saturated with an unthinking and unrepentant violence, because in the streets of Caracas the hope of Baudelaire is erased by the certain knowledge that everything is fatal, even chance, but who were we to contradict the owner's great enthusiasm and his hopeful generosity and so expose the truth behind the mask, so we went back to our drinking, so I think that's why we were going to Pérez Bonalde, because there was a hospital a few blocks from the station and if there were any survivors from the massacre that afternoon, that's where they would have been, except there was no fucking hospital, how we got this idea into our heads I can't imagine, and there probably hadn't been a massacre either, but what the fuck, in retrospect the whole damn thing was fucking hilarious, the whole sequence was rather like something out of an absurdist play by Fernando Arrabal, Bolaño talking about his idea for a new book at three in the morning, the two of us bathed in the erratic glow of festering, fluorescent lights in a deserted Metro station in lonely, mythic Caracas without even rats scratching about, somewhere beyond the known boundaries of reality, I suspect, and then Bolaño out of the blue remembering about the imagined gunfire from before, no warning, just bam! and then he became obsessed with the need to talk to a survivor of the imaginary riot that had taken place only in our collective brain that afternoon, this need surging through his arteries like a bolt of lightning, the fluorescent lights flickering with a more visible intensity as his obsession grew, and then bam! just like that the lights went out, also without warning, the two of us now waiting in a hazy, humid darkness backlit by the faint red glow of half-a-dozen emergency lights floating in the blackness of the Metro tunnel like the eyes of Cerberus guarding the black Gates of Hell, the two of us waiting for the train to Pérez Bonalde so we could go to a hospital that did not exist, so our plan was pretty much fucked from the start, but like I said, we didn't know. I'm pretty sure that was the reason, but we were both fairly drunk by then. I'm not even sure if we made it to Pérez Bonalde. I guess we must have made it because how else would I know the hospital didn't exist, but I don't remember. But while we were waiting in the darkness for the goddamn train I told Bolaño I wanted to see his right-wing writers' encyclopedia when he was done, and he said he'd send me a copy. After that we didn't talk any more about literature. We were too tired to talk about something so heady and yet so insubstantial, so unreal as literature. To tell you the truth, I think we were just plain exhausted. And then all of a sudden it was Friday night and we had arrived at the last stop on our whirlwind journey through this terrifying yet seductive landscape of dark nights and even darker treachery. We were sitting in a seedy dive on Calle Los Apamates, a stone's throw from yet another*

Metro station, a café where humanity's darkest intentions were made visible. It was the kind of place that served horrible dinners until nine or ten, and anything you wanted to drink until five in the morning. The patrons were mostly prostitutes sitting on the laps of drunken, overweight, mid-level businessmen, the prostitutes playfully tugging at ties and rubbing with surreptitious skill the bulges that had started to grow and spoon-feeding the hungry businessmen until their plates were empty and then the girls whispering words that promised a night of unending joy coupled with eternal absolution (¿Pendiente de una vuelta?) and the businessmen whispering back words that echoed with the hope of unrestrained passion (¡Chévere!) and then two by two the newly formed couples would begin heading for the door and the crystallized obscurity of the dark Venezuelan night, only to be replaced by more playful prostitutes and more eager businessmen. There were also a few out-of-place University students who had abandoned their studies days earlier and were now teetering on the brink, hoping for table scraps, perhaps, their eyes glazed over with the luminous, impenetrable anxiety of drug addiction, certain to end up the victims of some unspeakable crime. Bolaño and I were sitting at a small, triangular table next to a narrow aquarium that had been shoved into the back corner. Our tiny table was partially illuminated by the dim light from the hallway that led to the bathroom. The aquarium was supposedly filled with all sorts of tropical fish, though it was hard to see, perhaps it was only a few half-starved piranhas, and every now and then someone on their way back from the bathroom would toss a few coins into the aquarium and stop and stare for a while at the murky darkness of the water and the faint, greenish glow of a tiny light bulb lodged inside a porcelain deep sea diver. Everyone who tossed a few coins into the aquarium seemed hypnotized by the tiny deep sea diver. Then they would shudder and shake their heads and the spell would be broken. They would mutter a small prayer for good luck, or maybe they were cursing someone under their breath, hoping to cast the evil eye on an enemy, and then head back to their tables. I think we were the last ones to order dinner. We were eating pabellón, a meal that consists of carne mechada, black beans, sweet fried plantains, and queso blanco. We were also drinking a spicy, dry, dark rum, Pampero Anniversario, glass after glass after glass. We ate in absolute silence because we were very hungry, but once we finished eating, we began talking with the same fervor we possessed at the beginning of our journey. We talked about the ever-expanding galaxy, and we wondered at mankind's insufferable egotism to suppose that our star alone of all the stars in the sky possessed planets that supported sentient life. We lamented the lost beauty and obscured significance of those unheralded beings from distant planets whom we would never know. We wondered if they were flesh and blood creatures like we were, or if perhaps they were instead made of gas or water or frozen light and simply floated like nebulas or clouds from one place to another. We cursed our inability to soar through the heavens, except by using our puny, febrile imaginations, towards the unfathomable purity of those unreachable stars. We talked about the technology of spaceships. We talked about time travel. Who will be left far behind? I asked Bolaño. We all will, he replied. Then we talked about Simón Bolívar and Venezuela's struggle for independence. We talked about Bolívar's relationship with the famous German explorer Alexander von Humboldt. Why is it the Europeans, especially the Germans, but also a few Venezuelan myth-makers, insist on perpetuating the story that Humboldt gave Bolívar the idea of a free Venezuela when they met in Paris in November 1804? Wasn't Bolívar a bit too young and inexperienced to absorb such weighty advice at that point? Isn't it more likely that their first meeting was a bit more frivolous in nature, that perhaps all Bolívar wanted to know was the name of a good restaurant? Isn't it more likely that the political intent of El Libertador was stamped upon his psyche after his return to Venezuela, where he was ultimately confronted with the inescapable tragedy of life as a bonded servant to Spain? Wouldn't this realization have been enough to spur his political ambition? And what of Bolívar's strange, almost legendary meeting with José de San Martín, the great Argentine General, the Protector of Peruvian Freedom, who had liberated not only Peru but also Chile and what is now Argentina? What actually happened at that fateful conference in Guayaquil? Who was the puppet master? Why did San Martin accept the defeat of his political hopes to install a new monarchy in Peru (or was this hope also a fabrication of later historians) in favor of Simón Bolívar's dream of a series of republics? Was the banquet and ball given in honor of San Martin a political demonstration of Bolívar's complete victory? Is this why San Martin soon abdicated, leaving South America for good in 1829 for the shores of idyllic France and a life of quiet retreat? Can the riddle of Guayaquil only be pierced by two historians whose very existence is limited to the pages of a short story of the same name written by Borges? Is all reality suspect? Does the successive, ordered use of language by its very nature tend to exaggerate the importance of what we are saying? And what of Bolívar's own claim that he was in Milan in 1805 and attended the coronation of Napoleon? We were both fascinated by the swirling eddies of myth and deception that surrounded Bolívar. We wondered if his lover, Manuela Sáenz, a patriot and hero of the revolution in her own right, minded all that much that her beloved was taken from his initial resting place in the Cathedral of Santa Marta and put on permanent display, so to speak, in the National Pantheon in 1842, becoming thus a symbol of the impervious commitment to the competing ideals of liberty and equality, while she herself died in 1856 of diphtheria and was dumped with unceremonious disdain, and no small measure of fear due to the possibility of contagion, into a mass grave. We wondered who actually created these fantastic stories that we now take for history. We wondered if we ourselves could create such stories. Who will be left far behind? Bolaño said. We all will, I said. We were filled with sudden troubling premonitions. Or perhaps we were having simultaneous attacks of gastroenteritis. Then we were talking about Venezuela *under Pérez and how it was a ticking time bomb. The day that shook the country had only exposed the problem for the whole world to see. There was no brutal rupture with the past, no collapsing sky, no need to invent a new metanarrative to superimpose upon the universe. It was the same story that had plagued Venezuela since the days of the Spanish Empire, the same story that plagued all of Latin America. Everyone with eyes to see could see that the gap between the rich and the poor remained, and so did the frustration that fragments the lives of those living at the bottom. The streets of Caracas were still home to thousands and thousands of 'buhoneros' (vendors) who continued to scratch and claw with desperate enthusiasm just to stay alive, selling everything and anything from Rolex watches to rock-and-roll t-shirts to handbags to empanadas to raw oysters to pistols to drugs. The upper crust still hid out in their fortified castles, protected by barbed wire and surveillance cameras and German mercenary bodyguards armed to the teeth with fully serrated army knives and semi-automatic machine guns. And all over the city, in the slums of Caucaguita and San Agustin and Monte Piedad and Sierra Maestra, dozens of hastily built, ramshackle apartment buildings and burnt-red ranchos were still washed away in the muddy torrential rivers that followed on the heels of severe thunderstorms, in spite of the tangled black net of cables and wires that seemed to hold the barrios in place when it wasn't raining. The tears that were shed only months earlier for those who had died in the name of freedom had already evaporated like desert raindrops. But Pérez cannot wash his hands of that blood, nor the blood that is to come, I said. He cannot forever blame the leftist guerrillas and criminals and drug lords and counter-revolutionaries from Cuba and other politically undesirable elements for the plague that has already arrived on his doorstep. And it is not just a Venezuelan issue. It is a global issue. We must focus on helping everyone meet their basic needs, I said. It is time to put Marcel Duchamp's urinal back on the wall. And Bolaño naturally agreed. Then we talked about the explosive violence of the Caracazo itself and the burning buses and the looting that had spread like an Egyptian pestilence, like a fucking plague of locusts, and the government declaring marital law, and just like that Bolaño wanted to know all about the burn victim I had met in October, in fact it was more like an interrogation, like he was pumping me for information, what was his name? said Bolaño (Ernesto Peralta, I said) and where did he live before the riots? (in the neighborhood called El Marques just off Avenida Boyaca in the shadow of Cerro El Avila, the lungs of Caracas because of all the greenery) and where did he now live? (I did not know, I had not seen him since that first time) and how extensive were his injuries? (the entire left side of his face and neck and shoulder were burned very badly, I could not see the skin beneath his shirt, but the skin that was exposed was still very black, almost a charcoal color, and it was leathery, I mean it seemed like his skin was actually a piece of leather that had been left to rot in the elements, and it was also cracked in many places, and it was clear that his arms and his legs from the knees down had also been burned, but not as badly, but the overall impression was of someone with a rare, festering, malignant form of cancer or someone suffering from leprosy, he didn't look human at all from a certain angle, in fact in the dim light of the Metro station where I met him he looked more like a creature from outer space) and did he possess any unusual smell? (an unusual smell?) yes, like formaldehyde or rubbing alcohol or ammonium chloride? (I do not know, I do not remember any unusual smell) and did he seem to have an aversion to direct sunlight? (that is difficult to determine, one could argue that was the case, since I stumbled upon him at the deepest level of the Metro station, but I only met him the one time, so it is impossible to perceive a pattern) and did he seem to have come to terms with his deformity? (you mean psychologically?) yes, or emotionally, or did it seem like he possessed a violent, sinister streak just below the surface? (yes, now that you mention it, he most definitely possessed an aura of maladjustment, the tremulous tremors that lull us to sleep, as if he were just waiting for the right moment* to slit someone's throat) good, very good, said Bolaño, and there were many more precise, journalistic, though slightly bizarre questions after that, nitty-gritty questions, an attempt to get at the hidden psychology of what it means to live out one's days as a burn victim, and I did my best to answer every question he put to me, it was actually kind of fun, like we were two detectives comparing notes, that is the impression I had, as if Bolaño had come face to face with numerous burn victims since he had left Mexico City and was cataloguing how each had responded to their deformity in the hopes of answering certain fundamental questions about the nature of identity and whether or not you could indeed remain yourself if the face you had been born with no longer existed. Yes, it was an interesting conversation. And then just like that it was over, but not because we had exhausted its possibilities. Bolaño was just about to ask me what might have been the most profound question he had asked all evening (that was certainly the look in his eyes sparkling with mischief), when we were savagely interrupted by two immaculately dressed local gangsters engaged in a furious discussion about a recent epidemic of UFO sightings in the skies above Caracas. I say gangsters because each gentleman possessed a small pocket gun, a Beistegui Brothers Libia 6.35 mm originally manufactured in Spain but purchased only God knew where. With a flair for theatric gestures, they had placed their guns on their table while they were arguing. These were not the kind of guns police detectives would have carried. Yes, they were deadly enough, but a Libia is more for show, a collector's item, more for the prestige of owning such a gun, more to announce to the world that the man who possesses it is a man of some stature, more the kind of gun a gangster on the rise would possess. What was more intriguing than their tiny showcase pistols, however, was that their argument seemed less like an actual argument than it did an occasion for arguing. It was soon apparent that both men believed in the existence of UFOs, and that their comments about the sightings and the possibility of being visited by aliens or even abducted were aimed at disarming the paranoid vigilance of their *opponent, thus creating an opportunity to get off a quick potshot. We were in fact witnessing a rarely seen ritual dance between two second-tier egomaniacs vying for power (and a chance to gain market share in gangsterland) in the dim, bluish, cavernous light of this seedy dive on Calle Los Apamates south of Solano. Both men seemed to be frothing at the mouth. What about the story of Emelino Gonzales, the truck driver? said the one. Ah, my friend, why do you need to go back to 1954? said the other. We are talking about alien encounters, are we not? What better example than Gonzales, who was forced to exit his truck because a nine-foot wide spherical craft was hovering six feet off the ground, blocking the road to Petare? said the one. Ah, yes, but some say Gonzales was a deranged drug addict. Who else would claim he was attacked by hairy dwarves? said the other. But you do not dispute the fact that his assailants emerged from the craft and sent him flying backwards some fifteen feet with a concentrated beam of light? said the one. No, no. But Gonzales did say his astral assailants were covered with hair and they were wearing loincloths. I dispute that. And he also said some of these hairy dwarves were off gathering rocks when he surprised them. I dispute that as well. What aliens wear loincloths? And why did they need rocks from the road to Petare? said the other. What of the story of Lorenzo Paz and Alberto Rosales? said the one. You mean Rosales the shoe salesman and amateur photographer and not Rosales the philosopher? said the other. Yes, certainly, the one who along with Paz took the pictures of a luminous oval craft zooming back and forth in the skies over Carora, with great orange flames shooting out from its underbelly, incinerating the landscape. Who could deny the truth of the pictures? said the one. Yes, that is certainly a truthful account. But it is also an old, old story. And it does not take place in Caracas, said the other. Very well then, let us return to the recent sightings. What do you say about the craft Mrs. Regina Rivero said she saw from the plaza just outside the Chacaito subway station? said the one. Yes, yes, this report has been on the news on every channel. A whitish blue light of great size and luminosity, much brighter than any other heavenly body in the sky. The light appearing stationary for five or ten minutes, and then accelerating at great speed and vanishing in the hazy, urban glow of the city and the darkness beyond. But a whitish blue light is hardly a spacecraft, said the other. What then of the small, circular black object seen in the skies above La Pastora, an object that was most definitely an alien spacecraft according to the witnesses, and there were thousands of reputable witnesses who said the ship crisscrossed the heavens, looking for unsuspecting victims to snatch away, slicing up the sky in odd, bewildering geometric patterns before it zoomed away at the speed of light and was lost in the clouds surrounding Cerro El Avila? What of that, my friend? But instead of responding with another criticism, the other gangster picked up his Libia in a motion so quick and easy it was difficult to believe the gun had not always been a part of his hand, and without even a backward glance at his friend, he fired in quick succession at three hanging lamps hanging directly over the darkly stained bar. There was an explosion of glass particles and shards of darkness as the lights were extinguished one by one, and then a roar of jubilant laughter followed by a competing roar, and then the voice of the first gangster saying watch this! as the light from several more hanging lamps (these were hanging above various tables) was extinguished, and then there was more roaring, robust, jubilant laughter, and then for some strange, unfathomable, possibly psychotic reason, the men turned their Libias on the poor forgotten aquarium nestled in the back corner and emptied their weapons in unison, an amazing feat of synchronous skill which suggested, among other things, that these two gangsters were connected telepathically, twins of body, mind and soul. The aquarium glass shattered with the impact of the bullets, and then there was a rush of murky, aquarium water, and soon after that you could hear the fish flopping about on the tiled floor. The gangsters started congratulating themselves on their marksmanship. Their laughter swelled with their joy. Then one of them (it was difficult to see who was who) tossed a large bill to the* table. *For the damage*, he said. *And then they were gone. Just like that. We barely had any time to reflect on what had happened. We were like fugitives, too tired from running to think, rubbing our sore feet, lost in the second desert of our delusions. We just sat there numbly, absorbed by the darkness. And it was very dark indeed. The interior of this seedy dive on Calle Los Apamates had been plunged into what I can only describe as a primeval darkness. A couple of hanging lanterns had survived, and there was still the dim glow from the hallway that led to the bathroom. And remarkably, the tiny porcelain deep sea diver was still intact, still standing on the pebbly though unwatery bottom of his domain like an exposed skeleton, and he was still glowing faintly with a soft, surreal greenish light. But that was it for illumination. It was almost like the world had been suddenly transformed into a grainy film noir gangster movie from the forties, except there was no femme fatale. So we sat there for a while. I don't remember how long. I do remember it was dark enough that I had trouble making out even the face of Bolaño, who couldn't have been more than two feet away. Then I heard Bolaño's voice swimming towards me through that ocean of darkness.* Who will be left far behind? *Bolaño asked.* We all will, *I replied. And then we were laughing hysterically, arm in arm with death, that impertinent lover who whispers only bitter stories. That's what it seemed like. That's the last thing I remember.*

One would be hard pressed to find a more compelling portrait of two writers on a two-day bender. But the passage is so neatly developed, so charged with purpose-driven, kinetic energy, that it seems more like a fictionalized account of what should have happened (an ideal version of reality) than what actually did happen (plain old boring reality). Both the obvious details and those hidden beneath the luminescent surface of the prose dovetail in ways that seem crafted, as opposed to accidental. The hotel where Zabala says he and Bolaño met is a case in point. Hotel El Conde is located on the very corner where the house of the Count of San Javier lived with his wife and extended family during the 18th century. That the name Javier lay at the historic foundation of the hotel where he and Bolaño began their epic journey must surely have appealed to Zabala's sense of irrefutable destiny. Likewise, the looming presence of Rómulo Gallegos as a one-time resident of the hotel carries a similar prophetic weight when one considers that Bolaño was virtually unknown as a writer until he won the Rómulo Gallegos Prize for his novel, *The Savage Detectives*, in 1999. The irony of this fact may indeed be a coincidence, given that the second meeting between Zabala and Bolaño supposedly took place ten years earlier, but this small but significant detail could just as easily have been inserted into Zabala's narrative after 1999 and we would be none the wiser.

Of course two questions emerge from this line of thinking. First, when was this particular passage actually composed? And why would Zabala engage in yet another deception, particularly since it seems unlikely that he ever intended for his diary to be published? To answer these questions, it is perhaps instructive to examine the texture of the passage as a whole. Zabala gives us dozens of clues that as a writer he is interested in blurring the lines between history and myth, between fact and fiction. He declares at the very beginning of this passage that he and Bolaño were engaged in 'a dismantling of reality of the first order, and then a reassembling of that reality.' Then Zabala comments on Gallegos' great novel, *Doña Bárbara*, which is a mythic exploration of the life of a cattle rustler and petty tyrant from Venezuela (who also happens to be a witch), whose sense of reality, which is shaped by the violent nature of existence on the plains of Venezuela, deteriorates over the course of the novel as a consequence of both her struggle to find peace and love for herself and her struggle against the legitimate government of Venezuela. For Zabala, Hotel El Conde and Gallegos' novel are each an ideal 'jumping off point,' a trampoline, if you will, for the journey Zabala and Bolaño are about to make into unknown territory, and thus they also serve as appropriate symbols of the 'crossroads between the past and the future.' Reality is thus ever malleable. Bolaño listens to 'unseen music' and vanishes in the glare of the lamp light. They talk about the nature of reality and the meaning of existence. Bolaño describes a book he hopes to write that will be an encyclopedia of fake writers but everyone who reads it will think they are real. They go to 'some café or bar or restaurant in Catia, just off Calle El Cristo, or maybe it was closer to Parque del Oeste.' Zabala doesn't really remember. They imagine they hear gunfire outside this café and assume a riot is taking place, or at least Bolaño makes this assumption. The owner of the café wears a 'mask' to hide his melancholy disposition. Nothing in this account is precisely located either in memory or, seemingly, in actual fact. Zabala and Bolaño wait for the train to Pérez Bonalde in a Metro station 'somewhere beyond the known boundaries of reality' so they can 'go to a hospital that [does] not exist.' Zabala compares their experiences to something that might exist in the world of an absurdist play by the Spanish writer Fernando Arrabal. They curse the limitations of their imaginations, limitations which make it impossible to comprehend the 'unfathomable purity of [the] unreachable stars.' They talk about the myth and deception that surrounds the life of Simón Bolívar. They wonder if the riddle of Guayaquil can 'only be pierced by two historians whose very existence is limited to the pages of a short story of the same name written by Borges,' a writer who was himself a master of blurring the lines between myth and history. They talk about 'the hidden psychology of what it means to live out one's days as a burn victim' in an attempt to answer 'certain fundamental questions about the nature of identity and whether or not you [can] indeed remain yourself if the face you [have] been born with no longer [exists].' They witness a lively debate between two local gangsters about the truth of various UFO sightings in and around Caracas, but the sophisticated intellectual tenor of this debate seems well beyond what we would normally expect from gangsters, especially with its half-buried reference to Alberto Rosales, a Venezuelan philosopher and an expert in both Kant and Heidegger who was particularly interested in Heidegger's distinction between the notion of Being (*Sein*) and being (*Seiende*). Finally, everywhere Zabala and Bolaño go during their epic two-day journey, light does not truly illuminate. More often than not the two writers are surrounded by a hazy, murky, mythic, at times primordial darkness, as if the 'world had [indeed] been transformed into a grainy film noir gangster movie from the forties.' In short, Zabala seems to be saying that what we understand as reality is not reality, what we think of as our identity is perhaps something else. Everything is up for grabs. Of course many writers have tackled such themes. Understanding the nature of reality and identity have become the cornerstone themes of the post-modern era. What distinguishes Zabala from most other post-modern writers, however, is that he seems to embrace the joy of not knowing (as opposed to wallowing in the swamp of confusion and despair) because he is seeking spiritual enlightenment rather than intellectual certainty, which he viewed as something of a red herring. Zabala makes the search for identity and the search to understand reality the same search, but in the end he abandons both because, as he writes in his diary in an entry dated April 14, 2001: 'to search to the exclusion of all else for something that changes before our very eyes is a waste of breath and prevents us from experiencing the incalculable joy and ephemeral beauty of life.'

In May of 1996 Blanca Barutti went to South Africa with a group of one-hundred Cuban doctors as part of Cuba's ongoing commitment to share the country's medical personnel and medical expertise with countries in need. Blanca spent several months in the KwaZulu-Natal region of South Africa working in a rural clinic that had been abandoned since 1993. But by August of 1996, Blanca had disappeared. What happened to her is anyone's guess. Her name does appear on a list of doctors working at the Médecins Sans Frontières mission in Kigali, Rwanda from September to November 1996. The list contained the names of perhaps thirty Cuban doctors. But many of the doctors who worked with Médecins Sans Frontières ultimately went to the refugee camps that had sprung up along the border between Zaire and Rwanda as a result of the First Congo War, so their precise movements are difficult to track. There was also an unconfirmed report that the body of a woman matching Blanca's description was found among the bodies of several hundred Rwandan refugees that had been massacred by members of the Rwandese army near the temporary refugee camp at Chimanga, some forty miles west of Bukavu in the Kivu region of Zaire. But whether Blanca was at Chimanga or not is probably irrelevant. In all likelihood she just happened to be in the wrong place at the wrong time and so fell victim to the unrestrained violence that had become an indelible part of the African landscape.

News of Blanca's disappearance had an immediate effect on Zabala. He simply stopped writing. For two years he did not work on his book. And while he did manage an occasional entry in his journal, these were mostly copied excerpts from poets he admired, poetry that spoke to his unarticulated grief.

According to his daughter, Cecilia, Zabala lived the life of a zombie for those two years, struggling to come to terms with Blanca's absence. She said he was up at all hours of the night, wandering through the tiny, vacant rooms of the house in La Boca, a ghost without anywhere to go. Sometimes during the day he would sit beneath an Acacia tree near the water and stare out at the Caribbean Sea for hours without moving a muscle. She would follow him, fearing for his safety, but he would just sit by the water and stare out at the sea. 'I did the best I could for him during those two years,' Cecilia said. 'I made sure he had enough to eat. I brought him books to read. I made his bed. I washed his clothes. But I could not go where he had gone. And I could not help him get back.'

Eventually, Zabala did begin writing again, and he did so with a renewed sense of purpose, a renewed vigor. It was almost as if he believed he would see his beloved Blanca again, but only after he had finished his masterpiece. This was Cecilia's opinion. The end came quickly. In April 2002, he finished writing *The Mad Patagonian.* In May, he told his daughter that when he left this world he wished to be cremated and have his ashes scattered out in the Caribbean. That way, he said, they would perhaps find their way to Africa. He also asked that Cecilia burn his manuscript and mingle its ashes with his. 'We are the same thing,' he told her. 'My life and the book are the same thing. We are both seeking to return to Blanca.'

One month later, on June 26th, Zabala died when an undiagnosed cerebral aneurysm suddenly burst. Cecilia found him sitting up against the same Acacia tree where he had spent hours staring at the sea in the wake of Blanca's absence. 'He seemed to be at peace,' she said. 'And then I realized that he was with my mother, and they were in whatever paradise he had spent his life imagining.'

It is one of those quirks of history that *The Mad Patagonian* survived beyond the death of Zabala. To begin with, Cecilia was unable to fulfill either of her father's wishes. She could not bring herself to cremate his body. Instead she had him buried in Circuito Sur cemetery near Trinidad. And she could not burn his great book either. Then in 2003, with the help of a friend, she managed to get a copy of the manuscript to the editors of a now defunct literary press (Ediciones Pequeña Luna) in Caracas, Venezuela, and they agreed to publish it, but in 2004 the press went out of business, a casualty of the riots that rocked Caracas in February of that year. So the novel was never officially published and seemed destined for oblivion. Then in 2011 fate intervened. In January of that year, the unthinkable began to happen: relations between the United States and Cuba began to thaw. Cecilia began to communicate with her uncle, Emidio, who had moved from Miami to Pensacola, Florida and worked at the Naval Air Station there. It was Emidio who suggested they try again to get the novel published, but he suggested they publish it in English, not Spanish. Six months later, in June 2011, I received a letter from Emidio and Cecilia asking me to translate the book. How Zabala's masterpiece actually ended up in my hands and the challenges I faced during the four years I spent on the project is the subject of the Afterword to the current edition. Let me just say here that I have endeavored to preserve Zabala's vision as faithfully as possible. I have also endeavored in this introduction to give the reader some sense of who Zabala was by quoting generously from his diary because I believe the glimpses they provide of Zabala's soul are useful anchors for appreciating his novel. If the English edition fails to live up to the spectacular, audacious, linguistic brilliance of the original Spanish, then it is the fault of my ability as a translator. But I do believe the essence of the novel has been preserved. Zabala himself believed that all books were ghosts of some greater reality, so a translation is in fact a ghost of a ghost. But like any ghost worthy of recognition, *The Mad Patagonian* lingers in your imagination long after you have set it down.

Tomás García Guerrero,
Adjunct Professor of Linguistics, Emeritus
Communications Department, University of Tamaulipas, Mexico
August 24, 2015

The Mad Patagonian

Part One
An Echo of Paradise

Tout est vol, tout est concussion dans la nature; le désir de s'emparer du bien d'autrui est la première... la plus légitime passion que nous ayons reçue d'elle. Ce sont les premières lois que sa main grave en nous, c'est le premier penchant de tous les êtres et, sans doute, le plus agréable.

De Sade, L'Histoire de Juliette, ou les Prospérités du Vice

BOOK ONE

the house at the beach

-1-

Three weeks after my dad died I headed south to Florida. I was heading to Jacksonville to be a teacher. It was my first job. I don't remember what I was thinking on the ride down. To tell the truth, I have never been so disconnected from myself in my whole life. I drove a junky white Toyota and the air conditioning wasn't working, so the choices were either you boiled your brains with the windows rolled up, or you left the windows open and you couldn't hear the radio with the wind flapping in your ears.

That's about all I remember. The whole trip was one gigantic blur. Except I do remember I picked up a hitchhiker. He was too old to be hitchhiking, but there he was, a damn lunatic, standing by the side of the road, along the edge of the shoulder where the road sloped away, a duffel bag by his feet. He didn't look like he even knew where he was, like maybe he might just walk out into the middle of the highway and get hit by a semi. So what else could I do? He was holding a metal detector by the handle and he was wearing a fisherman's hat to keep off the sun. I picked him up somewhere in Georgia. He said he was heading down to Miami, he had heard the beaches down there were real good for treasure hunting, he wanted to try his luck, and then he smiled a ridiculous smile and held up his metal detector so I could see, but I didn't care.

I don't think we spoke again till I turned off the Interstate and let him out at a gas station. He said I seemed like a nice enough fellow but I shouldn't let that go to my head. There was already too much insanity in the world. Then he wanted me to remember that nothing was ever what it seemed to be, but I didn't say anything. You sort of expect old guys to say clichéd shit like that. Then we got out of the car and I started filling up and he walked over to a tanker that had just dropped off its load and he started talking with the trucker like they were old friends. They shook hands after that and the trucker helped the old guy climb into the cab, but I swear, just before he got in, he turned to me and waved and smiled, and then I heard him speak, which he was fifty feet away so I shouldn't have been able to hear him speak. I mean he wasn't shouting. He was just talking in a normal tone. He said 'Life is a lingering fever' in this hoarse, raspy voice. It was almost like his voice was coming out of one of the metal boxes you use to talk to the gas station attendant when your pump isn't working. Then he climbed up into the tanker and they pulled out. That was the last I saw of him. I don't know. Maybe I made the whole thing up. Like I said, the whole trip down was one gigantic blur.

The next thing I remember is standing in the auditorium of this fairly glitzy prep school with a floor-to-ceiling window like you see in the churches of those lunatic television evangelists. The window looked out on a grassy lawn and some live oaks, and then there was a tangled mess of vegetation and the St. John's River beyond that. You couldn't really see the river, partly because of the vegetation, but mostly because of the way the sun slashed through the glass. The Dean of the Faculty was saying how glad he was to be back to start the new year, and then he was introducing the new faculty to the old faculty. Since I was one of the new ones, I had to parade myself across a red-velvet platform stage. Then I sat down at a round table up against the television evangelist window.

There were only three of us sitting at the table, me and two doe-eyed, help-me-cause-I'm-caught-in-the-blinding-glare-of-oncoming-traffic bombshells who were going to teach intermediate Spanish. Everyone else was sitting away from the window, so the glare and the heat weren't too bad, but where we were it was pretty awful. The sun was just pouring in. It was the middle of the afternoon in the middle of one of the hottest Augusts on record. Wave after wave of relentless heat pouring through the glass. I was certain the air conditioning wasn't working, and after a while I was sure I was hallucinating. It felt like I was back in my junky Toyota with the windows rolled up, driving across the Deep South, but no matter how much time passed, I wasn't getting anywhere. It felt like the sun was stuck in the sky. I was drunk with the heat and I nearly passed out. There wasn't even a pitcher of water or bottles or anything. One of the Spanish teachers kept saying "it'll be all right, Travis, it can't be much longer," but the other one gave us a look, and with that the first one sort of swallowed the sound of her own voice and sat back, blinking.

Then the introductions were over and the Dean was done with his stories and the faculty had been dismissed. I must have been pretty dehydrated from the sun pouring in through that window because the next few hours vanished just like that. I felt like I was choking on dust. I was trying to remember what water tasted like. Then the dust settled and I could breathe more easily, but we were nowhere near the school. We were standing inside a small Japanese restaurant in downtown Jacksonville, me and the two Spanish teachers. It was kind of surreal. It was like we were the only people left on the planet. Like we were stuck in an episode of *The Twilight Zone*. Our restaurant was squeezed in between a discount tanning salon on one side and a Christian Scientist's Reading Room on the other, but they were both closed. The street outside was deserted, except for our cars. We were waiting for a couple of other teachers, a stocky, ex-marine named Ed Glaser, who taught Junior English, and Mick Haggerty, an ex-hippie who taught Senior Honors World History.

It was a pretty nice restaurant. I had never been to a Japanese restaurant before. There was a goldfish pond when you first went in and several bloated fish lolling about in the water with these lazy, unhappy eyes, poking their mouths up at the surface and blowing air and then bubbling back down, all of them with scaly, whitish, discolored patches, like they were going bald, except it was their color. They looked like the victims of some slaggy, tropical fish disease. There was also a short, rugged-looking bamboo bridge that went over the pond, and on the other side there was a fake bamboo hut, which is where they kept the cash register, but there was no one there. Japanese lanterns hung everywhere, purple, blue, lavender, dozens of them, and a few orange ones way in the back, which gave the place a smoky, festival look.

After a while a woman in a blue kimono tiptoed across the bridge and asked if we wanted a table and we said we did but we were waiting on two more and she smiled and said "Okay, okay, but you sit now please," and then she waved for us to follow. All of the tables were about two feet off the ground with flat pillows scattered all around so you didn't have to sit on the floor. The tables had a nice cherry finish.

We were the only ones in the whole place. She took us all the way to the back, I guess because it was closer to the kitchen. But she was very nice about it and brought us ice water with lemon and menus and then disappeared out front.

By the time Mick and Ed got there we had already ordered, but they didn't care. They said they had stopped off for a quick drink at a place on Beach Boulevard and had lost track of the time, but they were there now. Then Mick started talking about the good old days when he had been a hippie and how he had crisscrossed the country with Abbie Hoffman and his psychedelic entourage. I don't know if I believed him or not. Abbie Hoffman was a pretty long time ago. But just the possibility that Mick might have known old Abbie impressed the two Spanish teachers. And you could not deny that Mick actually looked like an ex-hippie. Or what I had always imagined an ex-hippie should look like. He was gaunt and gangly, with tangled threads of reddish-brown, beach-smelling hair that stretched halfway down his back, like seaweed or snakes or something, a Pancho-Villa style moustache that he liked to twirl, and a tiny pair of pale blue eyes, impetuous, unrelenting eyes that stared out at you from the dark of two cavernous sockets. I had never met anyone quite like him.

We ate dinner at that Japanese restaurant pretty much every Friday for the next nine months, the five of us. At first we talked very little and we ate tons of sushi. We commiserated over the long, interminably long, gloomy hours behind a teacher's desk and the gloomy smallness of our bank accounts. The dippy kids we taught spent more on clothes in a week than we made in a month. They drove BMWs and Mercedes convertibles and flew to Buenos Aires or Madrid for long weekends, and we drove around in junky damn Toyotas and old beat up Chevrolets and went to Baltimore or Tuscaloosa or Birmingham just to say we had been somewhere. But then we talked about other things. The two Spanish teachers were from Brooklyn. They had read a great deal about Cuba and the stultifying oppression of the Cuban people. They wanted to fly down to Cuba with Pastors for Peace and bring food and clothes and build houses. They wanted to *destultify* the Cubans, I guess. That was why they had come down to Florida. Then there was the stocky, ex-Marine from Charleston, South Carolina. His full name was Edward Saxton Glaser. He had been to Vietnam. He said he had been in a shithole he called Da Nang. He'd been in the Engineering Corp and done three tours and would have done a fourth, but by then the war was over. Ed didn't really talk a whole lot about the war except to say he'd "rather eat goddamn sushi than end up looking like it." The two Spanish teachers squirmed with weak, persecuted looks on their faces when he said that and stared down at their plates. Ed talked like that a lot. Man, he sure didn't think too much of those girls and their high-minded fixation with Cuba. He smirked gloomily whenever they opened their mouths.

And then there was Mick. The first thing that caught your eye about Mick was his smile. He smiled carelessly, effortlessly, without provocation, and often, and when he did you could see that several of his teeth were chipped. He said his teeth had collided with a Billy club one summer in Chicago during a week-long rally he had set up with old Abbie. Nobody could afford a hotel room, so they started hanging out in some park along Lake Michigan. Pretty soon there were thousands of hippies sleeping on the grass or on top of these ratty old Mexican blankets. Some were doing it right out in the open, but the rest didn't care. And every night the cops would try to roust them. There were cops everywhere. Hundreds of cops in their shiny, silver helmets like you see on *The Jetsons*, all of them with Billy clubs and talking into their walkie-talkies and some of them were even wearing gas masks. You could tell they were preparing for a major assault, and then all of a sudden they would let loose, not everywhere, the park was too big for that, so the cops picked their spots, they would appear here and there, a flurry of spastic motion followed by furious bursts of clubbing and shouting and screaming, and every once in a while a few gunshots. You never knew when they were coming. They just sort of materialized right out of the air, like they were jumping from black helicopters and sliding down ropes in the dark. The next thing you knew people were running into the streets, looking for anywhere to hide, even a garbage can. The cops were grabbing everyone they could and throwing them into trucks and hauling them away. But there weren't enough trucks. And some of the hippies were fighting back, throwing rocks, bottles, anything they could find. But most were running for their lives and shouting "pigs are whores" and "hell no we won't go" and shit like that. You didn't know what to expect, like one night an old man carrying a Marshall Field's bag got his head caved in for jaywalking. Another time a twenty-something mother and two little kiddies were pulled from their car and hauled off to jail because the kids were saying bam, bam, bam and pointing their fingers at the cops and the mother was laughing. Cars were stopped all over the fucking place because of the riot, but none of them belonged to the hippies from the hippie camp. Then there were the camera guys from the TV news, and they were just taking pictures, trying to capture a few good shots of democracy in action for good old Walter Cronkite, but then they were getting clubbed by the cops like everybody else, and one of them even got punched in the stomach right on national television. Then the cops let loose a couple hundred German Shepherds, and they would go right for your throat, and then somebody said there were tanks coming down Michigan Avenue. That was the coup de grâce for Mick's teeth. Mick tossed a ragged old American flag over his shoulders like a cape and raced into the street shouting "Death to the fucking Fascists!" That's when he got smacked right in the mouth with a Billy club. That's how he got his teeth chipped. He didn't say how it felt getting smacked like that. I guess maybe he didn't remember from being unconscious. But he said he made the six o'clock national news.

    I think the reason why Mick smiled so much was because he was kind of proud of his chipped teeth. Just about everybody loved his smile. The two Spanish teachers were in love with him. So was practically every teenage girl in the school. But you could tell old Ed didn't love him. You could tell old Ed secretly wanted to take a Billy club of his own to Mick's teeth. But he didn't. There was something about Mick. You just couldn't say anything against him. Even the Reverend Dubois, the Dean of the Faculty, even he kind of swallowed his tongue when Mick was around, which was pretty damn odd if you think about it. Mick lived in a brown-shingled house at the beach, a confirmed bachelor during the school year. But every summer a couple of girls who had been in his Senior Honors World History class moved in with him. Two new girls every summer. But whenever this was brought up to the Reverend Dubois, however damn tactfully, his tongue would half fall out of the side of his mouth, like you see in cartoons of people getting hung, and then he would start turning a purplish blue color and the veins in his forehead and neck would start quivering uncontrollably, wriggling like tiny eels, and then he'd be waving his arms in the air in erratic, angular fashion, and strange, drowning, gurgling noises would come popping out of his mouth the whole time, like he was really, truly getting hung. You never saw anything like it in your life. But the Reverend never said a word to Mick about his rotating harem, not that anybody ever heard anyway. When I told Mick I had been born in Chicago, he invited me over.

"So, you were born in Chicago, is that right Lauterbach?"

My full name is Travis Everet Lauterbach. A lawyer's name, maybe, I'm pretty sure that's what my parents had in mind, but not a teacher's, at least not the Travis part, which might have been the reason Mick just called me Lauterbach. It was the last week of May, one week after graduation. We were standing on the rugged bamboo bridge in the Japanese restaurant, looking down at those slaggy, lazy, diseased goldfish. The middle-aged woman wearing the silky, blue kimono was standing behind the register in the bamboo hut, but she wasn't looking at us. She was changing the register tape, her body sort of twisted awkwardly to one side to avoid getting ink on the silk. Then she clacked the little door shut and sat back on a stool. There was no one else in the restaurant. It was too early for dinner. We were the first ones there.

"Do you know what Chicago is all about?" Mick asked.

I wasn't sure. I was born there. But we had moved pretty early.

"Do you know about the Black Panthers?"

We looked up at each other. I had heard of them.

"The Chicago Seven?"

I had heard of them too. But beyond a few names I didn't know much. Mick smiled, and several chipped teeth flashed against the darkness of his mouth, and his whole being flashed against the smoky dim light from the Japanese lanterns, the softly glowing purples and blues and lavenders and oranges. I looked again at the fish, and there, suddenly, was Mick's face as well, on top of the fish, among them, now half-submerged, now rising again, wavering, a watery face looking up at me, still bright and smiling, almost laughing. "Your knowledge about your own city, my innocent Lauterbach, is sadly, fucking deficient," the watery face said. "You come out to my place tomorrow afternoon and we'll fill in the gaps."

-2-

Mick's brown-shingled beach house was at 17 Shell Street, a narrow street with cracked pavement and sandy patches and shells scattered about. The street ended at Mick's house. On the northeast corner there were a couple of scraggly, ornamental trees with flutey wind-chimes hanging from thick, brittle branches, like the outlaws in old Westerns after they've been caught and lynched. There was a small, iron gate directly out front, a rusty greenish color. The gate was attached to a partially finished stone wall that went several yards and ended in a bunch of palmetto. The front yard was covered with red cobblestone bricks, though you could see the sandy soil between the cracks, and in some places there were patches of spongey grass sprouting up. Mick also had some ferns growing out of these Pueblo Indian style clay pots, and they were all over the damn place, so you could hardly walk. If you wanted to go down to the water, there was a narrow macadam path that went from the sidewalk out front down along the side of the house and disappeared into the dunes and the sea oats and the afternoon sun shining on the sand. No matter where you were, you could hear the Atlantic smacking up against the beach.

Filling in the gaps of my knowledge about Chicago started with drinking margaritas. Mick came out almost to the gate as I was getting out of my car, bright and smiling and his chipped teeth catching the rays of the sun. Then he kicked the gate open and grabbed hold of my arm and hauled me inside. Mick was a pretty impulsive type. The margaritas were waiting on a small Formica counter with the kitchen on one side and the living room on the other. The next thing I knew I was sitting on a bar stool, my back to the counter top, a frosty strawberry margarita in my hands. Mick was standing in front of a sliding-glass door, looking out at the sun and the sea oats shimmering on the dunes in the distance. Man, you should have seen him. He was like a damn guru or something. He was wearing a striped T-shirt and baggy string shorts with the strings untied, dangling, and his scraggly old hair hanging down like it was, and he was twirling his moustache and then gulping down some of his drink and then lecturing about the travesty and absolute injustice of a culture, any damn culture, dominated by the idea of sin. Mick had a thing about sin. He didn't mention The Black Panthers or The Chicago Seven. I think he forgot why I'd come out to his house in the first place. Then again, I wasn't really listening too closely to what he was saying. He could have been saying anything. I really wasn't paying attention, if you want to know the truth. I was sitting there with this Paleolithic grin plastered across my face, drinking my drink and looking at the two recently graduated girls who were now living with Mick for the summer, and thinking some pretty raunchy, self-indulgent thoughts.

The girls were curled up on a maroon colored sofa on the other side of the living room, sipping their margaritas. They were wearing these flimsy, yellow bikinis, though with their legs pulled up off the floor and the sexy angle of their hips against the curve of the sofa, it looked like maybe they were wearing just the tops. Above them was an oil painting of a mermaid lounging about on the edge of a weather-beaten dock, a brunette with starfish and shells in her hair, and a sea gull standing on one of the posts and a couple of drunken sailors in the background leering at her. It was the kind of painting you can pick up for twenty greasy simoleons in the parking lot of an abandoned Denny's with thirty or forty Persian rugs strewn about on the asphalt and a rusted Winnebago pulled off to one side. I remember thinking how Mick's two girls looked exactly like that mermaid the way they were sitting, except for the starfish and the shells, but which had come first, the mermaid or the girls, I didn't know.

When the girls finished their drinks, they set their glasses on the floor. They were looking at Mick with an unashamed, devoted kind of awe. But Mick was still looking out at the dunes and the sun and sighing, pretty much ignoring them, talking and twirling his moustache and gulping and gesticulating wildly, like any would-be guru would. He seemed absolutely oblivious to the effect he was having. "It's nothing but fucking Fascism in a robe," he was saying. "Now you look at the indigenous peoples of South America. They don't drape their adult insecurities all over their kids. They let 'em run around naked. The boys in one group, running around with their miniature bows and arrows, chasing after green iguanas and their little wee wees dangling and they don't even know," Mick turning from the sliding-glass door and smiling his bright smile at the girls and his margarita sloshing up over the rim and onto his bare feet, "and the girls, they're too busy with their little girl stuff, making baskets and going down to the river with their mothers to fish and shit like that. And they're not thinking about the boys, not about doing it, anyway," Mick slipping into the kitchen, still blabbing away. "Not until they're older. Not until it's time to make babies," Mick drinking the last of his drink and then sliding his glass onto the counter. "And then that's what they do. They make babies. And they don't give a goddamn fucking crap who the father is or how many of their kids have different fathers, what the fuck, everybody is everybody's father, even their gods have a collective ancestry," Mick opening the refrigerator door, pulling out a pitcher, "it's all communal," then refilling his glass, nodding the pitcher at my own half-empty glass, and then at the sagging maroon sofa and the mermaids sitting there, "you want some more, Lauterbach, girls?" and then my glass appearing on the counter and Mick pouring and then the two girls appearing on either side of me, suddenly, like in *Star Trek* or something, their empty glasses next to mine and Mick still pouring and then "girls, this is a dear friend of mine, a dear friend and classroom compatriot, Lauterbach, dear, sweet, innocent Lauterbach of the Chicago Lauterbachs," the girls turning as if only then did they notice me, as if Mick's speaking my name and directing their attention had suddenly brought me to life, the two girls now smiling in imitation of Mick, wedging me in with their curt, approving nods and their flirty, vulnerable, mermaid smiles and their flimsy, loosely tied, ready-to-be untied yellow bikinis, and then the two of them laughing and blowing questions into my face and the spicy, strawberry smell of the margaritas like a fog welling up and my eyes itching and watering, so I couldn't tell who was saying what, "Hello Mr. Lauterbach are you really from Chicago Mr. Lauterbach what brought you to Florida Mr. Lauterbach say you're pretty quiet Mr. Lauterbach cat got your tongue Mr. Lauterbach we can do something about that if you like, say how old are you Mr. Lauterbach do you have a girlfriend Mr. Lauterbach would you like a girlfriend Mr. Lauterbach we're old enough Mr. Lauterbach we're way past eighteen, if that's what you were wondering Mr. Lauterbach, say what kind of name is Lauterbach anyway, where's your swimsuit Mr. Lauterbach, you did bring one didn't you or did you think did you think you could borrow one of Mick's, well Mick doesn't believe in swimsuits Mr. Lauterbach, do you Mick, and neither do neither do we," and then some dippy, giggly, girlish laughter, and then Mick was standing over by the sliding-glass door, as if he had been there the whole time, "come on you three, let's go down to the beach," and then Mick and the girls were gone and the sliding-glass door was open and a warm, salty breeze was blowing in. I left my empty margarita glass on the counter top next to the others and ran down the macadam path.

  The following September we decided to limit our Japanese dinners to every other Friday. We said it was because of money. But it wasn't. The truth is you can get pretty damn apathetic if you see the same people every single Friday. What can I say? But there were other reasons as well. One of the Spanish teachers had married a banker named Walter over the summer, and since they only had the one car, a mostly blue Chevy Citation (the two front fenders were painted black from two separate accidents), and since her husband was one of those vigorous holier-than-thou, self-motivated, nut jobs (he had been promoted to Assistant Vice-President at the age of twenty-four, an achievement which he had supposedly earned for bringing in the business of a large boat manufacturer, but which was more probably the result of his having caddied for the bank's Grand Pooh-bah when he was a boy), she had to sacrifice every other Friday and pick him up from the office. Then he would drive them both over to one of those festively decorated meet-and-greet beer bashes sponsored by the Downtowners, which was mostly a group of twenty-something, neo-Nazi bankers like Walter, with a couple of restaurant managers and a girl who had started her own nail salon thrown in for diversity, and maybe get some shrimp and pasta afterwards.

Once she brought him along, but all he could do with his sushi was move it aimlessly about his plate with the chopsticks until it was time to go. But he did make one, sort of reluctant, obviously distasteful stab at joining the conversation. During the middle of the meal he looked up somewhat uncertainly at his wife, and then at the rest of us, and then he said that he had met with the owner of some small bakery out in San Marco about lending him some money, and we shouldn't say anything just yet because he needed to get the loan approved, but boy, they sure made some pretty tasty croissants, we should try some. But he didn't get a chance to say anything else because that right there really ticked off old Ed. You see Ed had been trying to get a car loan for seven months, but they wouldn't give him one. Ed said they wanted him to fill out a truckload of these bogus personal history forms, and he did that, and then they had some more forms they forgot the first time, which you know they don't forget procedural stuff like that, and then they wanted to know did he have any kids and where could they reach his ex-wife and were his parents still living and what did they do and who should they contact in case he died, the kind of intimate, bathroom revelations nobody has a right to demand, and, well, right there, Ed decided he'd had enough of all the rigmarole, it didn't look like they were going to give him the money anyway, so he dumped the whole mess of forms in a metal wastepaper basket and lit a match and watched his car loan burn right there in the bank. That's what he told us happened. Sometimes Ed was a damn lunatic. He sure didn't have any use for banks.

"Is that what you do, then," he asked the young banker husband. You just knew Ed had been waiting since he sat down to light into the guy, and drinking Takara Sake while he waited. His face seemed red and swollen. "You go around eating fucking croissants and if you like them you go give the guy some money. Fuck. That's fucked."

Then Ed got up slowly, rubbing his bow-legged, ex-marine legs to work out the cramps from sitting on pillows for so long, and then he stood there a moment, sort of teetering, looking down at the table and a second bottle of Sake the waitress had just brought out and the clump of uneaten sushi on Walter's plate and him pushing it around some more, and then not pushing it.

You could see in Ed's eyes the fierce, unthinking, animal viciousness of his Vietnam years coming back. We all thought for sure he was going to pick up the inarticulate, young banker and hurl the poor, dippy bastard head first into the glass-case counter out front by the pond. But he didn't. He said "just fuck it" a couple of times, but under his breath, as if he were suddenly embarrassed. Then he swooped up the waiting bottle of Sake and carried it off to the bar in the back and plopped himself down on a stool, and there the smoky, orangeish light of half-a-dozen Japanese lanterns descended upon him, gloomily.

No one said a word in the suddenness of this angry departure, or for many minutes afterwards. Then Mick started twirling his moustache, and then he smiled his careless, bright, mischievous smile, and his tiny pale blue eyes had this drunken sailor's glint to them. He pointed out that such raging outbursts were not uncommon in vets suffering from posttraumatic paralysis of the brain, which was clearly Ed's problem, and this sparked some embarrassed laughter, and then a feverish, pretty juvenile debate about the actual causes of such a malady, how many deaths you had to see and torturings and such, and if your childhood mattered, and really, what in the world had happened to Ed in the city of Da Nang anyway, which was the only place we had ever heard him mention, it must have been horrible. Even the newly married Spanish teacher wanted to root out the cause of Ed's distemper, and then, maybe, she said, we can cure him. Of course her banker husband didn't offer an opinion. He had succumbed once again to the aimless misery of maneuvering his sushi about his plate. Every so often he looked at his watch. When it was finally time to go, he took off two steps in front of his wife. He left without even a look at the goldfish.

That was it for excitement as far as our dinners went until Mick invited a couple of students to join us, a couple of wiggly, brainless girls, kind of like the two mermaid look-alikes who had been living with Mick the summer before and who had moved out in August to go north to school, or maybe west. Mick was never absolutely clear about where.

So there we were sitting on the bench up against the wall opposite the cash register. Me, the two Spanish teachers, and Ed. It was early October and warm enough outside so you didn't even need a sweater. Mick marched in wearing rope sandals and shorts and the hair on his legs beaded with sweat. He wore a fraying poncho out of old Mexico with blue and yellow and orange stripes instead of a shirt, and a straw hat with a string. He stomped over the bamboo bridge, his tiny blue eyes bouncing up to the rim of his hat and then down. The two girls bounced after him, looking with these dippy looks at the goldfish as they crossed and then looking away somewhat abruptly, like they had never seen diseased fish before. They were wearing jeans and plain cotton shirts. Modest shirts. Tucked-in shirts with black belts around their waists. Their names were Laurie and Sonya. I figured they were auditioning for next summer. I was somewhat surprised they weren't wearing bikinis.

"*Buenas tardes, señoritas, muchachos,*" Mick said. "*Viva la revolución! Viva la revolucionario!*"

Laughing as if he hadn't a care in the world, he stopped in front of the bench and looked down at the four of us still sitting there silent and bewildered in the glint of his pleasant buffoonery. "What the hell are you people waiting for?" he said. "Let's eat some raw fish."

All through dinner I stared secretly at Laurie and Sonya, but I wasn't really looking at them. I was looking through them, back to that day at Mick's from the spring before. We had been all afternoon on the beach. It was a perfect day. The water was a bright, sparkling blue, like you see in postcards. There was a clothesline strung up between two poles and we played volleyball, boys against girls. Mick had a thing about boys against girls. He had been alternately savage and then charming, but in a playful, campy, theatrical way, spiking the ball at their smooth, girlish knees and watching them flop down in the sand, giggling, their flimsy tops slipping, and then Mick rushing to their aid if they took too long getting up, which they almost always did, and him apologizing, smiling softly, shyly, trying to help them with their straps, the sunlight bouncing off their nipples, but them pushing him away as they got to their feet, but they were still giggling. I couldn't believe what I was seeing. It was pretty erotic, like a pornographic version of *Beach Blanket Bingo*.

Later, when they were paddling around on a couple of dolphin floats, he ran up to the house and came back with some more margaritas. He waded into the water and they were laughing at him and calling him 'Grandpa Joe,' but in a cute way, and they grabbed the drinks and drank from a sitting, half-sinking position, and when they were done Mick tipped them over and it was his turn to laugh, and then he fled to the safety of the towels on the beach, which is where I had been since the volleyball because I didn't have a swimsuit.

"Ain't those two something, Lauterbach," he said, and there was an invigorating, trembling admiration in his voice. "You should get yourself a couple."

Then he sat there a while watching them. Like he was standing outside of time or something. I couldn't help thinking about what he said. I mean I'd only had two dates since coming down to Jacksonville. But you had to wonder what he was doing with a couple of giggly teenagers. He was over three times their age, which you have to admit sounds pretty damn suspicious, a little too much like something out of the pages of *Lolita*. But maybe it was the rest of us poor, dippy bastards that didn't get it. I mean both those girls were over eighteen, and they didn't have any trouble with him. They seemed happy enough. Maybe you couldn't really be happy until you gave in to your animal side. Maybe happiness wasn't something you thought about. You just had to experience it, instinctively. You ate when you were hungry and you slept when you were tired and you did it with girls whenever you could and you didn't worry about it later because it was all just a matter of animal magnetism anyway, and if it was warm enough you didn't wear any clothes, like those South American kids Mick knew about. Maybe if you thought about your own happiness at all, you couldn't ever really be happy, which I guess would mean that everything they said about God and self-sacrifice and the good of the country was just a lot of damn hype.

Then Mick had laughed and raced back into the noisy, splashing surf, and there was some shouting and the voices getting mixed together, and a couple of yellow bikini tops came flying off and they got mixed in with the spray and all you could see were naked arms and naked legs, and just like that I decided to go for a walk.

I started walking along the beach. I was headed in a generally southerly direction. After a while, the houses along the water gave way to a boardwalk with an arcade every two blocks and hotdog stands and souvenir shops and kids slurping down ice cream, and in the distance I could see the shimmering cloud of a couple of hotels, like an oasis in the desert. I was thinking it looked a little like paradise, not the kind Mick had, but the way you see it in those MasterCard commercials and you're sitting in a lounge chair beneath some palm trees, some exotic island somewhere in the Caribbean or the South China Sea, only with fake coconuts all over the place (it is a commercial after all), and then a waiter in a tuxedo comes with one of those ice cream drinks with a blue parasol and he smiles and you smile back and you slap your plastic on the tray and off he goes. That's what I was thinking, but when I got to the hotels, it was already turning dark, and the hotels didn't seem quite so shimmery, and I didn't even have a gas credit card, so I turned around and headed north. By the time I got back to Mick's place, Mick and the girls had gone up, but I didn't blame them. It had been a long day. I don't know how late it was, but it must have been pretty late because the house was dark.

They must have thought I'd come back sooner or later

because the sliding-glass door was open. But I didn't go in. I just stood there in the dark, listening to the wind chimes when the breeze came up and the silence when there was nothing but the dark, shimmering heat, and then I thought I heard Mick murmuring something and the girls murmuring back. I listened to their voices for a while. Then I went around to the front and got in my car and drove home.

-3-

It's hard to believe I had only two dates that first year down in Jacksonville. It sure does sound terrible, like I'm disfigured or speak with a lisp or have lice. But the truth is I don't know why. August to April of that first year was a steamy, rainy, suffocating blur of dippy, school-kid faces looking at me to teach them something they didn't already know and lost homework by the truckload and weekly chapel services in that television evangelist style auditorium and the goldfish at the Japanese restaurant and the bright smile of Mick and the gloominess of Ed and the bubbly, sensitive, relentless vulnerability of the two Spanish teachers. I can't even put the months in order.

But then it was April and the blur of those first months was gone, and there I was out on this date, which I guess you'd have to call it a date since there was just the two of us, but I have to tell you it was pretty much a fiasco from the word go. I don't remember the girl's name. Maybe I didn't even know it to begin with. I sometimes have problems with names.

I met her by accident late one Saturday afternoon down at the Jacksonville Landing. I was looking at the murky, dark blue river and the blue bridge that went across, and there were four or five dolphins jetting along, making their way back to the Atlantic, and the way they were going through the water, first two arcing up into the air and their wet milky-gray skin flashing in the sunlight and the spray and then both of them splashing down, and then two more and then one more and then back again to two, well, it wasn't at all like you see in the tourist shows with the dolphins jumping through red plastic hula hoops and ringing a bell twenty feet above the surface of the pool and the tourists thinking they're getting a privileged glimpse of this sandy, sunny, palm-covered mecca called Florida. It was just unadulterated, unthinking, relentless joy out there in the river. You couldn't help but watch. Then the dolphins were gone and I pushed back from the green iron railing and whammed right back into this girl. She sort of flipped back from the physics of it and landed on her rear guard, and two of the bags she was carrying spilled out all over the boardwalk, but the third bag sort of flipped itself up over the railing and spilled itself into the river. I guess maybe she hadn't seen me standing there. I guess maybe she had too many bags in her way.

I helped her pick up the bags from the boardwalk, and then we were both standing at the railing, looking helplessly at the third bag floating on the surface, slowly filling with water, and beneath the bag you could see the boxes or packages that had spilled out, a shadowy brownish blur in the blueish-brownish water, making its way towards the bottom. There wasn't anything we could do. It was really pretty scummy where the water came up to the boardwalk and the brown foamy bubbles smearing the cement and the brownish-green algae that grows there, which meant you knew there was no use trying to climb down and salvage a damn thing. We stepped back from the railing, and you could see she wasn't happy, so I apologized and offered to buy her back everything she'd lost. She accepted my offer, but she still wasn't smiling, but later, after she had a brand new third bag in her hands, and after I had apologized a second time and told her my name was Travis, after all that she was smiling like she hadn't lost a thing.

I must have been absolutely out-of-my-mind possessed. She had this toothy sort of gummy horse-mouthed kind of smile, and she wasn't a whole lot better with her mouth shut, but all the same the next thing I knew we were going out on a date. We drove in separate cars because she had hers from shopping. She gave me directions where to meet her, and she was in a desperate, almost lunging kind of hurry, like we should have been there already, which should have been my first clue. My second clue should have been where we went, which was a country and western bar, the kind just off the highway with a big red neon cowboy boot dancing out front and lights blinking all around. The sun was just beginning to set and the parking lot was almost full. Everybody there was wearing designer boots and Stetsons and silky shirts studded with rhinestones, except me, and there was smoke all over the place so it was difficult to see, which meant you were always getting bumped, except where the DJ sat, but he was behind some Plexiglass. The main drinks were beer and whiskey, which I didn't mind so much, not at all in fact. We listened to some old Waylon Jennings songs while we drank, and then some Tammy Wynette, and then a bunch of others I'd never heard of, which after you've been drinking beer and whiskey a while you can hardly tell the difference. I drank a goddamn truckload of beer and whiskey, which made the waitresses pretty happy. Then the DJ said he was putting on a new somebody called Travis something, and we listened to some song about a girl in a pick-up truck driving to Durango, and all the while we were listening, this girl I'd whammed into at the river was squealing and squeezing my arm, and her fingernails dug in so hard she gave me a couple of scars. I figured this Travis guy was maybe why she had wanted to go out with me in the first place. That's how it seemed to me, anyway, after the Durango song and my date had gone off to the Little Cowgirls room to powder her nose. I was standing along a rail that overlooked the dance floor of that smoky barn. I was just standing there rubbing my sore arm and wondering how many other guys my date had lured to this spot. Maybe she figured since my name was Travis, I had a country and western fetish just like her. How else could it be with a name like Travis? I bet that's what she thought. People are always trying to squeeze you into their own personal fictions.

  I never saw her again after that. I left her at the bar. They started doing some line dancing, and she was right there in the middle of the dance floor with the rest, about a hundred counterfeit cowboys and cowgirls with their happy horse faces and their too-happy rodeo smiles and their silk shirts studded with sequins and their designer boots clomping all over the parquet. If you've ever seen wild horses going loco, stomping around a corral and snorting and kicking up dust, which maybe you've only seen it in television westerns like me, well that's what it looked like. I paid for one last beer, but as soon as the waitress came I changed my mind. I left the beer on the rail and pushed my way through the smoke and didn't look back. Only once on the way home did I even think about leaving that girl like that, but it wasn't a big deal, I told myself. She had her own car. She was probably a lot happier without me.

  The next date I had was on another Saturday, one month later. It wasn't as bad as the first, but that's not saying a whole lot. To begin with, it was arranged by the two Spanish teachers. The one who was eventually going to marry the banker, her name was Emily Lavigne, she thought it would be a good idea if I went out with the other Spanish teacher, Tommie Rodriguez. It was a Tuesday when I found out about the whole thing. The Tuesday before the Saturday. It was already extremely hot, in the nineties, which isn't all that unusual for Florida in May. But it was pretty damn hot for me. I was sitting in the teacher's lounge in a ratty, old lounge chair someone had dug out of their grandmother's garage; it was cloth-covered, a dirty pinkish color with the fuzz beading up. A couple of other teachers were sitting at the glossy, greenish Formica-topped work table on the other side of the room. One was Janet Rainey, a shriveled-up raisin of a woman, from too much sun, who taught Religion part time, and who snapped her teeth like a cancer-stricken Doberman whenever you said or did something she didn't like. The other was Harvey Collins, an aging, too-fleshy math teacher with age spots on his wrists and neck, and stringy, white hair that he combed ear to ear. Harvey had the reputation, whether he deserved it or not, for pinching unsuspecting female behinds whenever he was waiting in a grocery checkout line or roaming around a Laundromat, waiting for a machine to open up. He was supposedly able to do this even with his arms full of milk and razor blades and cans of Campbell's Soup, or even a basket of dirty laundry and a box of Tide. Supposedly, Harvey only went after the really curvy ones.

So I was just sitting there. I had pushed the chair up against the air conditioner, which had been working when I came in, but then it had sputtered and whined and there was a shudder and it had started blowing dust and then it had stopped working altogether. Harvey Collins looked up and said something I didn't hear and then laughed. Janet Rainey didn't look up at all. I was still sitting there, half-glancing at a couple of memos and half-looking out the window and the glimmering, suffocating heat outside. I was just beginning to perspire when Emily Lavigne came in.

"Travis, Travis, Travis," she said. "What in the world have you been doing with yourself?"

She was wearing a clingy, yellow sweater dress, and when you looked at her you couldn't help but think about peeling bananas. She sat down on the arm of the chair.

"Travis, you are impossible, my dear," she said. "We've been looking for you everywhere!"

"What?"

"We tried calling you last night. Where were you? And then you didn't show up for first hour. Travis, Travis."

"I was late."

"You're a very naughty boy," she said.

Then Emily scooted herself a little bit closer, even as she looked away towards the work table. I just stared at her. If she had scooted any closer she would have been in my lap, which I have to admit I wouldn't have minded. I could see little bits of pinkish fuzz stuck to her dress from the chair. I thought that in spite of her upcoming marriage to the neo-Nazi banker Walter Dooley, she was still very much a girl. What did she see in Walter Dooley anyway?

"We decided it was time you and Tommie went out."

"Who decided?" I said.

"Why, Tommie and I," she said.

I started to feel dizzy with that, even though I was just sitting there, and it seemed like the world was losing its color, like a photograph that has been overexposed. For a moment it was like I was somebody else.

"Oh don't worry, Travis. She likes you just as much as you like her. It's written all over her face. We thought we'd all go somewhere on Saturday night. You know. You and Tommie and me and Walter."

There was very little I could say against the bubbly, self-assured almost blinding brightness of Emily Lavigne, with her shimmering, dark brown hair flopping about her head as she spoke, and her flirty, familiar, gesturing eyes. But I gave it a try, one try, to be precise. I guess maybe her pounding away at me like that was a little more than I could take. In spite of the way she looked. I mean it didn't matter what a woman looked like if she didn't leave you alone. It kind of felt like getting slugged in the nose.

"Will you tell Tommie I can't make it?" I said.

"I most certainly will not."

"Why not?"

"Because you are being absolutely, unforgivably absurd, Travis Lauterbach. For eight months now we've been going to that dull, chintzy little Japanese restaurant of Mick's, and for eight months you've been mooning uncontrollably over that girl, and she's been behaving the same way about you. My God, the two of you can't even have a decent conversation you're both so thunderstruck, and it's been that way since the day you met. You almost passed out when the Dean introduced us to the faculty, if you remember, and it wasn't from the heat. I keep expecting one of you or both of you to jump in the river. I don't know which would make me happier."

Then Janet Rainey spoke up from the work table. She spoke with a kind of veiled contempt, without inflection, without even her lips moving. At least that's how it looked.

"Would you two kindly be quiet," she said. "People are trying to work."

"Lighten up there, Janet. You be quiet yourself," said Harvey Collins. He had probably stopped working when Emily came in. He had probably been thinking for the last five minutes about Emily and grocery store checkout lines or Laundromats. "Go on there, Travis. Go out with the girl for God's sake. She's just a little bitty thing. She won't bite your head off like this one here," and he nodded at Janet.

This was followed by a moment of embarrassed silence. At least I was embarrassed. It was a pretty rude thing to say. And then I was thinking that Emily couldn't possibly have been right about Tommie Rodriguez and me. If I had been mooning over anyone, I said to myself, it would have been sweet Emily herself. She was the pretty one. Or prettier. Then Harvey and Janet returned to their work, and Emily was giving me a stern, dark probing look, as if she had guessed by my silence what I was thinking. She was pretty even in her displeasure. Then the look vanished and Emily nodded politely, a curt but categorical nod, and smiled.

"Well, then," she said. "It's all settled."

"Sure," I said. "It's settled."

"We'll pick you up at seven-thirty, give or take. Walter is driving, so you won't have to worry about a thing."

The next thing I knew I was going out with Tommie Rodriguez. She was my second date. And when Saturday came we went bowling. Me and Tommie and Emily and Walter. I don't know who the hell picked bowling. Probably Walter. We were all pretty rotten bowlers, but Walter was the worst. I think maybe he was looking for a little sympathy from Emily because of them having to go out with me and Tommie. But he didn't get any. But you could tell he sure wanted to be somewhere else from the minute they picked me up, him and Emily driving up in their black and blue Chevy Citation, sitting stiffly in the front seat like they'd just had an argument, Emily then turning to the window as I hurried out to the car, glistening and red-eyed and you could see the streaks on her face but she was smiling bravely anyway and out popped a "Hello Travis sweetie," and then me getting in and the dark shadow of Walter hunched over the wheel, sullen and composed and superior. "Well, well, if it isn't Travis Lauterbach," he said. "I wouldn't have known you." Then he hit the gas, barely giving me time to shut the door.

Maybe Walter thought if he was going to be miserable he might as well make everybody else miserable too. He didn't say boo the rest of the night except to order watery rum and Cokes from the bowling alley waitress and make rude comments whenever one of us threw a gutter ball, which seemed inevitable every time one of us stepped to the line. But the girls pretty much ignored him. They talked for a while about Cuba, and then they started rambling on about their own personal shortcomings as far as bringing food to the poor and building homes for the homeless. Yes, of course they'd done some good. A group of them had flown down to Havana during Easter break, that was a good thing, wasn't it? They had brought canned goods, pineapples and beans mostly, which is kind of funny if you think about it because the place is loaded with pineapples and beans without the cans, but they also brought some Campbell's Chicken Soup, which I guess you can't get there, and some Easter chocolate for the children. They had built fourteen houses, each house with a fence, but then again they weren't so sure if the people were better off. One of those poor Cubans had tried to climb aboard their plane when they were leaving, his daughter supposedly lived in Miami, but he had been discovered by the police and they had cuffed him and taken him away. The rumor was he had been dragged behind one of those portable airport latrines and shot and then stuffed in a garbage bag. Emily and Tommie didn't know for sure. Nobody knew anything for sure. The truth was maybe nobody wanted to know, that's what Tommie said. What was the good of building houses if it ended up they didn't want to live in them, and what good was flying down there for a week or two if it meant that somebody would get killed?

  I tried to break into their conversation a couple of times, but since I'd never been to Cuba, to build houses in Havana or for any other reason, I couldn't very well share in their misery. And I sure as hell didn't want to share in Walter's misery. He was sitting behind me and the girls, sitting stiffly, brazenly, like he was glued to the aquamarine molded-plastic bowler's bench, still trying to make his discomfort known, glaring icily at the lanes. He was a goddamn nut job if you asked me. I could have socked him a good one. I could have maybe broken his nose. I mean I was almost angry enough to do it. But that wouldn't have looked too good with Tommie and Emily there.

  So I drank bottled beer and bowled gutter balls and watched the two girls bowling and watched their curvy, unsuspecting, Harvey-Collins-type behinds, which almost made up for the rest of it. But I know if I had gone in my own car, I would have left just like the first time.

  Emily Lavigne fixed me up one more time after that,

but that was after I started going to Mick's house. It was in the middle of October during my second year. It was with the sister of one of Walter's friends, and it's funny, but I don't remember her name either. She was wearing so much blue eye shadow she kind of looked like a drunken, demented raccoon. And she had on this chintzy white blouse with ruffles, like maybe she had always dreamed of being a go-go girl and now was her chance. She was also wearing a pair of silver stilettos with a spiral loop that wrapped around her ankles, which meant she had trouble walking three feet without grabbing onto something, and a pair of designer jeans with glittery rhinestones down the sides, but the jeans were a little too tight so the rhinestones looked like rivets about to pop.

First we went out to dinner. Then we saw a movie I don't remember. Then we ended up at some glitzy night club in the corner of a grocery store parking lot. The place was overloaded with hype. The building was a square, cement block with a narrow strip of sidewalk along two sides, but there were strings of blinking lights hanging down from the roof, yellow and purple and green, to jazz it up, and a couple of fake palm trees just inside the door. A heavy-set bearded guy in a blue Hawaiian shirt was letting the girls go in for free, but he made me cough up a ten-dollar cover.

I think they called it The Paradise Club, or something exotic like that, but for ten dollars it didn't come even close. Everywhere you looked you saw guys in pin-striped shirts and khakis or jeans standing in fours and fives and these overly boisterous grins on their faces and talking big and extra loud and drinking frosty banana daiquiris, and there were girls flitting from group to group and accidentally bumping their hips up against these grinning big-talkers and giggling when they did it and the guys looking at each other and smirking and their boisterous grins becoming more boisterous, if you can believe that, like you wouldn't think a face could normally stretch that far, and then they were buying the girls drinks, and then the girls would be flitting off to somewhere else. Man, everybody in that place was drinking like mad.

As soon as we got to the bar, my date waved at a couple of the big-grinners, you could tell she knew them, and they came over and then they all started talking. I ordered a couple of beers and fished out a twenty and paid the man, and then I started looking around. I have to say I was pretty bored. They were playing some early Elvis Costello or something, but nobody was dancing. They had the stage set up for a Midnight Karaoke Contest with red and blue floodlights lit up so you couldn't see the audience, and a couple of bar stools for the singers and a couple of glittery microphones with long black cords, like the kind you see on reruns of *Star Search*. Any minute I was expecting Ed McMahon himself to come waltzing out and start the show. Not the older Ed McMahon who lost a fortune trying to prop up his wife's clothing company, but the younger one who kept bouncing around the country with that million-dollar check. But nothing happened right away, so I finished my beer and ordered another. My date was still talking with the two big-grinners, and I remember thinking if she ever did want another beer, they could be the ones to buy it. First they were talking about college and how they had cheated on this exam or that one and who they'd been going out with, and then it was about going down to Key West for a week at some place called the Blue Parrot, or maybe jetting off to Cancun, they were going to have a real good time. They had the kind of faces you wanted to just haul off and hit. You knew it was bound to happen one day. Simpering, snub-nosed baboon faces with fat red cheeks and fat, glittery eyes sort of just stuck there. It made you sick just to look at them.

    Then the karaoke contest started. I couldn't see who it was very well on account of the floodlights, but you had to say the guy was absolutely terrible. I mean with his croaky old voice it sounded like he was drowning in radio static. But then the simpering, snub-nosed baboon faces started laughing, and one of them said they should toss the drunken jerk in the dumpster with the rest of the night's garbage and put a girl on instead, which it kind of ticked me off he said that. Not so much because of what he said. I mean his sense of the aesthetic was absolutely dead on the mark. I guess I just didn't like the way he said it, like they were having the damn karaoke contest just so he could screw up his simpering baboon face and make rude comments about the contestants.

    So I was thinking what to say to him, because you really should try and talk with these big-grinning bastards before you go breaking their noses, but I couldn't think of a thing to say. Then I felt my fingers curling up and my arm pulling back, and I swear I was just about to let one fly, when a hell of a scramble broke out on the karaoke stage, and my arm relaxed. You wouldn't have believed it. The guy on the stage wouldn't leave. He was standing there, still croaking out his song, and when they tried to usher him off politely, he grabbed hold of the cord and swung the microphone at them. He was actually kind of whipping it around like he was in a god damn kung-fu movie or something. Then some dippy drunk leaned in too close and got clobbered on the forehead, and then everybody rolled back from the stage. You never saw a space clear out so fast. It was like Charlton Heston rolling back the Red Sea. And right there in the middle of all that emptiness and the red and blue floodlights and the sound of that microphone whipping around, well, like I said before, you wouldn't have believed it. It was surreal. I could hardly believe it myself. It was good old ex-Marine Ed standing there on the stage.

You could see plain enough he was drunk. The way he was swinging that microphone around and there wasn't anybody even near him. I don't think he even knew where he was. He probably thought he was back in Da Nang. He was probably looking out on a sea of Viet Cong faces. Then these three bouncers rushed him from behind, and poor old Ed, he couldn't do a thing. Bouncers are always these big, truculent nut jobs, six-foot-six and three hundred pounds and always they started out playing linebacker in the NFL and then they got kicked out for knifing some guy at the bottom of the pile and ended up in prison, and when they got out they became bouncers. One of them was the bearded guy from the door, and he had Ed in a Chinese choke hold. Another nearly ripped off Ed's arm to get that microphone. Then the third came around and gave Ed a swift chop in the stomach, I guess because there was nothing else left to do. It was damn cowardly, if you ask me, but you should have heard those snub-noses cheer when he did it. You could tell they wanted to get in on the action. Then the bouncers dragged Ed from the stage, but only a couple of steps at a time, because Ed still didn't want to go. Then he got one of his arms free and started swinging it, but he couldn't connect, and the bouncers kept grabbing hold of that arm, but old Ed kept shaking it loose, which was probably because of his all-purpose, martial-arts, jungle marine training.

Of course the whole time they were grappling with Ed they were closing in on those palm trees and the front door, and you knew they were going to toss him out. All the big-grinners in the place were cheering like mad, waiting for it to happen. But not me. I got to the door first, and I was trying to tell those bouncers I knew the guy and if they let him alone it would be all right, he was suffering from a paralyzed brain, but they just pushed me back.

Then Ed finally did connect, and it was one hell of a punch for being smothered by all those grappling-hook arms. Hell, it would have been a hell of a punch if he had been standing by himself. But it didn't land where he wanted it to. Ed connected with one of those fake palm trees instead, which I guess were probably made of cement, and he pretty much quieted down after that. It was like all the rage and persecution he had felt a moment before had been sucked out of him. To tell you the truth, I think he must have broken his hand. Then one of the bouncers held open the door and they threw Ed out and everybody cheered and laughed, and some even clapped. Poor old Ed, he must have sailed fifteen feet through the air. Then they turned on me, the bouncers, all three of them. I guess I was still trying to tell them Ed would be all right if only they left him alone.

"We'll leave him alone all right," they said. "We'll leave him alone right on his fucking ass."

They all seemed pretty pissed.

Then the cowardly bouncer, the one who had chopped Ed in the stomach, said I had better watch myself or they'd toss me out just like Ed. It was actually kind of funny because you could hardly understand a word he was saying the way he mumbled. It was like listening to the way they talk in those old 1930s Popeye cartoons. Then I guess I must have said something about that cartoonish resemblance because the next thing I knew I was sailing out the door myself.

I landed on the sidewalk, maybe two feet from Ed, but I don't think he noticed. He sure didn't look up. He was just sitting there on the curb, not moving, holding his broken hand up close to his chest, and with the other he was picking at bits of glass stuck in the pavement. You could see he was still pretty drunk. The act of getting tossed hadn't sobered him up any. But there was really nothing else to do but sit there with him. Even with a broken hand you wouldn't want to startle old Ed. If he didn't know you were there you just left him alone. I mean it took three damn bouncers to throw him out. So we sat there. The lights from The Paradise Club were blinking yellow and purple and green, and we just sat there. A couple of cars pulled up and a cab and they let some people out and drove off, and we sat there, still.

Then Ed looked over at me and broke into a sort of gloomy, maniacal grin. I think he had just realized it was me sitting there across from him.

"You all right Ed?"

He grunted something. "Yeah, I'm all right," he said. He stopped picking at the glass and held onto his broken hand. "Are you all right? How about you, Travis fucking Lauterbach? Are you all right?"

"Sure, Ed. I'm all right."

"Well me too. I never felt any better in my goddamn life."

I'll tell you one thing about old Ed, he could be a raging lunatic at times. There I was sitting on the curb outside a grocery store parking lot nightclub at one o'clock in the morning and thinking maybe he might all of a sudden forget it was me sitting there and smack me like he did that fake palm tree. Even if I didn't do anything he might smack me, right? But he didn't. He got real quiet for a while, like he was embarrassed, and I was thinking he sure embarrassed himself a lot. Then he started telling me about Vietnam, which I guess had something to do with him getting thrown out of The Paradise Club. Maybe once he had this idea about paradise, and he'd been looking for it, and maybe he thought Vietnam was going to be it. I mean before he got there. I mean Vietnam's pretty hot and there are jungles and beaches and the South China Sea, which is paradise to some people. But when he got there it wasn't like he had thought, which it almost never is. Maybe.

"I'll tell you something about Vietnam, Travis," he

said. "Vietnam was one fucked-up place to be. Maybe not as fucked-up as here," and then he laughed. "But it sure was fucked. It was a goddamn cluster-fuck. You really didn't know what the fuck you were doing. You just did it. I remember one time they dropped us in the middle of the jungle, I don't know where exactly. It was south of Da Nang, I know that much. But I don't know how far. They flew us in one night, and then they flew in some trucks and graders and bulldozers and told us to build some roads. Now you tell me where in the fuck were we going to build roads to? But that's what they wanted. But the truth was you couldn't build roads there anyway. It was too damn hot, for one thing. We'd cut a path through the trees and pour concrete at night, but it was still too damn hot, you could see it in the morning, the road, bubbling up in places, all over, hell, it looked like some drunken bastard had poured some goddamn pancake batter all over the fucking ground. And then there was the rain, and maybe we had us a couple hundred yards of road, but the rain would wash it away, piece by fucking piece, and then you'd be standing in water up to your waist and the whole fucking jungle looking like one big VC bathtub that had been blown to bits, and after the rain there was the mud, and that was the worst, like the plagues of fucking Egypt, that goddamn mud could suck you under faster than anything, cows, dogs, trucks, marines. I heard it got a Lieutenant Colonel once, which would have been all right by me. And on top of all that shit you had the fucking Viet Cong trying to blow your ass to hell. They said it was a secure area, but every fucking night the VC would lob in a few mortars. If that's secure I'm the goddamn fucking Pope, but what were you going to do, somebody wanted a goddamn road in the middle of the jungle, so that's what we set out to do, and to keep us happy they'd send in some girls every couple of weeks, and then there'd be a lot of fucking and drinking beer, but there were never enough girls to go around, so you had to wait your turn, and some of the guys didn't like that, and some of the guys didn't want to stop once they started. I remember this one guy, he had this pretty little piece by the ass, she was strutting around in this blue silk bathrobe with the flaps wide open and a pair of cowgirl boots with white fur, and he was fucking the hell out of her from behind and that blue silk bathrobe was flapping and she was laughing some and then moaning, and then just like that she said her time was up, she had another appointment, and then she was gone, but this guy, that really pissed him off. He picked up his M-16 and followed her, and he didn't see which hooch it was exactly, but he started firing anyway, and he kept on firing till that goddamn rifle jammed, fucking M-16s were a piece of shit, and when the MP's came for him he was swinging that M-16 like a club. But that's the way it was, Travis. It was fucked-up."

Then he stopped talking. The Paradise Club closed at two, but I guess the karaoke contest was over because people were already spilling out into the night, mostly big-grinners in pin-stripes, but some girls, too. I thought about my date and wondered if she knew I'd been tossed and if she cared and if she had done any karaoke or just watched and if maybe she had thrown me over for one of those two snub-noses. I didn't care if she had. I figured by then they had probably bought her a truckload of beer, which meant that they were the ones who had to drive her home.

"Come on, Ed. Let's get going." I grabbed hold underneath his shoulders. He was pretty heavy. He was a lot heavier than he looked. "Come on you drunk."

Ed grunted something, but he didn't resist when I helped him up. I probably would have asked him where he had parked, since he lives out by the airport, but he was basically inert. So I lugged him over to my car and shoved him into the back. He sort of flopped over head first, and then he lay there on the seat, a lunatic grin pasted on his face. Then I got in the front and turned the key and gunned us out of the lot.

-4-

By the first week in November that second year I had become a native Floridian, at least in my appreciation of subtle changes in the weather. I could smell a faint, salty coolness in the air, and I remembered thinking that the year before I hadn't noticed any change, the whole of Florida had been one suffocating, steamy, brownish-greenish, sultry eternal summer. But there it was now, the coolness, and a sense that life was about to change, my life, perhaps. The feeling was pretty damn invigorating.

We were at the Japanese restaurant as usual. Mick and I were sitting on one side of the table and Laurie and Sonya were on the other side. They were both taking Mick's World History class, and they were both still living with their parents. I remember wondering if they were still auditioning or if they had already passed. Tommie Rodriguez was stuffed unhappily in between them. Emily wasn't there and neither was Ed. Emily had gone with Walter to some tennis tournament out in Ponte Vedra, or maybe it was golf, and Ed had gone home early. He said his hand was hurting from the cast, like he just wanted to chew himself free, that's how bad the pain was. Not even a bottle of Sake had helped. He said he was going to go home and drink till he passed out.

"So you had a good time, then," Mick was saying.

He had just opened a second bottle of Kirin beer.

"Sure we did."

It was Sonya. She was wearing a pale blue lambswool sweater, and her shoulders were turned slightly towards Tommie as she spoke, it looked sort of like they were mirror images of each other, but her eyes were squarely on me and there was nothing I could do. With the soft, smoky light of the lavender Japanese lantern on her, illuminating her, highlighting her youthful, unconscious beauty, and the way she was showing herself off, it looked like she was up on a stage.

"But I know if there'd been more of us along, it would have been a lot more fun," Sonya said.

"Sure," I said. I looked over at Mick but he just ignored me. "Where was it you two went exactly?"

"Oh, Mr. Lauterbach, you weren't listening."

It was the other one, Laurie. She had this bubble gum bounciness with her blond ponytail and the flash of a pink ribbon and a pink Minnie Mouse sweatshirt that was just a little too tight and an un-Disney-like button that said Kiss

Me Mickey, I'm a Mouseketeer. I wondered just how many Mickeys she had kissed, and how many Micks.

"We went on a tour of some college."

"She never would have got back without me," Sonya said.

"Oh, good God! That's not true. I just wasn't ready to go home when she said."

"She means she wasn't ready to pass on all the free beer."

"Well I do like beer. So do you. Why I bet even Miss Rodriguez has a beer every once in a while. Do you Miss Rodriguez? Do you have a beer every now and then?"

"You would have been sick yourself just to see how much she drank," Sonya said. "And then she passed out and I dumped her in the car and drove home."

"Touché!" Mick said, finishing off half of his Kirin and looking me square in the eye. "That's what friends are for. Isn't that so Lauterbach?"

"Is that what you think, Mr. Lauterbach?" Laurie asked.

"Sure he does. Mr. Lauterbach's a genuine sweetie."

"Would you have done the same thing as Sonya?" said Laurie. "Would you have dumped me like that in the back seat of your car and then taken me home?"

"Sure he would have," Sonya said. "And then he would have dumped you on your own front lawn."

"Is that what you'd do, Lauterbach?" Mick said. "Who the hell taught you about driving a girl home?"

"Me? No one taught me."

"Man, I can see that."

"Don't let them get to you, Travis," said Tommie. "All you need is some practice."

"Well now," Mick said. "I do believe the young lady is making a pass at you." Then a leering, drunken sailor's glint came to his eyes and he started twirling his moustache and then he started to grin. "Yes, it is most definitely a pass. Ah, my friend. My poor, dear, lonely, Travis Lauterbach. He will go off with this Tommie Rodriguez and then he will be lost to us *por siempre y para siempre*," him picking up his half-empty bottle of Kirin, "of course he will be missed," looking at the beer inside, "*Si*," looking at us through the glass of the bottle, *"nadie sabe lo que vale el agua hasta que falta,"* and then back at the beer, swirling it around, "but we will not grieve, for this Tommie Rodriguez is a very pretty girl, deliciously pretty, why, if it were not for our dear friend Travis Lauterbach, we would have a go at her ourselves." Mick polished off the rest of the bottle and set it deliberately, delicately on the table. "*Este, tambien, es paraíso, eh?*" he said.

"What?" Laurie asked.

Then Mick was laughing a loud, boisterous laugh because he was drunk and because he thought he had made a joke, and Tommie was laughing from absolute embarrassment, but kind of like she was coughing, but whether it was from Mick's comment about her being delicious or Mick having a go at her or for the way he spoke Spanish, I didn't know, and I was laughing because it's pretty hard not to laugh when Mick starts acting like an idiot, and the two Mouseketeers were laughing these giggly little piggly-wiggly laughs, probably because they didn't understand a word of Spanish and they thought he'd said something dirty. Then the waitress came and the sudden breezy, rustling of her silky blue kimono sort of hushed us and we stopped laughing. She was the same one from behind the register. Mick ordered another beer and I ordered one and the girls and Tommie had Cokes.

"Mick, something happens to you when you drink beer," I said. "I swear all of a sudden you think you're Pancho Villa taking pot shots at the Federales."

"Who is Pancho Villa?" Laurie asked.

"A Mexican revolutionary," Mick said.

"So it was Spanish you were speaking,' Sonya said.

Sonya started to giggle.

"I could hardly understand a word you were saying."

"Ah, you are saying I mangled my Spanish."

"It sounded like Spanish to me," Laurie said.

"I learned my Spanish in the streets."

"What streets?"

"Ah, I am not permitted to speak about this. A good revolutionary abandons the past completely once it is past."

"Go on," Sonya said. "What streets?"

"Come on now, Mick," I said. "You've provoked their interest. You might as well make up something."

"Yes," Tommie said. "I'd like to hear about the streets and this secret, revolutionary past of yours."

Mick looked directly at Tommie and smiled and the light from the lanterns was bouncing off his teeth.

"It is mostly about why I learned Spanish in the first place."

"Why is fine."

"Okay then. I'll tell you. It was in the sixties."

"Oh, God no," Sonya said.

"Not another boring sixties story," said Laurie.

Mick just smiled.

"We had gone up to New York City," he said, "to help Abbie set up these free stores. We were living in this rat-trap of an apartment building on the Lower East Side, and I have to tell you it was like living in goddamn fucking South America. Like in Bolivia. Nobody spoke any English. Even the goddamn signs. It was all *"hombre!"* this and *"hombre!"* that and *"El cuarto de baño está al final del pasillo,"* which usually meant there was a hell of a party going on in somebody's apartment. But when we first moved in we didn't know jack! We couldn't even buy rice without thumbing through a dictionary. But the kicker was this one night. I'd been going all over the place that evening handing out leaflets and stopping sometimes to talk and pass around a joint, and I guess that went on for hours. But then I must have passed out or fallen asleep or something because the next thing I knew I was stretched out on the floor of some vacant room in a bombed-out looking apartment building. I had no idea where I was, but the sun was just coming up, so I headed over to the window. There was group of people setting up a street market. Old men in butcher's aprons and old women in scarves were setting up fruit carts and vegetable carts, right there in the middle of the street, and there were more people waiting for the market to open, they were leaning against the buildings or standing under the trees, not saying much, nothing I could hear, a sort of low, far-away murmuring. Well right then I knew I was in exactly the right place. These were the people we had come for, this is what we were about, feeding the people. It was a goddamn beautiful realization. It was like some sort of Robert Altman vision of hippies helping all of God's children find their way back to

Eden. Fucking beautiful. But the moment I had that thought, I realized I wasn't wearing a goddamn thing, which isn't all that unusual for me, but the floor in that apartment was a cold, linoleum floor, and I don't even want to mention the stains and the rat droppings. I must have been blitzed. Then I realized somebody had stolen everything I owned. They had stolen my leaflets and my joints. They had stolen my watch, a gift from my grandfather, and a gold chain that Abbie had given me. And they had stolen all of my clothes, all the way down to my socks. The fuckers cleaned me out. They even took my underwear."

Mick took a swig from his beer.

"Oh my God," Laurie said. "What did you do?"

"What do you think I did?"

"God, I don't even want to guess."

"Ladies, there's not much you can do when the Universe is jerking you around. I wrapped myself up in a pair of orange curtains from the window. I was hoping somebody else still lived in the building and maybe I could borrow some pants and a shirt. So I went across the hall and knocked on the door. Pretty funny, right? I'm standing in the hall in these orange curtains and they won't stay up unless I hold them, and they're pretty sheer to begin with, like you can almost see right through them, and I hadn't even taken a piss yet so I was pretty hard to boot, hell, I was about to burst. So I'm knocking on this door and then it opens and I'm looking at this fairly sexy *chiquita* wearing a t-shirt that's just a little too tight. She was holding a spatula in her hand and you could smell eggs or something from the kitchen. We just stared at each for I don't how long. Man, she didn't even blink. Then I started to say something about how I was embarrassed and did she have any pants I could borrow, but my Spanish wasn't so good and I used the word *embarazar*, which means to make pregnant. It's incredible the noise a simple misunderstanding can cause. She started screaming with *mucho disgusto* and waving that spatula in my face, but she didn't shut the door. She was just standing in the doorway screaming and shaking that spatula, and the next thing I knew I was running down the stairs, trying to keep those orange curtains from flapping up too high or falling off."

Mick finished off his beer.

"Hell, I wasn't about to wait around and see if maybe she had a husband with a baseball bat. I took off and never looked back."

And with that we knew the story was over and it was okay to laugh, which we all did a little bit, except Tommie, who was more or less groaning.

"Mick, I've heard that joke a hundred times," Tommie said. "And it's not any better now than it ever was."

"He was joking?" Laurie said.

"I was not," Mick said. "Maybe it sounds like a joke to the jaded and pretentious among us. But I swear it's the goddamn fucking truth. Mucho fucking."

"What did you think when she was screaming?" Laurie said.

"I was thinking, my dear, unjaded little girl, that if she hadn't been screaming, the two of us could have had ourselves a very nice little party. She was a very good looking *chiquita*."

"Jesus!" Tommie said. "That's all you men ever think about."

Laurie and Sonya looked at each other and burst out laughing.

We left soon after that. Mick and I each with a bottle of Kirin in hand, and the girls without. The two Mouseketeers were parked right outside and Tommie a few spaces in front of them. The street rose sharply after that and came to a crest at a stop light. It was pretty late, and the stores and other businesses were all dark except for the glow of the stoplight reflected in the windows. A bus went by and stopped at the top of the hill and several people edged away from the darkness of the buildings and got on, and as the bus pulled away you could see them plainly in the yellow light of the inside looking for just the right seat among all the empty seats. Then Tommie got in her car and drove away. The two Mouseketeers talked with Mick a moment, and at first they were looking very serious, but then they brightened and Laurie laughed, and then they were in their car and Laurie leaned out and waved good-bye.

"Come on," Mick said.

We crossed the street and walked half a block down the

hill to an alley parking lot overlaid with a whitish, powdery, concrete rubble. There was a harsh, white security light up on a telephone pole near the entrance to the lot and another light fixed to the side of a brown-brick building in the back, but it was broken. There were four tinny-looking cars in the lot and a two-tone pickup truck, gold with a white stripe, which was parked under the broken light. You could see a man and a woman were in the pick-up, or maybe it was just kids. You couldn't really tell. They were groping each other, squirming on the seat and slipping and regaining their balance, and the window was rolled halfway down, it was probably stuck, so you could hear them murmuring softly and moaning and him telling her to move her legs this way or that way because the buckles were in the way or he needed to shift himself to get a better grip.

Mick started laughing when he heard them, and by the time we got to our cars, a dull orange Datsun for Mick and the same old dirty white Toyota for me, the two in the pick-up had roared out of the lot. We had parked next to each other. Mick was leaning back against his own car, laughing again, waving away the whitish dust and drinking from his bottle of Kirin. I was sitting in my car with the window rolled down. I was drinking too.

"You going home?" Mick said.

"Yeah. I'm pretty tired."

Mick started to grin. He took a quick swig and his beer started to bubble up.

"Listen, next week I'm giving a little party, and you're going to be there, right?"

"Sure, Mick."

"It's sort of a farewell party."

"For you?"

"This one's going to be wild. Beach bums, bikers, a couple of jazz musicians I know, a couple of ex-Catholic priests, some girls in bikinis. It's going to be one hell of an eclectic bunch, with plenty of existentialism and margaritas and Bob Marley, and a joint or two if you're into that."

"You know where you're going this time?"

"Not yet. Maybe South America. Maybe all the way to Patagonia. But it doesn't matter. I've just got to get away from the strip-center, shopping-mall mentality that dominates this wonderful fucking paradise we've made for ourselves."

"How long?"

"As long as it takes. I told Dubois I'd be gone the rest of the school year."

"Damn, Mick. You're out there on the lunatic fringe."

"Hell, Lauterbach. Why don't you come with me?"

"Sure, Mick. And what'll I do for cash?"

Mick started tapping his almost empty bottle of beer against the side of the Datsun. He was smiling now and his teeth flashed in the glare from the one working security light. You could never tell if Mick was serious or not.

"Forget it, man. You don't have a reason to go yet."

"Did you tell the Mouseketeers you're going?" I said.

"The what?"

"Sonya and Laurie. The Mouseketeers."

"Man, you're all right, Lauterbach. No. I told them about the party. That's all they really care about anyway. There's not much else in their heads. They're pretty aimless. They're even worse than you, if you can believe that."

We laughed.

"At least think about it, Lauterbach."

"Sure, Mick, I'll think about it."

We finished our beers. Then Mick got in his car and drove off. He'd put on his straw hat with the string for the drive. I drove home in my dirty white Toyota. The coolness in the air had become a motionless, brittle kind of cool, like ice, except it was probably in the fifties. I drove along Riverside Avenue, and through the trees you could maybe catch a glimpse of the heavy blue St. John's River and the short choppy waves glinting in the moonlight. There weren't any boats out at this hour. Sometimes I liked to sit along the river at night and watch the waves rolling across and it was like I was the only person alive on the planet. But this only seemed true if you looked south, where the river seemed to disappear into the cloudy, mottled darkness of the sky. If you looked north, you could see the downtown lights, the neon blues and greens, the shimmery whiteness of the Jacksonville Landing, and you knew you weren't alone. Downtown there were always people out and about, maybe heading back from dinner or shopping or a movie, whatever people do anywhere, and there were all sorts of drunks and boozers and homeless guys shuffling around Hemming Plaza, even at two in the morning you could see them, and maybe a couple of guys in raincoats or an oddball gap-toothed prostitute now and then hanging around the restrooms at the bus station, and always there were the cops.

 Looking south or looking north was the difference between where you had come from and where you were going. But to tell you the truth, it didn't matter all that much to me. I took the job in Jacksonville after my dad died so I wouldn't have to focus on shit like that. He was always telling me to look where I was going, keep my eyes open, opportunity only knocks once or twice, you've got to grab the bull by the horns, close only counts in horseshoes and hand grenades, it's not enough to know how to ride, pretty much every cliché in the book. I guess he didn't want me to end up like him. My dad was a clerk in the army, a career man who spent his career counting inventory. My mom gave up on him pretty early, which sort of proves that life is a cliché, if you think about it. When he got transferred to Fort Dix, she stayed in Chicago. In a way, I guess my dad never left Chicago. He was stuck between coming and going the rest of his life. But I wasn't thinking about any of that shit the night Mick told me about the party. I was tired. The alcohol had worn off. I just wanted to get home.

 I lived in a pinkish, orangeish cement block apartment building with an aqua-marine colored roof about five blocks from St. Vincent's hospital. It was pretty much a dump, without even a view of the river, but it was cheap. I pulled into the parking lot and walked up the path and up the outside stairs. I lived on the second floor. You could look out through the sliding glass doors of the porch and see a row of one-story bungalows on the other side of the street. The houses were surrounded by oaks and magnolias with their waxy green leaves, and masses of overgrown azalea bushes. Above the houses you could see the spire of a Baptist church two blocks away.

 I went inside and flicked on the hall light and the kitchen light, and suddenly I wasn't tired. I grabbed a bag of pretzels and a couple of Cokes and sat down in front of the TV and turned on some western I was sure I'd seen before, and then the western faded and I was watching MTV and the first thing that came on was a Depeche Mode video. They were dressed in black and wearing black cowboy hats, it sort of looked like they were gunfighters, or maybe they were Mexican revolutionaries, it was hard to say, and then I was watching the news, and then some other movie I didn't know, some damn love story or something like that. I watched television all night, but I don't remember what I saw. I don't even remember turning the channels. Mostly I was thinking, and the television would sort of drift in and out of my mind while I thought, and after a while it was like my thoughts were right there on the screen, in living color.

The first thing I was thinking was about Mick going to some South American country to join the revolution, it didn't matter which country since it was one big revolution no matter where you went, and Pancho Villa was heading down from Mexico to help out, which I know is one big impossibility since Pancho Villa was assassinated in 1923, but in my imagination anything was possible, so there he was, the Pancho Villa of my imagination, slapping old Mick on the back and handing him a rifle and a few straps of ammunition, and then the two of them, Pancho and Mick, smiling at each other, and they both had these crazy, jagged, chipped teeth, like you could only be part of the revolution if you had once had your face smashed in with a Billy club. You could feel the excitement in the air. And then Mick was in Mexico fighting against the Federales, and then he was back at his beach house telling war stories to a couple of brand new baby Mouseketeers and then fucking the hell out of them.

I couldn't help but think that Mick was a lousy goddamn hypocrite. If he didn't like the shopping malls and all the theme park commercialism, why the hell didn't he stay and fight. Wasn't there plenty to fight about right here in the good old USA? Why did he have to leave the country to do his damn revolutionary thing? He was a damn hippie, after all. Well, an ex-hippie at least. Isn't that what they did in the sixties? They stood up and fought for what they believed in because that's what the founding fathers said they should do.

But then maybe you couldn't do that anymore. We had created a sprawling, rotting, festering urban ecosystem of video outlets and airfare price wars and happy, smiley-faced concrete clowns handing out burgers at drive-through windows, and everything was so tangled up in everything else that if you attacked one thing, you attacked everything. Maybe there was no place any more for revolutionaries in America. They either ended up in jail or dead, a footnote on the national news. Maybe people like Mick had to go somewhere else, at least for a while, so their brains wouldn't rot away.

Then I was thinking about why I didn't want to go with Mick, which I have to admit sounded pretty damn appealing. But I could see myself getting abandoned in some South American city because Mick had gone north with Pancho Villa to fight for the peasants, and all Mick would have said before he left was 'you need to find your own fucking cause to fight for, Lauterbach, whatever gets you pissed, that's the only way you'll ever grow up,' but he would have been smiling with his gleaming, chipped-tooth smile and clapping me on the back like finding a cause to fight for was the easiest thing in the world, so it would been hard to gainsay his advice, and then I could see myself wandering up some hilly back alley and smack dab into some guerrilla outfit that didn't know Pancho or Mick or anyone else north of the equator, a dozen grisly-faced, toothless bastards, gringo-eating deviants with tattoos on their arms and the backs of their necks and riding mules and empty ammunition belts slung around their waists, and all of them bloody from fighting the night before, and then I could see my dead body on some bricked-over back alley road because they didn't like gringos who couldn't speak Spanish. I could see it all on the six o'clock news, only they wouldn't know who it was, just some poor, dippy American tourist who didn't have a MasterCard. That's why I wouldn't go with Mick. It wasn't like going all the way to South America would make me any happier. Who said South America was paradise?

Then the love story came on and I was thinking about Tommie Rodriguez and the bowling date and her curvey behind, the kind Harvey Collins liked, and then I was thinking about those other two dates, and God what a mess they were.

And then I was thinking maybe I hadn't given Tommie a chance. Mick thought she was delicious looking. And I guess maybe she was. A guy could do a hell of a lot worse than Tommie Rodriguez. Maybe it had been so long since I had felt normal that I didn't even know my own mind. Maybe I just didn't like everybody I knew trying to push me and Tommie together. It had been practically non-stop since Emily Lavigne had tried. And now there was Mick and the party to think about, and I was pretty damn sure Tommie was going. What Mick had said at the restaurant about me and Tommie going off together, well, if he hadn't told her about the party yet, he was sure as hell going to. There was something perverse about Mick. But maybe Tommie and me wasn't such a bad idea. I had to admit I liked Tommie. I mean maybe Tommie was just what I needed.

Then the love story was over and some cartoons came on. You could see the sun coming up through the window and the dewy green of the trees and the gleaming white spire of the Baptist church. I still wasn't tired, but I was kind of numb from thinking so much. I went into the kitchen and dumped the empty pretzel bag in the garbage and the empty Coke cans. Then I fixed a bowl of cereal and went back to the TV.

-5-

The party at Mick's was one hell of a party. It was supposed to start at four in the afternoon, but I must have got the time wrong. I got there at quarter to and had to park three blocks away. I couldn't imagine Mick's little beach house with its matchbox living room holding three blocks worth of people. But there was no other explanation for all the cars. Man, they were everywhere. Beat up Chevy trucks and perky little red Ford Escorts and several BMWs, which meant students, and then there was a Volkswagen van and a bunch of regular bugs, a couple of blues and a yellow and a lime green convertible. And then about a block away someone had set up three sawhorse roadblocks, and on one side there were half a dozen Harley's, and then a few more cars, and then smack in the middle of the street was a stolen road construction sign which had been painted over. It said: "Warning! Party Ahead. Proceed At Your Own Risk." But Mick didn't need the sign. Already you could hear people laughing and talking loudly and shouting, and underneath it all was the steady reggae hum of Bob Marley.

The first thing you saw when you actually got to Mick's house was a farewell banner hung over the front door, and a couple of loudspeakers set up on the roof with wires running down into the house through one of the windows and reggae music pouring out like rain. I have to say one thing: Mick sure had a thing for his music. There was no getting away from it either. He had two more speakers inside the house and two more on a rotting redwood picnic table down at the beach. And everywhere you looked there were people having a good time. In the front yard there were several groups of people scattered among the potted ferns, a few sitting on the sandy, cobblestone brick or on folding chairs, and some on a wooden Swiss Miss-style bench shoved up against the house. Or maybe it was just the one group with the ferns getting in the way. But either way there were several different conversations going on at once and girls running in and out through the front door with beers and banana daiquiris and margaritas, like they were waitresses or something. Two bikers were arguing with some ditzy redhead about a bike trip they took out to Rapid City, South Dakota the summer before, all the way out to Sturgis on their Harleys for some bike rally, there must have been a million bikers, they said, roaring through the Black Hills for a fucking week, it was something to see, it was a goddamn millennial event, and she was saying if they had really gone, then where were the t-shirts to prove it, and they didn't seem to know how to handle that, but then one of them mumbled something about they didn't sell any goddamn t-shirts at the rally, the rally didn't have any shit like that, it wasn't infected with any goddamn commercialistic assholes, Jesus fucking Christ, but you could see he wasn't telling the whole truth.

Inside it was just as crowded as the front yard, maybe

more, and a hell of a lot noisier. People were sitting on the sofa and over by the kitchen counter and leaning against the walls and drinking and listening to the music and talking and smoking, and I thought it was pretty damn rude them smoking indoors like that instead of out, but I guess they thought they were in some Spanish biker bar out on U. S. Highway 1 or somewhere like that. I have to admit it felt like a bar with those waitress girls running around with drinks and getting flirty with the guests and then wiggling their rear ends up to the kitchen counter and then back out to the front yard, and behind the counter there was this guy named Rinaldo wearing cheap sunglasses and his hair slicked back, a tuxedo t-shirt top, swim trunks and Roman style sandals. He was mixing drinks in a blender and handing out beers, and just for a joke people started tipping him nickels and dimes and pennies, all of which went into a Mickey Mouse coffee mug or bowl or something right there on the counter. I guess after a while people forgot he wasn't really a bartender.

    Mick wasn't around the house so I grabbed a margarita and tossed a couple of quarters into the Mickey Mouse mug and went back out through the sliding glass doors. Down at the beach there was about a truckload of people. Some were playing volleyball and some were watching and they were all drinking mostly beer because there was a keg half-buried in the sand next to the net, and every now and then some girl got picked up and carried to the water, laughing and screaming and wiggling with welcome hysteria, and then she'd get dumped in, and then everybody had these dippy looking grins on their faces, even the girl. But Mick wasn't with the volleyballers either, so I headed back up and there was Ed with his hand still in the cast and next to him was his ex-wife, Joyce, who had this shrill, flutey voice which kind of stabbed at your brain, and three others I didn't know. I guess they had just got there. They were sitting on a makeshift patio in the middle of Mick's sandy, grassy backyard, just before you got to the dunes. They were sitting in these white molded plastic chairs, which Mick must have borrowed or stolen because they hadn't been there before, and they weren't exactly the kind of chairs Mick would buy anyway. Mick wasn't into plastic. There was a pile of chairs stacked up against a scraggly old palmetto. I nodded a hello and pulled a chair off the top and sat down.

Everybody but Ed was smiling these easy-going vacuous smiles, as if they'd been drinking for days and were happy just to have chairs to sit in. They broke off their conversation just long enough for the unknowns to introduce themselves. First there was Iggy and Imants, both ex-priests, ex-Catholic priests, with shiny bald heads and viciously red necks from where they'd been shaving too closely for years, and next to them was this girl with hair that kind of looked like Spanish moss hanging from her head, and she was Joyce's sister, which I couldn't help thinking maybe she meant ex-sister, since everybody else there was an ex, but I didn't say anything.

So I sat there in that plastic white chair and the sun splattering down, listening to these people talk, and except for Ed, and Joyce, whom I had met once before, and except for Mick's farewell banner hanging over the front door, I would have sworn I'd gone to the wrong house. I had never seen the rest of these people before, at least that's what it seemed like, not Joyce's sister or the ex-priests, and certainly not the bikers or Rinaldo the bartender in his tuxedo top or the dippy looking volleyballers at the beach, which was by no means exclusive proof that Mick didn't know them. But it was a little weird all the same, a slow motion *Twilight Zone* kind of weird where the people are talking in low, garbled voices and then the sound goes out completely and it feels like you're stuck in quick sand and then all of a sudden you can't see a goddamn thing and then you hear Rod Serling's voice, only it sounds like the voice of God, and old Rod he's saying "Ladies and gentlemen, you have just witnessed what happens when the aimless, hopped-up hope of youth is overwhelmed by the frenetic despair of an over-urbanized and mechanized society, a clash of opposite energies that pushes us beyond the limits of our imagination, a beach party somewhere on the outskirts of what we call the modern world, an unexplainable sojourn between the here and now and what we might call the edge of tomorrow. You have just entered *The Twilight Zone.*"

That's how it felt. But who can say for sure? Maybe most of these people had just seen the stolen construction sign and come off the street. Or maybe they'd heard about the party from some of Mick's friends. I guess it didn't really matter. I drank some of my margarita and tried to focus on the slow-motion conversation.

"Oh I went with a priest once," Joyce was saying. "He was an older one, I'd say. Nearer sixty than fifty. But he was absolutely ferocious in bed. I never saw a man like that. I guess abstinence makes the throbbing stronger." Both Joyce and her sister laughed, and Iggy and Imants sort of half-snickered, each of them grabbing and rubbing the red of their closely shaved necks. Ed sat back in his chair looking vaguely troubled. Then Joyce leaned away from Ed and touched her sister delicately on the knee. "Let me tell you something sweetie, if you're ever thinking about a priest, go after one of the older ones. They've been abstaining the absolute longest."

Joyce and her sister laughed again.

Old ex-husband Ed stared at Joyce, a look of bewildered disbelief becoming one of comprehension.

"You mean Father Adleman?" he said.

"Yes. Father Adleman. Who else would it be?" Joyce said.

"Was this before or after we got divorced?"

"Before, of course."

"Shit," Ed said.

You could tell Ed wanted to lash out at someone. He looked squarely at Iggy, who was still rubbing his neck. "That's pretty rich, aint it, Iggy," he said. "You goddamn horny priests."

"Horny ex-priests," Iggy said.

"Or ex-horny priests," Imants joked.

"Oh, I wouldn't go that far," Iggy said.

Joyce laughed, and then everybody else was laughing, except Ed, and then nobody said anything for a while. Probably it was only a couple of seconds, but it seemed a hell of a lot longer. The sun was warm against my face and I drank from my margarita. The others drank from their drinks. From where I was sitting I could see a sliver of the beach through the dunes and the bright wild blue of the Atlantic and the surf kicking up. The volleyballers had stopped playing and were heading down en masse to the water with another ultra girly-girl victim struggling playfully above their heads, and then there was a burst of gleeful, giddy, pseudo-sacrificial laughter, and then the volleyball girl was floating in the surf and the rest of them went back to their game. Good old Bob Marley was singing *Stir It Up*.

"Do you guys know this fucking Father Adleman?"

Old ex-husband Ed was shifting about in his white plastic chair, trying to get comfortable. The chair didn't seem all that sturdy with Ed in it. His face was turning red from the sun and from drinking and from being embarrassed and angry, all at the same time. It was pretty damn red. It was about as red as it could get.

"The fucking who?" Iggy said.

"It's a stage name," Imants said. "Like the Singing Nun or the Beef-Eating Bishop."

"Oh," Iggy said. "The Fucking Father. I remember. Yes, I knew him. But vaguely, vaguely. He didn't seem the type."

"What type? He was banging my wife."

"Your ex-wife," Joyce said.

"Shit," Ed said.

Ed sank back into the white plastic chair. He didn't know what else to say. He finished his beer, and with a flick of his wrist he sent the empty bottle spinning some ten feet through the air towards a Rubbermaid trash can on the grassy, sandy edge next to the stack of chairs. The bottle fell short and kicked up a poof of sand, but Ed didn't care. Brushing the wrinkles out of his shirt and pants, he headed down to watch the volleyballers, who were playing again. The others barely noticed Ed leaving. Joyce and her sister popped up from their chairs and happily flounced their way to the house to get refills. Iggy and Imants turned on me with these mockingly grave, ex-priestly eyes.

"So, Travis," Iggy said. "If you were this Father Adleman character, what would you have done?"

"What do you mean?"

"He means," Imants said, "if you were a priest and you wanted this woman, or any woman for that matter, would you quit being a priest just so you could have her, or would you stay a priest and screw her when you could?"

"Did Father Adleman quit?"

"I don't know. It doesn't matter. What would you do?"

"I guess if I wanted her," I paused. "Do I love her?"

"Love, want. It's all the same thing in the end."

"So I love her."

"Sure, you love her."

"Then I guess I'd have to quit. I mean if I loved her I shouldn't be a priest, right?"

"Right," Iggy said. "You see?" He was laughing and then poking at Imants with his beer and sloshing some on Imants's shirt. "That's the moral point of view of young America speaking there."

"Christ, Iggy," said Imants. The sun was glinting off the spilled beer and also off Imants's bald head, and for a moment all I could see was Imants's grave glinting eyes coming at me through the glare. "Suppose that you loved being a priest as much as you loved this woman," he said.

"Can you do that?" I said. You could see that Imants was getting a little irritated with my clichéd bewilderment. I thought I'd have some fun with him. "If you're Catholic."

"Sure, you can do it. So what would you do then?"

"You mean I have to give up something. Like a sacrifice?"

"No, no, no" Imants said. "You don't have to give up a thing."

"Well, I don't know," I said. "I don't see how I could marry her if I were a priest. Not a Catholic priest anyway. I mean I suppose if they changed their minds and said priests could marry. I mean if they issued a formal edict or a Papal bulletin or something like that, then it would be different. But the way it is now, I guess I'd have to join the Episcopal Church."

Iggy started laughing.

I drank some more of my margarita and watched Imants pretty much choke on my words. I'm not like a lot of Catholics. I wouldn't hold it against you if you wanted to be an Episcopalian. I mean I teach at an Episcopal school, for God's sake.

"Good God, Iggy. What's the matter with these people?"

"Face it, Imants, yours is a morally untenable position."

"Ahhhg!" Imants coughed on the last of his beer and then tossed his empty bottle after Ed's and reached below his chair and brought up another one. He had a stash of three or four bottles in the shade of the chair. He had apparently decided to waste as little energy as possible in his efforts to get drunk. He would avoid going back and forth between Mick's house and this circle of white plastic, sun-splattered chairs for as long as his stash held out. He opened the second bottle and started drinking and immediately started coughing again. Laughing, Iggy clapped him on the back a few times and the coughing stopped. The girls came flouncing back from the house. Joyce plopped down in her chair and began scolding Iggy and Imants for their obviously misguided reliance on beer, holding up her very own strawberry margarita as proof of a reliable alternative. Joyce's sister scooted her chair next to mine.

"So which type are you?" she asked.

She was sitting with her shoulders turned slightly away from her sister, but her head seemed to be floating directly above the arm of my chair, like it was detached from the rest of her body, and her Spanish moss hair was dripping down my arm. At first I couldn't tell if she was talking or not. She spoke in a soft, eager, whispery voice, and she was holding up her strawberry margarita as if to ward off interruption. The others were arguing playfully about whether to drink beer or margaritas.

"How's that?" I said.

"Which type? Joyce and I figured as soon as we left Iggy and Imants would pounce. They're always after people to settle this debate of theirs. They're both a little loony. They both think it's perfectly natural for priests and women to, you know, to do it. But Iggy thinks they should leave the priesthood if they want to and Imants doesn't. I think Imants has been losing the argument more than winning recently. At least he's been getting ticked off at Iggy a little too easily lately. It's pretty funny."

"Yeah. He got so mad before he started choking on his beer."

Joyce's sister sipped her drink and leaned her Spanish-moss covered head even closer.

"So what did you say?"

"I said I'd have to become an Episcopal priest."

"Oh, good. I like that. It's kind of romantic."

She sat back in her white plastic chair and her hair went with her, and then she was smiling at Iggy and Imants and her sister, a happy, contented smile, and it seemed like her smile was reflected in her margarita. Or maybe her margarita was reflected in her smile.

"They're gay, you know," she said. "That's the really funny part. The whole thing is just theoretical to them."

Joyce's sister started to laugh, and Iggy and Imants and Joyce were laughing also, but probably for a different reason, and while they were laughing they traded drinks and Joyce started guzzling Iggy's beer and Iggy started sipping from Joyce's strawberry margarita, and then Imants had a turn, and then they were laughing some more. These people laughed a hell of a lot.

Then old ex-husband Ed came back from the volleyballers and stood squarely behind his chair.

"You all just have to see this," he said.

"See what?" Iggy said.

"There's a dolphin washed up on the beach."

"A live dolphin?" Joyce's sister said.

"I don't know. I think it might be dead. But it's a goddamn beautiful animal anyway."

"What do you want see a crummy old dead dolphin for?" Joyce asked. "Good God, Ed. You must be drunk."

"Sure, Joyce."

Grinning fiercely, Ed headed back to the beach. He was pumped up by the dolphin and not even Joyce could take away his joy. He walked through the opening in the dunes and the salty, fishy smell of the ocean coming up with the wind and the glaring, burning sunlight fluttering in the wake of a few cloud puffs moving across the sky, and you could see a sudden tallness about Ed, as if he had grown three inches. He now seemed to possess a fierce, energetic, wide-angled brightness, like you see in the movies, which suggested, among other things, the absolute, religious, even mythic importance of looking at a dead dolphin.

"Come on everybody," Iggy said. "Let's go see it."

"I'm game," Imants said. "It sounds goddamn existential."

So that's what we did, all of us except Joyce. She sat

there in rigid, damning defiance of the very idea that we should bother with anything that had washed up on the beach. She sat there silently in her white plastic chair, drinking her margarita, and also Iggy's beer. But the rest of us ran after Ed, and we caught up to him at the dolphin itself. There was a whole crowd of eager onlookers, mostly volleyballers, but also a few retiree-type beach-walkers up from Atlantic Beach, and one old sea-captain bum with a metal detector who looked like the kind of bum you might see anywhere. Everybody was sort of encircling the poor animal, leaning over it, leering, poking at it with their fingers, which they'd probably tell you not to do if it were some old lady passed out on the street from a heart attack, but it's different with a dead dolphin right there in front of you. I don't really know why we came down to look at it. But you know, I have to admit Ed was right. It was a beautiful animal, even in death, with its milky-grayish skin glistening in the sunlight and the brownish-yellowish hard-packed sand beneath it and the purple strands of seaweed and the sudsy wavelets coming in from the blue Atlantic. It sure didn't look dead, but it was. You couldn't really see why it had died. You could see it had scars all over the place, like purplish-gray welts, but they were old scars from old dolphin battles and were long ago healed, so why this animal had died was a mystery. It didn't seem that an animal like that would just give up. Then I started thinking of it as a living, breathing animal. I could see it churning through the cool depths of the Atlantic, slicing this way and that in search of adventure, calling out to his dolphin buddies to join him and then all of them shooting up towards the glimmery surface, unthinking in their animal joy, their unrestrained lust for life, and then arcing up into the warm, sunny, salt-sprayed air. And when I thought of that I remembered the dolphins I had seen in the St. John's River. I wondered if this dolphin was one of them, and then I was sure that he was. And then I started thinking some slightly weird thoughts. Some very weird thoughts, if you want to know the truth. All of a sudden I could see in this dead dolphin the happiness that had been its life and I started thinking that maybe this dolphin was a message to me. Like maybe God was trying to tell me that there was indeed happiness out there, my happiness, if only I looked in the right place.

"Here comes Mick," somebody said.

"Hey, Mick, where the hell have you been?" shouted one of the volleyballers. "Do you know about this dolphin? You can't play volleyball with a dead dolphin on the beach."

"Why not?" the volleyballer's girlfriend said.

"Look, will you. It's too distracting."

I don't think Mick really heard what anybody said. He came down from the house, his chipped-tooth smile beaming a soft rosy glow in the late afternoon sun, and he was wearing his straw hat with the string, but not on his head, it was bouncing against his back with the string tight around his neck, like he was a bandit in *The Magnificent Seven*. Mick bent down and looked at the dolphin and patted it a couple of times on the flank and then he looked up at the crowd.

"I came to tell you sun gods and goddesses it's time to eat."

Mick looked down at the dolphin again.

"What, you mean the dolphin?"

It was the one volleyballer's girlfriend.

"Jesus, Lilly. Think about it."

Mick ignored the volleyballer and his girlfriend, patted the flank one last time and stood up.

"There's plenty of burgers and hot dogs," he said. "And there's tofu for all you vegetarian freaks. And the drinks are still on the house."

Then Mick headed towards the savory, sizzling meat smell of the grill, which only then did we notice, and man did that smell just open you up. I mean snap, just like that, I could hardly keep from running I was so hungry, and it seemed that everybody else was feeling the same kind of hunger the way we all of a sudden forgot about that dead dolphin. So we followed Mick up to the house, all of us except the retiree-type beach walkers, and a couple of overly zealous volleyballers who went back to the net and started batting the ball back and forth some more, and the sea-captain bum with the metal detector, who gave the dolphin a slow going over and that little box was beeping a steady, slow beep, I guess because he wanted to make sure it hadn't swallowed any quarters or something.

By the time we got back to the house, it was a maddening jumble of people with plates and drinks, trying to keep themselves from spilling. You had to squirm your way through to the grill, which was against the back wall of the house, right next to the sliding-glass doors, and then it was inside to the kitchen counter-top bar if you were thirsty, and if you wanted to eat anywhere near the house you had to stand because there wasn't anywhere to sit, but nobody except maybe Ed seemed to mind with all the food and people joking and laughing. Some were even dancing to Bob Marley while they ate. Mick liked Bob Marley a hell of a lot. I fixed a Paper Mate plate with a couple of burgers and some potato salad, grabbed a beer and sat down with Ed. We sat down where we were before, but the plastic white chairs were gone so we sat on the ground. I didn't know what happened to Iggy and Joyce and the others, and I guess Ed didn't care. He didn't talk about them and I didn't ask. The truth was Ed didn't seem too interested in talking at all. So we ate our burgers in a sort of gloomy silence and watched the others eating and laughing and dancing some, and then Mick came bursting out through the sliding-glass doors with two guys in short-sleeved khaki style uniforms with baseball caps and black Vandemere sunglasses and green patches on their shoulders with a deer and a bird and a fish like some kind of merit badge, like these guys were a cross between the Secret Service and the Boy Scouts. They were both carrying shiny, metallic kits with the letters FWC marked on them. It was about the dolphin. Mick said something and was pointing towards the beach and the Boy Scouts nodded and took off, and then you couldn't really see them, but you could see the glare of the sun bouncing off their metallic kits, but almost immediately they were back jabbering by the sliding glass doors. They were telling Mick the dolphin was dead, they only handled injured animals, live ones, he had called the wrong people. But Mick only smiled his chipped-tooth smile and his pale blue eyes were bouncing around in the dark of his stubbly face and he said, "Come on, man. You can see we're having a hell of a party here. Couldn't you do us a favor?"

You just knew the Boy Scouts were going to give in, they were Boy Scouts for God's sake, probably trying to earn the next badge to add to their shirts. Mick gave them a couple of beers and they headed around to the front. Ten minutes later they were driving down the macadam path in this official looking silver colored truck with blue lights on top and the same green and white patch with the deer and the fish on the doors. They drove through the opening in the dunes and the sand spitting up behind them and then they disappeared down the beach. You could see them drinking the beers and laughing as they went by, which it got me thinking some more about the dead dolphin and how happy it had looked, but when those two Boy Scouts came back you could see him, or it, or whatever, stretched out in the back of the truck on some kind of dark blue leathery, aquatic-type gurney, and it was tied down with about a dozen white nylon ropes crisscrossed like shoelaces, to keep it from falling out if they hit a bump. It sure didn't look happy any more. It was like the happiness of that dolphin was connected to the ocean and the rivers where it swam, and when the two Boy Scouts scooped it up, the happiness part just kind of drained away into the sand. They were left with nothing but a dead animal carcass.

After dinner, the sun started to set and the sky turned a bright tangerine color, except way out over the water where it was a dull, heavy blue. Mick said it was time to build the bonfire before we couldn't see a thing. He took us around to the corner of the house to a pile of driftwood. I have to say there was a hell of lot of driftwood there. It looked like Mick had been collecting driftwood for months. We carried some of it down to the beach, me and Mick and a few bikers and Iggy (but not Imants, who was rummaging through various abandoned coolers in search of a beer), and then Iggy and Mick started digging a pit in the sand and the rest of us went for more wood (at which point Imants joined us with a bottle for himself and another for Iggy).

By the time we got the last of the driftwood down to the pit, Mick had a pretty good blaze going, and it was dark too, the sky was pretty much black all over, and the water was especially dark, except for the running lights of a few shrimp boats off shore.

The bonfire was a good time. People came down with their drinks and stood around it and watched the sparks and cinders fly up into the night sky. If you stared long enough at the shimmering heat of the fire it looked like the whole world was melting. Then a few people lit up cigarettes or maybe some joints and started passing them around. There wasn't much talking and laughing at that point. There was a quieter, more sensual feeling about the day and the beach and the night unfolding, opening itself up to us. You could see people dancing slowly along the edge of the firelight, moving into the shadows, almost like they were shadows themselves, and the happy, redemptive sound of Bob Marley mingling with the faint, swishy sound of the surf.

I don't know how long I stood there just watching and listening and breathing in the smoky smell of that fire. I don't remember thinking a single thought in the smoky, surreal serenity of being there. But then all of a sudden it was like the movie version of myself standing there and the light glinting off my face, but I wasn't looking at the bonfire any more. I was looking up towards the house and the redwood picnic table with the speakers, and there was Tommie Rodriguez. She was walking towards me, walking, hell, it looked like she was gliding, like she was one of those angels in a junior high Christmas play and they were moving her through the air on strings.

Tommie waved and then smiled, and then she held up a margarita to show me and then drank some, and then just like that she was standing next to me.

"Hi stranger," she said. "I've been looking all over for you. Where've you been?"

"I guess I've been here," I said, nodding at the bonfire. "What about you? I didn't see you before."

"I came late. I even missed the barbecue."

"You didn't miss much."

She drank some more of her drink, and the next thing I knew she was holding on to my arm and we were both of us looking at the fire and listening to the reggae. I didn't have a drink so she gave me some of hers, and then we were sharing back and forth and laughing and squirming. I don't know what happened to the empty glass. Then I guess we must have got tired of standing because we were sitting in the sand and the bonfire wasn't quite so bright any more, or hot, and you could feel the cool, salt breeze blowing in, which felt pretty good, and after a while we were talking about some pretty weird late-night stuff. Theoretical, Iggy and Imants kind of stuff. At least I was. I must have been out of my mind.

I think Tommie thought I was drunk. But she was real nice about it. She laughed a couple of times, but all the while she kept holding on to my arm.

"Tommie, did you ever wonder about dolphins?"

"Mmmmm? No. Not recently," she said.

"Did you ever think that maybe dolphins have souls?"

"No," she said, and she laughed softly. "I don't think I've ever had that thought. But who knows?"

"People have souls, right? So why not dolphins?"

"You know you're very sweet when you're drunk."

"No, no. There was a dead dolphin washed up on the beach this afternoon. Before you came."

"And you were wondering if it had a soul?"

"Yes. I was. We were looking at it before they carted it away, and it looked so happy even though it was dead. Then the Boy Scouts came and it didn't look happy after that. It was just a dead thing in the back of their truck."

"Boy Scouts?"

"Yeah, I mean they weren't really Boy Scouts. They were two fish and game guys I guess."

"So where does the soul come in?"

"Well, I've got a theory about that. Maybe that dolphin wasn't quite dead when we saw it. Maybe that happiness I saw was the dolphin's soul. But when the Boy Scouts got to it, it really was dead. Its soul had left."

"That sounds terribly mystical," Tommie said.

She snuggled some closer to me.

"Yeah, I guess it does. But that's how it seemed."

"Very mystical."

We must have sat there in the sand for almost an hour, looking at the dying bonfire and talking softly and the smoke drifting up into the sky. I felt like I had known her my whole life. I don't remember the rest of what we talked about, but there was a lot of giggly, squirmy laughter and Tommie going "shshshsh" and putting her free hand over her mouth because her other one had my arm, but she was still giggling anyway.

Then Mick came down, but he didn't see us. He had a shovel or something and he started shoving the larger pieces of driftwood around, and then there was a burst of cinders and the bonfire grew suddenly brighter and warmer, and then Mick went down to the surf and you couldn't see him. The reggae was still going, only it didn't seem as loud as before, and nobody was dancing anymore, but you could see maybe five or six couples stretched out in the sand or sitting, at least you could see their shadows all mixed up with each other, sort of like me and Tommie with her holding on to my arm. Then Tommie and I were just staring at each other, like I was falling into her eyes and she was falling into mine, it was like being in *Vertigo* or something, being at the top of that church tower and nowhere to go but down and then that black and white pinwheel thing starting to spin, and right then Bob Marley was singing about the shelter of a single bed and all I wanted to do was kiss Tommie as hard as I damn well could, right on the mouth, and then not so hard, a softer kiss, which she seemed to want the same thing. But we didn't move. Neither of us. We just stared at each other like two dippy high-school idiots. And then a dozen pairs of running legs went by on their way to the water and the sand skidding up into our laps, and that pretty much broke the moment. We both turned as they went past and watched until you couldn't really see them, but you could still hear them, laughing and murmuring and joking around and then splashing in the waves. Then we heard Mick's voice booming out from somewhere in the darkness. "Buckle up boys and girls," Mick said. "This show's just getting started." And then: "If you're going to get wet you might as well get naked."

Then the laughter and the splashing seemed to move on down the beach. It was very dark. All you could see were the tiny green lights of the shrimp boats.

"Come on," Tommie said. "Walk me to my car."

"You're going?"

"I have to go. Come."

She grabbed both my hands and somehow we pulled each other up and headed towards the house. But we didn't bother going inside. Dozens of people were still going in and out through the sliding glass doors. Mick had strung these yellow and blue and purple lights around the back so it looked like you were on a cruise ship to Jamaica or somewhere. Everyone was still drinking their beers or their margaritas and slipping off into the shadows and then back into the yellow and blue and purple streams of light and these sexy coy smiles on their faces. But Tommie had to go, so what was I going to say, don't go, I've fallen madly in love with you and if you go I'm going to jump into the Atlantic and drown myself, which it may have been a pretty fair approximation of my feelings at the time, but it didn't seem too practical a thing to put into words. So we followed the macadam path around to the front of the house, past the bikers sitting among the ferns, past the stolen construction sign and the sawhorse and the Volkswagen Beetles parked at odd angles. We weren't walking all that fast either. I kept thinking I'm going to do it, I'm going to kiss her when we get to her car, an opportunity like this doesn't come along every day. But there really wasn't a chance. For one thing, there were way too many people around. Some were running back and forth between the bright, tinny, festival frenzy of Mick's beach house and the parking lot of their cars and motorcycles and the hazy, whitish glare of the street lamps and the swirl of insects pooling around the light. Others were sitting with legs hanging out of the windows of nearby houses, as if the party had somehow migrated to the whole neighborhood, and they were smoking cigarettes or joints. And everybody was jabbering away, laughing, calling out to us as we went by, a bewildering melee of late-night voices, drunken or sleepy or angry or surprised or merely curious, and everywhere there was the sexy, serene inescapable hum of Bob Marley and The Wailers.

"I had fun," Tommie said.

We were standing next to her car, somewhat awkwardly. Tommie was sort of half-leaning back against the front door and I was standing sideways, straddling the curb, but it was like I didn't have any control of my hands. My one hand was fumbling with my belt buckle and the other one was flopping around on the hood and then fiddling with the antennae and then back on the hood, but all the while I was hoping I looked roguish and tough and worldly and likable, all at the same time, like Humphrey Bogart in *To Have and Have Not*.

"I wish I had come sooner," Tommie said.

"Me too."

"Are you going to stay long?"

"No. I'm going to try and find Mick though. I haven't really seen him since I got here. I better at least say good night. I bet he's still swimming.

"And naked, too!" Tommie laughed.

Then Tommie leaned forward and gave me a quick, darty kiss on the cheek, and before I had even the slightest chance to react, she was sitting behind the steering wheel and the window rolled down.

"Good night, Travis Lauterbach," Tommie said.

"Good night, Tommie. See ya."

And that was that. Tommie drove away and I headed off in search of Mick. Of course I didn't find him right away. I spent the better part of the next hour searching for him, mostly down along the beach where I had last heard his voice. But he wasn't there. Nobody was. There was nothing but the grayish water and the waves coming in. Even the shrimp boats had left. But not finding Mick didn't really bother me. I mean not at all. I was so pumped up from Tommie kissing me like she did, even though it was the exact opposite of the way I had wanted to kiss her, that I felt like I was going to explode, like I was some kind of comet streaking across the sky. Tommie's kiss was all I could think about. I breathed in the salt water air and felt in myself a reckless, unrelenting joy. It was goddamn poetic.

So I walked until I couldn't hear Mick's party, and then I walked some more. I could see a few of those blue bug lights from the other beach houses, the light filtering out through the trees and an occasional zap when an insect got too close. I decided to cut through by one of the bug lights and head back by way of First Avenue. By the time I got back to Mick's house it seemed that most everybody had left. The string of yellow, blue and purple lights had been disconnected. Bob Marley was barely a whisper. The sawhorse roadblocks and the construction sign were gone. Only a few cars were left. The front yard was empty except for the ferns, but there were maybe a dozen people inside. I finally found Mick, fully dressed, sitting in the sand by the bonfire, cross-legged. He was staring at the charred pieces of driftwood and the orange flecks of fire deep within.

"Hey, Mick," I said.

"Hey there, Lauterbach," Mick said. He did not look up. He was twirling his moustache and contemplating the stillness of the beach and the almost dead bonfire.

"Man, I didn't see you hardly at all today," I said. "It was a hell of a party, wasn't it?"

"Yeah, Lauterbach. It was one hell of a party. One hell of a hairy shindig, that's what Abbie would've said."

Mick flipped his head back and gave me his chipped-tooth smile. Even in the dim, orangey glow of the fire you could see his teeth glinting.

"Say, Lauterbach, how would you like a beach house?"

"You mean look after it while you're gone?"

"No, man. I'm giving it to you. I'm heading down to Patagonia and I'm not coming back. I'm going to find me some Patagonian girls and fuck them till my balls fall off."

"What if I don't want it?"

"Then I don't know. I guess it'll just rot on the beach, and it'll be on your conscience, Lauterbach. Don't forget!"

"Okay, Mick. But when you get back it's all yours."

"Yeah. Sure. If that's the way you want it. But I'm really not coming back, Lauterbach. There's this little voice inside my head that says it's time to move on. So I'm moving."

"So maybe it'll tell you someday to come back?"

"Maybe, Lauterbach. Maybe I'm dancing this little dance all by myself. Maybe it's all just one goddamn eternal circle and no matter what I do I'm going to end up right back where I started. Is that it, Lauterbach?"

Mick started to laugh, but it was a strange kind of laughter. I couldn't tell if he was laughing because he thought something was funny or for some other reason.

"If that happens I'll be dancing my eternal circles in jail."

"Jail?"

"Sure, Lauterbach. Fucking j-a-i-l! Do you know how I paid for this farewell frolic at the beach?"

"No."

"I sold my car, and boxes and boxes of old books, and

the stereo equipment is going too. And then I maxed out my credit cards. I'm fucking twenty thousand dollars in debt, Lauterbach. I've got a one-way bus ticket to Miami and a suitcase full of cash like a goddamn bandito, and I'm twenty thousand in the fucking hole, and I don't give two goddamns about it because I'm leaving for good. The sky is opening up right in front of me. The Universe is saying it's time to go. So why would I come back?"

"But you didn't sell the house."

"It wasn't mine to sell. The guy who built it was a friend of mine, one of the few. He didn't believe in owning property, just like he didn't believe in banks or in any of that bullshit. He said we were all just renting space for a while and then we died or moved on and somebody else took over. He left fifteen years ago for Mexico, just one day he hopped on his motorcycle and took off. He was the real Pancho Villa, Lauterbach, a goddamn demagogue. He even had a carbine strapped to his back. Not like me and my costumey gringo lingo. He gave me the house. He told me to pay the taxes. That would be my way of paying rent. He told me to give it away before I left. If you want, Lauterbach, I'll toss in a couple of girls, too, with or without their bikinis."

I must have smiled because Mick laughed and clapped me on the back. It was a real laugh this time. You could tell. But Mick didn't know why I was smiling. I was still pretty psyched about Tommie, and now with Mick abandoning his beach house that very minute because the Universe was calling, well, all of a sudden it was like I was diving headlong into the surf and then popping back up with the shimmery brightness of the sun on my back, and I realized everyone was exactly where they were supposed to be. Everything that was happening, everything that was going to happen, it was all supposed to happen. It was a hell of a feeling. So why wouldn't I be smiling? Then we got up and raced towards the dunes and beyond that the soft yellow glow of the sliding-glass doors and the people inside. Mick beat me by a step, and then we stopped just outside and we were laughing and breathing heavy and each of us with a hand on the side of the house, and it sounded like Mick was actually wheezing. Then some girl came out and whispered something to Mick.

It looked like one of the teenage Mouseketeers. It looked like Laurie. She and Mick stepped into the shadows for a moment, and you could hear Mick saying something in a low whisper, but it wasn't clear what, and then Laurie was giggling, and then they stepped back into the glow of the light coming through the sliding-glass doors. "Say, Lauterbach," Mick said. "Can you do us a favor? Laurie has been abandoned by her ride. Jilted, in the vernacular. Can you take her home? She's looking for a knight in shining armor."

"Sure, Mick," I said.

"Thanks, Mr. Lauterbach. I could just kill that Sonya."

We went inside, Mick first, and he went directly behind the kitchen counter and grabbed a beer, and then me and Laurie followed him. It seemed pretty warm in the house with everybody just sitting around on the floor and on the bar stools and squished together on the maroon colored sofa beneath the mermaid and all of them looking at us with these pleasant, slightly puzzled expressions, as if their brains had melted and they couldn't quite comprehend who we were or where we had come from. I said a couple of goodbyes to people I didn't really know, and then a voice piped up from the sofa.

It was Joyce's sister.

"So that's your type, eh, Travis?"

Then she started laughing and spilling some of her frothy strawberry margarita on the people next to her. I didn't say anything. I was suddenly conscious of Laurie sort of hovering there right by my elbow. I didn't even look at her. Then Laurie and I were out the door.

I don't think I said a word to Laurie all the way to her house. She lived in a development about fifty minutes away. We drove along this lonely stretch along Butler Boulevard where there's nothing but trees and this sort of grassy, swampy nothingness and these thin, wiry highway lamps that glow with a strange soft pinkish glow, like radiation or something. It's a pretty lonely, eerie stretch of road, desolate. Like alien abduction desolate. But I didn't say a word to Laurie the whole time we were in the car. I could feel her squirmy, teenage Mouseketeer presence there on the seat next to me. She kicked off her sandals and curled her legs up on the seat

so her skirt was riding up along her thighs, high enough
so you could see her bikini bottoms. It seemed like she was
trying to get my attention. But I didn't really have anything
to say. What would I say, thanks but no thanks Laurie, I'm
madly in love with someone else, which was the absolute
truth, but there was no need to share my intimate bathtub
secrets with this girl.

I'm not sure what time it was when we pulled into
Laurie's driveway. Laurie lived on the river on the San Marco
side. You couldn't really see the house in the darkness, just
this heavy lush shadow and trees all over the place and heavy,
thick bushes, but you could feel the richness of the place.
It was sort of like being chloroformed. The only light was
coming from this seventeenth century Spanish-style cast iron
lantern fixed to one side of the front door, and it was glowing
a soft green light and it cast these shimmery greenish shadows
down a narrow brick walk, and then the walk widening and
a marble fountain with sculpted laurel leaves all around and
a Greek god or goddess or something in the middle, but the
water was off, and then the walk narrowing again. It looked
like something from *Twenty Thousand Leagues Under the Sea*. I
kept the motor running, but Laurie didn't get out of the car
right away.

"Do you want to come in, Mr. Lauterbach?" she said.

And then: "My parents won't be home for a week."

Then she kissed me.

I was sitting there sort of stunned by her question and I
wasn't even sure if I had heard her right, and then she kissed
me. Or maybe I kissed her. I don't really know how it happened. But the truth is I really wasn't kissing her at all. I mean
my body was. But my mind was kissing Tommie Rodriguez.
I know that sounds pretty lame, but it's the truth. I was so
pumped up from Tommie and the party at Mick's house and
then I was kissing Laurie but I was thinking it was Tommie
and my body just sort of took over. This was the kiss I had
wanted to give to Tommie. I was Humphrey Bogart in body,
mind, and soul, and I wasn't going to let Tommie escape so
easily a second time, even if it wasn't really Tommie, so I
wrapped my arms around Laurie and kissed her hard and
long until she gave this breezy, moaning sigh, and then it

was a softer kiss, our lips barely touching, feathery, moist, like clouds floating by, floating away, dissolving, and then her whole body shuddered and her moaning sigh from before became a cooing sort of sound, and then it was quiet. I don't know how long we sat there with the motor running. Then Laurie invited me in a second time, but I said no. I couldn't. I hadn't even meant to kiss her. But Laurie just sort of giggled and said, "It's all right Mr. Lauterbach. Don't worry about it."

And just like that Laurie slipped out of the car, her sandals dangling in her hand, and ran up the narrow brick walk with her blond ponytail bouncing and her whole lithe body moving effortlessly through the soft, hazy greenish underwater glow of the lantern, the way dolphins move through water, and then she disappeared inside. I watched her go, and after she was gone I stared at the soft green light of the lantern for a while. Then I left.

-6-

You always hear old guys talking about how time just keeps slipping away, faster and faster, and you don't really believe them because you think it's all just sour grapes now that they're old and can't get around like they used to. But it's true. Before I knew it, Thanksgiving was over and the kids were back in class with these dippy, bloated smiles from too much turkey and stuffing and cranberry sauce, and their brains were turned off by then because there were only two weeks left and then finals and then Christmas. It was all pretty much a blur. I tried calling Tommie a couple of times, but she was busy one night with grading Spanish papers, and the other night I guess she was out. We were supposed to have Thanksgiving at the beach house, just her and me, if you can believe that, and you just knew it was going to be one of those clear bright days when you feel that everything is possible, clear and bright like a photograph, and you knew there was going to be a warm breeze blowing up from the water and the sliding glass doors would be open so we could breathe in the salt spray, and maybe we would even eat our turkey outside on the makeshift patio so we could watch the waves coming in, but then Tommie's grandmother got sick and Tommie had to head up to Brooklyn because her grandmother was at that age when you wake up one morning with a cough and the next morning someone calls a priest. She headed up there the Wednesday before, and she was supposed to be back for classes on Monday, but she was gone almost three weeks. So it was me and Ed for Thanksgiving, but Ed didn't want to come out to the beach, and neither of us felt like cooking anyway, so we went out. The only place that was open was the Japanese restaurant downtown.

    I have to say Ed was pretty damn gloomy. He had been in a pretty gloomy state ever since he found out about the affair between his ex-wife and Father Adleman. It didn't matter that it was from years ago or that he wasn't married anymore and he didn't even like his ex-wife to begin with. It went deeper than that. It was like he had just found out that God didn't exist, that the whole thing with Christ and walking on water and heaven when you die was a sham cooked up by some guys drinking whiskey in the back room of some seedy bar called Gus's down in Miami and laughing their heads off at the rest of us. You had to feel sorry for old Ed. When Catholics slide off the map they've got nowhere to go. So there we were sitting on pillows and our legs cramping because even after a year and a half of eating sushi we still weren't used to sitting cross-legged on the floor, or trying to. The silk pillows they gave us were no help. And poor old gloomy Ed was drinking Takara Sake by the gallon and leaning across the table and leering at me and pushing a shot glass of Sake across and watching me drink and then laughing and sitting back. This went on for a while, an endless loop. But at one point Ed seemed to sober up for a few minutes, like he was suddenly back in the Marines, and he said, "I'll tell you what, Travis, everybody gets fucked sooner or later, especially if you don't play along, then you get fucked before you know what hit you, and if you do play along, well, you get fucked then too, it just takes a little longer, but there's no way around it, so what the hell."

I was staring at Ed's face while he was talking, and the blue and orange light from a couple of lanterns was washing over him, and maybe it was the Sake, I don't really remember how many I'd had by then, not as much as Ed, but it must have been more than enough because all of a sudden old Ed reminded me of one of those slaggy, diseased goldfish in the pond out front blowing bubbles. His mouth was moving, but it was like he was under water or something because you could hardly understand him. Wave after wave of orange and blue light washing across his face and him waving his arms and his mouth moving but you could only make out a word or two, like he was drowning, and the more I focused on I trying to hear what he was saying, the worse it got, until I couldn't hear a thing except this sort of gargling sound way off in the distance. Then Ed seemed to forget I was even there and he was back at the Sake. I don't know how many bottles we put away. It was one hell of a Thanksgiving dinner. The woman from behind the register kept bringing us Sake, and every once in a while she brought out a tray of sushi and we gobbled it up while she was standing right there, smiling in her silky blue kimono and bowing slightly and then shuffling off the way those geisha girls do in the old Japanese movies, back and forth with trays even when we didn't ask and jabbering her broken English and smiling some more. After a while she became sort of a blue blur, like a ghost or something that you can only see out of the corner of your eye. I guess we were the only customers in the place. I guess Thanksgiving wasn't one of their big nights. Then the trays stopped and you could hear she was back at the register ringing something up and then the sound of the drawer banging shut, but you couldn't see her because of the fake bamboo hut.

Sometimes I think Ed knew all along what was going to happen, but he didn't know how to tell me. That's why he started in on the Sake like he did. Nothing much matters after a couple of bottles of Sake. You feel like a god damn samurai warrior after a couple of bottles, like you are mother fucking invincible, and even when you sober up the next day the glow of that feeling lingers a while, sometimes for days, even longer, depending upon the weather. For me, I was feeling invincible up until eleven a.m. on Friday, December 17th. It was the last day of the term. I had just given my last final and was walking across the courtyard. I was almost skipping across, like I was one of my dippy-faced kids heading down to Disney World. Glassy-eyed aimless kids drinking up the soma of the modern world. But I guess I was just like them. I had no clue what I really wanted or how to get it. I wanted to believe that my very own happiness was out there somewhere, if only I just looked in the right place. I wanted to believe in the unadulterated joy of dolphins and the search for paradise and two souls spinning across the universe. I guess I was glassy-eyed in my belief. I had talked to Tommie the night before on the phone and she said she was coming back on Saturday, her grandmother was much better. She said she had a lot of Christmas shopping to do and decorating the apartment and baking cookies and she wanted a tree and a whole bunch of Christmas-type stuff, and everything she wanted to do included me.

    I have to say now that whole day and the next two weeks afterwards keep spinning through my mind like a slow-motion movie, especially that first day. I try to slow things down, freeze the frames, reverse everything, but it just goes on and on, and when it gets to the end it loops back to the beginning, all the way back to the very first day I started teaching, and then I have to live through everything all over again.

    So there I was practically skipping across the courtyard, and the gloomy smallness of my bank account and the eternal oppressive heat of the Florida sun was washed away because I would see Tommie the next day. I remember thinking I could live in that moment forever, with hope stretching out beyond the horizon. There was no other place I would rather be. I crossed the one courtyard and then zigzagged between classrooms and across another courtyard. I breathed in the scent of pine trees. The school was a series of oblong red brick one-story buildings, some going north to south, some east to west, all of them connected by a maze of roofed walkways. There were courtyards all over the damn place with scraggly aspen trees propped up by stakes and cedar benches with plaques that said *Alumni Gift Class of Whatever* where you could sit, but the outer edge of the school was surrounded by towering pine trees. Pine needles covered the ground. I once told Mick the school looked like a rat's maze, which made him laugh. First hour would end and the bell would ring and the dippy-faced kids would scurry out of their classrooms and down the walkways, and for five minutes it was like rats trying to escape the water in a sinking ship, and then the bell would ring a second time and you could see through the windows of each classroom, the kids once again trapped behind their desks, their bewildered dippy rat faces looking out at the pine trees and the patches of sky and the pine needles and the courtyards and the benches and wishing they were somewhere else. But today was different. I didn't notice anybody. I breathed in the scent of the pine trees and I felt the world opening up before me, and then it felt like I was standing outside of time. I felt a sense of freedom and pure joy I had felt only once before, that day at the Jacksonville Landing when I had watched those dolphins swimming up the St. John's River. I was going to see Tommie the very next day. Nothing else mattered.

The next thing I knew I was standing in the middle of the teacher's lounge. The place was already deserted. You could tell everybody had been anxious to get out of there. The mailboxes were mostly empty and the wastebasket was crammed full of extra exams and pens that didn't work, and there were half-drunk mugs of coffee all over the work table, and someone had left a perfectly good lunch in the microwave. The only other somebody in the lounge was Harvey Collins, but he was asleep in the fuzzy pink lounge chair. The air conditioner was on the fritz again and it was so damn hot that Harvey's white scalp was streaked with perspiration, and the few strands of white hair he had combed across his head were pasted to his skin. It was probably his lunch in the microwave, but he didn't seem to care. He was in short sleeves and his arms were covered in pink fuzzy beads and he was just snoring away, blissfully unconcerned with the real world, a ludicrous smile plastered across his face, like he was dreaming about grocery store lines and Laundromats and big beautiful curvy behinds. When I think back on everything, I'm not really sure why I went to the teacher's lounge anyway. When I think back on everything, I try to stop myself from going in. I guess a part of me thinks that if I hadn't gone in, if I hadn't noticed a small white envelope in my mailbox, then things would have turned out differently. I know it's a foolish thought, but I was a glassy-eyed aimless, dippy-faced kid same as the students I taught, like I already said. I didn't know what I didn't know. So there I was, standing in front of an avalanche of empty mailboxes with a small white envelope in my hand and my name scrawled across the middle in black ink, and then in parenthesis it said "urgent."

My first thought was it was from Tommie. My second thought was if it was from Tommie, how did it get there? My third thought was why was it marked urgent, and did I really want to find out? I don't remember what I was thinking after that. The letter wasn't from Tommie. It wasn't even a letter. It was a memo from the desk of The Very Reverend Richard Dubois, and it said I was to report to his office immediately, it was a very urgent matter, underlined twice for emphasis.

I read the memo three times just to be sure, and then I looked at the clock on the wall, one of those old fashioned General Electric clocks with the heavy black trim, and I knew it was eleven a.m., or close to it, but I couldn't make out the numbers. I thought maybe I was going suddenly blind, like I had been stricken with some strange, alien disease. It sort of felt like the fabric of reality was melting, like maybe I had slipped into an alternative reality universe like in *Blade Runner* and I was a replicant and Harrison Ford was gunning for me. A wave of nausea swept over me, through me. It seemed like my eyeballs were beginning to bleed. My teeth started to ache. I could hear Harvey Collins from the fuzzy pink lounge chair and he was laughing in his sleep, but it was a slightly hysterical, robotic kind of laughter, and then he wasn't sleeping any more, he was calling out to me, he was asking me if I was going to the faculty Christmas party on Saturday and was I still dating that little Spanish spitfire, Tommie Rodriguez, but his voice was distorted, thin, it had a tinny sound to it, it sounded staticky and very far away, like his voice was coming out of an old RCA Victor FM radio from the 1940s, like when my dad was a kid.

Then Harvey fell back asleep, or maybe he got up and went over to the microwave. I don't know. I was just standing there in front of the empty mailboxes, unable to move, staring at the memo. Probably it was only a few minutes, but it seemed a hell of a lot longer. After that a couple of happy, goofball teachers came in. They sounded as happy as clams, if you can imagine clams telling private jokes and then twittering away like no one else was around, but I didn't recognize them, which was pretty damn odd, if you want to know the truth, because there were only about a hundred teachers in the whole damn school, which I guess was just one more example that I had lost my grip. A couple more goofballs came in, as happy as clams like the other two, and I didn't recognize them either, and about then it felt like the whole goddamn world was closing in. I could hardly breathe. My eyesight had gotten worse. It was like looking through gauze. I could feel a tightening in my chest, and then a relaxing, and then a tightening again. My shirt was pretty much soaked through from perspiring. I was sweating bullets. I could tell the four happy-as-clam-types were looking at me with the memo in my hand like they were trying to read it over my shoulder. They were swirling around me, acting like they wanted to get to their own mailboxes, which even in the delirium of my going blind I could see were empty, I was close enough to see that, but they kept on swirling, and all the while they were laughing about their students and how many had failed their exams, and pretty much sounding like every other happy-as-a-clam teacher talking politely about the dippy kids they had to teach. Then there was a snapping sensation, like the frame of the universe had been tilted and some janitor had come along and grabbed hold of the frame and snapped it back into place, and just like that I could see again, only I was looking down at myself this time, like I had become detached from my body. I was sort of floating just above the mailboxes and the four teachers still swirling and still jabbering, and I was looking down at myself looking at the memo and blinking and the sweat still rolling down my back. I wondered if I was dead. I wondered if I had had a heart attack from one of those congenital conditions nobody knows about until it's too late, which you have to admit is an understandable reaction when you are floating above yourself, but if it had been a heart attack, my other self would have collapsed to the floor and the four goofball teachers would have switched to good Samaritan mode, and one of them would have started CPR, and another would have called for an ambulance, and the other two would have stood there, hunched over, looking at an almost dead body with eager, horrified expressions on their faces because most likely this would have been their first experience with death. But this did not happen because it wasn't a heart attack. I had not died. I think it was just the shock of the moment replayed a thousand times in my mind, which after a while you sort of detach yourself from what really happened and you start watching the events of your own life like you're watching a movie. That's why I see it now like I do. Sometimes I can even hear my own voice narrating the sequence of events.

    Harvey Collins had retrieved his lunch and was sitting at the worktable spooning in macaroni stew, and he was talking to the other four and they were answering him back, but I still couldn't make out what they were saying. Probably some more about the Christmas party. I watched my other self head for the door, but then the door whooshed open and Amy Baxter whooshed in with a basket of last minute holiday announcements, and Amy almost knocked my other self over on account of she's one of those impulsive types that never look where they're going, which I have to say makes her the perfect secretary for the Reverend Dubois, but she caught herself at the last moment and just sort of bounced to one side. She started to say excuse me and was looking up with these two fiery green eyes that always look like they are about to explode and her red hair tossed about in a tangled mess, but when she saw it was me, which is to say when she saw my other self with the wrinkled memo in his hands and the blood dripping from his eyes, she swallowed her words and her eyes went dark with disapproval and she whirled away and began stuffing white envelopes with little green Christmas wreaths on the front into the mailboxes, one after another, like she was punching tickets. My other self didn't say a word. My other self headed out the door. But I stayed behind for a few moments, floating above the mailboxes, watching Amy Baxter and the other four and the pink-faced Harvey Collins with his arms still covered in pink fuzzy beads shoveling in macaroni stew. The next thing I knew everyone was reading their last minute holiday announcements, apparently Amy Baxter thought they should read them right away, only they weren't about the holidays, they were about me, both myself and my other self, and then the four teachers were shaking their heads and saying it was hard to believe, a nice fellow like him, how does something like that happen, you think you know people, but you never know people, not really, and then Amy Baxter piping up how she knew all along, there was something peculiar about that one, you could see it in his eyes, and the other four nodding in reluctant agreement, and Harvey Collins not saying much of anything, just sitting there blinking at Amy and the four happy-as-clam-types, and then back to his stew.

    I didn't wait around after that. I floated up through the ceiling and headed outside. It was a cool, sunny bright day, but not too cool, which surprised me, I have to admit. You always imagine bad news arriving on rainy days, but that's not the case. Bad news almost always comes on the sunniest, brightest day there is, which I guess means the universe doesn't really bother about what happens to anyone. The universe could care less. I mean why should the universe care one way or the other, no matter what happens, life goes on. Of course I wasn't thinking all this back then. I wasn't thinking much of anything. I looked around to get my bearings. I was pretty high up by then and could see the whole campus. The red brick buildings were clumped together on one end, and beyond that there was a paved parking lot full of Datsuns and small, tinny Toyotas and old Chevys and dented Buicks for the teachers, and then a sandy parking lot beneath the pine trees for the students and Mercedes convertibles and BMWs pulling out, kicking up little puffs of dust and tires screeching when they hit the pavement, and on the other end of the campus there was a grassy stretch and the television evangelist style auditorium and the live oaks and the ground sloping away and then the heavy dark blue of the St. John's River. It almost looked like a painting, like the kind they sell in grocery store parking lots at the beach for the tourists. I could see a few students still hanging out in the courtyards below, and a few teachers trudging about with boxes of exams to grade, all of them heading for the teacher's lounge before they left for the day. My other self was heading for the office of The Very Reverend Richard Dubois, but I had no interest in joining him. I preferred the open air and the sunshine. From my vantage point above the trees the horizon seemed to stretch to infinity. I lost myself in the infinity of the moment. I lost myself in the silence of floating above the world. But it didn't last. After a while, I don't know how long, I heard the Reverend's voice, a faint, slightly nasal, squirrelly voice pricking at my ears. "I'm afraid you don't realize how serious this is Mr. Lauterbach, it is quite serious, and while it is not criminal, and believe me, Mr. Lauterbach, our investigation of the matter was quite exhaustive, if there had been even the barest hint of criminality, we would be having this conversation down at the police station, a statement, I think, which Ms. Daly and Ms. Pearsons sitting here beside me can both heartily endorse, but all that aside, Mr. Lauterbach, your actions are an irreparable breach of your moral responsibilities as a teacher at this educational institution, you were supposed to hold the interests of the students above your own at all times, which is to say that you were to understand what is in the best interest of the students at all times, there can be no exceptions, no excuses, did you not imagine, Mr. Lauterbach, what would happen, did you think the girl in question would remain unprovoked by her emotions, if you did you were naïve, she recorded every thought, every hope and dream in a diary, a diary, Mr. Lauterbach, which her mother found and read and brought to our attention in a state of panic not seen since the Chicago riots of the sixties when the police were armed with tear gas and assault rifles, yes, Mr. Lauterbach, that was the effect you had upon this young girl and upon her mother, unwittingly or no, you have brought this upon yourself, and it does not matter that most of what she wrote is a fabrication, it does not matter if the only crime was a single kiss, no indeed, the fact of the kiss is not the issue, and we have gone around this point for some time now, Ms. Daly and Ms. Pearsons and myself, no, the crime was that you put the girl in question into a situation where such a crime could occur, you assaulted her imagination with your presence, and you did this when her parents were away on an extended vacation, your abandonment of strict moral principles is quite extraordinary, Mr. Lauterbach, by which we mean to say it is totally unacceptable, we cannot tolerate this kind of behavior in our school, not under any circumstances, and so we have no choice, Mr. Lauterbach, but to terminate your employment, said termination to be effective immediately, the faculty and staff have already been notified, yes, Mr. Lauterbach, yes, the white envelopes with the Christmas wreaths on the front, yes, I suppose it is ironic at that, no, no, the announcement to the faculty merely states that you were terminated for unprofessional conduct, it does not define the nature of that conduct, no, Mr. Lauterbach, there are no mitigating circumstances, no, Mr. Lauterbach, what the faculty chooses to believe about what happened is entirely up to them, no, no, please, Mr. Lauterbach, no hysterics, the time for hysterics has passed, please take this box and gather up your things, you have one hour to vacate your classroom, after which time if you are still here we will call the police, what was that Mr. Lauterbach, why yes, of course, we are not without compassion, we are, after all, a Christian school founded on Christian principles, but remember, Mr. Lauterbach, you are to have no contact with this girl under any circumstances from this day forward, she is still a minor, or if she isn't, well, she is still a student at this school, so if you do try to contact her, well, that would be unfortunate, we would have to consider such behavior harassment and you would be charged under the law, and to the fullest extent of the law, do you understand what I am saying, Mr. Lauterbach, do I make myself clear, Mr. Lauterbach, yes, yes, good, very good."

Then the nasally, squirrelly voice of the good Reverend faded completely. It was almost as if it had been a figment of my imagination. But the silence of floating above the world did not return. At least that's how I remember it. I continued to float above the school for a while, but the silence from before was gone. I heard some kids shouting in the student parking lot and then some laughter and then the sound of someone leaning on a horn and then a couple more horns blaring away and then more laughter and then they drove off. I heard the heavy thud of a door slammed shut and then I saw my other self emerge from the shadows of the administration building, frowning a pinched-face frown, clutching an empty box. I saw my other self cut across the grass by the flagpole and then disappear into the maze of roofed walkways. From somewhere there was the sound of a bell. I could see a dozen or so colleagues at various points around the campus, some of them heading to the faculty parking lot, some of them cutting across courtyards or heading back to their classrooms. Some of them were murmuring to themselves, a low steady rumble that drifted up into the air. But all of them were reading the holiday announcement of my sudden termination, some of them reading as they walked, some of them walking and reading and then sitting down on one of the many alumni gift benches to catch their breath. You could tell some of them didn't know what to think. You could also tell that some of them had their own ideas from the very beginning, from before even the very first sentence.

 I closed my eyes and tried to forget what was happening. I knew I wasn't dead. I knew if I waited long enough, everything would settle. I had seen enough documentaries on the Sci-Fi channel to know how out-of-body experiences worked. But it sure as hell made you think. Maybe when you died you were floating above yourself same as I was, and you could go anywhere you wanted to, take a look at any moment from your life, but after a while you would forget what you were looking at, and that's when you really died. Maybe that's how it had been with that dolphin. Maybe when I was looking at that dolphin on the beach, maybe it was floating in the air just above me, maybe its soul was still close enough that I could see its reflection in the body it was leaving behind, like one was a mirror to the other, and since the dolphin's other self, its soul, was brimming with happiness, that's what I saw.

 I guess you can't say for sure about anything. My own experience didn't come close to what I thought might have happened to that dolphin. For one thing, I wasn't dead. I sure as hell knew that. I was floating above everything with my eyes closed, but at the same time I was rooted to the earth. I breathed in deeply. I heard the distant wavering cry of a blue jay. I heard the dull incessant whoosh of traffic moving along Atlantic Boulevard. Then I heard the sound of a car starting up. It was my own dirty white Toyota Corolla. I opened my eyes and watched my other self drive away, a flash of white through the dark green foliage of the pine trees. But I wasn't ready to descend just yet. I wanted to linger a while longer in the pure clean sunshine that existed beyond the naked ache of my dismissal. I wanted to float away on the breeze of my future. I wanted to know, at least for a moment, that the horizon, my horizon, stretched beyond the shadows of my imagination to the bright edge of infinity. I know that sounds pretty god damn lame, a bit too poetic. I don't usually go in for poetry. But that's pretty close to what it felt like. It's as close as I can get to it.

-7-

I no longer lived in the pinkish, orangeish cement apartment building five blocks from St. Vincent's hospital. I no longer lived in Jacksonville proper. After Mick left I took over his bungalow at the beach, and I stayed there through the end of December. I think it was the warmest December on record, that's what the paper said.

Mostly I didn't do a hell of a lot. Either I moped around the house drinking beer and eating cereal, or I walked up and down the beach thinking about Tommie and the dolphin and dolphins in general and that night by the bonfire. Sometimes I would get bored and head out to the beach with a couple of buckets of crushed seashells and toss handfuls to the seagulls and watch them scramble, thinking it was food. Sometimes I would watch the tourists from New York or Michigan take a dip in the ocean because they were the only ones who didn't think the water was cold and their kids screaming bloody murder all the way down to the edge and then laughing when they got wet and then they didn't want to leave.

That very first Saturday night, when the rest of the faculty was whooping it up at the faculty Christmas party at the Reverend Dubois' house, I was sitting in a white plastic chair wedged into the sand watching a handful of shrimp boats heading south along the horizon, dark shadows against the fading blue sky, and then it was just their green running lights winking in the darkness. I had brought down a cooler stuffed with beer. I was thinking some about Tommie and wondering if I would ever see her again. I didn't even get a chance to tell her what had happened. I hadn't really even talked to her since Mick's party. And now there was no chance. I was sure of that. I was pretty sure Emily Lavigne and Walter had filled her head with all sorts of crap, they were just the type. I could see old Walter hunched over the steering wheel of that goddamn black and blue Chevy Citation when they picked Tommie up from the airport and Walter smirking as he told her all about my depraved nature and everything I had done. I bet he told her I had raped the girl but the girl wouldn't talk and not even her mother or her aunt, who flew up from Miami, could get her to open up, and so they couldn't prove a thing, which was the only reason I wasn't in jail. I'm pretty sure Walter said something like that. I was pretty pissed about that. I was pretty pissed about Emily and Walter in general, but I didn't know what to do. So I sat in my white plastic chair and looked out at the swirling darkness where the sky meets the sea and I let my mind wander. I still felt kind of disoriented. I certainly wasn't happy about the way things had turned out, but then again, I was exactly unhappy either. The shrimp boats had moved down the coast a mile or so. It was hard to tell exactly how far. You had to really strain to see their green lights, and even then, it could have been your imagination. I gave up after a while and drank another beer.

 I drank beer until I couldn't see a thing.

 The next Monday Ed came out to the house. I guess he came out to see how I was doing, but he didn't want to come inside. I don't know why. Maybe he felt guilty about not telling me the trouble I was in when we were at the Japanese restaurant. Or maybe he thought I had a couple of mermaids stashed inside like Mick and the less he knew the better for him. Ed was funny like that sometimes. So I brought out my last four beers, even if it was only ten in the morning, and we stood outside in the middle of the street. We were close enough to the beach that parts of the street were covered with sand. The air was still cool, but the sky was a bright, warm, robin's egg blue, so you knew it was going to be a real scorcher.

For a while we didn't say anything. We just drank our beers and looked up at the sky or out at the beach, shading our eyes because of the brightness of the sun.

Then Ed started to open up.

"They're a bunch of fuckers," Ed said.

I grunted some into my beer.

"All of them," Ed said. "Every last goddamn one."

I still didn't know just what to say, and with Ed, well, you have to be careful. I began to think Ed had started his drinking for the day a few hours earlier.

"You know it's all anybody who works at that goddamn school can talk about," Ed said. "Hell, it's probably all over the goddamn town already."

"What's all over?" I said.

Ed glared down at his beer.

"Ah, just fuck it," he said. "Fuck everything."

"Yeah," I said. "That pretty much sums it up."

He drank some more of his beer.

"I hope to God you fucked the hell out of her," Ed said. "All of those girls, that's all they want anyway, the way they wiggle their tight little teenage asses so you can't help but stare at them and pushing their titties right into your face and looking up at you and their eyes getting bigger and you can almost taste it. They know exactly what they're doing."

Ed took another swig.

"Goddamn teases," he said. "What do they expect you to do?"

"Yeah, well, nothing happened, if that's what you're asking."

"What do you mean nothing happened?"

"I mean nothing happened. I mean I drove the girl home and then she leaned over and kissed me and said her parents were away and I said no thanks and that was that. She went inside and I went home. Nothing happened."

"But that doesn't make any sense."

"Nothing makes any sense."

Ed looked like he wanted to hit something, but he didn't.

"Fuck it," he said. "I guess you're right."

There wasn't much left to say between me and Ed after that. I was leaning up against my Toyota Corolla, which was parked sort of crooked, half on the sidewalk about two steps from the front of the house and the gate and the cobblestone walk and the potted ferns. The potted ferns were a dry brown color and you could tell they were pretty much dead. The next thing I knew I was looking at Ed's shadow. I wasn't looking directly at him. I was sort of looking at his shadow there in one of the sandy stretches on the street, but I wasn't feeling gloomy or anything like that. There was a slight breeze blowing across the street and Ed's shadow was sort of shimmering and I was looking at his shadow and thinking maybe our souls were like shadows and you could only see them in bright sunlight, but even then they were sort of shimmery, like Ed's shadow was, and the moment you realized you were looking at someone's soul it would disappear. I guess it was probably the beers doing all that thinking. I don't usually go in for beer at ten in the morning. Then Ed shifted himself away from the sun and his shadow was gone and he was leaning up against the Toyota, same as me. It was starting to get hot. We didn't speak for a long time. We looked out at the beach. There were a few Northerners running down to the water and a couple of beachcomber types wearing khaki bucket hats and sweeping the beach with metal detectors, sifting through the sand for loose change, and a few seagulls flying up into the air and flapping a while and then settling back down. We finished our beers, but we didn't move. We were hanging on to our empty bottles, the sun flashing against the bottle glass, but we didn't wince. We kept looking out at the beach and the salt water and the waves flashing silver and then curling and the sand pipers running up and then back out.

That was the last time I saw old Ed. He said maybe we should get together for New Year's, and then he said we would definitely get together, he would be out on the 31st with a couple of cases of beer, and we would drink until the moon fell into the fucking sea. Ed was a lunatic like that sometimes, but I couldn't tell if he really meant it or not. People are funny about things like that. They say they want to get together just to be polite but inside they're squirming like eels because all they want is to be let off the hook. I don't know if Ed was on the hook or not, but I let him off anyway. A couple of days before New Year's Eve I packed up my dirty white Toyota and headed south for Miami. Mick was in Miami. Or at least he had been. About one week after the party, I got a postcard from Mick. It had a Miami postmark. It was one of those vintage postcards from the 1930s with a picture of some kind of 18th century Spanish estate somewhere in Miami, somewhere overlooking a causeway with a couple of three-story stone buildings with red tile roofs and old-style iron lanterns fixed to the outside walls, and the water was a greenish, aquamarine blue and the sun setting in the background, and there was a flagstone walkway and a couple of steps up and then a small stone bridge arching over the water, the kind of bridge with an iron railing. There were about a dozen palm trees all over the place. At the top, printed in a very fancy type, were the words: *Venetian Casino, Coral Gables, Florida*. I guess it was supposed to be the Florida version of Venice. On the back Mick wrote: "I'll be here a few weeks. Can't say after that." He didn't say exactly where 'here' was. Maybe he had just been passing through Miami and was shacked up somewhere in the Keys drinking New Orleans-style Hurricanes night after night, drinking himself blind. Or maybe he really was going to Patagonia and he had already boarded a steamer and he was halfway there. It didn't matter. I was going to head south and find Mick no matter where he was and start my life completely fucking over, and at the same time I was going to let Ed off the hook whether that's what he wanted or not. That's pretty much what I was thinking. So I packed up my car, which didn't take all that long because I didn't have that much stuff anyway, a worn-out green army issue duffel bag that my dad gave me, filled to the brim with shirts and underwear and shorts and a few rolled up pairs of jeans; a shaving kit, a couple of pairs of khakis and three white shirts and two good jackets, preppy jackets, the kind I had to wear in the classroom, three boxes of books, everything from Kafka to Rod Serling to Hemingway, and a bunch of cassettes and a boom box. Then I scribbled a note to Ed and told him about the house and how I was giving it to him and he could do what he wanted just so long as he paid the taxes but if he didn't want it he could let it rot but then it would be his fault. I taped the keys and the note to the front door and started up the car, but then I just sat there for a while, looking at the reflection of the beach and the sky in the rear view mirror. It was a cloudy morning but you could see the sun sort of shimmering behind the clouds. I don't know how long I sat there. It was like my brain was trapped inside the clouds and I was waiting for the sun to burn them away. I thought about Ed and I wasn't sure if Ed wanted anything to do with an ex-hippie beach house. Then again, I wasn't even sure if Ed would get the note. It almost seemed like a joke, like stuffing a message into a bottle and chucking the bottle into the sea. But I didn't care. There was this little voice inside my head and it was telling me it was time to move. I think it was probably Mick's voice inside my head, but I guess that didn't matter too much. I was already moving in a direction that went beyond Mick. With my sudden termination I was now moving beyond anything and everything I could possibly have imagined. I was once again floating high above the world, higher even than the clouds, hardly able to breathe in the cold, thin atmosphere, dazzled by the sun. That's how it felt. That's how I saw myself. I was moving towards a limitless horizon. I was moving towards the bright edge of infinity. Then I leaned closer to the rear view mirror and saw my own reflection. I hadn't shaved in two weeks and the stubbly hair that grows on my face was pretty thick. My face looked almost black, except for these two brightly glowing eyes staring back at me from two sunken eye sockets. It was like the eyes of someone with radiation sickness. I was almost smiling, but it was a strange, twisted smile. I almost didn't recognize myself. I smiled back. Still smiling, I shifted the car into drive and hit the gas. I don't remember a thing after that.

BOOK TWO

the heart and soul of Calle Ocho

-8-

We are standing on a small stone bridge looking at tinted water. Across the water there are palm trees and an immaculate stone building with a red-tiled roof. We are waiting to see what we will do. It is almost like waiting for a funeral. I am beginning to think we are already dead.

We have never been here before. Correction. I have never been here before. The two teachers were here before. That's what they said. The one showed me a postcard. Venetian Casino, Coral Gables, it said. That's why I went with them. I wanted to see this Venetian Casino in south Florida. A taste of Europe with the barest hint of happy, unrepentant sex, like a spice, raw decadence, uncrushed, waiting to be crushed, the rush of breathing it in, the blood boiling, one brief hour of madness and joy. It has been a long time since I have been in Europe.

But the postcard was an illusion. It was a charlatan's ruse. There is no casino. It is a swimming pool instead. The Venetian canal so elegantly captured on the postcard is in reality a swimming pool. The stone building across from the stone bridge contains changing rooms and showers, a counter where you can buy hot dogs and sodas, a gift shop where you can buy suntan lotion and swimsuits, and a window where you pay to get in. If only I could have stepped into the painting on the postcard. There's a second stone building in the foreground, a Spanish style building like the first one, just before the bridge, with an old-time iron lantern fixed to the wall. The lantern is glowing in the postcard. It is sunset. The sky is streaked with a salmon pink color and the clouds float across, white wispy clouds, like white lace, virgin lace, the white lace dissipating, evaporating, leaving the naked, virgin, salmon pink sky to fend for itself. It is a delicious sky. It is the perfect sky for having sex. I am certain with the sky like it is that the stone building in the foreground is a bordello. I can smell a bordello a mile off, at least a mile. The whiff is unmistakable. That and the color of the sky. But I am getting ahead of myself here. To make sense of what happens next, I need to go back to before I even knew the Venetian Casino existed. Before I first crossed paths with the two teachers.

We live in Little Havana where Calle Ocho vanishes into the glare of the midday sun, a good thirty-minute walk to Domino Park, at least for me. By "we" I am referring to myself, Xavier Mendoza, and Soledad, who has been with me since before I care to remember. We live on a bright, clean street in a bright, clean neighborhood. The buildings are painted bright pink and bright yellow and there are bars on the windows. It is always midday where we live, even in the middle of the night. We own a small café called The Patagonian Café and we live on the second floor. I do not remember if we chose the name, if my beautiful and resilient Soledad chose the name, or if it has always been The Patagonian Café.

We employ eight beautiful *chicas jóvenes* to serve plates of roast chicken and rice and red pimentos and sweet potato pudding for desert, or cornbread and chunks of fried pork and ripe plantains, which I don't care for myself, or black bean soup, or spicy beef hash and fried potatoes. There is always plenty to eat. No one complains. And always we are serving drinks, mojitos and caipirinhas and Cuba Libres and mango martinis, and also beer and wine, plenty of wine. We make most of our money on the drinks. After the drinks the girls are on their own.

One Friday night last year the police poured into our café and lined up all the men on one side and all the girls on the other side. We wondered if they were looking for someone in particular, or if anyone would do. It is not always easy to tell who is a criminal and who is not, especially with the men. Some of them were wearing white shirts and thin yellow ties and brown suits off the rack and suede saddle shoes, like they were accountants from downtown. Some of the others were a bit greasier in appearance with ratty leather jackets and shirts with sequins and dirty jeans and moccasins or maybe black boots, and always lice crawling through greasy hair, their hair is dripping with grease, like bacon grease, and always they have a knife or two or three up their sleeves. But for some reason these *greasy gamberros* never seem to carry guns. It is the well-dressed accountants who carry the guns. But the police were not overly concerned with the men. Their primary focus was the girls. They made the girls spread their legs wide like so, so they could make sure nothing was hidden, and the girls were giggling with their breezy chiffon skirts riding high and their meaty brown assess pushed out away from the wall and wiggling with the promise of something juicy, and some of them wearing only thongs underneath, and some of them wearing nothing at all. Later they said it would have been fun, except it was the police. The police said there was a lot of crime in the neighborhood, a lot of whores looking to score, a lot of johns with loose change ready to plug a nickel or a dime or a quarter into any open slot, any moist, wet, titillating crevice. They searched everyone's pockets and purses, but they didn't keep track of what came out of whose pocket or which purse. They dumped everything on a table in the middle of the cafe. Knives, pocket books, wallets, rosaries, keys, money clips overflowing with crisp new greenbacks, old photographs with yellow around the edges, doodads, loose change, dice, cigarettes, bottles of aspirin, condoms, rings, bracelets, an ivory handled revolver, a couple of pipes, a couple of dime bags. But they didn't find what they were looking for. After they left, the men and the girls rushed the table. A few girls got scratched, clawed was more like it, an earring pulled from a lobe, the flesh dangling, a budding black eye. A few men got punched in the stomach, clocked in the back of the head with the ivory handled revolver, a few missing teeth, a few broken noses and the blood gushing out. Pools of blood on the floor. But nobody got shot. Nobody was hauled off to jail.

    The next day we swept the sidewalk out front as if nothing had happened. It is a clean street we live on. We sweep the sidewalk once in the morning, once every afternoon, and again in the evenings. It is good for business to keep the sidewalks swept. And business is good. We are filled to the gills with Cubans from around the corner and Nicaraguans from over by the cemetery and Dominicans and Hondurans who come down from Allapattah and a few Rastafarians mixed in. People come and go and we can hardly keep track. The night is over before we know it. We have forgotten to eat and drink ourselves. We end up eating raw oysters at six am and washing everything down with warm beer and then we go to bed and we sleep in the raw. We slip inside of each other and dream of raw oysters. We become raw oysters, wet, moist, slippery. This is not just how I remember it. This is how it is. We live in an eerie and seductive neighborhood, a festival atmosphere, Spanish trilling in the air, guitars strumming, the music flying about, troubadours with flutes and bangles and maracas, mystics, ghosts parading their pain, gigolos, prostitutes, drag queens, divas, drug dealers with neon running hot through their veins, hypnotists, palm readers, ex-priests, ex-nuns, Zen Buddhists, clairvoyants, clowns, all of history exists in this tiny enclave, this irrepressible paradise, this dot on the map, this broken landscape where men and women gather naked and unashamed and howl at the moon, all of eternity gasping its last gasp on this sun-burnt grid of asphalt and strip malls and abandoned churches and doughnut shops and chain-link fences and palm trees and children splashing in the urine-streaked fountains in the park, a seemingly endless progression of brightly painted streets and brightly painted streetwalkers between the airport in the west and the bright blue sun-sparkling bay in the east. It is the past, the present and the future all mingling together.

-9-

I confess this is more difficult than I thought. I am not a storyteller. What I mean by that is my stories are for Soledad. My stories erupt from the depth of my bowels, unbidden, unasked for, and to get rid of them, to purge myself, I tilt my head back and howl at the moon. That is what my stories sound like. A dog howling at the moon. Where they go after that I do not know. Who else hears this howling dog? Who else can capture the meaning and the chaos? Who else can share it with the world? Who would even dare do such a thing? I do not know. Perhaps I do not care. Perhaps I do not even give a fuck. Who can say? I am used to howling at the moon with Soledad spread eagle beneath me on the bed or on the floor and only a roughly woven braided rug to prevent splinters. It is only when I am inside Soledad and I am howling at the moon, or when I have just finished and then I am howling at the moon with greater intensity, it is only in these moments that I remember I have stories left to tell. That is where the past, the present and the future come together for me. Or sometimes we open the window and the moonlight is streaming in and from somewhere you can hear the sounds of a merengue floating on the wind, the rhythmic push and pull of sex, steamy and hard and then steamy and soft, the music then fading, a single note from a single moaning saxophone hanging in the air, wavering, lingering, then barely a whisper, barely a breath, and then from somewhere else it is a bolero, and a bolero is for hard, slow fucking, very hard, and very slow, so Soledad braces herself against the window sill and arches her hips to meet me and I plunge into her heaving, steaming, dripping *conejo*, a sliver of pink flashing in the moonlight, pink and fresh and bright with juice like a freshly peeled grapefruit, and then I pull out for a moment to feel the cool night air against my foreskin, swirling like silk, my shaft stiffening, my greedy, thirsty tongue lapping up the perspiration rolling down Soledad's moonchild of an ass, a luxurious ass, the fragrance of musk oil and lavender pricking my nostrils, and then again I plunge in and howl with glee. But I do not howl in all my fury even then, and I tell her this, I might send her through the window, I say, if I really let loose, and without her plush ass to hang on to, I wouldn't be far behind, the two of us hurtling through the window into the dark void, it would be inevitable, I tell her this also, and there are a few patches of weedy, spongey grass in the backyard, but not enough, it is mostly cracked cement down there, it would be a very long, hard fall with nothing to cushion the severity of the impact, one can only imagine how many cracked bones, but she only laughs and says she is strong enough for anything I can dish out. My Soledad says her big beautiful ass would cushion the fall for me. Then she smiles and says her big beautiful ass cushions every fall. Then she says I wouldn't be able to knock her out of the window anyway, even if I had a running start. I suspect she is right. And then I am sure she is. I am just past eighty, after a while it is hard to know how old you are, skin like dried leather and bones that you can see cracking and creaking beneath wax paper skin and flat feet and flabby arms and a flat ass like a boy of ten. My face is covered with so many wrinkles I sometimes think the mirror must be cracked. But Soledad is perfection. She is a curvaceous, meaty, goddess of the Pyrenees. She is my goddess. She will always be my goddess, with her curly brown hair pulled back tight and her greenish-gray eyes the color of a stormy sea and her smooth as porcelain, sun-washed skin. She flashes me a superior, haughty, indifferent smile now and then, especially when her juices are flowing and she is feeling good and my tiny explosion has come and gone and I am flaccid and shriveled and useless, a sun-dried fig, the eunuch of my deepest fears. It is then that I howl at the moon as loudly as I can, and she, like a priestess who has renounced her vows, flashes me her haughty, indifferent, superior smile, but then it is not so indifferent after all, for she is howling right there with me, beside me, the two of us looking up at the moon and howling, and she is holding on to me, playing with me, caressing me, until I grow again. So it is Soledad I am thinking of as I tell this story.

Let me begin by saying that they did not look like teachers. But this thought only came to me later. When I first saw them, they looked like everybody else who sat at the tables by the plate glass window and ate pork and cornbread or bean soup and drank beer and whistled at the beautiful *chicas jóvenes* and grabbed at their plump brown asses peeking through, the girls laughing and whisking away plates. So I gave them no thought at all. They were the kind of men you easily forget because they were like everybody else, especially if you did not see them again.

That first evening it was the usual assortment of Cubans and Nicaraguans and Dominicans and Hondurans. The air was thick and heavy from cigarette smoke. The sun had set. Darkness fell quickly in south Florida. A few street lights popped on, which gave the street outside a hazy, grainy quality, like an old photograph. The fluorescent lights inside the café crackled and hissed, but nobody cared. Everyone was eating black bean soup and drinking beer that night because it was the Wednesday night special. No one bothered the two teachers. The one teacher looked like a crazy Mexican with his hair all wild and flaming like the snakes of Medusa, and he wore a tattered Mexican blanket for a shawl and his teeth flashed like diamonds through the smoke. The other teacher was a lumbering mad dog it seemed, a mastiff foaming at the mouth with a beard that covered half his face and continued all the way down his neck, and there were bits of bean soup and foam from the beer caught in the hairs. So the Cubans and Nicaraguans and the Dominicans and the Hondurans left them alone, and you could not blame them, especially with people you didn't know, especially because these two had wild, crazy, dancing eyes, lunatic eyes filled with a psychotic kind of charisma that promised an immediate and violent death if you had not been initiated into their inner sanctum. At least that's how it seemed. But even as the teachers were left alone, their presence had broken the normal routine for a Wednesday night. The entire café descended into an uneasy, anxious, waiting silence, punctured only now and then by an occasional request for more soup or beer, and a sort of background mumbling that was difficult to decipher. There was no laughter, and the café was normally filled with laughter, loud, raucous, passionate laughter, and there was no flirting with the girls and grabbing their asses and then the girls squealing and then maybe a couple of *greasy gamberros* hurtling themselves into the space between tables in the spirit of a fist fight. There was none of that. Even the girls were quiet. There was just an anxious, silent waiting. The very air seemed grave and brittle. The world, this mosaic of dogs howling at the moon, was about to shatter into a million pieces.

It is not that I minded the world shattering, you understand. I am something of a born-again anarchist. The idea of the world shattering is appealing. What bothered me was the lack of humor. The situation was so tense that no humor seemed possible. So I turned up the radio, thinking to ease the tension, restore the jovial atmosphere I was accustomed to on Wednesday nights with a salsa or some Latin pop, but this only seemed to magnify the inherent threat of this lunatic fringe sitting by the window. I suddenly felt like I was watching a movie and there was nothing I could do. The Cubans and the Dominicans were now in a constant state of agitation, all of them glancing over at the two teachers to see if anything was about to happen, to see if one of the teachers had pulled a stiletto, or the other one a gun, one after another they looked at the two teachers, a continuous barrage of eyeballing, like they were taking turns keeping a night watch, table after table, dozens of heavy brown eyes blinking through the fog of cigarette smoke, and then back at their bowls of soup, mumbling about the presence of these two lunatics, their words garbled, barely intelligible, how it was difficult enough to eat your dinner in peace in a neighborhood like this but now there were these crazy white Mexicans to contend with, and then their heavy brown eyes blinking through the fog once again.

    One wonders how long such tension can exist without someone coming to the breaking point. At least that is what I was wondering. Where is the breaking point here, I said to myself? What will the catalyst be? How long can you stifle the sound of howling dogs? How long can you sit on the edge of infinity, about to fall into the abyss? Yes, these were the questions rolling around in my brain. It is enough to drive you crazy, thinking about such questions. Fortunately, I did not have to wait long for an answer, which arrived in the form of a drunken, dirty white-skinned Rastafarian who called himself Malachi. He was the catalyst. But to fully appreciate the irony of Malachi as the catalyst, I need to share with you the sorry soap opera drama of Malachi and Gisela.

    Malachi sometimes came in on Wednesdays, but I had not seen him in a month. He is a lunatic himself. He is in love with one of our girls, a young whelp of a whore named Gisela who has not yet grown herself an ass, but who more than makes up for that deficiency with her massive titties, which are always spilling out of her shirt. As the owner of a café given to late night whoring, I often need to step in, shove her titties back in her shirt and tell her to keep it buttoned until the witching hour. Sometimes, many times, I am shoving her titties back in as early as four in the afternoon when the sun is still bright and yellow in the sky and the long heavy hot shadows of the evening are but a figment of our diseased and degenerative imaginations. Not that I want to quell her enthusiasm, mind you, it is a rare quality these days that a girl wishes to share her titties for free, just because she is so in love with the beauty of a bright clean day and the sidewalks have been swept and the kitchen is getting ready for the evening's customers and her titties are to her only a part of the natural order of the world's unending, eternal, bright clean brightness, you could not hold that against her. She really does have tremendous, voluptuous titties, the kind you can sink your teeth into and imagine yourself a leopard on the edge of the African savannah, and sometimes I do just that, I nibble a little around the edges of her nipples and pretend to growl, or give her a hard squeeze, a viciously juicy squeeze, just before I shove them back in, and Gisela squeals with delight and apologizes and wiggles all at the same time and promises to keep herself clothed until after the drinks have been served and the customers drunk enough to pay just for the pleasure of sitting there, drunk as proverbial skunks, watching Gisela's titties bounce about carelessly, effortlessly, her bubbling, enthusiastic laughter bouncing everyone's eyeballs off the walls.

    Gisela shows an interest in everyone who notices her, but she is particularly fond of those who live on the edge of the world, beggars with limbs missing who roll around on skids, masochistic thieves who sleep on beds of barbed wire as penance for their thievery, college students who have lost their way after drunken brawls at the beach, sex fiends driving brown metallic El Dorados with the horns of Texas Longhorns on the grill who have a taste for shaved pussy and girls with whips, toothless vagabonds with breath that smelled like stale fish and whose mucousy laughter can be heard several blocks away, lawyerly ex-cons and mealy-mouthed bastards of every shape and size and ethnic persuasion, her radar for such men is infallible, she loves them all without exception, without expectations or condition, all of them except poor, unfortunate Malachi. It is, as I have said, very much a sorry soap opera drama for our little corner of Calle Ocho. Malachi used to come into the café around three in the afternoon and drink beer, waiting until Gisela would let her titties pop out for a breather, and then he would watch with the schizophrenic attention of a late-night zombie, his eyeballs wiggling with every gyration, his mouth open, beer dribbling out of the corners, collecting in tiny pools on the table. When the show was over, which meant when I decided enough was enough and shoved Gisela's titties back in, he would laugh and clap and whistle and say it was the best damn show anywhere in Little Havana, even if there wasn't a stage for strutting, even if there wasn't a pole and purple lights flashing and the audience jerking themselves off like greased lightning in the blue shadows, and Gisela would smile shyly and sometimes even blush. He was always a gentleman, in spite of his language. He never approached her in a menacing way. He always clapped.

And so one afternoon, partially, I suspect, to show her gratitude for his obviously restrained yet undaunted adoration, and after she was fully clothed once more, she sat down at his table and they started talking. I don't remember what they were talking about. He was ranting and raving, waving his arms wildly in the air above his head, talking about the ancient sun god, Amun Ra, and the Egyptian pyramids and the sacredness of dolphins and the search for paradise and the second coming and the destruction of the Fascist state of America and the end of time, and Gisela was listening with the rapt fascination of one who is generally bored with life except when her titties are doing the Can-Can. It was a slow afternoon. There were a couple of greasy gamberros loading up on rum before they hit the streets, a bored looking accountant who must have got off early or been fired waiting on a late lunch, a couple of the girls wiping down the tables and Soledad in the kitchen and myself and Malachi and Gisela.

The next thing I knew Gisela was on her feet, two steps back from the table, holding one of her high heels with the spiked tip pointed straight at Malachi, saying if he took one step closer she would gouge out his eyes, and stabbing at the air with her shoe, and then she took another step back and settled into a sort of half-crouching state, her eyes burning holes in the air. You could almost smell the smoke. Malachi didn't say a word. He stood up, his face swallowed up in a sort of greasy, black shadow, like he had been smiling but the smile had been choked out of him, leaving him angry, frustrated, the taste of stomach acid rising up, his eyes watering as if his prick had been caught in a zipper. He stood there a moment, looking at Gisela, chewing his tongue some, swishing the bile around in his mouth and then swallowing, and nobody moved or said a word, not even the greasy gamberros, who are usually looking for a fight to wash away the slag of their early afternoon hangovers, and then Malachi blew Gisela a kiss and made his way out into the bright clean sunshine of the afternoon, whistling a reggae tune as he went.

That kiss seemed to linger in the air like swamp gas. It was almost Biblical, an ancient pestilence descending, the curse of an idiot-savant.

That Malachi chose to return to the café the very night the teachers appeared seemed one of those rare moments when the sky opens up and we are given a glimpse of the inner workings of the universe, the machinery of God. At least that's how I later came to see it. But when it was happening, well, my mind was completely drained of thoughts. I was only a reflection in the plate glass window, a frozen witness to the coming apocalypse. The moment I turned up the radio, you could see a change come over Malachi. His body stiffened. He was very drunk. He became as if mesmerized, his eyes fixed, indifferent to his immediate surroundings, his right hand twitching, his fingertips tapping lightly the handle of a gun stuffed into his shorts, the clutching, infinite loneliness of the world glittering like a halo about his head, the second hand of the clock slowing to an occasional tick. He was staring at these two teachers who resembled two crazy, white Mexicans, the one laughing, his flaming, Medusa hair dancing sparks against the window, the other one not laughing, sopping up soup with his beard, and all the while a stream of words was streaming out of Malchi's mouth, almost unintelligible, under his breath, but I was close enough to hear, the words half-formed, half-heard, tormented words, that's how it seemed to me. It was them, he said, they were the reason Gisela turned on him like she did so there was no reason to take it out on her, no reason to waste a bullet on her skinny little ass, he would save all of his bullets for these two, it was these white devils all along, six bullets for two, three for each, they were the ones who had slipped inside his skin, stolen his words, forced him to say things he didn't mean, they were the reason he had insulted the woman he loved, they were the reason he had taken out his prick that afternoon and started jerking off right there under the table, and the beautiful Gisela had wondered what he was doing and had dipped down to take a look and had started laughing, she had almost peed herself she was laughing so hard, that's when he had started spewing his venom, insulting her pedigree, her family, her mother and grandmother, that's when he said he'd rip out her heart if she didn't stop laughing, he'd rip out her heart and tear it to shreds, and the look in his eyes had been cold, hard, unforgiving, heartless because his own heart had been shredded by her laughter, and she had believed him, she had looked at him and all she had seen were snapping teeth, he saw the image of his snapping teeth reflected in her eyes, and suddenly she believed him capable of infinite cruelty, that's when she had threatened him with her shoe, the once happy, laughing girl with exuberant breasts, consort of the sun god, his consort once upon a time, for he had once been the sun god, this is what he believed, but not anymore, but it was not her fault, she was not responsible, he saw that now, they were the ones who had stolen his divinity, he said, along with everything else.

That's when Malachi fortified himself with the dregs of his fifth beer, a burst of warm alcohol soaking his chin and time speeding up, and then he pulled his gun from his shorts and exploded through the glittery clouds of stale cigarette smoke, a wailing banshee of divine vengeance wearing a red and yellow and green striped cap and black nylon biking shorts, barefoot, shirtless, unshaven, bleary-eyed, and before a single eyeball had blinked twice, he was sitting at the table of the two teachers, holding the gun with a steady, unwavering hand, the barrel pointing directly at the temple of the one with the flaming, Medusa hair.

One rarely encounters such situations, except in books. Immediately you could see that Malachi was unsure what to do next. He suddenly seemed to realize that he was temporarily the center of the universe. But he also seemed to know that his position could change with a sudden gust of wind. It was like walking a tightrope a mile up in the air. If he pulled the trigger, well there was nothing heroic about pulling a trigger, it was like butchering pigs, there was no honor in butchering pigs, but if he chose this course, then the exhilaration of these few moments, the sense that he was sowing the seeds of destiny among the stars, would vanish, a beggar's chalk painting dissolving in the rain. He would be left with nothing but a swirling, discolored memory, a river of chemicals, a cancer, a scar. But if he surrendered the gun it would be worse. You could tell this is what he was thinking. You could see this in his eyes also. If he surrendered the advantage of the gun he would find himself floating in the gutters of an inhuman world, a part of the daily flotsam and jetsam of a hundred thousand abortions whooshing down the wormhole drain, drowning in a sea of pus streaked semen and warm piss and menstrual juice and dead fetuses and radiator fluid and bloody diarrhea, seeking refuge inside the cathedral ruins of an embryonic sac, curling up to say his prayers then whispering goodnight, God speed, good riddance, gadzooks, the sac shrinking, disappearing into the frigid, humpbacked void of sodomized angels, wingless now, lecherous gargoyles sporting skeletal appendages without feathers, it would be a birth in reverse, the collapse of the universal soul. He wasn't sure how to save himself.

"Tell me why I shouldn't pull the trigger," said Malachi.

The one with the Medusa hair smiled, at least it looked like a smile coming through the glittery, shape-shifting cloud of cigarette smoke, but he said nothing. He stared across the table at the other one, who did not look up from his bowl. Malachi's arm began to tremble, a slight quivering.

"I can't think of a thing to say," said the one.

His smile widened. He turned to look at Malachi, the snakes of his flaming Medusa hair were now writhing in the air above his head, rattling against the plate glass window, sparks beginning to fly.

"If you need to pull the trigger then you need to pull the trigger," he said.

Then he guided the barrel into his mouth, took hold of it with his teeth, and continued talking, hissing was more like it, his lips barely moving, the sound squeezing out through the gaps.

"It doesn't make a bit of difference what you do. We are all dancing in one god damn eternal circle. Like angels on the head of a pin. So what the hell, let's get this goddamn fucking dance over with."

The smile became an explosion. The light from this explosion was so powerfully bright that no one could see for several minutes. It was a wonder the whole café didn't burn to the ground. Then the brightness faded. The familiar crackle and hiss of the fluorescent lights could be heard, the flickering, whitish light seeping through the glittery, cigarette fog. Everything had returned to normal, it seemed. The Cubans and the Dominicans were busy slurping up bowls of soup and drinking beer and grabbing at the girls passing by, their chiffon skirts wafting up as they swooshed past and a flash of beautiful brown flesh. One of the regulars wanted a flank steak, which isn't on the menu, but Soledad cooked one up anyway. Bursts of raucous laughter rattled the tables. When the men got hold of one of the girls they pulled her closer and gave her ass a squeeze like it was a fresh loaf of bread and the girl would laugh and push herself away until the next time.

Malachi and the two teachers were sitting at the table up front near the plate glass window. They had become old friends. There was no sign of the gun. The table was covered with empty beer bottles. Malachi was saying he knew of a club up in Allapattah where you could dance and drink all night for twenty bucks. They played a lot of bachata and merengue, but sometimes a salsa, he said. It was a pretty rough place. Everyone carried a knife at least. The women had stony, scarred horse faces, but they had very beautiful bodies, not flaccid and shapeless like the sack of shit whores down here. Malachi said if all you could see were the faces he wouldn't go. Every Saturday night they had a dance contest where the women would dance for the men, it was sort of a striptease, he said, where the men would throw money at the women and clap and shout until all the women were naked. The one teacher said that was the kind of free-spirited paradise he'd been searching for all his life. Malachi said he would take the two teachers there some time.

-10-

The next morning came quickly. I don't remember when we went to bed, but it was early, just after three I think. The girls were still busy downstairs and someone was singing, maybe it was the radio. I have never needed much sleep. I am certain this is a matter of instinct, a remnant of our primordial past. It is one of the few things that makes absolute sense. As long as we are awake, we are not dead. I climbed down the backstairs and headed down the alley, and then I turned up 22nd Avenue, which is always bustling. The sky was a hazy, whitish gray. The air was unusually cool. There was even more traffic than usual, mostly late model cars, a few vans with the windows blacked out, a garbage truck, a city bus, but it was already a few minutes after nine so most people were at work. The morning ahead was expansive, infinite, a time for lingering, for sampling the delicacies of this earth, for imagining the farthest corners of the Universe. I was headed for Café La Nueva for a pastry and an espresso. I have been going to this café for quite some time. It has become a habit. The old one burned down years ago. The new one takes up the first floor of a small red brick building with French doors trimmed in white and a blinking neon sign in the shape of a coffee cup with steam rising and the word 'Open' blinking in bright red. The new one is three blocks from where the old one had been.

Every day they set out some wooden tables and chairs, even if it is raining. The tables and chairs are partially protected by a yellow awning, and there are a couple of almond trees off to one side. A flock of small birds (perhaps they are warblers, they are usually winter birds, but who knows) takes up residence in the almond trees.

I used to go down to Domino Park to play dominoes, or sometimes just to watch, but I do not go there anymore. They are mostly Cuban there and I am not Cuban, so there is always a razor edge of animosity. Besides, I do not even like dominoes. So I go to Café La Nueva.

Some mornings I sit outside and drink my espresso and read the paper. Some mornings I watch the traffic go by. This particular morning was for watching traffic. The girl brought me the coffee and lemon cakes and some chocolate sauce on the side and she smiled. She has full red lips, very full, but I was not thinking about her. I was thinking about the two teachers from the night before, though I still did not know they were teachers. I was wondering what kind of magic spell they had cast over Malachi and how they had made the gun disappear. I have seen many strange things in my eighty-some years, things I question even now if they really happened or if it was just my imagination.

I used to think I came to this country from Hungary. I was fairly certain of this. But my memory of the past has become a slippery thing. I used to think I was born in Ružomberok, a town that was part of the Austrian-Hungarian empire until 1919, when it was given to Czechoslovakia, but now I think that is a rumor I planted in my own brain after watching *Casablanca* with Humphrey Bogart and Peter Lorre, because Peter Lorre had been born in Ružomberok. I have watched that movie several times, countless times on the small television we keep in the back. The Peter Lorre character was named Ugarte, a thief who helped exiles who wished to escape. It is a shame he murdered the German couriers. But I can understand that about wanting to kill Germans during the Nazi years. I do not remember when I acquired the belief that I was Hungarian. It is a ludicrous thing to believe. Everything about me says I am not Hungarian, the fact that I speak Spanish, not Hungarian, is not my only clue. Perhaps I needed to hide my identity for a while, and now I have forgotten when and why. I wish I could make sense of my memories.

The strangest memory I possess is one of tanks rolling down a long boulevard. I am standing with my father, I am a very young boy and it is very hot, but I am not sure where we are. Sometimes I think the two of us are in Zaragoza, but why I cannot say. Sometimes I think we are in San Sebastián in '36 during those final days before it fell to the Nationalists, but there is none of the lingering carnage that is evidence of a great battle. And everyone is smiling and laughing and singing songs and clapping their hands. It is like a celebration. And besides, there were no tanks at San Sebastián, only a few armored vehicles. It is a very strange memory.

I remember the tanks were like a parade of garbage trucks and we were lined up along the avenue, there were many, many people. It was a normal looking street, except for the tanks, with apartments and shops and cafes and churches. We were watching these tanks like garbage trucks roll past, and suddenly a young boy made a dash to cross the avenue and fell down, and you could see he had skinned his knee, but it seemed a tremendous amount of blood for a skinned knee, and the people on both sides of the avenue were shouting for him to get up, to cross before the next tank smashed him to a pulp, but he did not move, he just held out his arms, imploring someone from the crowd to have pity on him, and truly it must have been more than a skinned knee, for the amount of blood was far more than a knee might contain, there were rivers of blood, rivers and rivers of blood pouring out of his knee, running down along the gutters on both sides, causing the sewers to overflow, the bloody sewer water beginning to lap over the shoes of those standing along the curb, we thought perhaps the boy had been shot, or that many boys had been shot, even though there were no soldiers in my memory, only the tanks, even though there were no other boys in the picture, but whatever the case, we were certain this one was doomed, but at the very last minute a young woman flashed across and rescued the boy, a flash of light between two tanks and the boy was saved, an angel doing God's work.

Of course none of that is really strange. It was routine for the times. It was almost expected. A parade of tanks that looked like garbage trucks. Unseen soldiers shooting boys. Rivers and rivers of blood and the sewers overflowing. An angel appearing when all hope is lost. But what is truly strange came later. What is truly strange is when I think back on that moment, it keeps changing. Sometimes the boy in the street is my own young son, who left us long ago, and the woman flashing by is my very own Soledad. Sometimes in this memory where I am standing with my father, I am almost a grown man, and we are both carrying rifles and shouting obscenities as the tanks roll past and then the boy is crushed. And sometimes I am the boy in the street and I am reaching out to the crowd, but I see that there is no crowd, there is just an empty street, and there are no apartment buildings, there is only a great emptiness where the buildings should have been, and then I look up again and I can see that someone has planted thin trees in the empty spaces, and they are just beginning to show tiny green buds, and behind the trees, you can see a heavy burning sun behind gray clouds, but the sunlight does not penetrate all the way, just enough so the green buds look like they are glowing, like they are just catching fire, like the trees are beginning to burn, and then I look up a third time and I can't see a thing because the air has grown dark and heavy with smoke and the smell of burning oil and the sounds of the tanks, and there is a heavy, creaking, cracking sound, and then the world goes black.

What does it mean to have a memory like this? What does it mean when the past changes before your very eyes, or slips away so completely, so effortlessly, that what you once thought was a fixed, eternal truth might never have happened at all? I find it easier now when I am sipping my espresso and nibbling my lemon cakes to think that nothing has happened in my life except what is happening now. I was born only yesterday. My name is Xavier Mendoza because this is what my wife, Soledad, my sweet goddess of the Pyrenees, this is what she calls me. She is God's breath upon my soul. She is the only reason I am still connected to this earth. She has been with me for longer than I care to remember. But as long as she knows who I am, then I know who I am.

The girl brings me a second espresso and another plate of lemon cakes.

"*Hola Señor Mendoza,*" she says.

"*Hola a usted mi pequeño pollo.*"

She laughs.

"No, no, no Señor Mendoza. I am no small chicken anymore."

"Ah, you are mistaken," I say. "At my age, every woman I see is *mi pequeño pollo.*"

She laughs again.

"Do you like my lemon cakes," she says.

"Very much, yes."

"I made them fresh this morning."

"They are very good."

"I was thinking of you when I made them."

"Now you are making an old man blush."

"No, no, no Señor Mendoza. I do not think there is anything that would cause you to blush."

She laughs a third time and whirls around, her curves slicing through the air, and disappears into the café. The aroma of her lemon cakes is swirling all around me. The warblers are chirping from the almond trees, hopping from branch to branch. They are beginning to annoy me. They are like a Greek chorus with all their chirping. Then the girl pokes her head back out through the door and the birds fly away. "If there is anything you want, Señor Mendoza, anything at all, just ask."

I am not fast enough to answer and now she is gone. I want everything from her. I should have told I am in love with her, which is true, at least for today. I should have told her I wanted more lemon cakes, but I have already eaten too many. I am remembering her heart-shaped ass as she whirled away and it is hanging there in my memory, suspended in the air and the soft sunlight filtering through the leaves of the almond trees and the lemony smell of the lemon cakes and the sound of her laughter mixed with the sounds of the birds, and I am thinking how very much I would like to sit her on my lap and lift up her skirt and squeeze her ass and breathe her in and then spread her legs so I could diddle her a while and feel her wetness gushing forth and hear her moan. Right there sitting outside the café I would do this. But then I am thinking of Soledad. Not that Soledad would mind, she wouldn't. Soledad encourages me. She says a healthy appetite needs variety, a table covered with exotic cuisines to sharpen the palate. She would probably even like to watch, maybe have a taste herself. But I am thinking of Soledad because it takes energy to sample other women, even when they are young and willing and full of heart, and I am old now, and some days I have little energy left. Today I am thinking of Soledad because I want to plow into her again and again. I want to make sure I have the stamina. I am very hard just thinking about her.

I must have fallen asleep. The girl is back with another espresso. She is wiping down part of the table and smiling and clearing away the other cup. I do not know if I finished drinking it or if I knocked it over when I fell asleep. I feel badly she is expending so much effort on my behalf.

"Are you feeling better Señor Mendoza?"

I nod and smile back at her. On the other side of the street someone shouts and waves but I cannot see who it is. The someone I cannot see continues on their way. I am taking the last sips of my last espresso and watching the traffic some more. The air is very warm now. It is almost noon. A car whooshes past, then several more. Every now and then a dozen or more warblers fly low beneath the speeding cars and come out the other side. They are flying further and further away, down the street, back and forth they go beneath the cars. They must be the same warblers from the almond trees, I think. They are like flashes of light. Then one of the warblers gets clipped. I see the car whoosh past and the clipped warbler is now spinning in the dust of the street, spinning and flashing like a silver coin, and then I can no longer see him. I take the long way home. When I get back I go straight around to the front and go in through the café door.

"Hello Mr. Mendoza," says a voice.

"*Hola Señor Mendoza*," says another.

I am not sure what I am looking at. Or at least I am not sure why. The first voice comes from the lumbering mastiff with the full beard from the night before. The second voice comes from the one with the Medusa hair. They are both holding brooms. They seem to have worked up a good sweat. The next thing I know they are both outside sweeping the sidewalk and I am sitting at a side table, away from the windows. Soledad has brought me a bowl of thin barley soup and a few Saltines and a plate of pisto.

"They fell asleep downstairs," she says.

I am eating my soup, dipping the crackers, savoring each spoonful, but I am listening.

"I came down this morning and there they were, so I gave them both brooms."

Later, we are back upstairs. We are lying down in bed. It is the middle of the afternoon and I am very sleepy. The blinds are slanted shut and the shadows are dark and cool and there is air blowing from a small fan on the dresser on the other side of the room. The air is coming in waves. You can hear the motor of the fan growing louder as the fan spins closer, and then fading as it spins away. On any other afternoon I would have Soledad flat on her back and I would be pounding away at her. But my erection from before is no longer there. Besides, I am very tired. I curl up against Soledad and close my eyes and she wraps her arms around me. It almost seems like I am curled up inside her. She is talking to me in her soft, sweet, kitten's voice. Her voice fades in and out with the spinning of the fan. She tells me she came downstairs that morning and I had gone for my coffee and there they were, sleeping at the table up front by the plate glass window, and they were very nice, very apologetic, they had a long talk together, they said they were teachers, but she could tell in a few minutes that the one with the Medusa hair, the older one, had the appetite of a Picasso, the kind of sexual depravity Picasso was known for, and she laughs at this and pokes me in the ribs, and the other one would be very beautiful if he cleaned himself up, she says, he is very young and fresh, and she is smiling but it is a sad smile and I know she is thinking of this young teacher as a mirror image of the son we had always wanted, but our son had died, he was a small, oddly deformed baby boy born a thousand years ago, and he spent only a few days on the planet and then his tiny eyes clouded over, the spirit of death filling his lungs, and then he died and we buried him in a small grave in Caballero Rivero without even a stone, without even a small white cross, and we never spoke of him after that, but we never forgot, this is how she is thinking of the young teacher, I am sure of it, she is looking at this young teacher as if he is our son and he is no longer buried, he has returned to us, without the deformity that caused his death, and she gives me a gentle kiss on the cheek as if to remind me that life is too short to question the gift of second chances, she tells me these two teachers will only be here a short while, they are trying to figure out what to do next, especially the young one, she gave them the brooms and told them they could stay for a while if they swept the café three times a day, and also the sidewalk, she gave them the room across the hall, she will see after them, she says, and after that I don't remember what she is saying,

I don't need to remember, she is my universe exploding, the tanks are coming and she is the angel of my last hope, and I am painting my newborn self across the sky.

-11-

The two teachers and Malachi have been restless for days, and their restlessness is infecting everyone else, the girls, Soledad, even me. It feels like sand coursing through my veins, and I wonder if it feels that way for the others, but it is Sunday today and we are closed and we are ignoring this feeling of being restless. Most of the tables are covered with chairs. We have cleared off a few and we are sitting around and drinking beer and sangria and the ceiling fans are spinning because of the heavy, dull heat of the day. We are chewing the fat, all of us, except Malachi is not here. He has been coming around a lot lately, but he is not here now. Soledad has turned the radio on in the kitchen and when we hit the quiet spots in the conversation we can hear the sounds of Latin pop. It is like the sound of a quick, hard rain at the beach.

"That is precisely why I'm heading to Patagonia," says the older teacher.

"Don't believe him," says the younger teacher.

"Fascist!" says the older teacher.

"He's been talking that garbage for years."

"Fucking Fascist!"

One of the girls laughs. It is a short, chirpy laugh.

"Mickey, Mickey, Mickey! You are such a bad boy."

She is still chirping. She is too young to know what a Fascist is, but she already knows quite a bit about fucking. She is sitting in a chair next to the older teacher, leaning herself against his shoulder, playing with his stringy, Medusa hair and drinking her sangria. They are sitting at one corner of the table. There are two other girls sitting cattycorner. Soledad is behind them at the counter filling a bowl with chips. She brings the chips out and a jar of salsa and goes back to the counter. Everyone digs in.

Soledad is always taking care of many small things.

"That's a hell of thing to say," says the younger teacher.

"It was just a raw observation," says the older teacher.

"After all we've been through together."

The older teacher polishes off his beer.

"Forget about it. We have bigger fish to flay."

He slides the first girl on top of his lap and buries his head in her chest, but he continues talking. All you can see is his wild, flaming Medusa hair flying about while he talks. The girl is no longer chirping. She is now giggling.

"You mean fry," says the younger teacher.

"No I don't. I like my fish raw. That's a prerequisite if you want to live out your days in paradise."

"What a load of garbage."

"And after you eat your fill of fish, then you're ready for the eighty vestal virgins. Also raw."

"And then what?"

"What more do you need after eighty vestal virgins in the raw?"

The older teacher looks up for a moment from the chest of the girl and looks across the table at the young teacher. The girl also looks at the young teacher. She is smiling with great enthusiasm.

"Then why are you always talking about going to Patagonia?" says the younger teacher.

"Travis, my fucked-up friend, you are definitely confused. Patagonia isn't just a place. It is mostly a myth, which is another way of saying that Patagonia is mostly a state of mind."

The older teacher squeezes a nipple and dives back in. The girl does not mind a bit.

"Oh, Mickey," she says. "You are very, very bad."

The eyes of the older teacher once again vanish from view. The girl presses her lips against his neck and begins moaning softly, or perhaps she is sighing from her obvious love sickness. The younger teacher is smiling at the catty-corner girls and they are smiling back. They shift in their seats and spread their legs a bit and smile some more and drink some more sangria. All three girls are wearing tight-fitting t-shirts and short shorts, their brown, cheeky asses spreading out where they sit and their smooth bright legs flashing in the dim light. It is hard to tell them apart. The younger teacher pushes his chair back away from the table. I suspect he wants a better view of the legs of the cattycorner girls.

"The thing about Patagonia is this," says the older one.

His face is no longer buried in the first girl's chest. She has shifted herself. She is now sitting in his lap, leaning back against his shoulder. She is smiling, content, oblivious.

"It's the last place on the fucking planet where they've never even heard of the Judeo-Christian concept of sin. Or the Muslim concept. Or the Buddhist. Or any fucking concept at all. All they care about is fucking each other and eating fish from the sea. They don't even know fire exists, that's why they eat their fish raw, just like the gods intended. That's the way it's supposed to be my friend. All they're doing is just living. That's paradise. But you don't have to go there to get there."

"I want to go." says the first girl. "I like it raw."

"We all like it raw," say the other girls. "Can we go too?"

"You hear that, Travis? Everyone wants a little piece of paradise."

The three girls are laughing, softly, happily. They polish off the last of the chips and salsa.

"Sure Mick, that's easy for you to say," says the young teacher. "Look at you! God damn guru. Anything you want."

The first girl starts wiggling slowly in the lap of the older teacher, it is a slow, hard dance, *un baile erótico de regazo*. It is very professional. You can see he is becoming aroused.

"It's never been that easy for me," says the young teacher.

"You'll get there, my friend," says the older one. "But you have to learn to relax. Let go. Forgive yourself."

The young teacher doesn't say anything, drinks some more beer. The two cattycorner girls are sipping their sangrias, heads bent close towards each other, murmuring, looking at the young teacher, licking the rims of their glasses, slowly, drops of sangria juice lingering on their tongues, and then they are laughing some more, soft and sexy. The young teacher slides his chair back to the table. He drinks more beer, looks at the girls. They are exceptionally skillful, these girls. They have been with me for a long time.

"We forgive you, Travis," the cattycorner girls say.

"Forgive me for what?"

"For whatever you're thinking right now."

"How do you know what I'm thinking?"

"Never mind about that, Travis."

"Yes, never mind."

"And what if I don't want to be forgiven?"

"Don't listen to those sirens," I say.

The cattycorner girls send me daggers with their eyes.

"They have no intention of forgiving you," I say. "They will use everything you think and say and do against you until they get what they want, and on that day, make no mistake, they will leave you lying naked in the gutter, hands tied behind your back, penniless, broken, a shell of who you once were stinking of rum and piss.

"We would not do that, Travis."

"Don't you listen to this old fart, Travis."

"Yes," I say. "I have seen it a thousand times before."

"He is just jealous."

"And old."

"Yes, he is very old, and very forgetful."

"Yes, yes, this is all true," I say. "But I am not talking about my shortcomings. I am talking about theirs, and they do not know the first thing about forgiveness. It is like your friend says. All you have to do is forgive yourself."

There is a lull in the conversation. It is almost like falling asleep. I am wondering if the older teacher has slept with all of my girls. He seems very capable, *muy macho*. I am even wondering if perhaps he has taken them on two or three at a time. The other one I am not sure about. Well that is not quite true. I am sure he has not slept with anyone but himself since he has been here. Then I am not wondering about anything. The blinds are up but it is cloudy outside and the light inside the café is very dim. I am sitting at a table separate from the others, drinking from a small, dark brown flask. I am drinking dark rum all the way from Puerto Rico. Sunday is the only day of the week I drink my dark rum. I am drinking and the world is a drowsy world and no one is talking and the only sound is the sound of the radio. The radio is playing a samba. Then the samba stops and a man starts talking. He is ranting and raving about a little boy who was found floating in an inner tube three miles off the coast of Florida. His mother had died in the crossing so the government had sent him back to Cuba to be with his father. The man is speaking with the voice of outrage. He is speaking for thousands who feel the same way. But I wonder about all that. I wonder how the man would feel if the boy was his son. Would he not be overjoyed to have his son once again in his arms? Who has the right to deny a father such joy? Then I wonder about the hundreds of young boys, perhaps thousands of young boys, who have perished in the ocean between Cuba and Florida, all of them desperate to escape to America, clinging to flimsy boats or inner tubes, all of them food for the sharks. We do not know about these boys. We do not know what happened to them. We do not know if they truly existed. They are only phantoms in our imaginations. But I am greatly troubled by their deaths all the same. Then I am thinking that we are all exiles, refugees, trying to cross an ocean of trouble to find a better life. It is the same no matter where we come from. Then I notice the man has stopped talking. The radio is now playing some Gloria Estefan. I have always liked Gloria Estefan, but you can barely hear her, the music is very faint, hardly a breath at all, it sounds a million miles away in the dim light and only adds to the feeling of drowsiness.

After a while, I noticed that the conversation had resumed. Everyone was pretty much where they had been before, except the lap dance girl was back in her chair. She was leaning against the shoulder of the older teacher. Every so often she punched him in the ribs or pinched him with a hard, vicious, twisting pinch, and she was saying *porecito*. When he leaned over to kiss her she tried to bite him, or maybe she already had and I had missed it because his lip was bleeding. She wiped away the blood with a napkin.

"Does it have to take place in a bedroom?" said one of the cattycorner girls.

"No, no, my young coquettish nymphomaniac," said the older teacher. "It can be anywhere two people can get naked."

"And more than two?"

"Of course. The more the merrier."

"Then we, my girl Thérèse and myself, we have a story."

"We do?" said the other cattycorner girl.

"The painter," said the first cattycorner girl. "The one who lived by the Tower Theater."

"Ooooooohhhh, him, yes, I remember him."

"It was before I knew Thérèse."

"It was the way we met. It is a crazy story!"

"Two young girls and a painter," said the older teacher. "Who said romance is dead? Fucking outstanding! Now if only there were a few newly converted anti-religious cynics in the audience."

"I'm an anti-religious cynic," said the young teacher.

"You don't count, Lauterbach. You were born a cynic. And anti-religious to boot. Go on girls. On with the story. I'm getting hungry."

The cattycorner girls drank some more sangria. They smiled and made eyes at each other. Everyone else drank their beers.

"What an amazing, unforgivable fucking *cabrón* he was," said Thérèse. "This painter. A gifted bastard. Always fucking around. But ooooooohhhh me, what eyes he had."

"She is getting ahead of the story," said the first cattycorner girl. "It did not start with his eyes."

"For me it started with his eyes. Ooooohhhh, yeeeess."

"It really started with the Tower Theater," said the first cattycorner girl. "This was years ago, four or five years before they closed down the first time. Maybe more. I didn't go there a lot, a few times. But whenever I was there, I saw him hanging around, sometimes at that little place next store getting a sandwich, but most of the time I'd see him hiding out in Domino Park. He would set up a small table like everyone else, but instead of dominoes he'd cover the table with ceramic miniatures of the theater. I mean it was chock full. I guess he was trying to sell them to anyone who wanted to buy. Or trying to. But he wasn't trying too hard. He really wasn't into the miniatures. To tell the truth I don't think the theatre knew what he was up to. He was into painting. Like Pablo Picasso and all that artsy shit. That's what he said when I got to know him. But I didn't know what to think the night I met him, oh baby, it just doesn't seem real even now, I didn't know what the fuck was happening. I had just walked out of a movie. It was an American movie, but we had only been in the States a few months and my English wasn't so good yet. I mean half the time it sounded like they were underwater or something. Fucking gibberish. Anyway, this movie I walked out on sounded like that. And I didn't give a fuck about the subtitles. I didn't want to read at the movies. Reading gives me headaches. I go to the movies because I don't like reading. So I was trying to explain this to the girl at the ticket booth and get my money back, but she just laughed, so I flipped her off, and then she flipped me off, and then the booth went dark and she went away, and then she was standing in the lobby like there was a spotlight on her and I was pissed, I don't know what else I was thinking but I was so pissed, but what was I going to do, and then I heard a voice from the sidewalk, and it was saying, 'That's not the way to get your money back,' and it was a really deep voice, the kind that flows through you, like a bassoon, like something musical, and the next thing I knew I was walking arm in arm with this guy and he smelled like orange spice and I couldn't get away from him, but I didn't want to get away either, and we walked for a while, I really don't remember how long, and then we sat down at a café, they had these sidewalk tables outside with Tiki torches and he wanted to sit at one of those because they reminded him of Gauguin, that's what he said, so that's where we sat down, but I wasn't a complete idiot, so I was saying 'I still don't see my money,' and he laughed and gave me a cigarette to keep me quiet and flashed back to the theater, and then another flash and he was back at the table with my money. What do you say when something like that happens?"

"You say yeeesss!" said Thérèse. "What else can you say?"

The light from outside was glowing a soft, hazy red. Soledad brought out some nachos with jalapeños and some more chips and salsa and another pitcher of sangria. The cattycorner girls filled their glasses and drank some more, and everyone else kept pounding their beers.

"So there I was sitting at this table and staring at my money and he ordered us a couple of coffees, and then I was thinking what the hell was I going to do, this guy was absolutely gorgeous with his thick, curly black hair and the way his cheekbones caught the torch light outside this café, and I could see just a hint of the devil in his smile, and when he looked at me with those searing brown eyes of his, it was like hypnosis, *mirada fuerte*, my grandmother would say, the strong gaze, something to be avoided at all costs, especially if you are a hot young whore walking the street, you have to be strong against such eyes, but I was not strong, I felt my whole body melting away, he could have me whenever he wanted, I had never seen anyone like him, not up close, it was like he was straight out of the movies, like he was Antonio fucking Banderas, but this all happened a very long time ago, so he couldn't have been Antonio, and I was thinking this just doesn't happen, not to me, so then I was thinking he was probably just another fucking *chamuco*, had to be, and he was playing a pretty good scene, I mean it was Academy Award caliber, but he'd done this a thousand times before, I was sure of that, all he wanted to do was take me to bed and fuck my brains out and that would be that. That's what I was thinking."

"That's how he operates on your mind," said Thérèse. "That's part of his mystique."

"I could barely say thank you."

"You never say thank you," said the lap dance girl.

Everyone laughed.

"A couple of weeks later was the next time I saw him. It was very much like a dream. He was sitting at his table in the park. It was a very lazy mojito kind of day with the sun beginning to set, a very orange sun, and he waved at me to come over, so I did, and there were a couple of old farts in polo shirts looking at the miniature towers, I guess they were done with their dominoes for the day, and he had to keep an eye on them so he couldn't talk right away. So I was walking around the table same as the old farts and looking at the towers, and the way they were shining there in that orange sunlight, dozens of them laid out in rows on a wooden folding table, all of them with the tower part sticking straight up in the air, and I was trying to keep myself together, but it was very difficult, but then the old farts were gone and all of a sudden I started laughing. I couldn't control myself. It just came bubbling out, because those miniature towers looked like dozens of cocks, dozens of long, thin glittery cocks glittering in the sunlight, all of them ready to explode, raring to go, like they were all on a mission, ready, aim, fire, like pronto."

Everyone laughed again.

"Reina is the one on a mission," said the lap dance girl. "Everywhere she looks she sees cocks raring to go."

"Yeeeesss she does, doesn't everybody?" said Thérèse.

"Only if you know where to look," said the older teacher. "Then you'll see gods and goddesses themselves walking around with tremendous hard-ons."

"Even the goddesses?" said the young teacher.

"Especially the goddesses. They're walking around with strap-ons with golden tips. And these strap-ons are at least two feet long."

"So what happened next?" said the lap dance girl.

"The next thing I remember is I had one of those towers in my hands and I was inspecting it at close range, just to be polite. I was very methodical. I was turning it this way and that, examining it from every angle."

"Stroking it, you mean," said Thérèse.

"And he said I could keep it if I liked it, it was a gift, and we started talking and I told him how the towers looked like glittery cocks and he burst out laughing, and then he said it was deliberate, of course, the phallic nature of the theater itself, the design of it, he said it was an art deco experiment, and I didn't know what to say to that, I don't normally go in for all that artsy, fartsy, cheezy, feezy crap, that's the last thing I need, to tell you the truth, *lo último que necesito es un catarro*, and that's when he told me he was a painter, a serious artist like Picasso or Balthus or Bernini or Gauguin, he said, and that all serious art was about sex and sexuality and the freedom to fuck whoever you wanted, which I had never thought about before, I mean who thinks about stuff like that, and then he said it was the ones who thought sex was a crime that were the real perverts."

"A man after my own heart," said the older teacher.

"That's when he invited me up to see his studio," said Reina. "He was unbelievably bold."

"Aaaaahhhh, me, but you knew this was coming," said Thérèse.

"We did indeed," said the older teacher. "It's exactly what I would have done."

"And you went to his studio anyway," said Thérèse.

"He said maybe he'd even paint me, if I didn't mind sitting naked on a pedestal for a couple of hours so he could see every inch. He said he liked the rounded curve of my shoulders, my large, billowy breasts, my dark hair. He asked me if I shaved my pussy. Are you kidding me! What balls to say a thing like that! That's what I was thinking. He said he only worked with models who shaved their pussies."

"Let me tell you it wasn't much of a studio," said Thérèse. "He lived on the second floor of the old liquor store across from the costume house. Before they went out of business. Paintings all over the fucking place, on the floor, stacks of them along the walls, beneath the windows, piled up on the one sofa, on chairs. Paintings and empty bottles of wine."

"But he kept his bed clear," said Reina. "As I remember he was very much on a mission about his bed. I don't remember him doing much painting. But we drank an awful lot of red wine. And we did an awful lot of fucking. He was breezy as you please when it came to fucking. As soon as it was light he wanted to fuck. And then as soon as he took a shower. And then as soon as he ate. And then as soon as he took a crap. As soon as he drank some wine. As soon as he turned on the television. The radio. As soon as the sun set. As soon as the stars came out. *Siempre estoy arrecho contigo*, he would say to me. He was always horny. Christ he was horny."

Reina made the sign of the cross and smiled.

"He was a vampire," said Thérèse.

"He needed plenty of sex and plenty of red wine," said Reina. "He said that's what his doctor had told him. It was a hell of a line."

"Or one hell of a doctor," said the older teacher.

"He was a bastard," said Thérèse. "He could party all night long and pick up a new girl for breakfast and another one for lunch. He would suck the life out of you before you even knew what was happening."

"She's just pretending to be mad."

"*Aye ke la verga.*"

"I mean she was mad at first."

"I was."

"But it didn't last long."

The two cattycorner girls looked at each other and then burst out laughing.

"It was all pretty funny at the end," said Reina.

"It was wickedly funny," said Thérèse.

"I get wet just thinking about it," said Reina

The two laughed some more, their eyes glistening.

"You see I had been sleeping with this painter for several months," said Thérèse. "I knew he was a pig, a very gifted pig, but still a pig, but I forgave him because I never ran into these other girls, these hairy, smelly, tuna cunts, that's how I thought of them. But the day I met Reina, well, I just wasn't expecting her. It was the middle of the afternoon and I figured he was just waking up so I headed over to the studio. He always made me use the side stairs so I wouldn't attract any attention, but only a total fucking *pendejo* does such a thing, there's nothing more obvious than a young whore in a mini skirt and a tube top sneaking up the side stairs in the middle of the day. But up the stairs I went and I popped through the screen door with a mini-mart bag with coffee and cigarettes, and there were the two of them over by the sofa, grunting away doggie style. She was holding on to the edge of the sofa to keep her balance and he was ramming into her as hard as he could, so hard a pile of paintings fell to the floor from the shock, and the next thing I remember he had rolled away from her and was sitting bow-legged on the floor, scratching his balls, and he said 'Hola Thérèse! Did you bring me my cigarettes? Come on, don't just stand there, come and join the party!' It was strange like a dream is strange. I hurled the mini-mart bag as hard as I could at this one here, swinging it round and round a couple of times before I let loose. She was dripping wet from his cock and looked at me and smiled and I let that bag fly. I was aiming for her head, but the bag sailed to the right and knocked over an easel with some of his paints instead. I looked at him and I said 'Okay, which one of us goes,' and he said 'I am very much satisfied with things as they are, but if that's the way you want it, then the two of you will have to fight it out for yourselves.' All I could see after that was red. I was on top of her before she could take a breath. I wanted to strangle her till her eyes popped, but I didn't have a good grip. Then she shoved me into another stack of paintings and there was more paint on the floor, and pretty soon the two of us were rolling in paint like mud wrestlers, we were covered in it, and she was clawing at me and I was clawing at her, and then one of us would get free, but only for a moment because the other one would come charging after, and then the two of us would fall to the floor again, and all the while I could hear his slobbering, laughing voice saying 'Toro, toro, toro' and laughing and laughing and then 'olé' and then laughing and slobbering some more. And then snap, just like that the cobwebs cleared and I stopped seeing red, I mean the whole scene was just ludicrous beyond belief, and I looked at her and she looked at me, and I can't quite explain it, but in that moment we became sisters."

"It was telepathic," said Reina. "Like telepathy."

"In that moment we knew we were finished with the painter."

"It was like we were inside each other," said Reina.

"All of our love for him was gone," said Thérèse. "But we also knew the afternoon was not yet over."

"It was like we were thinking each other's thoughts," said Reina.

"Mmmmmmmmmm, yeeeeessssss it most certainly was," said Thérèse.

The cattycorner girls poured themselves more sangria. They were beaming.

"The first thing we did we were all over him," said Thérèse. "We pulled off his pants and then his shirt and dragged him laughing and sputtering into our paint-filled arena, and we climbed on top of him, one at each end like bouncing on a seesaw, and I fucked him several times to keep him happy, and then we switched places and it was Reina's turn to fuck him, and he kept crying out, "More, more, more,' and we lathered him in paint while we were fucking him. Then we turned him over and tied his hands and legs behind his back, the way you tie up any pig, and we covered his back with as many colors as we could find, a patchwork of colors, a rainbow, and then we leaned him up against the sofa and shoved a pile of his paintings up under his chin so he wouldn't fall and turned on some reggae so people would think he was throwing a party, and all this while he was laughing and sputtering, he thought it was all part of the game, you see, his cock was ready to go once more, you could see that clearly in spite of the paint. He was begging us to fuck him one more time, this is what he'd been looking for his entire life, but we were through with him, and we told him so, but we couldn't keep from laughing ourselves. He looked like some sort of crazy voodoo doll with a blue and green head and red stripes down his arms and a purple stomach and a purple cock and orange legs. We told him he was a pig and that we were through with him, but he didn't seem to get it, he just wondered when we were going to fuck him again and how long we were going to keep him tied up, and we hadn't really thought about that last one, we should have left him tied up for good, but we didn't, we should have left him there until the paint had crusted over and his cock had fallen off, but we weren't so cruel as that. We each kissed him, a long, slow, sexy goodbye kiss that left him thirsty and panting, to let him know what he would never have again, and then we told him we'd send someone around in an hour or so to help him wiggle out of the ropes, and then we left. We didn't even bother about our own clothes. We just left."

"You didn't care you were naked?" said the young teacher.

"Why should we care about that?" said Reina. "We're naked a lot."

Everyone laughed.

"Besides," said Thérèse. "We were covered in paint. There wasn't much to see."

"What happened to the painter?" said the lap dance girl.

"I don't know," said Thérèse. "We ordered a pizza and told them to use the side stairs and walk right in."

"We never saw him again," said Reina. "He just vanished completely."

The cattycorner girls were smiling, wiggling, very satisfied with themselves.

"You better watch these two, Lauterbach," said the older teacher. "It's like the old man was saying, they'll chew you up and spit you out, leave you lying in the gutter."

Everyone laughed again.

The two cattycorner girls sipped their sangrias, their heads bent close towards each other once more, murmuring, smiling. They licked the rims of their glasses, slowly. Drops of sangria juice lingered on their tongues.

-12-

It was only after waking up that I realized I had fallen asleep yet again. When I was younger I rarely slept. But now it is sometimes difficult to tell if I am sleeping or awake. I must have been sleeping for a while because it was dark when I woke up, except for the kitchen light and the dim yellow counter lights and a candle glowing in a jar on the table we had cleared. The blinds were down by then, but it wouldn't have mattered. It was very dark outside. Everyone else was gone, except the young teacher and Soledad. They were talking in soft, low whispers, and the way the candle light bounced off their skin they almost looked like young lovers. I had been dreaming of Soledad. In my dream she was lying in the grass on a single silk sheet, a dark gray in color, or maybe it was black. She was naked and relaxed, as if she herself were dreaming, and there were vines sprouting up everywhere, each vine ending in a leaf of three leaflets and more and more vines were sprouting as the dream progressed. We were closed off from the world, surrounded by a blue curtain hung on a wire and fixed in place with orange clothespins. You could see the orange glow of the setting sun beyond the curtain, a darkly burning glow, just over the top of the curtain, but we were in the dark, in the shadows. Soledad was sleeping peacefully and there was a plate of apples next to her and the air smelled of honeysuckle and lilacs and damp earth and apples and sex all mixed together. In my dream I understood that my Soledad was the mother goddess of the earth come back from the land of the dead, and so she had abandoned her earthly body. Her skin was a soft, whitish, lilac color, a reflection of the early morning summer sky even though it was evening in my dream, or perhaps it was the soft, whitish afterglow of death. My Soledad did not look like herself, but I knew who she was, even with the changed color of her skin and her hair was now blonde, she was still my Soledad, her head was thrown back, her arms stretched out behind her head, curving away from me, curving into each other, becoming a pillow for her slumber, a halo to her dreams. I looked at this goddess of my loins and I could barely breathe. I wanted to fuck her more than I had ever wanted to fuck her. I wanted to pry apart her legs and climb on top of her and pummel her shaved whitish, lilac colored pussy with my cock. But in my dream I could not move. I had no arms, no legs, no lungs for breathing, no fingers to tickle her twat, no cock to pierce her with, I was a lonely, lifeless head, a piece of carved stone, vaguely Grecian, a white marble bust perched on a black pedestal. And then I realized my Soledad was in danger, though from what I did not yet know. I cried out to my Soledad to wake her, to warn her, to plead with her, but she did not answer. I pleaded with her for a long time, but she did not stir. Darkness fell. Then a warm breeze blew through the darkness and the blue curtain shimmied and shivered and two long shadowy arms reached out from the darkness and wrapped themselves around my Soledad, one around her throat, gently caressing her, the other pushing up against her breasts, her breasts bobbling like two gray pigeons from the pressure, and she stirred, and then sighed, and then she said 'I am wet, my darling, oh so very wet,' and then she sighed again, a long luxurious sigh, and the shadowy arms pulled her towards the curtain and the curtain shimmied and shivered again, and then the leaves of three leaflets at the ends of the vines became excited and started chattering, and only then was it clear that the vines did not end in leaves at all, or maybe things had just changed, for at the end of each vine was now a thick, juicy, stubby green cock with two rounded, greenish balls on either side, and the cocks that were once leaves were angry at the intrusion of the shadowy arms, they were shouting, an almost incomprehensible din, especially as they were speaking in Lapuridan, 'leave her be,' they cried, 'she belongs to us, we must impregnate her, we are about to burst,' but the two shadowy arms ignored the cries of the green cocks and pulled my Soledad through the blue curtain to the other side, and all the while I was shouting for her to wake up, to resist this madness, to come back to me, but my words were lost in the commotion, and I was so agitated, so beside myself from grief, that I did not notice I was rocking my sculpted stone head back and forth on the black pedestal, picking up momentum, and then I toppled myself from the pedestal and that was that. Soledad was gone and the warm breeze had vanished and the blue curtain was as it had been before and the vines were vines once more, and I was lying there now on the ground where Soledad had been, looking up at the heavy, suffocating nighttime darkness, wondering what had happened, wondering if I would ever see my beloved Soledad again.

I don't know exactly how long I was looking at the darkness, exhausted, useless, a spent cartridge, before I realized the dream was over, or perhaps reality had simply shifted once again, like the fog disintegrating when the sun comes out. I did not remember where I was at first, but then I did. Soledad and the young teacher were talking softly in the candle light. The rest of the café was consumed by the darkness. It was a very romantic scene. It was just the right kind of light for a merengue, and then later a bolero. Soledad was talking about when she was a beautiful teenage goddess in the Pyrenees Mountains and why she left. I knew this story very well because it was from the beginning of our life together. The young teacher was lapping up every word.

"Most of what I am telling you took place during the war against the Fascists," she said. "It begins the same year the war began. I myself I was too young to bother much about the fighting. We lived in a small village in the mountains in the north of Spain. We knew it by the name of Elzaurdia, though it had other names as well. If you headed north from there you would find yourself in France in no time. It was a very dusty, rocky road that took you past a farm here and there and the cattle grazing and the chestnuts and the beech glowing in the sunlight and then through the forest where the sunlight was streaked, and so on like that. Many people used this road during the war to travel back and forth across the border because the Fascist patrols did not usually go up that far. Except sometimes you might see a patrol heading up into the mountains, but they always kept to the road, and they always returned very quickly to Bera. My brother said you could take the road all the way to Saint Jean and the sea, though how he knew this I did not know. It was a very small village where we lived, four or five streets, some of them cutting up the mountain side at steep angles, some of them cutting across. It was a village with many buildings crowded together in a very small space, white buildings with stone archways and stone patios underneath where the sun did not reach, and all of the buildings had red roofs and red shutters or green roofs and green shutters, and red geraniums and white roses hanging from the balconies, and every now and then a flag from before the war, it was very picturesque, like a postcard for the *turistas.* But truly there was very little color in my village, not like here with the buildings painted yellow and bright pink and turquoise and green. There everything was white. And there was no church, and my father did not believe in church for his daughters anyway. There was a very dark room near the back of our house, away from the morning sun, and there was an altar there, an ancient altar from before the time of my great-great-grandfather, and that is where we went on Sunday mornings to pray and the candles burning on the altar, and you could see where the smoke from the centuries had soured the color of the plaster ceiling. It was a place without words, a place of gloomy shadows dancing on the walls, and we would sit in the gloomy silence and it felt like the silence was crushing the life out of us, except every now and then we would hear a lonely red-billed chough somewhere outside, the *chee-ow, chee-ow, chee-ow, chee-ow* way up in the sky, or maybe very close, or sometimes the droning whir of an airplane, but very far away, the sudden sounds shattering the moment, shocking us back into our normal selves, and we would breathe deeply and smile at each other as if we had been delivered up from the grave. But then the silence would descend upon us once again and our smiles would disappear under the weight, and to stop our thoughts from hurling us into the abyss of insanity, which is a place, the old men used to say, where not even God would dare go by himself, we would fiddle with our beads of the rosary until midday, at which time Elsa would bring to us lunch in the cool shadows of the patio if it was summer, or in the embalming warmth of the kitchen if it was winter, a plate of pisto and fried eggs or some cold almond soup or pickled eggplant and a bit of grilled fish, and cut fruit when we could get it, and then butter buns and lemon cakes and tea, and sometimes the priest who came once a month to give us communion would take his lunch with us, my two sisters and my mother and myself, but every time we would sit there in the shade of the patio and the warm breezes blowing past in the summer, or huddled around the smoky, clawfoot stove and the wind whistling through the lonely streets in the winter, until my father and brother would return."

Soledad had left the table while she was telling her story, had gone behind the counter and fixed up a tray. She returned with coffees for all of us.

"It has the feeling of a very long night," she said. "Is this not so, Papi?"

"It is so my love," I said.

She sat down opposite the young teacher, her face glowing youthful in the candlelight.

"Everything we do follows us everywhere we go," she said.

"Yes, my love, it is just as you say. There is no escaping it."

We sat in silence drinking our coffees, Soledad and the young teacher at the table and the candlelight washing over them, myself sitting in the shadows on the other side of the café at a table by the plate glass window with the blinds down. I felt invisible in the shadows. It was very quiet, even for a Sunday evening. The radio had been turned off and there was no music anywhere you turned your ear, except for the occasional car whooshing past with space-age woofers blaring and the window glass rattling. The young teacher finished his coffee and pushed his saucer to the center of the table. He drank much too quickly. He was like most young men. He did not yet know how to savor things. One knows a great deal if one knows how to savor things. But perhaps he would learn.

"Where did your father and brother go?" he said.

Soledad smiled her bright, exploding sun smile.

"Why they had gone to church, of course," she said. "Every Sunday they would head down from Elzaurdia through the forest and then they would pass through a village or two and then follow the river and then another village and then they would go to church, and sometimes they would stay after to play *pelota*, and sometimes they would be gone all afternoon. They would take a small white van my father kept for hauling firewood, always there was a stack of firewood in the back, and one morning I decided I would hide in the back with the logs and see this church where my father and brother went. It was only a short way from Elzaurdia if you were the wind, but it seemed a very long time in the back of that van. My father and brother did not speak until the van had stopped and there was a bell ringing and my father said "say your prayers quickly to the Mother Maria, my son, so she is not angry with us for being late," and then my father and brother got out. All I could see of the church from the rear window of the van was a white wall and the brown timbers holding up the roof and a side door with a stone archway. I could hear the voice of the priest working his Latin and the tinkling of bells and the moaning people with their 'Amens' escaping through the cracks in the walls like smoke, and then the Mass was over and the people were streaming out, spreading along the outside of the church in a thin, wavering line, like a shadow when it is very hot and the air is melting, some of the young boys and the older men getting ready to play *pelota* against the white wall, but my father and brother had no interest in *pelota*, they were heading straight for the van, so I crouched down behind the logs once again."

"Did they find out you were hiding in the van?"

"Yes, I was found out," Soledad said. "It was, what is the word, very traumatic. But all of that happened much, much later. You will hear all of it, I promise, but you must have patient ears. Do you have patient ears? They are very difficult to grow for one so young."

"Yes," said the young teacher. "I mean I'll try."

Soledad laughed and the candlelight flickered.

"Good enough," she said.

Soledad took a long sip from her coffee.

"All of this happened the year I turned fourteen," she said.

The whole room settled back into darkness, except for Soledad's face, which was lit by the candle.

"I spent many Sunday mornings the next year traveling incognito in the back of my father's van. But it is not how you might think. On that very first day I learned that my father and brother never played *pelota* after Mass. Instead, my father drove the van to the other side of the village where there was a stone wall from the time of the Romans, the last visible reminder of a fortress, that was the story that went with the wall, and beyond the wall you could see patches of wild fennel and then a grove of walnut mixed with oak and beech and the silvery flash of a small stream where the men went fishing, but no one was fishing on that day. My father pulled off into the grass and parked alongside the wall beneath a towering chestnut tree. On the other side of the road, across from the tree and the wall, there was a long, two-story stone building, an immaculate stone building with a red-tiled roof and a wooden balcony on the second floor that had been freshly painted. At first I thought we had stopped at a fancy hotel for the Americans who came up from San Sebastián before heading to Pamplona. But there were no Americans coming up the road for the fishing because of the war. Yet I could see many cars parked along the side of the road and in the grass. I remember thinking how very beautiful this hotel was with the mountain rising up behind it and flowers all around. I had never before seen so many flowers. There were flowers everywhere, along the edge of the building, along the road, stuffed into small pots on the balcony, everywhere you looked, red gardenias, roses, blue gentian mixed in, but mostly there were hundreds of bright yellow sunflowers. I remember thinking how unusual for my father and brother to stop at a fancy hotel. And then I knew. They had not stopped at a fancy hotel. It was a brothel."

"A brothel!" said the young teacher.

"Life does not stop just because of a war."

The young teacher was lost in a world of disbelief.

"Should I tell him all of it?" said Soledad.

"Whatever you wish to tell him, my love," I said. "He is old enough, I am sure."

Soledad laughed again, and it was a juicy laugh this time and the candlelight seemed to grow brighter.

"Then I shall tell you all of it," she said. "Every word."

"What kind of father takes his son to a brothel?"

"It was the custom with many fathers where I grew up."

"How old was he, your brother?"

Soledad went over to the counter and came back with the coffee pot and filled our cups.

"My brother was seventeen," she said. "A few years older than I was, but he had been going for many years by then. That is just how it was. He was thirteen the first time. But it was not something we spoke of."

"Lucky thirteen," said the young teacher.

"Yes," she said. "But he was always lucky, my brother. I was the one who was not so lucky. At least when I was a young girl that is how it seemed."

She filled her own cup and sat down.

"Everything we do follows us everywhere we go," I said.

"Yes, my love, yes," she said, and she laughed. "And that is most especially true when it comes to this story."

We both laughed.

Then she turned her eyes to the young teacher once again. One could tell he would soon have become lost were not Soledad there to guide him.

"I could not believe where they were going," she said. "Even though, as I already said, this was quite common where I grew up. So I got out to follow them. They crossed the road and took a path around to the side of the building and went in through a large wooden door that looked like the door to a stable. I did not go in right away. I clung to the corner of the building, half-hidden by the shadows of a blackthorn tree, and waited, and then I heard a door open and close from the balcony and a woman appeared. She was wearing a blue corset that fit her very tightly around the middle and her breasts were spilling over, and she was very beautiful standing there on the balcony in the bright, cool sunlight, leaning over the railing. She had very brown hair, brown like dark coffee, and very white skin, like the white ivory keys of my father's piano, and she had bright blue eyes to match her corset. I had never seen anyone so beautiful. In my mind she had been lifted out from the pages of a fairytale and deposited there, in the mountains of my childhood, so that I would see her and fall in love with her. She was humming softly to herself and smoking a cigarette and from somewhere there was music, a lazy love song floating on the air. Then she took a very long drag, and the smoke was curling up around her face, and then she flicked the remains of the cigarette over the edge and plucked a red gardenia and put it in her hair, but as she did so she saw me standing there below. I had stepped out into the bright, cool sunlight when she came out. She smiled at me and plucked a second gardenia and tossed it over. Then she went back inside."

Soledad stopped for a moment, my beautiful goddess of the Pyrenees, sipped from her coffee and looked at the young teacher and smiled, and then she looked over at me sitting in the shadows, all but invisible, but not to her, and her eyes hooked into mine and suddenly I felt as if I were standing with her outside the brothel and the heavy sweet smell of gardenias in the air, looking up at the woman in the blue corset from so many years ago. We have become very close over the years, Soledad and I. She inhabits all of my stories, and I inhabit all of hers.

"I do not know how long I stood there looking up at the empty balcony," she went on. "I put the gardenia in my hair and looked up at the spot where the woman had stood. I forgot my father and my brother. To me they were on the other side of the world. I passed through the very same wooden door they had passed through only moments before, but they were not there. They had become like a midnight dream that one forgets in the morning. I remember it was very dark inside, so I stopped just inside the door, peering ahead down a long hallway and a lantern hanging from the ceiling. I could smell all sorts of smells mixed together, lavender and musk oil and citrus and cinnamon spice. The lantern cast a blueish light on the walls and I could see old posters from old bullfights with the matadors sticking their swords in the bulls and their red capes flying and the horses of the *picadores* in the background, but the capes looked blue in the dim, lantern light, and at the bottom of the posters you could see the times and dates and ticket prices. At the other end of the hallway, past the lantern and the posters, there was a second door, a heavy brown door, which I did not see at first, but it was open and I could hear people laughing and soft, sad music, so I went through. It was hard to tell where I was at first. It felt like I had stepped into the past, into a room from before the war. There were no windows, or they had been covered up. I could see many vacant tables pushed up against one side of the room, and half a dozen more set up in the middle like in a café, and on the other side of the room I could see stairs. There were two heavy brass lanterns hanging from the ceiling and a few floor lamps and people were sitting at the tables and drinking and laughing loud boisterous laughs and then running up the stairs, and in the corner by the stairs there was an old man playing a guitar, strumming softly and singing. He was sitting on the floor, barefoot, his legs crossed, his head bent over at an odd angle, an impossible angle, truly, as if he were unable to hear his own guitar playing unless he bent over close to the sound. He did not notice the people running up and down. He smelled of *absinthe*, a heavy sweet smell that covered him like a cloud. I was standing there, very close to him, looking at him, but he took no notice of me either. I was listening to him strumming and singing, and it was the same lazy love song I had heard outside. There was a halting tremor in his voice, a sense of loss and lingering regret that drew me towards him, kept me listening, but it was a feeling I did not fully understand. That is when I met the woman in the blue corset. She saw me standing there by the old man with the guitar and she saw the gardenia in my hair and smiled and took my hand and led me upstairs to her room. She told me to be quiet and sat me in a chair by the window. I could see the balcony outside and some red gardenias stuffed into a pot, and I could see my father's white van on the other side of the road. I do not remember her name, but she told me she had many things to teach me, and that the lessons would begin that very afternoon."

Soledad began to clear away the coffee cups, the coffee pot, while she spoke. She was a vision, my Soledad. It was like watching a dancer. Then she continued with her story.

"The woman in the blue corset taught me that the most powerful men in the world will do anything you ask, if only you promise they may someday untie your corset. And if you bite off their fingers when they think that day has arrived, if you threaten to cut off their manhood with a razor sharp knife and push them out the door and turn the key on their heavy, musty, sweet *absenta* breath, they will come crawling back every day afterwards on their knees, for weeks and weeks and weeks, at all hours of the day and night, troubadours singing their lonely love songs, vagabonds, exiles, refugees, phantoms floating on the wind, miscreants pleading with you to tell them what they have done to displease you, begging your eternal forgiveness. She taught me that we are the true *Toreros*, that most men are just *toros de lidia*, the fighting bulls. The horns they possess are illusions. Yes, yes, they can carve you to pieces if you get in their way, they can trample you to death if you are unlucky, if you do not know what you are doing, but they are easily turned aside these men who are just the fighting bulls, a single flash of a blue corset and they fall away into nothingness."

Soledad returned to the table with a new tray. This time it was not coffee. It was a bottle of clear white liquid with the label Suisse La Bleue, three glasses, a bowl of sugar cubes, a covered pitcher of ice water, and three slotted spoons. The young teacher did not notice the tray.

"And is Señor Mendoza just a fighting bull like you say?" he said.

"No, no, no," Soledad said, but she was smiling a sly, mischievous smile as she spoke. "You are going ahead of the story again. First we must drink to the fairytale of my childhood. We will drink *absenta*. It is a drink for very special occasions. But it is also for drinking at the drop of a hat. Then after the drinking you will hear how I was found out and what my father said. And then you will hear about my Papi and how we met and whether he is just a fighting bull or no."

Soledad poured Suisse La Bleue into each glass, but not too much, a few fingers. Then she lay a spoon directly across the top of each glass and placed a sugar cube in the middle of each spoon and poured the ice water over the cubes very slowly, drop by drop, the sugar beginning to melt, slipping through the slots in the spoons, the liquor becoming a hazy, whitish, milky cloud. It was the way the old ones prepared *absenta*. It was the fire of God burning across the sky. It was the way to heaven while you were still rooted to the earth.

"There," she said. "Now you must drink slowly, *absenta* was meant for a very long moment. Breathe it in slowly."

We began to drink.

"Yes, that's it. Be patient. I will keep our glasses filled as long as there is reason to breathe."

"As bitter as wormwood," I said.

We drank some more. We laughed.

"If you go to Spain, my young friend," I said, "do not drink *absenta* where the *turistas* drink. They will give you an extract of wormwood that is the color of emeralds and tell you it is made from the same recipe they used a hundred years ago. But what they say will be a lie. What they will give you will taste like goat piss. This is much, much better."

We laughed some more.

The young teacher drank his first glass far too quickly and gagged and laughed and begged for more. Soledad kept her promise. She told the rest of her story. She kept our glasses filled, though even I did not see how she managed this. She was everywhere at once, she was an exploding star, she was a milky, cloudy blur, filling our glasses, drinking her own, sitting at the table, telling her story, her face lit by the soft, cloudy light of the candle, her voice washing over us, through us, cleansing us, liberating us, burning away the ties that bind us to existence, her words seeping into the deepest, darkest, most forbidden corners of our souls, drop by drop by drop.

-13-

This is the rest of Soledad's story. It is in her own words, which are also my words, as best as I can remember them.

"The woman in the blue corset became my spiritual guide," Soledad said. "That is the best way to describe her. She was a mirror to my deepest felt desires, my captive femininity, my heart and soul. I soon became adept at disrobing in front of strange, lonely, heart-broken men. I helped them find their way back to themselves. I became a burlesque show, a Ziegfeld Follies girl, a Hollywood movie star. I let them take me in the hot, stinking heat with their hot, musty, sweet *absenta* breath, my swollen, bright pink pudendum swollen with their milk, again and again and again I let them take me till their faces collapsed in puddles of joy. I gave them intimacy. I gave them love. And so they forgot about the war for a while and the weary troubles they carried with them everywhere they went. When they left they swore I had transported them to Paris or Monte Carlo or Madrid or Prague, at least for a few hours, they would never have to travel beyond the borders of this brothel again to see the world, this is what they swore, and though I had never been to those cities, not even through magazines or books, in my tenderhearted, ignorant faith of a kitten, I imagined that without me walking the lonely streets of those fabulous, fairytale cities, making love to the thousands upon thousands of lonely, broken, soulless men who lived there, these cities were desolate, bleak, forbidding places.

"I could not have been happier. Which is all very strange when I think back on it. Spain was at war with itself. For three years the people of Spain were tearing at each other's throats. My own father was gone sometimes for as long as a week, fighting against the Fascists. But we were isolated from the war in our tiny village in the mountains. Even the patrols they sent into the mountains rarely came within shouting distance of our home. And so I had no thoughts of anything but my own happiness. There was nothing else to think about.

Ah, what a luxury that was. I had never known such joy. I was my own woman at the tender, foolish age of fourteen. But my mother took note of everything that happened. She did not know much about the world. She still put the dried leaves of laurel and ash and the heads of dried thistles around our home to protect us from evil spirits. But she knew about me. She knew I hid each Sunday morning in the back of my father's van. She knew I returned home each Sunday evening singing with a joyful heart, but she said nothing, not to me, not to my father, not to my sisters. I was a very foolish fourteen and I thought her silence meant I was in control of my own destiny. But what did I know of destiny. I was not in control. A few months after I began my Sunday pilgrimages to the brothel, the woman in the blue corset left for Madrid. I was worried for her traveling alone, but she only laughed. She would be fine. She said her grandmother had once lived in Madrid and had known all sorts of writers and musicians and even painters with names like Ortiz and Madrazo and Rosales. She said she desired that kind of stimulation. So she left.

"One month after that my brother discovered my secret. He was as much a voyeur as a young initiate, and after he had satisfied his lust on the girls my father had purchased for him, instead of drinking with the other men downstairs and talking sex and sports and politics, he would wander from room to room, slipping in through doors that had been left open a crack, peeking through keyholes, sliding in and out of the fractured afternoon shadows so he could glimpse the sweaty, naked bodies flailing away in the dim light, arms and legs wrapped effortlessly around arms and legs, vague, unrecognizable faces, some with their eyes closed or their eyelids half raised like window shades and their eyeballs rolled back, others with eyes bulging, anonymous faces, almost inhuman. My brother could not tear himself away from what he saw, they were like extraterrestrial squids, my brother said, swimming in the primordial sea.

"I do not remember the exact day my brother discovered me. It was very hot. I was with a lumbering goatherd who had once been in the army. My brother said he did not recognize me at first from where he was watching, the shadows and the angle and the dim light made it difficult to see who was who.

I was to him just another squid at first. Then my lumbering, perspiring goatherd was finished and pulled away, dripping and smiling and soiling the air with his breath. He pressed his tongue against the back of his teeth to get the last taste of my juices still lingering in his mouth, and my brother was all but vanished, ready to move on to the next room, the next squid, but then the goatherd said the memory of that afternoon would stay with him till the grave and beyond, till the end of time itself, and then he saluted as if he were speaking to a Colonel and blew me a kiss as if I were the Colonel's wife, and I laughed. My brother recognized my laughter and stopped in the doorway. The goatherd pushed past a few moments later, mopping the back of his neck with a soiled handkerchief, and nodded at my brother, grunting and smiling bigger than before, *'ella merece cada peseta,'* he said, before he disappeared down the hall. My brother went over to the window and pulled up the shade, and suddenly I was sitting there on the edge of the bed, my skin pasted over in places from the goatherd's milk, naked and vulnerable and alone in the dazzling sunlight.

"I also do not remember what my brother said when he discovered me. I remember he stood there a while, taking me in, devouring me with his eyes as if I were just another squid for consuming. But I do not remember what he said. But he did not expose me to our father. He did his best to make sure our father did not find out. He kept me hidden. Sometimes just after Mass my father would discover a buyer for some firewood, but my brother would steer him away from the sale and the back of the van, reminding him that it was Sunday and it was very bad luck to sell firewood on a Sunday, did he not remember the anger of Kristo at the money changers, and my father would agree and laugh with my brother at this burst of foolishness, and then climb up into the driver's seat. Sometimes on the way back my father was very drunk and he would crawl into the back to sleep and I would sit up with my brother in the front and he would drive. Every time my brother hit a rocky part in the road or went round a bend too fast my father would mumble something, 'is anything the matter Xavi, did we have an accident, did we blow out a tire, is it a patrol, if it is a patrol you must say the Marxists are ravening beasts, just like General Queipo says they are, you must say everyone who sides with the Marxists deserves to be stuck like a pig,' but my brother would say no Papa, there is no patrol, no accident, there are no worries, it was only a cow wandering across the road but it is back in the field, go back to sleep. And so it went for months and months.

"My brother kept me hidden from our father, he was my shield, my guardian angel, my savior, always keeping for me a lookout. In time, he started calling me a very great talent, a prodigious talent, he said, which made me blush, and soon thereafter he appointed himself the manager of my very great prodigious talent and he began to collect money from every unshaven *putero* I slept with. But I did not mind. I did not sleep with these men for the money, so what did I care if my brother put a few coins into his pocket. I had never been happier. I had never known such joy, as I have said. Truly, I did not even think about the money. But my happiness did not last. On the very last Sunday in August, one month after I had turned fifteen, my father discovered I was in the brothel. That day is burned into my memory. It was bleak and rainy that afternoon. The rain came down very hard and cold, though September had not yet arrived. There were very few men that day, and by the middle of the afternoon all the men were downstairs drinking and talking and getting drunk. They were talking about the war, and they were very free with their opinions because the war was now over, but they were not as free with their opinions as they might have been had the Republicans won.

"I was sitting alone in a chair by the window looking out at the potted geraniums and the wind was blowing very hard, the rain sweeping across the balcony. I could hear the booming of thunder up at the top of the mountain where the storms came across, but then I realized it was not thunder, it was too close for thunder, it was my father.

He was very angry. His voice was rumbling through the brothel. Even the floors and walls were shaking from his anger. I could not hear his words distinctly, it was like listening to the mad bellowing of a bull after the banderilleros have stabbed him in the neck with their harpoons, but I knew what he was saying, what else would he say, '*non da nire alaba, puta arrain atsegin duten usaina,*' again and again, 'where is my daughter, that whore who smells like fish,' and then '*xerra ireki i bere sabela eta amaiera jarri bere lotsa, nire lotsa,*' and I could hardly breathe his anger was so heavy, his words as sharp to me as the knife he surely held in his hand, do you wish to know what he was saying, he was saying, 'I will slice open her belly and put an end to her shame, which is my shame,' that is what he was saying, and I did not know what to do so I sat there and did nothing. I waited for my father and his knife. I waited to be cut open like a fish. What else could I do?

"But my father did not smash through the door. He did not even make it down the hall. I could hear the voices of my brother and the old man with the guitar pleading with my father to spare my life. The old man was saying 'a daughter such as this is not worthy of the aggravation, come, my old friend, share with me a bottle of *absenta*, I have a bottle just for occasions such as this, we will drink it all the way to the bottom,' and then my brother joining in, 'yes, Papa, yes, she is not for you to worry about, I will take care of her, I will take her to Saint Jean, I will drive her across the mountains and take her to Saint Jean,' and then the old man saying 'yes, yes, my old friend, trust your son to speak these words of wisdom, let him take the girl across the mountains, and you and I shall drink away the rest of the day, we shall drink to the death of your daughter, to the death of daughters everywhere,' and I could not hear what my father said after that, his voice became a strange, strangled thing, I would have said it was someone sobbing, except my father never once shed a tear for anything, and then I could hear the sounds of dragging feet and the voices of my father and the old man and my brother drifted away, and then there was a deep, hollow silence, except for the rain. It was a very black silence.

"Then the door did burst open, but it was not my father. It was my brother. He did not say a word. He did not have to, the look he gave me said everything. I got dressed. I pulled out a small woven handbag and started to pack my things, a blue corset, a silk robe, a brush with an ivory handle, a bottle of perfume one of my *puteros* had given me, but I could not get the buckle of my handbag to work. I dropped everything on the floor. I was trembling and my face was covered with a matte of tears and I could barely make out the shadow of my brother standing next to me.

"I do not remember leaving the room. I do not remember getting into the van and driving across the mountains. I remember it was dark. I remember the road was very erratic, going this way and that way, and always there was a small stream on one side or the other, and we crossed over several small bridges, but I was crying the whole way and it was raining very hard, and after a while I could not tell the difference between the sound of the streams and the rain and my tears. I remember thinking it was the darkest night I had ever known, the darkest night one could imagine. And then I remember my brother's voice coming at me through the leafy darkness of the mountains and the weaving darkness of the rain, a moaning, distant voice like the wind through the branches of the trees, the wild beech and the walnut and the pine and the oak, and his voice was saying, 'yes, this night is very dark, but in the morning you will see a brand new day and the sun shining on the ocean and you will see a brightness you have never seen before and you will feel very much better,' and then later he said 'the worst of it is over, Tomásénéa is just up ahead,' and I looked out the window and I could see the lights of a small farmhouse twinkling through the trees.

"We drove the whole night to get to Saint Jean, and in the morning it was just like my brother had said. The sun broke up over the mountains behind us, a great explosion of light whooshing past us, ahead of us. We drove past a few whitewashed cottages on the outskirts, their red roofs shining in the sunlight, and the land sloped away towards Saint Jean, and we could see a thousand red rooftops below and a bright green river dividing the town, and then the flashing wetness of the sea. The rooftops were still wet from the rain and they also flashed brightly in the sunlight, and I could hear the sounds of trucks moving and people shouting and I could smell the salt spray of the sea.

"I had never seen such a beautiful morning. My brother drove as far as he could go, across a small bridge and through the narrow streets twisting and turning, and when we turned away from the sun, the sharpness of the morning shadows cut across our path, and when we turned again into the sun, we were dazzled by the sudden brightness of tall, white buildings with red shutters and green shutters and blue awnings, ancient stone buildings that had been freshly painted and decorated with colorful flags, and everywhere we looked there were almond trees and eucalyptus trees and lime, their leaves ablaze with moisture, sparkling like diamonds. My brother parked along a stone wall with a view of the bay, and the air smelled fresh and clean from the rain, and from somewhere there was also the smell of bread baking. We could see a few empty benches and a few cork trees for shade and the beach stretching out beyond the stone wall and then the greenish blue waters of the bay. It was still early, so we sat there a while looking at the water and the shadows of a few people walking in the distance, and we did not speak. There was nothing to say. It was a glorious morning.

"I don't remember how long we sat in the van, but I do remember it started getting hot, even with the windows rolled down and the sea breeze blowing through.

"Then my brother said it was time to go, and I smiled and kissed him. He did not smile back. He gave me a handful of coins and some paper money and I stuffed them into my handbag and slid out of the van. My brother did not even wave goodbye, but I forgave him instantly. He drove down the street and turned into the shadows of an alley, and then he was gone, but I was still smiling. I was walking through the streets of Saint Jean by the sea and I was smiling and the air was flooded with a bright sunlight washing through my hair and across my face.

"The next thing I remember it was late afternoon and I was sitting at a small café. Across the street was the river and on the other side I could see a few blue colored long boats, fishing boats, one with the engine running and the smell of diesel in the air, heading out to sea, a few others anchored in the water, black cormorants resting on the sides or flapping their slender black wings and flying away or diving into the green river water and then coming back with a silver-blue fish. Another boat was tied to the dock and half a dozen men in yellow or green workpants and blue shirts were unloading the catch of the day. All of the men wore black caps. One was standing alongside the pilot house with a red hose in his hands and the water rushing out all over the deck. He was talking to another man who seemed to be in charge of the boat. I remember thinking how wonderful it was to sit there at this café and drink a coffee and watch the cormorants flying about and the blue fishing boats and the fishermen unloading fish, and I did not even mind the smells of the fish and the diesel mixing with my coffee. I remember thinking I was once again in control of my own destiny. But again I was mistaken."

Soledad then paused in the telling of her story and she looked directly at me, her eyes once again hooking into mine, and for a moment she and I were the only two people in the universe. We did not need words, she and I. We had lived inside each other for a very long time. Sometimes we even saw the world as if we were one person. Words were no longer necessary. Then she smiled a wistful but mischievous smile and laughed softly to herself. It was almost like she was sighing.

"*Urak dakarrena, urak darama,*' she said.

She filled our glasses with the last of the *absenta*.

"What water brings, water takes away."

We drank.

"I do not know what happened to the fisherman after they unloaded their fish," Soledad said. "I suppose they went somewhere to drink. In my memory the fishermen are just no longer there. They are suddenly and completely gone, and there sitting across from me was a smiling face. I did not see where he had come from. He simply appeared. We sat there looking at each other for a long time. We did not speak. There was no need of words. It felt like we had just met and it felt like we had known each other since before time began. I do not know quite how to explain it. You could say that our souls had been hovering around that café since before we were born, longing for that day to arrive. One moment I was looking at the fisherman on the other side of the river, and the next moment I was looking into the wistful, greenish-gray eyes of the most beautiful man I had ever seen. His eyes were like the color of a stormy sea. But it was like I had known him my entire life. It was like we had been born of the same womb at the same time. It was like I was looking at myself. We were linked from that moment in ways that are difficult to describe. We had lived and died a thousand times together. We knew each other's thoughts, each other's hopes and fears. We shared the same memories, the same history, the same struggles. Oh, maybe not in all the details. But the spirit of our lives, the pattern of our experiences, was the same. We shared the same soul. Do you know what he said to me sitting there at that café? The very first words he said when he sat down across from me. He was looking deeply into my eyes, so deeply it was like he was inside me, like we had switched places and he was looking out through my eyes, seeing the world as I saw the world, and then he said 'I have been searching for you all of my life. I have known you since before you were born. I was meant to find you sitting here, like this.' It was a most amazing thing to say, was it not? But the most amazing part was I was thinking the same words as he spoke them. They were his words, but they were also my words.

"We lingered at that café, my beloved and I, until well past dark and the orange street lamps came on and there was laughter and music coming from the row of windows behind us, above us, men and women leaning out over balcony railings, listening to the faraway smash of the waves along the coast, drinking wine and singing and laughing, drinking in the darkness of this village by the sea. But we paid little attention to what was going on around us. For a time we drank in each other instead of the world all around. But then he grew very serious. It was almost like he had become another person. We talked about the dangers of traveling in a foreign country. My beloved said it was best to travel under an assumed name, especially if you were an exile from Spain. He said he was no longer Spanish. He said he was now a Hungarian living in the Slovak Republic. Then he showed me a set of traveling papers that said he was born in a town called Ružomberok. But I did not like his Hungarian name. It was very difficult to pronounce, so I asked him if he would mind very much if I called him Xavier Mendoza, in spite of what his papers said, because Xavier Mendoza was the name of my brother, because I was still stinging from the loss of my life on the other side of the mountains and how quickly everything had changed, because the name of my brother, the name of my family, was my only possession and I did not wish to leave it behind, because when I looked into the stormy, greenish-gray eyes of my beloved, my one and only husband until the end of time, I thought for a moment I was looking at myself, because it pleased my vanity to do so, because I was crazy mad in love, because I knew without a doubt that my beloved was not one of the *toros de lidia*, one of the fighting bulls, that he was instead descended in spirit from the great *Toreros* of ancient Iberia, he was a man who wore his courage like iron, so he knew how to live his life to please himself, and what pleased him more than anything else was my happiness, for all of these reasons and more besides, I asked my beloved to keep and honor the name of my brother no matter what anyone thought, to become my husband under the name of Xavier Mendoza, and my beloved said 'Yes.' Then we finished our coffees and ordered fancy liqueurs and ate fancy dessert cakes, and then we shared a glass of *absenta*. I had never had so much to drink in my life and I could not walk. I could barely stand up. We did not stay that night at the Hotel Eskualduna with its ancient stone balconies and its thick, velvet curtains so no one could see into your room and a few well-heeled Spanish exiles sitting in the lobby, dreaming of revenge or new beginnings and then heading to the train station only a block away, or perhaps they would head into the tiny café on the first floor, which is where smugglers used to meet. That night we wanted nothing to do with Spanish exiles. That night we gave up everything Spanish except our names. We did not wish to remember the past. We wanted to focus on the future. So Xavier carried me to a tiny, three-story hotel three blocks from the river. The lobby of our hotel was bare except for a piece of red carpet spread across the floor and a couple of antique chairs made from black walnut against the bare plaster walls and a black walnut mirror with hooks for hanging coats. The light was very dim. Behind the front desk there was a row of small wooden boxes for the keys. There were also two cockatoos in the lobby, wild, unkempt, untethered cockatoos flying back and forth between the chairs and screaming out *'buenos dias señoritas'* as they flew, and I remember thinking what a strange and wonderful dream I was having, but it was not a dream. The proprietor appeared moments later and his face broke into a beaming grin when he saw my beloved Xavier holding me, my arms wrapped around his neck, like in the old movies when the groom carries the bride across the threshold, and he grabbed a green bottle and he spoke in French and he spoke very fast, but the meaning of his words was clear enough, 'welcome, my friends, yes, yes, welcome,' he seemed to be saying, 'a bottle of our finest champagne for the happy honeymoon couple, no, no, my friends, a bottle of champagne, please, please, do not worry, it is on the house,' and then he led us up the stairs.

"We woke up the next morning in a bed without sheets, the two of us naked, the empty bottle at the foot of the bed, our skin stained with the smell of sex and sour white wine, Xavier's arms still wrapped around me, the two of us curled up together like we had been sleeping that way for years. We woke just before dawn to the sounds of the cockatoos below and the proprietor grumbling and cursing, and then further away the sounds of the fishermen putting out to sea. Three days later we took the train from Saint Jean to Bayonne and then Bordeaux, and from there to Paris, but the whole trip was a blur of images, the train whizzing up the coast, the bright blue waters of the sea flashing by to the west and the stone architecture of bridges and towns, and then the train moved away from the coast and we were traveling through a sea of wheat on either side of the train and dark green trees in the distance, and the sunlight was now a deepening, amber color, and then the sea of wheat became a fortified castle high up on a hill and then more towns, more villages, people stopping to look at the train whizzing past, getting out of their cars or straddling their bicycles and waving at the train, schoolgirls wearing plaid skirts with tan blouses and matching sweaters and caps smiling from station platforms or cobblestone sidewalks, and then the ever-changing imagery of the wheat fields and the stone villages and the waiting traffic and the happy schoolgirls had all vanished, and the amber sunlight had vanished, and all I could see when I looked out the window was a reflection of myself and my Xavier, the two of us nestled close to each other, whispering to each other the rest of the journey, talking about love and children and making a new life for ourselves in America, and whether or not our destiny was written in the stars.

"Xavier said we would go to America and make for ourselves a new way of living. It would be our very own way, filled to the brim with an overflowing love. Our children would sing songs about our love. Our story would become a saga for the ages. This is what he said to me on the train to Paris. Then he produced a second set of traveling papers from his coat jacket pocket and handed them to me. 'We are both from the Slovak Republic,' he said. He was beaming. I asked him how he had managed to secure two sets of papers, but he just smiled and said we had friends everywhere. Then he covered my neck with kisses and moved up to my ears and then back down. I was so dizzy in the head that I almost passed out. I knew if we had not been still on the train we would surely have stripped to our skin and made love then and there. All of my fear and nervousness vanished. The next day we took a second train from Paris to La Havre, and the day after that we boarded a boat, the *Ile De France* with its two towering smokestacks painted red and black and the smell of burning oil and its flags fluttering in the breeze. We set sail for New York City at 5:05 in the morning. We have never looked back."

-14-

I have been thinking some more about our son who was born and who died. He was three days old, a tiny, oddly deformed shriveled-up peanut of a baby with short stubby arms and protruding shoulder blades that looked like folded-up wings, and skin stretched so tightly across his bones that you could see the blood moving through his veins. The day he died the world was struck by lightning. There was a great storm with greenish-gray clouds a mile high and great bolts of lightning like jagged pieces of bright burning glass to scorch the earth. My son was killed by a bolt of lightning. My son was killed by the hand of God. My Soledad said our son was an angel born by mistake, that was why he died.

God does not admit to mistakes, she said. I wanted nothing more to do with God after that, but she took my hand and pressed it to her heart and then we went to Gesù Church in downtown Miami to speak with a priest. Soledad wanted a fat, fancy stone with fat cherubs blowing trumpets and fancy words carved into it. My One and Only Angel, my Hope and my Salvation, the words would say. But we had no money for stones. She wanted a Mass of the Resurrection and a funeral parade with people dancing and singing like a carnival Sunday and the beating of the *txalaparta* sticks like the sound of horses running and a gilded coffin placed in a glass wagon drawn by two mules, and afterwards a lunch of barbecued lamb and everyone in the neighborhood visiting and sharing stories and warming our hearts with their laughter, all of this for our little one so he would be properly welcomed through the pearly gates. But a Mass such as this cost more than a fancy stone, and besides, the priest said it was not permitted to indulge in such extravagance, it was a sin before God, especially since our son had not been baptized.

Of course I did not believe him. I said to him there were many extravagant tombs in the cemetery, many fancy funerals, but he did not respond. Then I said there had been no time for a baptism, why would God be so hard on a little child, but he just shook his head, no, no, he said, his hands were tied, he was truly sorry, dreadfully sorry, there was no choice but to leave our son in the merciful hands of the angels and hope for the best. My heart was broken for my Soledad. As far as I am concerned, she is the heart and soul of Calle Ocho, but this priest did nothing to help her. I am certain he was a German priest. An ugly German priest with eyes like those of a frog. I have not been back to Gesù since. We found a renegade priest who lived in Riverside to say a few words over our son. Then Soledad lit a few candles and said a prayer to Saint Barbara, and I did not say a word because I could think of nothing to say, so I let Soledad be my voice. Then we buried our son in secret in a corner of Caballero Rivero beneath the branches of a flowering dogwood where the crepe myrtle grows along the fence. So I have been thinking about our dead son. Ever since we took the two teachers under our roof, I have seen the way Soledad has been looking at the younger one. I can see in her eyes that she believes our dead son has been reborn. He died before we even gave him a name, but I can see in Soledad's eyes that she believes he is sitting there now in the café, right there before us, a Mendoza through and through, but without the deformity of angel's wings. This is what I see in her eyes. He would have been older than the young teacher, a great deal older if one is to believe the passing of the years. But perhaps Soledad is right to think as she does. Perhaps she has no choice. Who can say? She is giving him all the love a mother could give a son, a love which she had buried away in the deepest parts of her heart and soul where not even the flowers of a flowering dogwood could reach, a love I swear I did not even know existed until this young teacher intruded upon our lives.

Except I did know. I have always known. And now I am feeling this same love for this same young teacher swelling inside me like a balloon. It is a tightness in my chest and a weakness in my eyes whenever I look at him, and I am surprised this balloon does not burst. Every day the feeling grows stronger and I am not sure what to do. How does one who has never been a father suddenly behave as one? I watch the way Soledad sits with the young teacher and talks with him and gently corrects his misconceptions about life, and every day now she makes for him a special plate of pisto and fried eggs or red beans and boiled pork or sometimes a nice juicy piece of albacore tuna grilled lightly with black sauce and a couple of beers to wash everything down, and always now they are talking late into the night about life in Miami, how there are plenty of schools in Miami if he still desires to teach the children, and if he does not wish to teach we can find him something to do around the café, and then she is asking if the older one is truly a teacher, the one the girls call Mick, she is surprised that someone with his appetite is given to teaching, and then she is warning him about the girls in the café, especially Gisela, who is now bringing in more customers than all the other girls combined and soon there will be cat fights, and also she is warning him about that crazy Rastafarian, Malachi, who is always hanging around, and sometimes she talks about life in Spain and her own childhood, but not often, and always they are drinking *absenta* the old way and listening to Latin pop on the radio and laughing and talking and laughing. She is smiling all of the time now, a thick, juicy, curvaceous smile, and even when we are alone in the darkness of our bed, I can feel her heart bouncing and I know she is smiling because she has found this young teacher who reminds her of our dead son, and who can say she is not right to think so, and then she kisses me good night, a gentle, loving, lingering kiss, and again she is reminding me that life is too short to question this gift of second chances.

-15-

Yesterday morning the young teacher accompanied me to Café La Nueva for lemon cakes and an espresso. It was Soledad's idea. It was she who planted it in my brain. I suspect it was she who planted it in the brain of the young teacher as well. But what is one to do? Soledad has only to ask and I would move mountains. Her smile is all the reward I need. So off we went. It was a very bright morning yesterday, but not too hot. We sat outside and the girl brought me a cup of espresso and a plate of lemon cakes and some chocolate sauce on the side. It is always the same girl, the same table by the almond trees, the same flirtatious small talk in the beginning. It is a ritual.

"Hola Señor Mendoza," she said.

"Hola a usted mi pequeño pollo."

She laughed.

"No, no, no Señor Mendoza. I am no small chicken anymore."

"Ah, you are mistaken," I said. "At my age, every woman I see is *mi pequeño pollo.*"

She laughed again.

Then she looked squarely at the young teacher and her eyes narrowed.

"It is all right," I said. "He will have the same."

The girl disappeared and then reappeared with a second

cup of espresso and a second plate of lemon cakes, but without the chocolate sauce. Then she whirled herself away, but she was looking over her shoulder as she went, smiling. "If there is anything you want, Señor Mendoza, anything at all, just ask."

We polished off both plates of lemon cakes in no time at all. Then we sat for a very long time. It is impossible to say how long we sat. But we did not say anything. In truth, it was a morning for watching traffic, so that is what we did. It was very noisy for a while with the amount of cars and vans and trucks crowded together, barreling down the street, the smell of diesel and gasoline swirling, the dust also swirling, and a few cars honking. The warblers from the almond trees were gone. Perhaps they were chased away by all the traffic. Then there were long periods of no traffic at all and it was strangely silent sitting there at the table by the almond trees because the birds were gone and there was very little to say just yet. We could still hear the people laughing and gossiping inside the café and coffee cups clinking, but these were muffled sounds, as if they were bubbling up from the bottom of the sea, or they had crossed the boundaries of eternity just to reach our ears. Then a few more trucks passed by and the girl brought us more espresso and another round of lemon cakes and the young teacher and I were deep in conversation.

"That was not the way he put it," the young teacher said. "It wasn't just any woman. It was a particular woman. He said if you loved a certain woman and wanted to fuck her and you were a priest, what would you do? Would you quit being a priest? Or would you stay a priest and fuck her when you could?"

"It is not a real question," I said.

"What do you mean it isn't real," the young teacher said. "He gives you a choice. Do you remain a priest or do you quit? The question is what do you choose."

"But this choice is meaningless. It is like at a carnival show. It is a shell with no substance inside. He gives up nothing. Either way he fucks the girl. No, no, if it were a real choice you would have to choose to either fuck the girl or give up fucking altogether? Now there is a choice that has some balls, no?"

The young teacher did not know how to respond. He sat there looking out at the street with a blank look on his face and said nothing. A few cars went by, and then a garbage truck, but that was all. Most of the traffic for the morning was finished. In the silence, after the last of the cars had passed, the birds returned to the almond trees. Awhitta whitta whitta whitta, they were saying. They were a Greek chorus with something to say whenever we paused for a breath.

"Who did you say asked you this question?" I said.

"He was an ex-priest. Ignacio or Ignatius or Immanuel. Something like that. There were two of them"

"Ah, two Jesuits. They are always asking such questions, the Jesuits. They are the worst of the religious. They are always pretending to search for the truth and they ask you such questions to trap you in their search, and all along they know there is no truth to discover."

"That sounds like them."

"And you, my young friend, I suppose you pretended to be honest but you were also playing a game, no?"

"Yes."

"And they found out?"

"No. I told them if I really wanted to be with the girl I would have to marry her. I said I would have to quit being Catholic. I said I would join the Episcopal Church. They didn't say much after that."

I could not help laughing.

"You rubbed their noses in their search for truth, these Jesuits," I said. "This is very healthy."

I laughed some more. The young teacher smiled.

I could hear the Greek chorus chattering from the almond trees.

"And who is this girl you wanted to marry?" I said.

"There was no girl."

"There is always a girl."

"No, I mean this was all theoretical to them. They go around asking this question all the time. It's a big joke. There was no girl."

"Yes, yes. This is the whole problem with all religions, is it not? They are always making their pitch in theoreticals. Hah! Priests pretending they know the mind of God."

"Ex-priests."

"Priests, ex-priests, they are all the same. They are jokesters. They are unwitting pawns of the Devil. They know nothing about God, that is for certain. And they know next to nothing about life and death. The rotten meat smell of it. The heavy, stinking, insufferably sweet-tasting smell of sex lingering in the air like old wine. Happy couples fucking late at night to the music of the bolero, young couples, older couples, men with men and women with women. The unthinking animal terror of being alone and rubbing the head of your cock until it bleeds because all you can do is masturbate. The heartache of living in a foreign country and you will never see the mountains where you were born ever again. You will never witness your father's death or know where he was buried, see the grave with your own eyes. God will not grant you this wish. But you know this. You give up the past and look to the future. You willingly embrace the struggle of a young man hoping to start a new life. But at the same time you are very much afraid, hiding inside your own language, uncertain how to speak this new language of fast cars and neon lights and greasy gamberros with their pockets stuffed full of new American dollars, uncertain how to get your hands on some of these dollars, uncertain if the luck you have always possessed will remain or if it will vanish under the weight of so many men looking for work, your hopes retreating into the shadows of these mountains made of concrete and steel, always just out of reach, unattainable, vanished, gone. It is a small miracle you were even allowed into this country with the immigration quotas that are in place, especially since your papers say you come from the Slovak Republic. 'Why didn't you head east towards the Soviets,' a man at Ellis Island sneers, 'there aren't enough jobs for those of us who are already here.' But you have forgotten this small miracle. You have been in this country three years, and still you are a young man finding his way, trying to find work. Your fears grow fat with the passing years. It is like looking at something through the magic of a magnifying glass. You take whatever odd jobs you can scrounge up, but the cities are flooded with exiles, refugees, for the whole world is now at war. But it is not enough. There are two mouths to feed and it is not enough. This is why you head south for Florida, for you and your beloved. You meet a man on a street corner handing out flyers. He says there are jobs in Florida, jobs building ships and rolling out ammunition, all kinds of jobs. He says they are in Pensacola and Jacksonville and Miami and Orlando, these jobs. You pick Miami because you like the name, and you pack up, you and your beloved, and head south, but you are still afraid. You start working for the Miami Shipbuilding Company but you are not yet an American citizen, but you have a piece of paper that says that you have a right to be in this country of free men, and so you work for the war effort, this is all you can do, but again you are afraid because the name on the paper is not your name. Your papers say you are Hungarian, but you are not Hungarian. You are Basque. You were born in Spain. You and your father fought against the Nationalists. But now you are afraid they will find out and you and your beloved might be deported, even though you have no idea who 'they' might be. And at the same time you are struggling with your own fears, which you never share with anyone, you are struggling also with the fears of your beloved, who has always wanted a child, but she is afraid that a child is a gift which God will not permit, however much she may desire one, but you cannot absorb her fears, you tell her to forget about children, but you do not really forget, but the years pass anyway, ten years pass under the bridge, then twelve years, and you have forgotten where you came from, you have always lived in this paradise called Florida with its strangely glowing sun and its pestilent heat, and then one day your beloved is giving birth in the back seat of a car parked along the side of a road, a narrow wet road cutting through a swamp, or a busy truck-filled road heading into the city. It does not matter. Your beloved is also a fugitive, disowned, an exile who will never again see the mountains where she was born, just like you, sitting in the back seat of your car, the heat of the midday sun beating down on the car and the air boiling inside and the leather seats searing her skin and her blood now boiling as well, spilling out across the leather. Your beloved screaming, an almost inhuman sound, unending, intolerable, like the glass of a thousand windows exploding, lacerating our ears. And then the unforgivable joy when the cord is cut and it no longer matters there was only a small pocket knife to do the cutting because you take your bloody son out of the car and hold him up in the air to show God, and he is shining red and glowing in the sunlight of this strangely glowing Florida sun, a defiant gesture, perhaps, but you are certain that God has blessed you beyond all measure. To these charlatans, to these men who know nothing and next to nothing, life is just waiting for the day when you put a cold body into the ground. Death to them is spitting out a few words to help us forget about the dead, to get on with the business of being alone, but their words evaporate like a summer mist as soon as they are spoken."

We were both silent for a while. We could not breathe. We could not hear the warblers chirping from the almond trees. We were caught in a vacuum of silence. A vast black hole eating up the universe. Then the young teacher blinked at me in the sunlight the way a small bird blinks and we were breathing normally once again.

"Men like these know nothing at all," I said.

"I am sorry. You were talking about your own life?"

"Yes. But it was many years ago."

"I did not know."

"It is all right. Besides, I am no longer certain if what I remember actually took place.

". . . ."

"Sometimes it feels like my life exists only in my own imagination. You will have to forgive an old man when he starts to ramble."

-16-

Sometime later it was the young teacher's turn to ramble. I wasn't sure if was the same day or if months had passed. I wasn't sure if his story was the product of one conversation or a dozen. After that first morning, the young teacher and I made many, many pilgrimages to Café La Nueva, and we had many long talks that stretched into the late hours of the afternoon. Hours and hours we talked, and after a while it was difficult to separate one day from another. The days blurred together. The young teacher said all he could think about was a young woman he knew when he was teaching and how he was madly in love with her but could never get up enough nerve to tell her, and then he was dismissed from the school and he never saw her again. He said he had come down to Miami to forget her, but this strategy had failed. All he had been thinking about for months and months was this girl. He said he wanted to talk to her, explain everything that had happened, but he never did.

    Anyone with half a brain could see this lumbering mastiff of a young lunatic was overwhelmed with the grief of a broken heart. You could not deny this truth. In spite of Soledad's motherly attention, his beard had become much worse than when he had first arrived. It was matted from sweat and smelled of stale beer and old coffee and cigarette smoke. His eyes had narrowed, becoming tiny pinpricks of blackness surrounded by a halo of red. He was up at all hours of the night, wandering up and down the hallway that went past our bedroom, into the green-tiled bathroom and you could hear the water running, the water spurting out in short bursts from the brass spigot because the pressure was no good, and then the sound of gargling and spitting and then the toilet running, and then back down the hall, sometimes tripping over the folds of the beaded imitation Persian runner in the hallway, slamming against the wall with a heavy thud and the photos hanging on the wall in our bedroom rattling, back and forth all night he would go, and sometimes if you looked out the window you could see him sitting out back in a rusted lawn chair in one of the weedy, spongey, grassy patches, an island in a sea of cracked cement and broken glass and soda tabs and the glass glittering in the moonlight, and he would be sitting there without a shirt, his pale white skin a ghostly white, looking up at the darkly glowing sky, a three story building on the other side of the alley and the windows on the third floor reflecting a few neon blues and greens from Eighth Street, and he would be sitting in the lawn chair for hours looking up at the sky but not moving, his mouth open, the sounds of a merengue or a bolero or sometimes even a tango floating on the wind, the sounds of people laughing, his head cocked to one side, as if he were a dog listening to other dogs howling at the moon.

Life is always very ironic. But this is true only if one has eyes to see and ears to hear. It is like the words of the old poet, 'those who were seen dancing were thought insane by those who could not hear the music.' My life has become like that. My life has become very ironic. The more time I spent with the young teacher at Café La Nueva, the longer I sat at that small wooden table next to the almond trees listening to his story, the more I realized that he and I were both cut from the same bolt.

-17-

"I kept wanting to talk to Tommie," he said. "I wanted to explain everything. I wanted to see where she stood and if there was any hope, but Mick just laughed at me, he said there were plenty of fresh tuna in the sea, so why worry about one that got away, and then he said 'Get real, Lauterbach, if she had really wanted to be with you she would've come looking for you,' and that just sort of gutted me to the bone, I mean what could I say to that, I mean the facts are the goddamn facts. After that Mick started taking me to clubs to get my mind off my troubles, strip clubs mostly with names like Club Zanzibar and Brandy's and The Pau Pau Club and The Alley Cat and Coco's Lounge on the Edge of the World, which Mick just had to go there with a name like that. But they were all pretty much the same. The same spinning red or purple lights and girls strutting across a stage with a shiny black linoleum floor and mirrors along the back and a pole in the middle. Smoke-filled lounges serving drinks till three in the morning or four or five, highball glasses of whiskey-and-Coke and rum-and-Coke and bottles of beer, trays and trays of alcohol floating from table to table and the men lining up along the stage with drinks in their hands, leaning over to slip a dollar bill inside a garter strap, their fingers lingering long enough to touch some naked skin, just their fingertips, their erections almost bursting through their pants. Lap dances everywhere you looked, friction dances for a little extra, the women in only their thongs and spiked high heels and blue pasties, bending over nice and slow, wiggling their asses closer and closer and then turning and pushing their titties into happy, eager faces, the men breathing in the lavender or lilac or lemon or cherry blossom smell of cheap perfume, and then the girls turning again before the men got too frisky and wiggling their asses even closer, rubbing up against hundreds and hundreds of hidden cocks until the men closed their eyes and moaned.

Some of the clubs had smaller VIP rooms like bathroom stalls with couches where you could get comfortable. Some had private booths with girls behind glass and when you paid your twenty bucks a spotlight would come up and a girl would start to grind away like a drugged marionette, her naked cheeks pressed hard against the glass, and she would finger herself so you could see her pussy and how wet she was. The clubs north of downtown catered to lonely businessmen and bachelor parties and off-duty police, and every once in a while you'd see a few Navy guys looking to blow off some steam or a Coast Guard recruit. Thugs and drug dealers and motorcycle gangs had taken over the joints south along Dixie Highway. The beach was for tourists and college kids. We went to all of them.

We spent most of Mick's savings and all of my severance buying drinks and watching girls jiggling their asses and squeezing their tits together and dripping with wet smiles and shaking a few drops our way, all for a few bucks. We stayed in cheap, concrete slab motels if we slept at all. It was the same everywhere we went. I have never been so fucking out-of-my-mind depressed in all my life. Nobody's kidding anybody in a fucking strip club. Most nights I wanted to climb into one of those cherry red dumpsters you see in alleyways all over and curl up with the garbage, and if I died before morning it would have been a good thing.

The very first night we went out we hit a club called The Cocodrilo Club a few miles south of Coral Gables. My skin was crawling the moment we stepped inside, like there was lice dripping from the ceiling, and every time one of the girls smiled at me I wanted to wash my hands or my arms or my face, whatever part of my body the girl had scorched with her eyes. Those first couple of weeks I couldn't even look at the girls for more than a few seconds, and then later I mostly just looked at their faces, but I was trying to get them to look into my eyes. I wanted them to see that I really didn't want to be there, that I was embarrassed to sit there watching them peel down to their skin, that it was Mick, a counterfeit Mexican revolutionary with an over-sized libido, who had dragged me inside, I wouldn't have invaded their privacy otherwise, I wanted them to see that I was different, I wanted them to see that I was still in love with Tommie Rodriguez and that I would have given anything to be able to call her on the phone or write her a letter, a long handwritten love letter like they wrote in the 19th century, just to tell her how much I really loved her and what had happened at the school and how I didn't really want to be down here in south Florida going from strip club to strip club in search of whatever, I couldn't even begin to guess, not even God knew for certain what Mick and I were up to, but as soon as I figured out how to wake up from this twisted nightmare of a movie, I'd load up my junky white Toyota and head back to the beach house and maybe we could try again. That's what I wanted them to see when they looked at me. That's what I wanted to say to Tommie. But even when I did manage to catch the eyes of one of the girls, it was only for a few seconds, and the eyes were always the same, sort of glazed over, unfocused, hesitating for a moment, but only because I had invaded their line of sight, and then the eyes moving on, mechanical zombie eyes that could only see movement.

"I never did get used to going to those strip clubs. There were too many people walking around with those mechanical zombie eyes, the girls dancing, the men watching the girls dancing, the bouncers flexing their forearms, smiling at the drunken bastards walking in and out, throwing a few quick good-natured punches at the air, the bartenders mixing highballs behind the bar. Everybody with their eyes stretched wide open, held open with tiny metal spikes was more like it, their eyes clicking with a mechanical click, click, click as they looked this way and that, but nobody could see a thing. I was sick to my stomach most of the time. I was ashamed of myself. I kept thinking about Tommie and what she would have thought seeing me in one of those clubs, and I wanted to write that goddamn letter or pick up the phone, but I never did. The nights kept clicking by, like a movie that's been speeded up, and with each passing frame I felt a little more disconnected from the world, a little more outside myself, and after a while it seemed that Tommie was something I had dreamed up, that she had never existed at all. My only reality was going to strip clubs with Mick and drinking till my eyes went numb, and most days I never even saw the sun, and when I did wake up during the day, everything tasted of salt, and it was so blurry and muffled I thought I was living at the bottom of the sea. Of course Mick didn't give two shits about what I was going through. Every time I tried to talk to him about it he just gave me a blank stare and ordered another drink. It was like bats or night birds flying out of my mouth instead of words. So I caved. I gave in. I dove head first into the spinning wormhole of my imagination and became somebody else. If Mick didn't give two shits then I wouldn't either. But I was just pretending. There was a part of me deep down inside that hadn't changed at all. It was the part of me that was sick of the way my life had turned out. The purest part of me. The part of me disgusted with myself. But what the fuck was I going to do?

And then one night I started thinking that if I only had a gun, my troubles would be over, problem solved with a flashing bullet, my brains splattered all over the wall of some pathetic, nameless club, because it seemed poetic justice to blow myself away in a strip club with the meathead bouncers grinning their stupid meat-eating, shit-eating grins and the zombie girls wondering what the fuck had just happened and then seeing all the blood and screaming and running for their dressing rooms. One fucking bullet and my problems would be solved. I would be somebody else's problem.

"I don't remember exactly when I started thinking like this. You have to be pretty much chemically imbalanced to go down that road. You have to be seeing tiny yellow worms swimming around in your soup and crazy shit like that. You have to be pretty fucked up. But I do remember where I was when this chemically induced epiphany first struck. Mick and I had gone to some shack south of the city that didn't even have a name. Just a pink neon sign that said 'Girls! Girls! Girls!' I don't remember how we even found out about the place. Probably Mick thumbing through the yellow pages. We got there around ten o'clock and went inside and it was pretty dead. It looked like somebody's garage with white cinderblock walls and bright white fluorescent lights, which must have been the house lights because they were way too bright for stripping, and a cement floor they had painted a shiny gray color and if you hit a wet spot you could barely keep your footing. There were a dozen black tables with black chairs scattered about, but they were mostly empty. We sat down and ordered whiskey. We sat down directly in front of a tiny stage crammed into the corner, a couple of rows back. The stage was maybe two feet above the shiny gray floor, without even one mirror to give it depth, without even a disco ball or glittery stars painted on the wall to give you something to think about if the girls couldn't hold your attention. Next to the stage there was an opening in the wall with a black curtain pulled across.

"We finished our drinks and ordered some more. There was only one other guy in the joint, an old wino with his own brown paper bag sitting in the back, staring out at the world without even blinking, talking an undecipherable gibberish to the empty chair beside him. We could hardly taste the alcohol in our drinks, but then we had been drinking since five o'clock so pretty much everything tasted like water. The DJ put on a George Thorogood tune with George singing in that scratchy voice of his about how he liked to drink alone, with nobody else, and we were looking at the old wino and laughing at the irony of it all, and then the house lights snapped off and a blue spotlight zoomed in on the curtain. You could see the dust floating in the air from the spotlight and a girl stepped out into the particles of dust. I don't know if you could really call her a girl. She seemed more like thirty-five, and when I saw her in the fluorescent light later on she seemed closer to fifty. She didn't have a clue how to dance to a George Thorogood tune. She probably didn't have a clue about dancing in general. George's tune played pretty well for a burlesque, which surprised me, but this girl couldn't make it work. She kept running into the pole, and when she grabbed it for a spin she lost her grip and stumbled backwards into the wall. The wino in the back was trying to sing along with George and drinking from his bag at the same time. A couple of grease monkeys who had just got off work came in and sat down right in front and started hooting and whistling, and the girl was encouraged by this and she started to do better. She regained her balance. She swung herself around the pole and tilted her head back so we could see her face upside down, and then she curled herself into a ball and twisted and turned and popped up again and then down and pushed her ass up into the air and flexed her cheeks, and then she was up on her feet again, but she had moved away from the pole, and she was doing something that looked like a Texas two-step along the edge of the stage, first one way and then the other, tapping her toes out and then in and gyrating her hips. After a while she almost seemed graceful moving through that dusty blue light, like she was swimming under water. But all the same it was pretty murky water with all of the dust particles floating in the air. You could hardly see a thing. Then the grease monkeys were shouting at the girl, telling her to take it all off. She flung her top into the audience and it landed on an empty chair, and then she started twisting her torso violently, trying to get her titties to jiggle, but her titties seemed fairly small and flat, though it was hard to tell in that murky blue light, but they sure as hell didn't move a whole lot in spite of her efforts. George was into another tune by then and he was singing about a landlady asking him for rent. This second tune wasn't nearly as good as the first for stripping, but by then the girl was really into it so nobody cared, and when she tossed her g-string into the audience the two grease monkey's stood up to catch it but it sailed past them and landed in my lap.

"I wasn't expecting the g-string. Mick started laughing, and the waitress who had just brought us another round started laughing too. 'That's your ticket, Lauterbach,' he said. 'Manna from fucking heaven.' The two grease monkeys glared at us, their eyes glowing a bright yellow-green in the murky blue light. You could tell they were regulars. Mick raised his new whiskey-and-Coke in the air and nodded in their direction and some of it sloshed on the table but Mick kept looking at them, grinning, and the two grease monkeys sat back down and looked back at the stage. Old George was done singing and the white fluorescent lights snapped back on and the girl had retrieved her top from the chair and was waiting by the black curtain, looking over at me with a helpless, yearning expression in her eyes. Mick gave me a nudge and I stumbled up from my chair, and then we were standing face to face, me and the girl, and I could see for the first time how really old and dried up she looked. Her pupils expanded and her helpless, yearning expression hijacked her entire face. She said they were running a special that night, three songs for the price of two, and then she slid her g-string from my fingers, gently, as if she didn't want to spook me, and pointed at two bathroom-type stalls that looked like closets on the other side of the room. I hadn't seen the stalls when we first came in. They were painted gray like the floor, which added to the impression that we were in somebody's garage. She said she'd be there in five minutes, she needed to change her costume. Then she tugged on my shirt sleeve so she could whisper into my ear, leaning so close I almost gagged from the fruity, peach-smelling teenage perfume she was wearing. 'Thank you,' she said.

"I don't know what I was thinking. I guess I wasn't thinking a goddamn thing. I wished I had gone back to Mick and the table, but I didn't. I found myself waiting inside the stall, sitting in a wooden chair with rounded arms and a leather seat cushion, like it had been stolen from a legal aid lawyer's waiting room. There was only the one chair, and a single light bulb with a string screwed to the wall. It was also very hot, very stuffy. The air conditioning, which wasn't very good to begin with, didn't reach into the stalls, but I was fairly drunk, so I didn't notice too much. The DJ started playing some country music, which presumably meant that another dancer had taken the stage. There wasn't a speaker in the stall so the music sounded sort of muffled, but it was loud enough that it probably didn't matter all that much, especially with a naked girl. I didn't have to wait too long and then the door opened and the girl slipped inside. She was wearing a black mini-skirt with pink sequins but without panties, and a black leather vest open down the middle and a cowboy hat and cowboy boots. She didn't waste any time. She started spinning around in slow motion, peeling back her vest and then dropping it on the floor, and then sliding her skirt down and kicking it away, and after a while I forgot how much time had passed, how many country songs the DJ had played, and then some rock-and-roll songs, and then the blues, all I knew was this thirty-five-year-old dancer who looked fifty was grinding away at me with her ass, only I didn't really care how old she looked, she was pushing her ass down into my crotch, wiggling back and forth, trying to find my cock, and then she started emitting a soft cooing sound, ooooohhing and ahhhhhing about how big I was and how good I felt even hidden away like I was, and I must admit I was ready to burst, I mean I was throbbing, it was almost becoming painful, and she must have sensed my agitation because she said I could take it out if I wanted, it was okay with her, and before I could say a word she had unbuttoned my jeans so I could breathe, my cock pushing itself out through my open fly, and then she was back at it, sliding the meat of her ass up and down, but with great almost tender delicacy, great precision, the tip of my cock glowing a bright red against her pale white perspiring skin, even in the dim light of a single light bulb the contrast was unmistakable, my shaft cushioned by the folds of her cheeks, and then her soft cooing became deeper, heavier, a low moaning late night sound like a lonely saxophone wailing in the distance, a single note hesitating, wavering, and she said I could stick it in if I wanted, she hadn't been with anyone in a very long time and it would feel so good to take me inside, I could have her for as long as I wanted, we could go somewhere else, she only lived a few miles away, we could spend the whole night together, if I wanted. But at precisely that moment I noticed the music had stopped. I could hear the clicking, humming buzz of the fluorescent lights and I started wondering when she would have to go back on the main stage again, and then I suddenly realized I wanted nothing to do with this woman. My cock wilted in an instant and I buttoned my jeans as quickly as I could. A great gnawing wave of disgust flowed through me. In another few seconds I would surely have squirted all over that woman's bouncing, sweaty ass, and I wondered if in coming so close to a climax in such a place, if God would spare me his vengeance, or if I might come down with some strange, slaggy tropical fish disease because of my lack of will power. Then I thought of Tommie and I wondered what she would say. I thought God might as well strike me down because once Tommie knew I had let a naked stripper push her naked ass against my naked cock, well that would be that, as they say. She would never look at me again. Just the thought of me would send her retching.

"The girl didn't say anything at first. She was sitting there on the gray garage-type floor on her black leather vest. She was still wearing her cowboy hat and boots and she sat there with her arms on her knees and her legs wide open. I could see how very old and dried up she was all over. I would never have been able to push my way inside her, no matter how big and hard I was. She had shaved her pussy, but it seemed like it was glued shut. I wondered again what I was doing there, but I just sat there in the chair, looking at her. She asked me what was wrong, didn't I like her, and she waited for me to say something but I didn't say a word. The clicking and buzzing sound of the fluorescent lights seemed to grow louder in the silence. Then her eyes misted over with that helpless, yearning expression again and she said she wasn't very good at this, she was sorry, this was only her third night, she had been an administrative assistant for a local bank for twenty-five years but then the bank merged with a bigger one from up north and she lost her job. She hadn't worked in six months. She didn't know what else to do so she took this job. She didn't know dancing was so hard. They only made their money on tips. The three songs for the price of two, well, all that money had to go to the house. That's the way it worked. She had him down for six songs in all, which came to ninety bucks, but all that went to the house, it wasn't hers. She said she was sorry if she had done something wrong, she didn't know what else to do. It looked like she was about to cry. The fluorescent lights snapped off and another two songs came on, which meant I was probably in for another thirty, but I didn't care. I pulled out my wallet and started peeling off bills, and all the while I was saying if she wanted to stick to this business she should find herself a better club to work in. I gave her three-hundred dollars and told her she should keep it all and clear out before they knew she was leaving and never come back. It was all the money I had left. Later I told Mick about it and he laughed a good long belly laugh, but it was also a welcoming laugh, like I had just been initiated into some sort of secret society. He said she was one hell of a professional to take me for three-hundred with that sob story. 'Congratulations, Lauterbach! You've just been fucking baptized.' That's when I started thinking about guns and bullets and splattering my brains all over the walls of some strip club. I thought maybe I'd do it in that garage-type hole-in-the-wall where my baptism had occurred, but I didn't because of the possibility that Mick was right about that girl and as soon as we would walk in we'd see her taking advantage of some other poor dope who didn't know any better. That was the worst part of it. I wanted to think of that woman as a damsel in distress and I had helped her find a better life before she had thrown everything away, like I had. I needed to believe that she had taken my money and was working in a Ruby Tuesdays and her kids were happy because she was home at night, and I didn't even know if she had any kids, but I sure as hell hoped she did. But deep down I knew Mick was probably right.

"I had to sell my Toyota after that just to goddamn eat. But I stopped going to strip clubs. Mick tried to get me to go a few more times but I wouldn't do it. I just sat by the window in whatever cement slab motel we had ended up in that day, looking out of a second-story window at the traffic rolling by, eating Chinese takeout, listening to *The Jetsons* or some other kid's cartoon on the television because you couldn't watch a damn thing without getting a headache, because the color settings were screwed up so everything on the screen was red. After a while Mick stopped trying, and then he gave up the clubs himself. He said we needed a change of scenery. He said maybe we'd overdone it with the strip clubs and getting blasted every night. We were no closer to finding any goddamn paradise than when we had first come to Miami, so what the fuck. But I didn't believe him by then. I was still fairly certain Mick didn't give two shits about anything that happened to me. But I figured it was probably a good idea to go somewhere else. I wasn't so deeply mired in a tragic, depressed almost vegetative state that I wanted to end my days in a cheap, cheezy, Miami motel. I knew the universe would help me find a better place to die. Two days later we were eating at The Patagonian Café and that crazy fucking bastard Malachi pulled a gun on us. I remember being puzzled by the fact that Mick was the one with the gun in his mouth and not me."

-18-

I am standing on a stone bridge looking at the water and I have been standing here for quite some time, it seems, looking at this strangely tinted water, but I do not remember how I got here. It is a lagoon of some sort. The water is sort of a teal color for a while, and then it changes back to pure blue. The two teachers are standing there with me, one on either side. It is funny but I can never remember their names. But it does not matter. A failing memory is one of the advantages of old age. The younger one is looking down at the strangely tinted water the same as I am, watching small eddies swirling past, or perhaps they are the bubbles of tiny fish. I cannot see where the bubbles are coming from. They head out away from the bridge and disappear in the dazzling sunlight on the surface. The younger teacher says something about how fabulous this place is. He wonders how long it has been here. But I do not answer him. I do not even know where we are. The older teacher is not looking down at the water. I forget about the water and the younger teacher and I follow the eyes of the older teacher. He is shading his eyes because of the sun. It is a very bright sun. It is early afternoon, maybe two o'clock. The older teacher is looking across the lagoon at a great stone building with a red-tile roof. It is an immaculate building with vegetation all around, palm trees and oak trees and magnolia and some pine mixed in. The building is somehow a part of my memories, but I cannot place it. Down from the building there is a red gate and there are hundreds of children on the other side. It seems strange that the gate is closed in the middle of the day and that we are on the inside and all of these children are on the outside. I have no memory of passing through the red gate myself. There seem to be many gaps in my memories. The world all around is strange and fluid like a dream is sometimes strange and fluid and you are expecting things to change in an instant, you are waiting for the change, and then it happens. But I am standing on this bridge and nothing happens immediately. The children are waiting to go through. The gatekeeper is late opening up and the children are fidgeting, laughing, running in circles like stray dogs. When I was a boy my father would take me into the mountains and if we saw a stray dog we would shoot it. My father said there were some men who made no distinction between dogs and children. During the war, many dogs and children were shot. But it is different in America. No one is shooting at these children. They seem fairly safe from bullets. All the same, I am wondering what they are doing over there on the other side of the red gate and if they are aware of the potential danger of men shooting them like dogs, and then it occurs to me that perhaps this is the reason I am standing there on the bridge, yes, perhaps I am supposed to watch over these children like stray dogs who are unaware even that they are being watched, perhaps I am supposed to watch over these children as a loving father would watch over them, once the gatekeeper opens the gate and lets them through, yes, that is certainly something I am capable of doing, I am deep down at the bottom of my soul a father, in spite of everything else I might have been or might have done or didn't do, even though I have no children of my own. Then the gatekeeper opens the gate and the children roar past him as a waterfall roars and I close my eyes to listen to the sound, and it is a comforting sound, soothing because it is vibrant, full of energy, so I keep my eyes closed for a while, squeezing in the darkness and the sense that I am still alive, but as I am standing there with my eyes closed, listening to the waterfall roar of the children passing through the gate, it suddenly occurs to me that perhaps I have died, perhaps I am already dead, perhaps this is why I do not remember where I am or why or how I got here, and then I am smiling a slightly puzzled smile. If one were looking at me, I suspect it would seem I had a touch of indigestion. If I am dead, I think to myself, it is nothing like I imagined death to be, I am still myself. I am untouched. And yet I am not myself. I am frozen in space and time, I am weightless, and as I move further inward, contemplating my weightlessness and the possibility of my death, the memory of the children passing through the gate vanishes as completely as if those children had never been born. But I am untroubled by this. I do not even feel the blank gap of yet another lost memory. I feel that everything is contained within this moment. It is now, suddenly, as if nothing else in the history of the world has ever existed, there is no buried past arcing away behind me and dropping off into sudden darkness, no labyrinth of pathways spreading out before me, offering the imagined solace and brittle hope of many possible futures. More and more I am struck with the notion that I am truly and irrevocably dead. The feeling becomes noticeably stronger. The air is laced with the sickly, sweet smell of gardenias. The feeling is itself something more than a premonition. It is almost a conviction. It is a feeling of being self-contained, existing only within the boundaries of oneself, impaled by the horn of my own thoughts, my memories bleeding out, but slowly, the moment stretching to infinity, the clocks of the world now useless, like deflated balloons that have spun around aimlessly for a while and then, sputtering, float lazily to the ground, their mechanical parts now draped over rocks and seashells, this is what death is. Then I remember the two teachers. I can hear them breathing. I can feel something like concern emanating from their lungs as they push out each breath. But it is more than concern. It is also agitation. I am wondering if they are also discovering their own deaths, surprised that this is what death feels like. I open my eyes and it is not as bright as I had expected. It is a strange, muted light that bends easily in the wind. It is like looking at the world through funhouse goggles. The faces of the teachers have become elongated, they have mushroomed into vicious, snarling snouts, they are in need of muzzles, and their eyes are beginning to bubble over with wonder at how their faces have changed. They are seeking answers, but I have no answers to give. Then the sun grows very hot on my cheeks and I feel flushed and thirsty, and their bubbling eyes melt away, and then their snarling, unmuzzled snouts dissolve, and all that remains is a shapeless piece of flesh where their faces had been and two black gaping holes instead of mouths, it is like they are screaming in agony, but they are not screaming, they are beyond pain, beyond words, they have become detached, weightless, like floating in space, and I am floating right there with them, suspended in the liquid gel of eternity, and then suddenly everything is moving again, very, very fast, so fast everything is mixing together, merging, converging, returning to some vague, watery point on the horizon, light and sound, the future and the past, the whooshing muddy rivers of all of us, the gray clouds that circle the earth with the satellites and the sun-speckled waters of the Atlantic below and the boats bringing in their catch and the matadors with their flashing red capes who flick their wrists and easily turn the fighting bulls aside and then plunge in with their swords gleaming and the blood splattering and the crowds chanting "Toro, toro, toro,' and the sounds of screaming cockatoos, and the sounds of small children singing hymns to the Virgin Mary, the Mother of Love, their small children's voices consoling us, absolving us, ringing out like tiny silver bells, cheering us on in beautiful days and in stormy weather, and then the sounds of Soledad singing her songs of joy as she dances around the kitchen, and I am listening to her sing and all uncertainty vanishes, all of this flashing towards us, flashing by, for we are now traveling thousands of miles per second, the two teachers and myself, like fiery, orange meteors with plumes of brownish-black, acidic smoke streaming past, we are burning up, burning away, dissolving, gravity is pulling us back into the atmosphere, back into ourselves, the deafening roar of re-entry swallowed up in the vacuum of a single instant, and then I am gasping for breath and I feel a tremendous ache in my ribcage, as if someone has been pounding away with a sledgehammer for hours. I am surprised my bones haven't cracked. Then I realize that I have come very close to dying. I am standing there on the stone bridge looking at the strangely tinted water, my head tilted to one side because the sun is too bright, it is strangely bright. I am wondering what is happening to me.

"Let's get out of the sun," says a voice. "It's getting hot."

It is the voice of one of the teachers, perhaps the older one. I am looking past him at the water. I can see now it is a swimming pool and there are children swimming. Around the pool there are several Spanish style buildings, white with red roofs. There are palm trees growing along the edges. Some of the palm trees seem to be growing straight out of the sides of the buildings. I am looking at everything as if for the first time.

"Are you okay, Señor Mendoza?"

It is the younger one now. The older one is silent.

The younger one is giving me a very long look. They no longer possess snarling, elongated snouts. They no longer need muzzles.

"Yes, yes, I think so." I say. "I am feeling a little muddled, that's all. Have I been sick?"

"Not sick exactly," says the younger one.

"It's the heat," says the older one.

"Yes," says the younger one. "And the bright sun."

"Yes, yes. But these things have never bothered me before," I say.

But they do not seem to hear me.

A very warm breeze blew across the pool and the stone bridge and he remembered once his father had taken him south and the wind had come across the plains all the way from the Mediterranean to Zaragoza, and it had been very hot against his face, like opening the door to an oven, and it felt like that now and he felt perspiration beading up along his forehead, but he was still cold and he shivered. He felt hands grab his arms squarely beneath the pits. They were not rough hands, they took hold of him gently and lifted him up. 'We'll be there soon, Señor Mendoza,' said a voice, and then a second voice said something but it was gibberish to his ears so he let it go. He could only see his feet at first, one foot forward and then the next, and so on, the white stone bridge receding. He wondered where he had left his shoes, but then the thought left him. His legs felt very heavy, but with the weight of his body suspended by the strength of the hands on either side of him, he felt as light and insubstantial as sunlight. He tried to raise his head, to see precisely where they were going, but the effort was more than he could manage. It was easier to let his head hang, to watch his feet go flashing by, and he hoped that whoever was helping him along would continue to do so.

"Have I been sick long?" he heard himself say.

"No, not long," said the first voice.

"It came on rather quickly," said the second voice. "I'm not sure I would even call it a sickness."

He closed his eyes and let the sound of the two voices wash through him. The gentleness of the voices and the sense of being supported by two sets of strong, capable hands revived him somewhat. He managed to look up and saw they had left the stone bridge and were passing along an extended colonnade connecting a small stone tower to a larger stone building with a heavy wooden door and window frames painted bright blue. There were green benches between the columns, facing the pool, but these were filled with children and bath towels and discarded socks and shoes and sandals and t-shirts and empty lunch boxes. After the last column there was no bench and they turned there and passed into the warm, thick darkness of a pavilion. He was talking the whole while, asking questions, but he kept losing his train of thought.

"What was I saying?" he heard himself say.

"You were asking about the festival in Allapattah," said the first voice. "You were disappointed you couldn't remember the big-head puppet parade, the Cabezudos."

He was shivering again and wondered what kind of sickness he had and he was suddenly afraid of this sickness, the way a small boy is afraid, and then he laughed at himself and he let the fear pass. It had been a long time since he had felt such a fear and he wondered if it would come again.

"That's when you took sick," said the second voice. "Later that day. But I wouldn't even call it a sickness. It was more like you just overdid things."

"That's exactly what you did."

They found an empty picnic table in the darkness and then they said they would bring him some water and they vanished into the brightness of the sky beyond the columns. He sat there looking at the bright blue of the water, a sharp rectangle against the black shadows beneath the pavilion. After a while the two voices returned. It seemed darker. The fear did not return. He had almost forgotten why he was sitting there.

"Here you go, Señor Mendoza. It's nice and cold, so drink it slowly. You don't want to shock your system."

They left again but he did not remember where they were going. Time moved erratically, jumping backwards in fitful bursts like tiny yellow birds taking wing, then sliding forward, then stopping altogether. He drank the water slowly, and then the bottle was empty. He could feel the water tumbling down his throat, the hollowness inside filling up. He was a prisoner inside himself, trapped in the cavernous darkness of his bowels, until he drank the water, and as the water level rose inside, he rose, up through the twisted curvature of his throat and out through his mouth into the open air, and then he kept on rising. He was looking down on himself. It might have been a dream, but the sensation of floating was very strong. It was like watching a movie filmed from the air. He saw himself sitting at the picnic table and simultaneously standing on the stone bridge between the two teachers and he was also floating in the air. He was in all three places at the same time. He wondered if his three selves were thinking identical thoughts or if they were each bound to a specific moment, and he tried to tune his ears so he could catch what was rolling through the brains of the other two. It was like trying to capture a radio station that is just barely in range. Then he was standing at the bridge again, only this time he was taking in the buildings that surrounded the swimming pool with a measurable degree of disappointment. He had not known the purpose of the trip was to take him swimming for an afternoon. He had thought he was going to a brothel of some sort. The picture on the postcard had reminded him of a brothel he had been to when he was younger. He had been hoping to dive into that memory of his youth for one final fling before he died, that's how he had thought of this trip. He was certain Soledad had sent him with these two so he could taste once again the freshness of his youth, of their youth. Then he was sitting once again at the picnic table and he could barely breathe. He had knocked the empty bottle from the table and it was bouncing on the cement floor of the pavilion in the darkness the way plastic bottles do, a hollow sort of clacking sound rippling up from the floor, he could feel the rippling waves pulsing through his body, and then the bottle settled. He could hear the sounds of the children in the pool and running through the pavilion, chattering and laughing. The children possessed very small, tinny sounding voices, very high up, it sounded almost like a ringing in his ears. Then from very far away he could hear the haughty, superior, compassionate laughter of his Soledad, and suddenly he could smell the scent of gardenias once again and he remembered how she used to wear gardenias in her hair, but that had been many years ago. He wondered if she were wearing a gardenia at that very moment. He wondered what she was doing while he was away at the pool and how hungry he was to see her face, and then he felt hungry in general, even though it was still early, nevertheless, he hoped she would make him a bowl of barley soup and Saltines and a plate of pisto, just the way he liked it, when he returned. He thought about how long he and Soledad had been together, and he could not remember a time when she did not exist. She was his beautiful goddess of the Pyrenees, always, his heart and soul for ten thousand years. He wondered how long this dream would go on and when he would see her again, and in the muted silence of his reverie he heard her voice calling out to him. There was a timorous, fragile quality about her voice, as if it had traveled across the centuries to reach his ears, and she was saying 'everything we do follows us everywhere we go,' over and over again, and then her voice was replaced by the sounds of the sea and the steady crash of the waves along the shore and he was reminded of their time in Saint Jean and that small café with its view of the river where they had talked about the future and then he had taken her to a small hotel only three blocks away, a seedy little hotel that did not compare in the least with the mysterious elegance of Hotel Eskualduna, but he could not help that, he had not wanted to attract attention, there were too many people at Hotel Eskualduna who would have recognized him, but he had never told her that, and then he heard the voices of the screaming cockatoos once again, but there were many more of them now, it sounded like hundreds and hundreds of white-feathered cockatoos, he could hear the rush of their wings as they wheeled through the dark open spaces beneath the pavilion rooftop, past the picnic tables and the benches and then back out into the bright blue sky and then down again into the pavilion, a frenzy of feathers, the cockatoos screaming *'buenos dias señoritas'* as they flew. And then the cockatoos were gone and he was floating in the air once again, rising with the heat, escaping, the atmosphere beginning to thin. He could see the first of his former selves, the one at the bridge, stumbling against the railing and the two teachers taking hold of his armpits. He could see his second former self in the darkness of the pavilion, kneeling down on the cement floor, his torso sliding forward, his arms sliding out to either side. And then he was very high up. He could see a few figures running along the edge of the pool and then dashing into the darkness of the pavilion. Sirens were blaring. Children stopped swimming to see what was going on. On the other side of the red gate, two police cars drove into the parking lot, and then several policemen were rushing towards the pool. But he had already turned his attention elsewhere.

BOOK THREE

the sex queen of the Moulin Rouge

-19-

Malachi Horatio Decosta lived in Allapattah just north of the river on a dead-end side street in a small shotgun shack of indeterminate color. No one paid much attention where Malachi went or the hours he kept. No one on his block even knew his real name. He looked like every other Rastafarian in the neighborhood with his yellow and red and green striped cap and his smelly dreadlocks flowing out from underneath. Except he was white (he claimed to have been born in the Caribbean, but whatever accent he pretended to have vanished completely in moments of great distress), and he also wore black bicycle shorts and rode a badly twisted ten-speed that must have been twenty years old. He had picked it up at a garage sale for ten dollars. One dollar for each twisted gear. You could hear Malachi's bike grinding and rattling and wheezing from three blocks away. It sounded almost cartoonish, like a demented accordion that played the same two sliding mechanical notes over and over again. The people of the neighborhood knew Malachi only as the man with the broken bike. But that was enough. They called him 'Broken Bike' for short. "Oye, man, I just zeen Broken Bike ride by." "Oye Broken Bike, what was you doing tonight?" "No, man, you aint wanna be messin with Broken Bike, you be in some jam you do that, he a crazy lunatic motherfucker. Even his friends say so. Heee'll put a gun to your head like he giving you a cigarette."

No one understood Malachi any better than Malachi understood himself. This was not saying much. Passersby might encounter Malachi standing outside a Laundromat in the middle of the morning, his bike leaning against an expired parking meter, ranting and raving about the horde of Castro hardliners in Congress, for Malachi held them responsible for everything from overpriced airline tickets to the Caribbean to the steady decline of the middle class to the lack of good beer in the grocery stores. Then he would descend into a weepy prolonged silence. After that he would begin waving his arms erratically in the air as if he were trying to describe the scene of an accident through pantomime. What would you think?

To be honest, most of the world thought him a lunatic. But he was not a lunatic. He simply danced to a music that few people heard. He noticed small things that others missed. He remembered what he saw with cinematic clarity, in living color. He forgot nothing. Clinically he was what some would call an idiot-savant, and so he often seemed crazy to those who did not know him. In other words, to most of the world, which is to say those who did not perceive the pattern in his madness, everything Malachi did seemed an afterthought, an invention of a drug-induced stupor, a chance phrase on a bumper sticker taken to heart, a warning in a dream caused by eating rancid pork, the word of God misremembered.

-20-

An example of Malachi's perceived lunatic behavior:

After ten years working for a local outfit hauling garbage, one day Malachi caught his reflection in the side view mirror of the truck. He was just sort of hanging on, his arm looped loosely through the sidebar, chewing on his tongue, and behind himself he could see flashes of sunlight coming through the trees, and thinking these flashes were Morse code from the ancient Egyptian god Amun-Ra (he had been reading a lot about Egypt at that point), he decided to quit his job, just like that. He decided he was going to branch out on his own. Why not? He suddenly realized he knew as much about garbage as anyone else in the trade. And he paid far more attention than most to the waste reduction habits of each household. The sexy chiquitas who had taken up residence in apartment 212B of the Dolphin Shores Apartment complex (the ones who were perfume girls at the airport mall), threw out sexy lace underwear from Victoria Secret after wearing them for only a single day and a single night, so he knew there was money to be made there. In the same building on the fourth floor there was a young father, an ex-Marine who had got his legs shot off in the desert. Mostly empty baby food jars and half-drunk bottles of whiskey. Opportunity there as well. And the Senior Center on 24th Avenue, they were always boxing up shoes and old clothes and costume jewelry when somebody died and leaving the boxes out back for the Goodwill truck. That was just a matter of scheduling. Yes, there was a great deal of money to be made if you just kept your eyes open, if you knew where to look. Malachi thought he was going to get rich sifting through the trash of everyone who lived north of the river between 27th Avenue and the Interstate. He thought he might even have to hire a few derelicts like himself. The boss man of his former crew, an enormously fat, happy man, laughed and laughed when he learned of Malachi's plans, but even this insult did not infuriate Malachi. Besides, the boss man wasn't even an American, he was a refugee from Kuwait, a casualty of the very same war that had claimed the young father's legs, and he did not speak English very well, so it was hard to be sure just what he was laughing at. So Malachi forgave him what was surely an unintentional slight. His hope soared. His hope was a bright smile that lit up the sky on even the sunniest day. He outfitted himself with an abandoned grocery store cart from Publix for hauling purposes and a lonely skier's pole for reaching objects just out of reach. He spent countless hours scouring back alleys and vacant lots and abandoned buildings, but after several weeks of back-breaking work in the sun, and unexpectedly fruitless work at that, Malachi decided to spend most of his time down along the river, investigating the shaded, vacant areas beneath the bridges, the hidden walkways, the shaded areas that bordered the numerous marinas but were separated from these enclaves of the extravagantly (absurdly so) wealthy by shiny, brand-new, chain-link fences. Mostly he found broken bottles and rusted toaster-ovens and empty paint cans and plastic bags stuffed with dirty diapers, but occasionally there was something worth saving, something he could polish up a bit and sell for a few dollars, something he could claim for himself, like his bike. He began to think of this alternative reality along the river as a paradise where the treasures of the universe lay waiting. If you asked him if it wasn't absurdly difficult and perhaps financially irresponsible, even ruinous, to expect to find treasure in this manner, wasn't he tempting fate, or at the very least, wasn't he embarked on a fool's errand, he would simply smile and say, "No, man, it's easy, man. Everywhere you look there are diamonds in the rough."

-21-

By the time Malachi met the two teachers at The Patagonian Café, he was no longer in the garbage trade. He was a part-time talent scout in the adult film industry, or at least he had been. In truth, he had only ever worked for the Velázquez brothers, a pair of local thugs who, according to some, had made their money running drugs in the eighties, and according to others, they were front men for the CIA, before they gave it all up (either the drug business or the spy business) and became pornography hustlers. Their company, which they named Coñazo Films (which translated literally meant Giant Vagina Films), turned out half a dozen adult films a week, sometimes more. But it was hard to say if Malachi would be working for Coñazo Films much longer. He had crossed the line, so to speak, and that was something you did not do with the Velázquez brothers.

How Malachi crossed the line with the Velázquez brothers:

The Velázquez brothers had had the rare misfortune to be born Siamese twins in a devoutly superstitious and homophobic Catholic family. They were joined at the hip (they shared a small portion of the iliac crest, the part of the hip that flares out), but slightly turned towards each other. All their grandmother could do when she saw them was wave a bony finger in their direction and scream *"hueva del Diablo"* before she fled, wrapped in the spider web of a black shawl, into the trembling shadows of her sitting room. Their father would not speak to them at all. They had been successfully separated as small children, but they carried the scar of their union as if it were part of a shameful, incestuous, homosexual past. The myriad psychoses they developed as a result of this childhood trauma laid the foundation for their later success as thugs, or as they preferred to think of themselves, modern day Mongolian warlords destined to conquer the world (they had watched with obsessive interest a movie about Genghis Khan when they were young boys and had never forgotten the riveting, ringing sensation in their ears that the graphic violence in the movie had produced). They were humorless men with black leathery, crusted-over skin, as if they were both burn victims or suffered from leprosy. They were identical, down to the minor indentations in their once conjoined hips. No one joked even about Siamese cats in their presence for fear of a bullet.

  The brothers called each other Bull and Horse respectively, but no one knew them well enough to know who was who. Even Malachi generally called them both Mr. Velázquez, and he had worked for the brothers for two years sending strippers their way, yoga instructors, lifeguards, massage therapists, substitute teachers, girls who worked at deli counters or florist shops or hair salons or out at the airport mall (two of the four sexy chiquitas from apartment 212B regularly appeared in orgy scenes in Giant Vagina Films). Anyone Malachi thought might look good in front of the camera, without clothes on, naturally, he sent along for a screen test. He was paid a small commission each time one of his referrals appeared in a movie, and he did quite well for a while, enough so that he began to find his squeezebox bike embarrassing, even shameful, and he seriously contemplated tossing it into the river, a sort of symbolic crossing over into the land of the dead, which appealed to his sense of the mythic (or perhaps pseudo-religious would be more precise). But he could not shake the feeling that getting rid of the bike would spell disaster. In his mind, the physical aspects of the bike were intimately linked to his own identity. If the bike were to suffer the agony of an untimely (or even timely) death, he thought, who could say he wouldn't be next?

  Malachi's coup de grâce as far as picking talent for the Velázquez brothers was persuading Gisela to strip in front of the camera and strut her stuff. It didn't take a whole lot of persuading. One afternoon at the café Malachi asked her if she would be interested and she said yes. He mentioned that there might be some fucking involved. She said she didn't mind, she liked fucking. He said there might even be a lot of fucking. She said okay. She made a total of seventeen films, all of which went straight to video, and was an instant smash. The video stores couldn't keep her movies on the shelves. The Velázquez brothers were suddenly flush with suitcases of cash and decided to bankroll a major motion picture with Gisela and her wonderfully voluptuous titties as the star. They were going to do a giant billboard campaign. They were going to open in 2,700 theaters across the nation and rake in millions. Suddenly they seemed less and less like burn victims or psychotic killers troubled by an unspeakable past and began to laugh at a few non-threatening jokes. They permitted Malachi to call them Bull and Horse interchangeably. And then Gisela decided she didn't want to be a film star anymore. For one thing, she said, it was boring. For another, she was raw from so much sex, she hadn't realized they were going to do it this much, it hurt even to pee. Finally, she said she had promised Señor Mendoza she would give up movies for a while to see if she really loved doing them or if she was only in it for the money. Señor Mendoza had been telling her that the only way to find true happiness was to make sure you were following the dictates of your heart.

"Happiness has nothing to do with money," that's what Señor Mendoza had told her.

By this point, of course, the Velázquez brothers had already emptied several suitcases full of ready cash to grease the movie-production wheels of their greatest venture. Their behavior had been entirely predictable, one might even say inevitable. They had hired a big-time director from Mexico City (who was watching the bright blue waters of the Atlantic from the balcony of a ninth-floor hotel room in the city of Sunny Isles Beach until filming began, smoking Cuban cigars by the box as if he were eating chocolates and dining on caviar for breakfast). They had engaged the services of an upscale production company six blocks from the hotel (the package they had purchased included two sound technicians, several actors on call in case they were filming a crowd scene or had a few bit parts left over, digitalized video equipment, which was pretty standard, a fully stocked bar, and a catering contract with the hotel that housed the director). They had hired Ambrosi Perugini, the flamboyant designer from Milan (who was also staying at the hotel), to oversee the artistic dimensions of the picture (costumes, set design, etc.). And they had hired a publicity firm headquartered in Austin, Texas to give them coast-to-coast coverage, mostly radio spots. They were shelling out eight thousand a day for a chance to skip the pearly gates and bask in the sun of their own private paradise.

Two days after Gisela quit Coñazo Films, the Velázquez brothers decided to lean on Malachi. They placed an unsigned message into a small green envelope with the Coñazo Films logo stamped in the middle (the logo was a picture of a thick-lipped hairless vagina that at various moments, depending upon the angle of the light, looked like a glistening mouth that was laughing, or sometimes crying, or sometimes getting ready to eat) and then they slipped the envelope under the door of Malachi's shotgun shack.

It was one in the afternoon when the envelope appeared on the other side of the door, where it met the resistance of a pair of rope-soled sandals and stopped. It was two o'clock when Malachi noticed the hairless vagina on the floor. But instead of a gaping orifice capable of expressing a range of human emotions (joy, sorrow, hunger), Malachi saw instead a giant eye staring up at him. He opened the envelope and read the message.

We need Gisela to get her fucking tits back in front of the goddamn camera. We are losing too much money and we are holding you responsible. You better have some idea how to fix this if you don't want your own goddamn fucking ass in a sling. Meet us up on the roof to discuss details. Do not be late. (P.S. Please excuse our fucking French, but we can't help it with things being the way they are.)

There was no mention of the time, no way to determine if he was already late or not, but this was typical of a Velázquez brothers' message. This kind of stubborn vagueness was deliberate. It was supposed to indicate a malicious, sinister intelligence lurking somewhere on the periphery of existence, getting ready to pounce, never quite visible until it was literally too late to do anything about it. Malachi was mildly disturbed. But he knew the message came from the Velázquez brothers, and in spite of their reputation, he had never witnessed them even roughing someone up, let alone killing them in cold blood. The feeling of being disturbed gave way to one of irritation. He threw on his shorts, a t-shirt and a baggy safari vest with two oversized pockets and headed out the door.

'Up on the roof' meant the roof of a corner video store on 22nd Avenue. The journey would take him twenty minutes by squeeze-bike. At one time this tiny one-story building had served as a getaway safe-house for the Velázquez brothers, and it still possessed the aura of a den of thieves, but now it seemed almost cultivated, as if it were part of a scene from a 1940s Hollywood movie. The air inside the store was stale and smelled of dried urine (the door to the bathroom did not close all the way, and there was no light, so many men dribbled on the floor) and cigarette smoke (they had set aside a couple of red leather armchairs in one corner for patrons who wished to smoke while they debated the merits of various titles; the chairs were always occupied).

Most of the patrons were wearing a hat of some kind, pulled down so you could barely see two eyes blinking in the shadows beneath the brim, and long trench coats of various styles and colors, which gave the impression that in addition to thieves from a 1940s movie, the store was also frequented by flashers recently released from jail. There was constant traffic up and down the rows and rows and rows of adult films with glossy covers depicting all sorts of lewd behavior — teenage girls with rather prominent jugs (though hardly worth noting when compared to Gisela's) dancing naked with ape-like creatures around coconut trees; twelve-inch or perhaps sixteen-inch schlongs ramming into heart-shaped asses; devil women wearing masks and collars with spikes whipping timid, fragile men chained to whorehouse beds in brothels that looked vaguely like medieval dungeons — that sort of thing.

The clerk was a wheezing fat man with greasy red hair tied in a ponytail who sat ensconced in a small Plexiglass cubicle behind an elevated counter near the entrance. Everyone called the clerk Paco. At times he looked like a desk sergeant in a police precinct nearing retirement, at other times he gave the appearance of a tollbooth collector struggling to stay awake. He spent most of his working hours playing video games behind the Plexiglass.

Somewhere between Malachi's shotgun shack and the video store, the sense of irritation Malachi had felt gave way to a feeling of untroubled enthusiasm. This was an easy thing to fix, he told himself. He was no novice when it came to women, and Gisela, at least as far as Malachi could determine, had fallen madly in love with him. The morning after they had finished shooting her twelfth film (a cheesy flick they had wrapped up in two days called *The Dickey Horror Peep Show*; Gisela played the role of Jeanette, the blind girl), Malachi had taken her out for a celebratory lunch of Mexican take-out (El Sombrero Hambriento, by the baseball park) and a bottle of El Coto Rosé. They had eaten their meal in the cool shadows beneath the 17th Avenue drawbridge, and when they were finished they lay back against a cement pillar next to the hydraulic machinery (Malachi had brought along a blanket for comfort). Then Malachi kissed Gisela for a very long time, and after that she had let him massage her enormously oversized breasts and then peel back the second skin of a wet t-shirt to gorge himself on her very brown, very erect nipples, and she had, in spite of an unexpected ejaculation on his part, which left a glossy watermark of a stain on his black shorts, squealed with unashamed delight. They had been dating ever since. No, thought Malachi, there was no need to worry. This was an easy thing to fix. Moments later he was flying up the stairs to the roof of the video store to tell the Velázquez brothers the good news.

    The conversation on the roof:
    "You're late," said the one, presumably Bull.
    "Very late, in fact," said Horse. "What shall we do with him, Brother?"
    The brothers paused, looked at Malachi across the crumbling tar of the rooftop. It was very sunny and all Malachi could see were their shadows.
    "That is up to him," said Bull.
    "Fair enough," said Horse. "It's worth one try at least."

"Yes, of course," said Malachi. "I mean there's nothing to worry about. I'm telling you. This is an easy thing to fix."

"We've spent too much damn money already," said Bull. "And we're losing more by the minute."

"Eight thousand dollars a day," said Horse.

"I didn't realize it was that much," said Bull.

"It could even be more," said Horse.

Bull looked at Horse for a moment with silent appreciation, as if only his brother could have determined the precise rate at which they were losing money.

"Of course we knew the risks," said Bull.

"In a venture like this there are always risks," said Horse.

"But it still knocked us for quite a loop," said Bull, with an odd mixture of admiration, incredulity, and intolerance.

"Yes," said Malachi. "I know. It was stupid of her to quit like that, without any warning."

"We don't respond well to warnings," said Horse.

"No, we don't," said Bull. "We're the ones who give them. Is that clear?"

Horse nodded with measured gravity.

"And the warnings we give are not easily forgotten," said Horse.

"Exactly right!" said Bull.

Malachi wasn't sure how to respond. He was perspiring profusely, from the heat, no doubt. His t-shirt was completely soaked, though his safari vest remained remarkably dry. His mind began to wander and he was unable to comprehend the direction of the conversation. Or perhaps there was no direction. He couldn't decide which would be worse and wondered if he were going mad. The whole conversation seemed to be taking place inside a hospital for the criminally insane instead of on a rooftop. It was clear the Velázquez brothers weren't listening to him. Occasionally they stared at him with a strange glowing look in their eyes, as if they had radiation sickness and did not recognize him, or perhaps it was an unusual mixture of compassion and paranoia Malachi had never encountered before, or perhaps, they too, were simply overwhelmed by the heat. Malachi wasn't sure. He hoped the brothers were just flexing their muscles, saying everything they had wanted to say to vent their frustrations over Gisela and the absence of her breasts from the big screen, but the subtle tremors of the conversation suggested something far more sinister was at work. Whatever it was, Malachi knew something was off. He had the odd sensation that he was watching the conversation take place and participating in it at the same time. He was both the observer and the observed. This would account for the strange waves of nausea that raced uncontrollably through his body. One of the brothers would say something, and then there would be a blank space in the air where his words should have been, and then the other one would speak and another blank space, and then he, Malachi, would open his mouth, and again there would be blank spaces, like miniature black holes sucking all of the oxygen out of the atmosphere, and then they would close their mouths with simultaneous finality, all three of them, as if they had just agreed that the end of the world was imminent, and they would stare off into space, each in a different direction, contemplating the limits of mortal existence, or perhaps thinking about some dry cleaning they were going to pick up later but now there was no use, and only then in the vacuum of this cinematic silence would the words that had been spoken come tumbling past his ears, an arcane gibberish all at once, as if someone had suddenly flipped a switch. It seemed like they were trapped in a scene from a poorly written, poorly dubbed spaghetti western.

"So you see it is in all of our best interests to fix this thing before it gets any worse," said Bull.

Malachi nodded.

"You do agree with us, don't you?" said Bull.

"Yes, yes," said Malachi.

Bull had his arm draped across Malachi's shoulders. The two of them were standing along the edge of the rooftop. Bull had one foot up on the rounded rooftop facade and was looking at the people walking back and forth on the sidewalk one story below, but Malachi was distracted. He had twisted his neck so he could see over Bull's bulging Popeye forearm and was looking squarely at Horse, who was standing on the other side of the roof in front of the doorway to the stairs. Malachi wondered if Horse had positioned himself to block his escape route should he make an attempt. Then he was certain this was the case. The Velázquez brothers never left anything to chance.

"Don't you?" Bull said again.

Bull gave Malachi a gentle, loving shake to encourage Malachi's complete attention.

"Yes, yes. I told you this was an easy thing to fix," said Malachi.

Bull smiled, the sunlight flashing behind his head, and Malachi noted several missing teeth. Malachi wondered why Bull didn't fix his teeth, and then it occurred to him that Bull's sinister reputation was defined in part by the dark spaces in his mouth. His was a twilight smile always submerged in the shadows.

"That's good to hear, my boy," said Bull. "We have always liked you. Isn't that so, Brother?"

Horse grunted from the other side of the roof.

"Loyalty," said Bull. "That's what we expect."

"Loyalty," repeated Horse, and it sounded like he was suddenly standing directly behind Bull. Malachi could feel the hissing, hot breath of the words on his own neck, but when he turned his head to look he saw that Horse hadn't moved an inch.

"Loyalty," said Bull again. "We could give a crap about results without loyalty. Do you get my meaning?"

Malachi assured Bull that he did.

"You wouldn't want to go flying off this rooftop head first, now, would you?" said Bull.

Malachi briefly considered the distance. They were only one story up, about sixteen feet from the sidewalk. He might survive the fall, but then again, he might not. Malachi was not certain about the physics of his situation. Besides, if he died from the fall there's no telling what the Velázquez brothers might do to his body. Chop it up for fish bait, he thought.

"Would you?"

Bull tightened his grip on Malachi's shoulders.

"No, man, I mean Mr. Bull, I mean Mr. Velázquez, no, no, I have to tell you I was born nervous about heights, everyone knows this."

Bull roared with laughter. It was robust laughter, neither malicious nor mocking.

"Horse, do you remember the taxi driver? What was his name?"

"Caballero."

"How did he die?"

"Drowning."

"And the accountant?"

"Alvarez. A boating accident."

"So again, drowning."

"Yes, I suppose so."

"And what happened to Eléna Montaño?"

"The reporter from Channel Ten?"

"Yes, what a fucking bitch."

"She drove off a bridge in that De Soto we gave her. Down in the Keys."

Bull roared and roared and roared. He could not contain himself. And one could not ignore the hearty sincerity of the sound. Bull's laughter embraced the world. A few passersby from below looked up, expecting to see happy, simple men working on the roof, but they became confused when all they saw was a two-headed shadow standing in the glare of the sun and hurried away, as if they had only then realized they were passing by an adult video store and feared someone might inform their husbands or their wives where they had been at three in the afternoon. They were also no doubt aware of the stories associated with the Velázquez brothers, and perhaps also their coincidental proximity to the original den of thieves, which may have given their flight from the scene an extra dash of velocity. But whether these thoughts were uppermost in their brains or not, it was always prudent (as the citizens of Miami and elsewhere most certainly knew, even if they professed otherwise) to keep one's eyes on one's own business and plod ahead in rigid lockstep with the unflappable silence of eternity (Whew!). The pedestrians fled. Bull's sincere, roaring laughter settled with impunity on the sidewalk.

"Is there anyone that didn't die of drowning?" Bull said.

"Yes, of course. You just happened to pick three that occurred near the water."

"Have we ever tossed someone off a rooftop?"

"Yes, but it was a long time ago. It was this very roof in fact."

"Good God, Brother, you're right," said Bull. "That fucking pipsqueak faggot."

Bull grew quiet for a moment, deadly serious.

"Serves him right the way he fucked up that deal with the Panamanians."

"Yes," said Horse. "I can still see his eyeballs bulging as he went over the edge."

"I remember, I remember," said Bull.

"Like in one of those Roadrunner cartoons," said Horse

"Stop it! You're killing me," said Bull.

Bull roared some more and stared down at the sidewalk again, presumably at the spot where the little pipsqueak faggot had landed, his head cracking open like a melon and his brains oozing out, a glistening, pulpy orange-reddish mass that eventually collected in the gutters and was washed away by the rain.

No one spoke for several minutes.

Malachi shifted uncomfortably and Bull relaxed his grip.

"Loyalty," Bull said again.

"Loyalty," repeated Malachi.

"But all the same," said Horse, "You better fix this thing."

"That's right," said Bull. "We're losing eight-thousand dollars a day. Loyalty don't mean crap stacked up against losses like that. Do you get my meaning?"

Bull and Malachi were heading for the door to the stairs.

"Yes," said Malachi. "It's an easy fix, like I said."

"Good, good," said Bull.

Horse opened the door for Malachi.

"But don't take too long," said Horse.

"No," said Bull. "We're losing eight thousand dollars a day, just so we're clear on that."

"Yes," said Malachi. "I . . ."

Horse gave Malachi a long, hard, silent look, as if to underscore what his brother had just said.

"Give him the script, Brother," said Bull.

Horse took out a wad of papers from his back pocket and gave it to Malachi. Malachi started to read the script. The pages were in no particular order but it looked vaguely interesting.

"Don't look at it now," said Bull.

Malachi nodded, somewhat surprised at Bull's reaction, after all, it was their movie. Bull grabbed the wad of papers from Malachi and shoved them into one of the oversized pockets of Malachi's safari vest. "If she asks what the movie's about, just show her the script."

"Sure thing," said Malachi.

"But don't take too long," said Horse again.

"Exactly right," said Bull.

Then Horse shut the door, leaving Malachi alone on the stairs, momentarily dazzled by the darkness.

Malachi emerged from the darkness of the stairs as if he were a wingless angel seeking shelter. He stood there for a while where the stairs ended, watching dozens and dozens of faceless, expressionless men in oversized trench coats and wide brimmed hats trolling up and down the aisles, looking for exactly the right video for the evening. Waves of nausea were still racing through his body, so much so that he had the distinct impression that he was vibrating. Paco was doing a brisk business for the middle of the week, or perhaps it was already the weekend. Malachi couldn't remember what day it was or even what month. He seemed to have stepped outside of time. He breathed in the familiar smell of stale urine and cigarette smoke to steady his nerves. He would decipher what had happened on the rooftop at a later point, he thought. But not now. At the moment he needed something to facilitate escape.

"Hey, Broken Bike," cried a voice.

The voice belonged to Paco.

"You looking for anything in particular?"

Malachi did not respond. The vibrating sensation had returned and he was trying to will it away through conscious, focused effort.

"We've got a bunch of new Salma de la Prada films," said Paco. "I mean they've been out for a while. They're classics, some of them. But they're new for us."

The vibrating subsided.

Malachi had not moved from the spot at the end of the stairs, but the crowd had thinned out and now Paco was standing next to him. Malachi wondered where the customers had gone.

"They're some really great films," said Paco.

Malachi looked up at the wheezing fat man and smiled a sad, anxious smile.

"I never heard of her," he said.

"She's a big deal in Spain," said Paco. "She looks sort of like Brigitte Bardot."

"I don't know her either."

"See for yourself," said Paco, grinning.

"Yeah, sure."

Paco was suddenly holding a stack of Salma de la Prada films so Malachi could see. Malachi was uncertain how they had appeared in Paco's hands so quickly. He looked them over.

"I'll take three," he said.

"Any ones in particular?"

"No, any three will do."

"That's the spirit," said Paco, somehow mistaking Malachi's anxious sadness for restless enthusiasm.

And then: "Just remember to get them back on time, will you?"

"Sure, sure," said Malachi.

"No sense paying a late fee if you don't have to, right?"

Malachi nodded. He gave Paco a twenty, following him to the counter, a steady wheezing sound ringing in his ears, and then watched fat fingers ring him up. He felt hollowed out inside, still a bit uneasy. His mouth was very dry. He looked through the narrow window above the counter. The blinds were up. The sky had begun to cloud over and he knew a storm was coming, but he still had time, he would make it home before the rain. Then he heard the rooftop door open and close and the sense that he was vibrating returned, only stronger than before, it was as if there was now an electrical current flowing through him, the blood flowing through his veins turning to quicksilver, it seemed that he could even smell smoke, and in this agitated state he found himself wondering what would happen if Gisela said no, how would the Velázquez brothers exact their revenge, and he tried to push this line of thinking out of his mind, it was counter-productive, but the vibrating sensation only grew stronger and he suddenly felt like the whole world was submerged beneath a sea of electricity, the very air was charged, his every breath releasing thousands of ionized particles ready to ignite, the ionized dust particles of small glories and larger halos, perhaps, a whirlwind of destruction. He didn't know what he was doing. Blindly he grabbed at the counter until he had his movies in hand, and then he told Paco to keep the change and he shouldered his way out through the padded black door into the street, holding his free arm up as if to shield his eyes. He sure as hell hoped things would work out.

-22-

Malachi did not sleep well that night. In fact, he did not sleep at all. He kept getting out of bed, checking the front door to see if there were any more messages from the Velázquez brothers, any more little green envelopes with gaping hairless vaginas watching him from the floor, or running to the bathroom as if he had to pee and flicking on the light but forgetting about the toilet, staring at his reflection in the mirror, splashing cold water on his face to make sure it was truly himself staring back, but then his face dissolving, sliding off into the sink. He trudged back and forth, from one end of his shotgun shack to the other, but the distance he traveled seemed immense. It was as if he lived in an endless maze of rooms, some with windows, some without. He forgot when, precisely, his face had disappeared. He wondered if his faceless condition were permanent or if there were something he could do, herbal supplements perhaps, but he could think of nothing that might help. He wondered how he could see his faceless face if he had no eyes. He closed his unseen eyes and tried to imagine what he knew he looked like, but all he saw was a blank, featureless mass like unformed clay. He assumed at that point that he had simply wandered into someone else's house, someone else's life. Strange greenish lights made sweeping patterns on the walls of this endless rat's maze, like helicopter searchlights, which the part of his brain that lay submerged beneath the waves of his insomnia took for the head-lights of a passing car flashing without apology through the windows, but as the lights continued throughout the night, no matter which room he was in, as if they were following him, he became uncertain, even suspicious. Somewhere towards the middle of that interminable night he began to panic and started chasing after the lights, shouting obscenities, letting the intelligence behind the lights know he wasn't afraid, laughing at their cowardice as they disappeared and the darkness returned, swifter than death.

When morning came he was lying in the middle of the floor, curled up in a fetal position, naked and covered in a bloody, viscous fluid, as if he had just been born. He lay there blinking stupidly for a while, the sunlight playing with the cool shadows on the floor. He could not remember the exact moment when the sun appeared above the horizon, but this would have been true even had he been waiting to record the event. It was very cool and pleasant there lying on the floor and he did not wish to get up. Then he got up anyway, for no particular reason, went to the bathroom and cleaned himself thoroughly. His face had returned, but he seemed to have forgotten it had disappeared during the night. He located his black bicycle shorts, a new t-shirt, his safari vest and his rope-soled sandals and got dressed. He did not notice several additional green envelopes on the floor, their gaping vaginas staring at the ceiling, indifferently. He now seemed immune to their effect. It was a bright, sunny morning, so bright that the world outside seemed a watermark reflection of itself. His heart was racing. He was thinking only of Gisela.

-23-

By three o'clock Malachi had crossed over the 17th Avenue bridge, and thirty minutes later he was a block from

The Patagonian Café. He had not taken his bike. Why he had not taken his bike he was never able to adequately explain. Perhaps, given the conversation with the Velázquez brothers the day before, his unconscious self was trying to warn that great unthinking imposter, his animal self, that they should both adopt a more unobtrusive mode of transportation, and should the opportunity arise, they should dive quickly and deeply into the nearest dark hole and remain there for some time. This explanation, at least, offers up some insight into the internal workings of Malachi the man. Then again, who can say for certain why anyone does anything? The air was clear and the sun was bright. That is all the explanation that is necessary. Malachi walked the roughly three miles from his shotgun shack in Allapattah to The Patagonian Café in Little Havana, and he took his time doing so, taking numerous detours just for the hell of it, reading every advertising poster and handbill he came across, watching a funeral motorcade rolling down the street, whatever street he was on he didn't remember, the motorcade then disappearing into a tornado of white dogwood blossoms swirling in the air, breathing in the thrill of pure sunshine, thinking of Gisela and what she would likely say. At precisely three-thirty he turned the corner heading into the homestretch. A few cars went past. A garbage truck. A bus. Malachi saw Señor Mendoza sweeping the sidewalk out front. But Señor Mendoza gave no indication that he saw Malachi (nor did he look up at the passing cars), perhaps because his attention was focused on the muddy streaks left by the thunderstorm from the night before (and which stubbornly resisted his heartiest efforts with the broom), or because he had never before said two words to Malachi and did not wish to alter his pattern of behavior, or because he was simply succumbing to the bewildering inertia of old age when even those we have known for decades are reduced to unrecognizable shadows. The only sound Malachi heard as he approached, apart from the background static of birdsong and automobile traffic, was the steady scratching of bristles on cement.

"*Hola, Señor Mendoza,*" said Malachi.

Señor Mendoza stopped sweeping a moment, as if he had been suddenly interrupted by a stray thought, a memory from his childhood, perhaps, and then shaking his head and muttering obscenities under his breath he looked back down at his feet and continued attacking the mud. Malachi's thoughts returned to Gisela. He peered in through the café window, cupping his hands around his eyes like he was holding binoculars, but the glass glowed darkly from the sun and all he could see was his own reflection. Malachi went inside.

-24-

Sitting with Gisela in the cafe:
"They really said that?" said Gisela. "I can't believe they would say that."
"Sure babe, we can all believe what we want, I suppose. But you'd be singing a different tune if you'd been on that rooftop."
"I really liked watching Eléna Montaño."
"Don't know about her. Never watched her."
"Channel Ten."
"That's why. Not my channel."
"I really liked her. Eléna Montaño, roving reporter. That's what they called her. They sent her everywhere. All over the city."
"Was she the red head with those dark Spanish eyes and the bright smile? The one who liked to wear those fancy silk halter tops with the black jackets and hoop earrings?"
"You said you didn't know her," said Gisela.
"Ooooh babe, she had nothing on you."
Gisela leaned her voluptuous chest across the table and smiled at Malachi, a softly glowing smile. Immediately Malachi thought of lightning at the beach, a brilliant burst of energy lacerating the sky, the pure, crystalline radiance of molten glass frozen in an instant, the time it takes to take a breath. This was the effect Gisela had on his libido. She was wearing a yellow tube top that barely covered her nipples.

Malachi was surprised that she didn't pop free just from breathing.

"She was on billboards all over town," said Malachi.

"She was a shooting star," said Gisela, sadly.

"That's too bad then. Hate to see it happen to anyone, but to a beautiful girl like that . . . ."

"I always wondered what happened to her . . . ."

"The Velázquez brothers said she drove off a bridge."

"Maybe they made it all up. They wanted to scare you."

"Nooo babe, that's just it. They sure as hell didn't sound like they were making it up. And they weren't trying to scare me at all. I swear on a stack of any Bibles you want they forgot I was standing there. They were just going through a list of people they had killed, in a very casual way, like they were trying to remember what they had for lunch. They were laughing about it, too. This one guy with bulging eyes they threw off the roof. The roof where we were talking. They were cracking up about his eyes. You should have heard them! They said it was like watching cartoons."

"Ordinary people just don't talk like that," said Gisela. "Only lunatics talk like that."

"That's what I've been trying to tell you, babe. These guys are the worst kind of lunatics there are. They are invisible men, like ghosts, you don't even know they are there, watching you, waiting, and then they see something about you they don't like, maybe it's the color of your hair that pisses them off, you can't know what you can't know, and then all of a sudden, wham, your ass is theirs, carved into little pieces for the fish, or maybe your boat blows up or your car goes over the edge of a bridge. How many ways can you kill someone? They know every one, so there's no escaping that. I'm telling you it's true. They are lunatics like God and the Devil mixed together. The way I see it we don't have much of a choice. You've got to do their movie, for both of us. I don't know what's going to happen if you don't."

It was at that point that Señor Mendoza came inside. He put the broom in the corner behind the cash register and sat down at a corner table opposite the counter. He was looking at Malachi and Gisela with an air of disapproval, but he said nothing. But his eyes did not waver.

"That's crazy talk, baby," said Gisela. "Now I gotta work some."

She pushed herself away from the table with such sudden force that this time everything did come spilling out. She seemed to have completely forgotten about the threat of the Velázquez brothers. Laughing a breathy, exuberant laugh, she gave her newly naked breasts a loving squeeze, as if she had been waiting for just the right moment to give her twins, as she called them, a breather. Then she rolled her tube top down so that it more or less looked like she was wearing a yellow belt and went to work, wiping down the few remaining tables that needed wiping, stocking the silverware tray, bringing Malachi a couple of beers and a plate of pisto (because there was always plenty of pisto at The Patagonian Café) to keep him busy, and then back at the kitchen window retrieving a bowl of barley soup and Saltines and another plate of pisto for Señor Mendoza, and all the while twirling to the sounds of Gloria Estefan or Albita Rodriguez or some other Latin pop diva pouring out of the radio in the back, twirling round and round with such uniform grace that one almost forgot she was practically naked from the waist up.

Then a couple of *greasy gamberros* (Señor Mendoza's words) came into the café. Perhaps they were not so greasy, just sweaty, tired, overworked, bored. They worked downtown on a skyscraper project, such skyscrapers as there were in Miami, but there had been a strike among the electricians so the bosses had told everyone to go home until they sorted things out, which the bosses said could take days, maybe even weeks. It was clear the two men had been drinking before they got to the café. They sat down at the counter and ordered beans and rice and rum.

At first they watched Gisela without saying a word. They could not believe their luck. They watched Gisela with contorted, happy grins. Their eyes shone like unreachable stars. You could pretty much guess what they were thinking.

Gisela disappeared into the kitchen and then returned with their order. She planted herself squarely in front of the two, her nipples pressing down against the countertop.

"Do you know the Velázquez brothers?" she said.

Yes, they said, they knew them.

"And these Velázquez brothers," she said, "they have killed many men?"

Yes, of course, they said, and many women too, and even children, that is what they do.

A great, glowing sadness swept over Gisela's face.

"What do you want to know about the Velázquez brothers for?" said one.

"Surely a sexy *chiquita* such as yourself has better things to think about, no?" said the other.

Gisela's sadness left her and she laughed. Always the flirtatious advances of strange men made her laugh. She seemed suddenly very happy. The two *greasy gamberros* also laughed. Their happy, beaming, sweaty faces disappeared momentarily into their plates of beans and rice, and then they slurped down their rum and asked for more, they were very thirsty, they said, they had worked up a very large thirst, a gigantic thirst, and they laughed as if they had just told a great joke. Gisela returned with a bottle of rum and planted it on the counter between the two men. The bottle was only a quarter full. The two men were no longer laughing, but they still seemed happy, and also content. They looked now at Gisela as if her happiness was their responsibility.

"You should be very careful not to ask too many questions out in public," the one said.

"This is true," said the other, and then he lowered his voice. "Word gets around."

"Whatever you can imagine about the Velázquez brothers is true," said the one.

"But also what you cannot imagine," said the other.

Then they turned their attention to the bottle, speaking in hushed voices, as if they were afraid of being discovered.

For a time, the café became a very quiet place. It was like a siesta. The radio was playing an instrumental version of "Livin' La Vida Loca," mostly guitars and horns, but you could hardly hear it. Señor Mendoza's soup had put him to sleep. In spite of the sunshine pouring in, he was dozing awkwardly in his chair, leaning back against the corner where the window and the wall met, snoring softly, almost inaudibly. The two *greasy gamberros* were communicating in a bizarre kind of sign language, their hands and fingers tracing intricate patterns in the air that only they could see. Even Malachi succumbed to the silence. He had suddenly remembered the wad of papers in the pocket of his safari vest and was now absorbed in the pages of the Velázquez brothers' movie script. The pages were scattered all over the table.

Then a lonely looking accountant wandered into the café and sat down at the opposite end of the counter from the two *greasy gamberros*. They looked at him with great suspicion and then averted their eyes and continued with their strangely animated pantomime. They had never seen him before. Their voices were still stifled by their paranoia.

The accountant ordered a beer (a bottle of *El Presidente*, which did pretty well at the café because of the Dominicans), and stared at the wall behind the counter. There was nothing to look at on the wall except a vintage poster of a bullfighter with a fancy silver sword gleaming in the sun and a fancy red cape draped over one shoulder. The bullfighter was staring down at a dead bull crumpled up at his feet with several darts sticking out of the bull's hump and blood streaming down the sides of the bull. The poster said El Cordobés, and then there was some small print, most likely in Spanish as well, but the poster was too far away.

Then the music seemed louder all of a sudden. The radio was playing some more of the Latin pop divas. Gisela brought the accountant his beer and he began to drink. The accountant didn't even notice Gisela. It seemed like he was identifying with the bull. "Poor fucking bull," said the accountant.

The *greasy gamberros* looked over and nodded with sympathetic understanding, expecting the accountant to say something more, but he grew silent, mesmerized by the poster. Then they asked for another bottle of rum. They wanted a full bottle this time.

Señor Mendoza woke up and resumed eating his soup.

Gisela brought out a full bottle of rum and the *greasy gamberros* thanked her. (Once again their eyes shone like unreachable stars.) She sat down opposite Malachi and repositioned her yellow tube top so it barely covered her nipples. He looked across at her glowing there, a bright yellow goddess swirling in sunshine, and smiled. He had barely noticed she had been gone. "It's the movie script," he said. "It's brilliant!"

-25-

The Velázquez brothers' movie script:
The movie didn't have a title yet. In the first part, Gisela would have played Nefertari, the virgin bride of the ancient Egyptian sun god Amun-Ra. Malachi became quite animated as he told Gisela about this part. In the past few years he had read *The Religion of Ancient Egypt* by W. M. Flinders Petrie, followed by *Eternal Egypt* by Pierre Montet, *The Tombs of Harmhabi and Touatankhamanou*, by Theodore M. Davis, and numerous articles on the High Priests of Amun at Thebes. In spite of the many historical inaccuracies (in the Egyptian part), which did not bother Malachi as much as he would have expected, but which he duly noted, he saw immediately what the writer of the script was trying to do.

"Amun-Ra is a fucking god," said Malachi. "He's like Antonio fucking Banderas. Everybody and their uncle wants Amun-Ra to fuck them, men, women, grandmothers, kids. They're lining up on the steps of the Great Pyramid, millions of them, the whole city, hoping to get picked, hoping to get whisked away in the flaming chariot of the sun god king and eat fish and roasted meat and raisins and dates and wild figs and drink wine and fuck and get fucked till the end of time, which is pretty much everyone's idea of paradise, at least in this movie, and you're the one who gets picked. Amun-Ra picks you."

Gisela liked the fact that she was picked above millions of ancient Egyptians, presumably waiting in the hot Egyptian sun for hours, days, perhaps months, just for a date with the Antonio Banderas of their time. She liked the idea of paradise. She also liked Antonio Banderas. But she would not have waited more than an hour herself, and she said so, and she wasn't all that sure about fucking till the end of time either, that sounded far too painful. But she was happy she was picked. But the rest of the movie was too confusing.

In the middle part she was supposed to be swimming with dolphins, or maybe she was having sex with the dolphins, she couldn't tell what was happening, but she didn't think she'd like having sex with dolphins anyway, not even one, it didn't make any sense to her, how would they do it, maybe if they had hands, like mermaids or something, but the idea of sex-starved dolphins groping her with their flippers was just disgusting. Of course Malachi was trying to explain first of all that it didn't matter about the flippers, dolphins could have sex eight or nine times an hour and they didn't need their flippers (except for obvious swimming purposes), but none of that mattered anyway because having sex with the dolphins was symbolic, nobody expected anybody to get mixed up in a dolphin orgy, not in a realistic sense, the point of the movie was that dolphins expressed their love with pure, unfiltered enthusiasm, that's precisely how Malachi put it, but Gisela had been dubious the moment dolphins had been mentioned, and then she got stuck on the word 'unfiltered' and all she could visualize were people standing in line to buy Brita water filters, which only added to her confusion about the story.

But it was the third part of the movie that sealed it for Gisela. In the third part it was the 1960s in America, but it was an alternative 1960s, the America in the movie was a Fascist regime, not a Democracy, and Nefertari and the Amun-Ra character were now hippie organizers trying to start a revolution and shouting 'death to the fucking Fascists' and political propaganda like that, but then they got sidetracked by all the free love parties floating around and all the sex they were having, and they were hallucinating from all the drugs in their bloodstream, so they had a difficult time remembering who they were having sex with, but no one expected they would be overwhelmed by jealousy, they were hippies for God's sake, but when the drugs wore off they got into a tremendously melodramatic argument about who was sleeping with who (this was the climax of the movie), and they were in a café or a restaurant when the argument took place, so there were all sorts of eyes watching and ears listening, and then Amun-Ra lost all sense of perspective, all he could see was red, and just to prove he didn't care about Nefertari anymore, he dropped his pants and started masturbating right there in the café (or restaurant), and Nefertari whipped out a stiletto and said she was going to cut off his prick and feed it to the pigs, presumably because she was incensed at his behavior, or maybe just disgusted, in any event their relationship was finished, and then he ran out of the café.

The last scene of the movie was him running down the street, and coming the other way was the revolution they had been working on (or perhaps it was the government response to the revolution, or some mixture of the two, the precise nature of what was happening was left open to interpretation). At the end the script said you could see the figure of Amun-Ra growing smaller and smaller against the looming darkness, and then you could hear bombs exploding and the sounds of troops marching and thousands of tanks rumbling down the streets, and then the camera was supposed to tilt up so you could see the black shadows of thousands of droning airplanes filling the afternoon sky. The airplanes were most likely Stukas, Malachi thought, like the ones that had come down from the Bay of Biscay in 1937 to drop their bombs on the beautiful town of Guernica. Wave after wave after wave. A hundred German Heinkel He 111s, he guessed, just like in '37, though the movie script didn't say, and hundreds of Dornier Do-17s and Ju-52 Behelfsbombers (also German), and a few Savoia-Marchetti SM.79 bombers (Italian) from the Aviazione Legionaria tossed in for the sake of international diversity. The script said the sky was absolutely black and you could hardly hear from the droning of the airplane engines. The movie was supposed to end with the total blackness of the airplanes.

In Malachi's mind, it was hard to distinguish the black shadows of the airplanes up in the sky from what he imagined were the black shadows of the falling bombs. Malachi thought it was a flaw in the script that you could hear the sounds of bombs exploding without first seeing the airplanes and the bombs falling. (He also made a mental note, though he did not share this with Gisela, that the black shadows of both the planes and the unseen falling bombs bore an uncanny resemblance to the shadows of Bull and Horse standing in the sun on the rooftop the previous day.) Gisela said the last part was just too weird, it gave her a shiver, like a ghost story, and she didn't like ghost stories. She said she wasn't interested in doing the movie. But then she saw the blank, caved-in look on

Malachi's face, and she said she'd think about it. Then Malachi suggested they act out the climactic scene, just for fun.

They read over the appropriate pages a few times and got into character. Gisela moved her lips as she read, but she was a consummate professional when it came to the actual performance. She took on every aspect of the roles she played, down to the tiniest nuance of feeling and expression that could never be adequately captured by the camera. She was wholly committed. Malachi, an amateur certainly, said he was ready to sell his soul to do his part justice.

They were seated throughout most of the scene.

Malachi was the first to speak but he was suddenly nervous. He needed the script in his hand to deliver his lines.

"'I have six bullets in this gun,'" said Malachi as the Amun-Ra character. "'Three for each of us.'"

"'Go ahead then,'" said Gisela as Nefertari. "'Shoot.'"

Malachi was surprised by the presence of the gun. He had missed that on his first reading of the scene and wasn't sure what to do. He held up his hand awkwardly, as if he were hoping it might be mistaken for a gun. Gisela suppressed a giggle.

"'Go ahead then,'" said Gisela as Nefertari, repeating the previous line. "'Shoot. I don't care.'"

"'No,'" said Malachi as Amun-Ra. "'I'm not going to waste these bullets on your skinny little ass. . .'"

Malachi was beginning to feel the pressure of potentially flubbing his lines. He forgot where he was in the script and was trying desperately to find his spot. Then he recovered and looked over at Gisela (forgetting she was Nefertari) and smiled. He was practically grinning, which was precisely the wrong emotion for the scene, but Malachi was just happy to be back on track.

"'Bullets are too good for you. . .'"

"'You, you. . .'"

"'I just want to know one thing. Why did you have to sleep with so many bastards?'"

Malachi stopped smiling. The line between fiction and reality was a blurry line.

"'You're the only bastard I know,'" said Gisela (Nefertari).

Malachi and Gisela were speaking in extra-loud stage

voices, as if the only way to convey the necessary emotion of each line was by shouting. They were still sitting at the table. The accountant had spun halfway around on his stool to see what the commotion was, spilling some of his beer on his shirt, and then he said shit and went to the bathroom. The two greasy gamberros were sizing up Malachi. They couldn't see the script from where they were sitting and were trying to determine if he were truly a threat and they might have to intervene. The fact that he seemed to think his hand was a gun suggested to them that he was indeed a lunatic, but probably capable only of harming himself. They calmed their heroic impulses with this thought.

As for Señor Mendoza, he woke up suddenly when the shouting started. He thought perhaps he was dreaming, but it was a very strange dream and he was troubled by it. He could hear angry, shouted words, but they were bouncing back and forth in the empty echo chambers of his brain. They sounded very far away. He could not tell for certain what was being said.

"'It was Arrabal's idea, wasn't it! Him and those dope fiends you call friends.'"

"'They are my friends. You can't tell me who my friends are. Not anymore. Just like you can't tell me who I can sleep with. We're finished, you and I. We run in different circles now. I'll sleep with whoever the hell I like, and there's nothing you can do to stop me. I'll take on a dozen new lovers every week and they can fuck me whenever they want to. I'm hungry for it, do you hear me? I'm hungry for it all the time.'"

"'They're white devils. But they'll get what's coming to them. You can be sure of that.'"

"'What are you saying?'"

"'You know what I'm saying. Everything comes full circle. Everyone gets what they deserve in the end. That's what we've been fighting for, or did you forget that Nefertari.* (And then an overly dramatic pause.) *But before you say another word, I'm going to show you what I really think of you.'"

This time Gisela could not help herself. She could see Malachi was going to play the scene all the way to the end and she burst out laughing. "I can't believe you're really going to do it," she whispered. Then Malachi (Amun-Ra) unbuttoned his bicycle shorts and took out his penis and started stroking himself. Gisela looked under the table to see for sure and then she popped back up and her laughter ballooned and she said "Malachi, baby, what are you doing?" but he just shook his head, trying not to burst out laughing himself, the two of them frozen in the scene, whispering back and forth, their words leaving only the faintest impressions in the air, like the ripple of a love song from centuries ago, "finish the scene, babe, finish it," and then "but I don't have a knife," and then "use your shoe, you're wearing high heels, aren't you?" and then "I am, you're right," and then "let's finish it," and then "okay baby," and then the scene resumed. They both stiffened as they got back into character.

"'*There, now you know exactly what I think of you,*'" said Malachi (Amun-Ra).

Malachi (Amun-Ra) shook his penis around a bit, as if to demonstrate that he had just had an orgasm, and then he shoved it back into his shorts and buttoned his fly.

"'*You're pathetic,*'" said Gisela (Nefertari), and she started laughing very loudly, a hollow stage laughter (part of the script) that also served to mask the waves of genuine laughter that rippled now uncontrollably through her body like a sickness in this theater of the absurd.

"'*If I could rip out your heart I would,*'" said Malachi (Amun-Ra.) "'*But you have no heart to begin with. You are a whore, like your mother and your grandmother were whores. You come from an ancient house of whores.*'"

"'*You, you. . .*'"

Then Malachi (Amun-Ra) stood up abruptly, mechanically, his suddenly extended buttocks knocking his chair to the floor with excessive though certainly unintentional force, and brandished his hand which was supposed to be a gun in the air. It was a bit melodramatic, even for this script. Gisela (Nefertari), stifling yet another wave of laughter, pulled her shoe off her foot and stepped quickly away from the table, half crouching, her arms raised to shoulder height, her elbows flared out, waving her spiked-heeled shoe in graceful counterpoint to Malachi's (Amun-Ra's) hand (gun). Malachi (Amun-Ra) was so focused on maneuvering his hand (gun) that he paid no attention to what Gisela (Nefertari) was doing.

The two of them looked almost like an amaurotic matador and a deranged perhaps crippled bull dancing in the arena. They looked like they had been doing this dance for years.

"'*If you take one step closer I'll cut off your prick and feed it to the pigs,*'" said Gisela (Nefertari).

But Malachi (Amun-Ra) said nothing. He stood there a moment, looking at Gisela (Nefertari) with a mixture of pride and contempt (which Malachi could not quite pull off; it looked more like he was suffering from acid reflux). Then he smiled a very convincing cavalier smile and blew her a kiss and ran out of the café.

-26-

Never before had Malachi felt so distraught, and yet at the same time so absolutely free. Gisela remained adamant in her refusal to re-enter the world of the Velázquez brothers and their pornographic movies, in spite of the obvious artistic merits of the film in question, which Malachi tried to point out with affectionate resolve every time they were together in bed. But within a week of the melodramatic episode at the café, Gisela hardly paid attention to anything that came out of Malachi's mouth. She distracted herself with thoughts of vacations in the rainforests of Brazil while he was on top of her pounding away, expressing in between the gasps that come from strenuous physical exertion his absolute need to fulfill her every desire and his indefatigable hope that she would soon change her mind.

He was utterly baffled by Gisela's inability to understand the importance of maintaining a cordial and gradually distant relationship with his employers. She did not seem to truly appreciate the kind of men they were. Then again, perhaps he was supposed to make an abrupt stand against the Velázquez brothers and everything they represented (though just what they represented eluded Malachi at the moment). Perhaps he had finally found his purpose in life.

He had always enjoyed thinking of himself as a Rastafarian rebel leading the righteous to justice in the face of certain death. Perhaps there was nothing to worry about, he would tell himself. Despair is only a point of view, after all. And while everyone knows with a certainty that could pass as faith that death is inevitable, it is equally true that at any given moment death is only one of many possibilities. Yes, that was the truth of it, he would say, and then he would feel suddenly and strangely liberated, as if there were no relationship between his current circumstances and how his life might turn out. Once again he felt detached from himself, as if he were trapped in a labyrinth of mirrors, watching events unfold and living them at the same time.

Of course some might argue that Malachi's thinking was muddled by the need to rationalize his difficulties in the face of Gisela's refusal to do one final film, but others might say that his logic was inescapably precise, and perhaps even prophetic.

When Gisela told him he was no longer welcome at the café, he responded with the wisdom of a television guru.

"He doesn't want you to come to the café anymore," said Gisela. "He was very concerned. He said he can do without your kind of riffraff."

"Who said this thing?" said Malachi.

"Señor Mendoza."

"It's no big deal."

"He said you're a crazy, lunatic. He thought the scene we did was real. He's afraid of you."

"Me? Malachi wouldn't hurt a fly."

"I know that, baby."

"When did he say this?"

"Yesterday. He took me aside and he said 'stay away from that crazy, lunatic, Malachi.' He was almost shaking when he said it."

"It's no big deal, babe." Malachi looked at Gisela and smiled his most becoming smile. "He will forget all about it soon enough."

It was at this point that Malachi stopped going home. He had only been to his shotgun shack twice since the scene at the café, partly because Gisela would only have sex with him in the privacy of her own bedroom. But mostly because, as far as Malachi could ascertain, a menacing, alien presence had taken over his house and had infected the entire neighborhood. The first time he went back was two days after they had shocked Señor Mendoza. Malachi wanted to retrieve his bike. He was not aware of anything out of the ordinary at that point and walked about as if in a dream. He was thinking vaguely about Gisela and how sexy she had seemed when she had acted the part of Nefertari, but his thoughts were unformed. He was lost in a labyrinth of shadows. Twilight was descending. The whirring sound of cicadas hovered in the darkness of the trees. Soon the stars would be visible. A few streetlights popped on and there were clouds of tiny insects, as frail and unaware as dust, bubbling up beneath the pale orange streetlight glow, their tiny lives disintegrating when they got too close. Malachi's own house was an ink blot of blackness, at least this is how it would appear to most people, but not to Malachi. He actually saw more clearly at night. The brightness of a sunny day sometimes overpowered his eyes. He felt as if he were looking at the world through a cloudy, dusty piece of gauze. But the darkness was a cleansing; it washed away the film.

    Malachi's first clue that something had changed was the presence of his bike in the middle of the street in front of his house. In truth, he did not at first even recognize that it was his bike. He saw a shiny, flat, disc-shaped object glinting in the light of the orange-glowing streetlights and wondered what it was, and as he stepped into the street for a closer look, the hairs on the back of his neck sizzled with electricity. It was his bike. Some unknown persons, it appeared, had placed his bike squarely in the middle of the street and then had proceeded to roll over it, back and forth and back and forth, quite possibly with a giant tractor or perhaps even a steamroller, until his bike had taken on the flattened, shiny, disc-shaped qualities already mentioned. He wondered how long it had taken to produce the uniform consistency of the object his bike had become. It was almost as if in the process of rolling back and forth over the bike, the metal had melted and then reformed. It was actually quite impressive.

Our hero stared at his bike for a long time. The electric hum of the streetlights and the whirring sound of the cicadas faded into the background static of his mind. He wondered why he had walked the other day from Allapattah to the café, he always took his bike, but he had left it at home that day, and he could think of no good reason why he had done so. He marveled at how fragile and unforgiving the mosaic of our lives truly was. One seemingly trivial misstep and the whole world broke into a million pieces. Malachi's expression became grim. It was the universe playing a cruel and pitiless joke. What was one supposed to do in the face of such cruelty, he wondered? But again, he had no answer. He shrugged, an unconcscious reflex, as if to say that even the world's most brilliant thinkers would struggle with this question. Then he noticed part of a wheel protruding from the disk and realized that his first impression had been wrong. (He often found that what he thought was perfect, in this case the uniform flatness of the disc, was not without flaws.) His mind went comfortably blank and he took hold of the edge of the wheel (about six inches of bent rim and popped rubber) and dragged the flattened bike up the walk and laid it against the side of the house. It did not occur to him that the unknown persons responsible for the crime might be lurking in the shadows, waiting to pounce. It was late and he was tired. He went inside without even turning on a light, and thereby missed the half dozen green envelopes with the hairless vagina logos stamped in the middle, the envelopes scattered about the floor, all of the gaping vaginas staring up at the blackness of the ceiling with unblinking vigilance. That first night Malachi went directly to bed.

    Several days later, perhaps a week, about ten in the morning and already the temperature was well above ninety, Malachi returned to his shotgun shack for the second and last time. An air of surveillance had descended upon the street. A seemingly abandoned white van was parked on the corner and there were strange clicking sounds coming from inside, like those from a Geiger counter or the rotating whir of an electric fan. As he passed by various houses he felt a fluttering of movement behind the windows, as if eyes had been glued to the glass and then curtains suddenly drawn, but he did not actually see anything out of the ordinary. Three doors from his house he saw a neighbor woman in a flowery dress (he could never remember her name) clipping her hedge, but she seemed less intent on pruning her azaleas (which Malachi had always felt was an odd choice for hedges, but to each his own) and more intent on observing his return. She seemed to have been purposely placed there to record if and when he should appear.

Malachi was not aware of her scrutiny at first, nor was he aware of the observers hidden behind their curtains or the two men inside the van taking photographs with a couple of wildlife cameras and a variety of zoom lens for when the quality of the light changed or they wanted a different angle or they were just bored with their assignment. It was only later that he realized the entire block had been mobilized against his return. While it was happening, he was aware of only a vague discomfort, as if the world was slightly out of focus and a headache was looming. Once again he was thinking of Gisela, but with greater clarity this time. He was certain that she would relent, and he allowed the illusion of his optimism to wash away the grime of negativity that had become embedded in his skin. In his mind's eye he saw Gisela suddenly on the big screen, and then he saw himself in a movie theater watching her voluptuous titties bouncing back and forth on a fantastic journey from ancient Egypt to the alternate America of the 1960s. He could see his future imagined self masturbating with uncontrollable delight. And he also noted, with some degree of pride, since he sometimes shared Gisela's bed, that most of the patrons of this future imagined theater were similarly engaged in pleasuring themselves, a natural reaction, to be sure, since the original script called for Gisela to play the entire movie naked from the waist up.

This was Malachi's state of mind as he pushed through the chain-link gate and headed up the walk. He took some comfort in the fact that the metal disc that had once been his bike was still leaning against the side of the house (we are always hoping that things will stay put where we place them), but he failed to notice that the disc had been moved to the other side of the front steps. To his credit, he did notice the more than two dozen green envelopes with gaping vagina logos now scattered across the floor when he went inside (though he took no interest in the messages he knew they contained). And he began to look at his present situation with a greater objectivity, what some would call fatalism, and what others would decry as a lack of faith. He wondered who the Velázquez brothers had hired to deliver the messages and when they would take on this duty themselves. He wondered how long he had before the next envelope would arrive.

It was a dicey game he was playing. He had fallen off the grid, so to speak, an ironic turn of the screw given that the world he inhabited was already off the grid. He was a ghost among the underbelly of ghosts until he could persuade Gisela to change her mind, or until some other solution presented itself. Without the faintest trace of humor, he began to wonder who was in charge anyway. He was still confident that things would work out. Malachi had always possessed psychotic levels of optimism. But the presence of so many envelopes had jarred his sense that God was truly on his side. He had been laboring under the assumption that he had an unlimited amount of time to set things right, and now he was almost overwhelmed with the dizzying sensation that time was short.

He forgot about closing the door. Staring down at the jumble of little green envelopes, he was suddenly struck by the way they were all piled one on top of another, the gaping, glistening vaginas all mixed together, a strange bouquet of paper flowers that seemed to glow with the stark funereal brilliance of orchids strewn across a casket. He could almost smell the fragrant, sickly sweet smell of ritual death hovering in the air. Then he remembered why he had come home. He had come for the Salma de la Prada films. He wanted Gisela to see these films, which had been viewed by millions, so she could appreciate the artistry of her own work and better understand the opportunity that lay before her. She could be the next Salma de la Prada. The world would be her oyster. That's what he was going to tell her. That was his plan.

Moments later Malachi emerged from the cool darkness of his shotgun shack with the three films in his right hand. The sun had become quite fierce and the air was thick with a blazing white heat. It was difficult to breathe. Malachi felt a sudden restlessness of the spirit, as if it were already too late to change his fate but he was going to die trying, and then his restlessness was replaced by a deep-seated paranoia. The world began to melt from the heat. He fumbled with the lock and then it seemed that the lock was melting and he jerked back his hand and left the keys dangling. Maybe he was dying, he thought. Or maybe the Velázquez brothers had already caught up with him and he was already dead. He stood on the steps facing the melting lock and the dangling keys until he regained his composure. The usual rigidity of the world returned. Then he headed away from his house, back down the street. He did not understand what was happening to his sense of reality, why he was plagued by these bizarre hallucinations. It was then he noticed the woman in the flowery dress moving away from her azaleas towards the sidewalk to intercept him. She was still holding her clippers.

"*Hola*, Broken Bike, *hola, hola*," she said, waving the clippers at him as she hurried along, then barring his path, at least partially, so he felt he had no choice but to stop as well. "You are going so quickly. And so soon. It is only the middle of the day."

He had never really looked at her before. They were neighbors, three houses apart, which meant he mostly saw her from a distance, trimming her hedge, setting the sprinkler at a certain angle so the water would not hit the house, carrying bags of groceries from the carport in through the side door. It was almost as if he had only seen her through the wrong end of a telescope. But now she was crowding up against his left shoulder, his left arm pinned against his side, the point of the clippers wavering only a few inches away. He could see that she had very wrinkled brown skin, especially her face, he had not realized she was so old, and her complexion was not uniform. One side of her face exhibited the normal discolorations and markings of old age, but the other side was horribly scarred with ridges that looked like someone had carved out pieces of her flesh with a knife. The ridges were glowing a bright bloody red from the sun. Malachi wondered if the pain of her disfigurement was fresh, or if she had long ago forgotten what had happened to her. He wondered what that kind of pain felt like. He wondered what she wanted with him. She looked up at him with childlike insistence, her eyes twinkling with a mirth that seemed out of place.

"Where are you going in such a hurry?" she said.

Malachi was uncertain what to say.

Then he remembered the movies and held them up with his unpinned arm. "It's nothing," he said. "Just returning a few movies."

She laughed with the same mirth reflected in her eyes.

"You young men are all alike," she said, and then she pointed at the movies with the tip of her clippers. "Always disappearing into the darkness to watch a picture show. Never looking out at the world. Never noticing what is real."

Malachi smiled and moved as if to depart, thinking the conversation was over, but the old woman was suddenly standing in the middle of the sidewalk, her clippers hanging ready by her side.

He was surprised at her unexpected agility.

She smiled back at Malachi, revealing the jagged remnants of perhaps three teeth.

"Do you believe in God, Broken Bike?"

"Yes, yes, I believe in God."

"Well that is only part of it, isn't it," she said, and she laughed some, a sort of a cackling, coughing laugh, and he could see spittle collecting on her three teeth and they began to glisten in the sunlight.

"And the Devil?" she said.

Malachi said nothing. He was trying to suppress a sudden urge to urinate. It was like being tempted in the desert.

"That's a bit trickier," she said, and then she laughed some more and rolled her tongue around the inside of her mouth and looked at him for a moment, studying his expression, and then she spat on the sidewalk. "It is hard to know if the Devil is even real," she said.

Malachi smiled weakly. The urge to urinate had passed.

"Especially if you spend all your time watching movies."

She pointed her clippers a second time at the movies he held in his hand and he followed her movements with his eyes. Then he heard the sound of an engine turning over and the white van on the corner pulled away from the curb, the dust of the street swirling. He watched the van speed up through the intersection and then bank suddenly left, the way an airplane sometimes banks after take-off, and disappear down a hidden alley. Then he turned back to the old woman, but she had vanished in the wake of the van's departure. Malachi heard the sound of a door closing shut and the heavy dull echo of the bolt sliding into place, and then there was only the sound of the white blazing heat and the lonely cry of a blue jay somewhere in the air above. He waited for a moment to see what might happen next, but nothing happened. Then he moved quickly, but not too quickly, down the street.

-27-

Word all over the city (at least the underbelly portion) was that the Velázquez brothers had put out a bounty on Malachi's head. It was not a "dead or alive" bounty just yet, but that was probably only a matter of time. Many felt that the only effective approach when it came to bounties was to make sure the wanted person was dead. The phrase "dead or alive" was merely an anachronistic formality, a holdover from the childish delusions of an earlier age. These progressive free-thinkers (what some would call anarchists) were certain that if they produced a dead Malachi, the Velázquez brothers would more than likely pay up. Then again, nobody could be quite sure what the Velázquez brothers would do in any situation. This element of unpredictability held everyone in check, even the free-thinkers. So for the moment the bounty on Malachi's head was more or less just a theoretical warning. The Velázquez brothers wanted Malachi alive, they wanted everyone to know they wanted Malachi alive, and since everyone in the city (the underbelly portion) thought Malachi was crazy, everyone left him alone. (Even the Velázquez brothers thought Malachi was crazy, this is why they liked him; they were the ones who first said "Heeee'll put a gun to your head like he giving you a cigarette," though whether this statement had any basis in actual fact or was simply a clever, preemptive marketing ploy by the Velázquez brothers, not even Horse remembered).

Malachi's only link with humanity was through Gisela, who provided him with a little extra cash as his resources dwindled and the comfort of her open legs to boost his spirits. He had become an expatriate rebel, which in some respects had been his goal for as long as he had worn dreadlocks, but he soon grew tired of living on the edge of the edge. It is one thing to seek complete isolation from the outside world, quite another to be abandoned by that world, or more precisely, by everyone you know.

Those who knew Malachi by sight (excepting Gisela) went so far as to cross to the other side of the street when they saw him coming, presumably so he wouldn't get the wrong idea. Malachi wasn't sure what was happening. His old life had vanished without warning. But perhaps he was too close to the events that were unfolding. Viewed instead from the detached, self-contained and very safe perspective of, say, sixty-thousand feet in the air (heaven by any other name, with or without clouds), Malachi's plight seemed a blessing in disguise. Indeed, it seemed as if the saints themselves were sitting on those cloud-covered steps leading up to paradise, watching every move poor old Malachi might make, conspiring with the universe to make sure he suffered no lasting harm.

If you can imagine asking one of those long-dead, no longer suffering martyrs what they thought they were doing, you can also probably imagine them saying in reply that "God was saving Malachi for better things."

There was no one, however, mortal or divine, real or imagined, who gave any thought to the welfare of the other parties involved in the Velázquez brothers' greatest venture, unless by welfare one meant pointing them in the direction of those heavenly steps noted above. (This was not true for Gisela, she was the talent, and therefore untouchable, and besides, it was rumored that Bull was secretly in love with her). Within three months of Gisela's decision to forgo international celebrity status in the adult film world, Horse supposedly informed Bull that they needed to pull the plug on the whole damn thing, they were bleeding to death, they couldn't go on like this forever, they'd lose every dime they had. They already had had to sell one of their speedboats, the Bertram. They didn't want to lose the two Cigarettes as well. Bull agreed. In spite of his psychotic enthusiasm for a life of crime (he supposedly said it was the only thing they were suited for), he no longer possessed the energy to start completely over from scratch, if it came to that, they had to think like businessmen, but all the same he wanted to tag at least one of the fuckers who had caused the bleeding, as a lesson to the others, something to remind them that the Velázquez brothers did not give a fuck about the rest of the world, he was adamant about that. Supposedly Horse said that went without saying.

  The big-time Mexican movie director was the fucker the Velázquez brothers decided to tag. They had no intention of killing the guy without first talking with him. The Velázquez brothers didn't like to be pinned down by their decisions. If they liked the guy well enough, they'd probably tell him to leave the country and they'd choose somebody else. Of course no one would ever know exactly what happened. One day the newspaper said that Juliano Manuelo Marquez, a big-time Hollywood movie director who currently made his home in Mexico City, had skipped town without paying his hotel bill. The newspaper said he had been in Miami for a few months to scout locations for a new film, but did not say what the film was about or who was producing it. The newspaper also said Marquez was wanted for questioning by the police on a separate undisclosed matter and that if anyone had any information as to his whereabouts they were to come forward immediately. A week later the newspaper ran a follow-up article that summarized all of the movies that Marquez had made, and listed all of his awards, including an Academy Award Nomination for Best Foreign Language Film for his film *The Old Guitarist* (the story of an old man who runs a brothel in the mountains of Northern Spain in the years leading up to the Spanish Civil War and is later killed by a corporal in the Civil Guard while trying to rescue one of his prostitutes — who it turns out is his only daughter — who was arrested for thievery and thrown in jail).

The follow-up article ended with the same plea for a member of the public at large to divulge inside information particular to an ongoing investigation, but not even the newspaper expected the article would get any results, which is probably why they buried it at the bottom of page nineteen opposite an ad for timeshares in the Keys. Two weeks after that, everyone (even the newspaper reporter who had written the articles) had forgotten the big-time movie director had even been in Miami, and Malachi would have been among this larger group except that he stumbled upon the truth one night in a seedy but popular drinking establishment called Gus's, a flimsy, shrunken-looking structure just north of downtown Miami that existed always and only in the shadows of the elevated Interstate. (Malachi had started drinking in random dives all over the city to make it more difficult for the Velázquez brothers to track his movements.)

The truth, as Malachi heard it, came dribbling out of the mouths of two drunken pool guys who worked for a pool cleaning company called Aqua-Clean. The Aqua-Clean headquarters was located three blocks from the bar in a building that looked like an abandoned cannery. The pool guys were still wearing their Aqua-Clean jumpsuit uniforms.

The conversation between the two pool guys:
"It's fucking hard to believe," said the first one.
He was clean shaven but had shaggy blond hair, and the sleeves of his uniform were rolled up, revealing a series of interlocking tattoos that looked like aquamarine-colored bolts of lightning slicing up each arm. It was possible that the lightning bolts were a symbol of some gang affiliation, but this seemed unlikely. The name Rudi was sewn into his uniform just above the left-side chest pocket. The company had chosen a very fancy script for the lettering, and also a bright aquamarine color for the thread, which you would expect, given the name of the company. The script was so fancy that if you weren't looking at the name too carefully, you might think it said Trudi instead.

"What about Jake," said the second one. He was half a head shorter than Rudi, with a full red beard but without the tattoos. The name on his uniform was Bert, or maybe Brett.

Malachi couldn't tell. Fancy script could be challenging in the dark. He settled on Bert.

"Jake doesn't know shit about what happened," said Rudi. "He wasn't even in the room. He was down at the pool draining the water when the Velázquez brothers drove up in their Hummer. It was Dominick who went up with them."

"Yeah, sure, Dominick told you all about it," said Bert. "How do you know what Dominick saw?"

"Trust me," said Rudi. "I know."

"Like shit you do," said Bert. "Nobody knows."

"Trust me," said Rudi again.

"Shit," said Bert.

The two pool guys finished off their beers (they were drinking Amstel, which Malachi didn't really like) and ordered another round. They were sitting at the far corner of the bar where the mahogany counter turned ninety degrees and ended abruptly at the stairs (only three steps) to a small storeroom. It was fairly difficult to see in the corner. The light bulb above the stairs was burnt out or broken, and there was no mirror behind the bar to reflect the light from those fixtures that did work, so the only effective illumination came from a small television set perched on the corner shelf above the door to the storeroom. There was a baseball game on with the volume turned down too low to actually hear, but nobody seemed to care.

The faces of the two pool guys were bathed in a soft, bluish glow from the game, but everything below their faces was submerged in darkness. From the other side of the bar they looked like two disembodied heads floating in the dark. And since the light from a television is never steady, the two heads seemed to shimmer constantly, and would sometimes even disappear altogether when the brightness of the game was replaced momentarily by a dark screen as the station went to a commercial break.

Malachi was sitting just before the elbow, pretending to watch the game. It was after eight o'clock and the bar was starting to fill up. Malachi's ears were buzzing with the sounds of waitresses clearing away empty bottles and the smash and shriek of broken glass and the cash register humming and the murmuring drone of many voices hanging in the air like smoke and the bartender ringing a brass sailor's bell whenever he got a good tip and the edgy, self-indulgent, drunken laughter of men who had scores to settle but became impotent when facing an opportunity for revenge. The bartender almost forgot to take Malachi's order.

"So you want to know what happened?" said Rudi

"Sure, what the fuck," said Bert.

"Dominick said they took the service elevator up to the ninth floor and went straight to that Mexican prick's room and they didn't even knock cause the Velázquez brothers had a key. Man, you sure as hell don't mess with those Velázquez brothers."

The bartender returned with two more Amstels for the two pool guys and a whiskey sour for Malachi. The two pool guys lowered their voices to a whisper when the bartender was there, hardly even glancing his way, and then resumed in normal tones when he left to settle a dispute at the other end of the counter.

"He just said it was in his contract, and one of the brothers said they didn't give a shit about contracts, except the ones they put out themselves, but the prick didn't get it, all he said was 'then we'll see you in court.'"

"Crazy dumb fuck," said Bert.

"You said it. Dominick said he couldn't believe his eyes the way that fat Mexican prick was talking to the Velázquez brothers, like they worked at the hotel parking cars. But the worst of it was the whole time the brothers were trying to talk to him rational like, this prick was sucking on a cigar and blowing smoke in their faces. Total fucking disrespect. Dominick said they were giving the guy plenty of chances to be reasonable, though in retrospect he said it was clear the brothers had made up their minds about the prick pretty early in the conversation."

"Crazy dumb fuck," said Bert. "He was probably fucked the moment he opened his mouth."

"You got that right. Dominick said he was the biggest prick he ever saw. And no one could believe how many cigars this guy smoked. The other brother wanted to know how many boxes of cigars he'd gone through, meaning the Mexican. Dominick said there were dozens of empty boxes of Cubans all over the floor and on the bed, he couldn't say how many. But the prick said he didn't keep track of trivial expenses like that, he was paid to create great art, and smoking cigars helped put him in the mood, and then he blew some more smoke at the Velázquez brothers and walked out onto the balcony. Dominick said the prick was standing there blowing smoke, and all he was wearing was a pink bathrobe and sunglasses like some fruity homosexual fuck, and then just like that he turned his back on the Velázquez brothers and went out onto the balcony. You bet he was fucked. Dominick said a breeze was blowing and you could see the fat, greasy cheeks of the guy's ass, but he didn't care, he was just smoking and looking out at the beach and the morning sun on the water. Dominick said he couldn't believe what he was seeing."

Bert gave a long low whistle, like a bullet that could bend around corners.

"Man, didn't he know who he was dealing with?"

"I guess not."

"What kind of dumb fuck turns their back on the Velázquez brothers?"

"You got me."

"And wearing a pink bathrobe to boot."

"The crazy shit people do."

"Some people."

"Yeah, some people."

The two men seemed to be glowing with amazement, even in the dark. Once again the bartender returned and the voices of the two disembodied heads sunk to a whisper. More Amstels appeared on the counter. A couple more whiskey sours. Then the bartender had to help some of the waitresses with a rowdy crew that had pushed three tables together in the middle of the bar and were watching a girl take off her clothes. The girl was already down to her panties. She was thoroughly enjoying herself.

The normal tone of the conversation resumed.

"Wait a minute," said Bert. "You mean to tell me the one brother lifted that Mexican prick off the ground with only one arm and tossed him over the railing?"

"That's what I said."

"Man, I would have loved to see that."

"Dominick said it was pretty impressive."

"What do you think he told the prick just before he did it?"

"I don't know. Dominick couldn't hear. They were talking together for quite a while. Just the two of them on the balcony, the one brother with his arm hooked around the shoulders of the guy and the breeze blowing, and then the one brother must have told a joke cause the Mexican prick started laughing. But he still didn't get what was happening. And then just like that the one brother lifted the Mexican into the air, like his arm was a goddamn cargo crane or something, and then he swung his arm back nice and slow, and then without saying a word he snapped it forward and sent that Mexican flying up into the air. Dominick said it was pretty amazing. He said it was like watching a slow-motion instant replay on television. The guy's legs were kicking and he was losing his pink bathrobe, it was sort of fluttering up above his shoulders, like a defective parachute or something, and the last thing Dominick saw was shit coming out of the guy's ass, like he was squeezing it out with his cheeks, like he was trying to stop it only he couldn't, and then he was gone. He was just fucking gone. Just the pink bathrobe floating in the air and a few ribbons of shit."

"Man, I would have loved to see that."

The two men stopped talking for a moment, staring vaguely into space, the bluish light of the game washing across blank faces. It seemed as if they had suddenly become hypnotized by the image of the pink bathrobe, as if they were now watching the death of the big-time Mexican movie director on a gigantic movie screen suspended in the blackness of their imagination.

"You don't think about that, do you."

"What?"

"Shitting like that."

"No, I suppose not."

"Sort of an involuntary reaction to the stress. You can't help it."

"No, I guess you can't. Nobody can."

"Man, what a fucked-up way to go."

"You said it."

"But that's what you get when you fuck with the Velázquez brothers."

"They're professionals, that's for sure."

"Damn right they are."

". . . ."

"Dominick said it sort of took you by surprise how easy they made it look."

The two disembodied heads paused again, looking more thoughtful now, aware, almost philosophic. They drank their beers, ordered more Amstels, drank some more. They seemed to have forgotten how to speak. The bartender came over and turned off the television and the two heads disappeared. After a while they were talking again, but they were just voices in the darkness.

"So what happened to the body?"

"Nobody knows for sure."

"What about the police?"

"The police don't know shit."

"I'll bet Jake knows."

"Jake doesn't know shit either. Jake was draining the water from the pool when Dominick went up with the brothers, and when the pool was empty a guy from the hotel told him to cover the bottom of the pool with a tarp. They were going to paint pictures of dolphins on the sides of the pool for kids to look at when they were swimming under water. They didn't want to get paint on the bottom. He could come back later when they were done painting. He could come back in a couple of days. So Jake covered up the bottom and then he left. When he came back the tarp was gone and there were dolphins just like the guy said. That's all Jake knows."

That was the end of the conversation. Malachi settled into the darkness of the corner. It was a comfortable feeling. He ordered himself one more whiskey sour and drank it slowly. He was thinking about the Velázquez brothers and the big-time movie director. In his mind's eye he could see the poor guy sailing through the air and then landing splat in the empty pool, his neck crunching up beneath him, his shit smeared across the tarp, the blood pooling out from various places where his veins had burst from the impact, and then the brothers rolling up the tarp and loading it into a boat and heading out to the Gulf Stream and dumping the body for the sharks.

The two pool guys were right about one thing, he thought, the Velázquez brothers were very professional. You had to admire them for that. Malachi thought for a moment about how much skill was required to toss a guy from a ninth-floor balcony so that he landed in the middle of an empty swimming pool. How many times did you have to practice that before you could judge correctly the appropriate angle of descent and the effect of the wind and a dozen other variables he knew nothing about? How long before you became an expert? Then Malachi was wondering if this one would count as a drowning victim because the guy had died in a pool at a hotel on the beach, or if it would be recorded as a near drowning, or maybe flying off a rooftop, or more precisely, a hotel balcony, since there was no water in the pool when it happened. Malachi thought about the death of the big-time movie director for a while. Then he finished his whiskey sour. He looked over at the pool of darkness where the two pool guys had been, but they were long gone. Malachi had not even seen them leave.

-28-

There is a warm wet wind blowing in from the bay. It is surprisingly strong, the wind. It is soon a ferocious wind, sweeping the streets. Garbage tumbles past, shredded pieces of newspaper, paper cups, candy wrappers, tin cans rolling with parabolic fury. A few cars whoosh by, but other than that the streets are empty. Everyone else is indoors.

Then the rain comes. It is only eleven o'clock in the morning and the rain is already here. A storm of tiny bullets rattling against windows and doors at a sharp forty-five-degree angle. The tiny bullets sting when they hit flesh, but they do not penetrate. Yet they burn all the same. The air is steaming from their passage. The ground is on fire. In spite of the rain, you can smell smoke. Wisps of blue smoke curl up from the sidewalk even as the downpour increases in velocity. A few shingles fly off a roof. A garbage can careens into a parked car and a car alarm goes off, then several more car alarms. Malachi is standing in the doorway of the video store during the storm, his back flattened against the black padded door to minimize the impact of the rain, but the doorway is too narrow.

Then the wind subsides, not all at once, but in short gasping breaths, as if it is too early in the day for such a storm. After a while there is a pale yellow glow from the east, and from somewhere the sound of seagulls. Malachi is soaked. He is holding three videos. He is clutching them against his stomach. The videos are also wet, at least the boxes, but the boxes are made of plastic so it doesn't matter. Malachi turns to face the door and begins pounding but nobody answers. As a last resort, he tries the door and the door opens easily so Malachi steps inside. For a moment he does not know where he is. He wonders if he is dreaming, but the sense that he is awake and looking out through the jelly of his two eyes is quite strong. Then he laughs, a hollow inwardly focused laughter that nevertheless bounces off the interior walls, which reverberate like the membrane of an African drum. He has been suffering from hallucinations now for the last few months, what some would call waking dreams, which every good Rastafarian knows is the source of all religious inspiration. Yet the reality inside these hallucinations has been no different than reality at other times. Malachi wonders if he is once more slipping into another altered state, but he does not panic. The world is a fluid place. And he has been under a lot of stress lately. And he has been eating poorly. If it weren't for Gisela, he thinks, but then he decides not to think about Gisela

He decides instead to inspect the fabric of reality inside the store. It is very dark inside. There is a deeply rooted stillness in the air. It is almost like entering an ancient tomb. He feels as if he is wandering through a grainy old photograph. There are only four windows, very narrow, and very high up, and they are protected by blinds that seem almost lacquered shut. Malachi has only been here when the fluorescent lights were on and there were people in trench coats and hats milling about. Odd that the store should be closed on a Wednesday morning, but maybe Paco is sick. He has only ever seen Paco sitting behind the counter, playing video games and offering up occasional suggestions about which videos to rent, which offer the greatest visual stimulation for private masturbation sessions, and which should be viewed with friends. Paco is the only one who works here. There is no one else the Velázquez brothers trust half so much.

Then Malachi breathes in the familiar odor of stale urine and cigarette smoke. His eyes begin to adjust. He is no longer confused. A pale glow seeps around the edges of the blinds. Behind the register on the wall a red glowing security light blinks steadily. There is just enough light to see by, a diffuse light, naturally, but it is enough. Malachi is satisfied that this is not the landscape of a dream. He heads over to the cubicle where Paco normally sits and stands and listens. He hears the stringy, mechanical whining of cicadas, which seems to him a natural sound even inside a dimly lit video store, but as he listens more closely he realizes he is listening to voices, not the sounds of insects. The voices are buried beneath layers of radio static, he decides, which means it is difficult to pinpoint their exact location, but he is certain the voices are coming from the roof. He does not think about the incongruity of a radio blaring away from the rooftop of a video store that is closed for the day.

He closes his eyes and follows the sound, moving by instinct now, stopping occasionally and tilting his head to make sure of his bearings, stepping with small, careful steps to avoid making any unnecessary noise and giving himself away. He marvels at his ability to move with such sure-footed confidence even with his eyes closed. He has never done this before and is elated with his success. Blindness is only a state of mind, he thinks, like despair. He tries to remember what he was doing before he came to the video store, but his memory is a blank.

Then he remembers the three videos he is still clutching. He stares at the videos in his hand, but doesn't remember how they got there. He wonders if they have always been there. He tries to shake them loose, but they are stuck, they are a part of his own flesh, like a cancer.

Then the sounds of the voices seem all of a sudden quite loud. He realizes they are not voices on the radio. They are almost on top of him, it seems, descending from the darkness of the stairs that lead to the roof. The voices are so close he can almost feel their hot breath on his face. He forgets about the cancerous videos and heads up the stairs and sits down on the top step, pressing his ear against the door. It is the kind of behavior one would expect in a low-budget gangster flick from the 1940s. (All he needs is a revolver in his free hand to make the scene complete.) He is not sure why he puts his ear to the door. He has never liked B-movies. Besides, there is no mistaking the fact that the voices are engaged in a private conversation.

The first two voices (a big heavy voice and a slow, steady voice) are familiar, but the third one is unfamiliar. The big heavy voice is doing more talking than the other two. This voice is asking about the photos and the unfamiliar voice is saying he only came back once, we took some pictures of the neighborhood and here's the photo of the old woman and the two of them talking, and then the slow, steady voice is saying the old woman already works for us, she's been on the payroll for years, she was that *piantada caja*, the one who danced at La Campana, at least until the fiasco with the Panamanians, she'll do anything we ask, and then the big heavy voice laughing a full, robust laughter, you mean that's the sister of the little pipsqueak, and then, she is, and then, she's so goddamn old looking, what happened to her face, and then, don't you recognize your own handiwork, you're the one who carved her up, and then, yes, I remember now, she didn't even make a sound, sort of felt bad afterwards, but it had to be done, still that doesn't explain how old she looks, and then, I guess not, perhaps it's premature aging from the stress, the first one bursting out with more laughter, the entire roof beginning to shake, you mean from giving up her brother, and the second one, I guess so, and then, what was her name, and then Isidora, and then, good old Isidora, put Isidora on him, and then, already did that, and then, oh God, it's too rich, and then the voices becoming a low murmur as various strategies are discussed.

Malachi begins pressing his ear against the door with

greater intensity, as if it is a suction cup and if he presses it hard enough he can pick up even the thoughts and emotions behind the words, and then the big heavy one again, reminiscing, his face contorted with visible pride (visible in the sense that Malachi can see a contorted, pleased expression in his mind's eye from the words alone), the voice recounting a time when he was down in Little Havana eating pizza at his friend Eduardo's place on 5th and a call came in for delivery but Eduardo was short-staffed, that bastard never had enough staff, always trying to cut corners, the one laughing some more, not so loud as before, but still thick and heavy, the slow, steady one saying you're going to love this, and the third, unfamiliar voice not really saying anything, just a short, squeak of a laugh, and then the first one, so I said I'd deliver the pizza, what are friends for, and Eduardo gave me the pizza and a note with the address, it was an everything pizza with Anchovies and pineapples and God knows what else, just a whole lot of garbage, everything you can imagine, and the second one now laughing, interrupting, just the way you like it, and the first one again, you wouldn't have believed where I took that pizza, some studio shit-hole on top of the old liquor store (the second one saying this was years ago, before they went out of business, and the third, unfamiliar voice saying, he remembered the place), and so I got there and I looked at the note and it said please use the back stairs, we're having a hell of a party, so I was expecting all sorts of naked pussy and all the booze I could drink and a whole lot of fucking, I was looking forward to having a really good time, you remember the kind of parties they had in that neighborhood, you'd have thought the same thing, and then the second one saying this is where it gets good, and the third unfamiliar voice not saying anything, and then the first one, but what a fucked up place that studio was, I walk in there all pumped up with this everything pizza and all I see is this fucked-up homosexual asshole, he's absolutely naked except he's covered with paint, all sorts of colors mashed together like some mascot hyped up on coke, and somebody had tied him up like a hog and left him leaning against the sofa, you had to wonder what kind of friends he had, so there I am and it looks like he's got an apple in his mouth or something and he's moaning and moaning, only I can't quite hear what he's saying, I'm not sure it was even words, he looked pretty out of it, but not all the way out it, I mean he was trying to look back to see who just came in only he couldn't turn his head far enough because of the rope, and I'm eating one of the slices of pizza now, because there's no way in hell this fruity homosexual bastard is getting a pizza from me, and I walk up to him, just behind him so he can't see, and I say what the fuck are you saying, just like that, a normal even tone, no belligerence whatsoever, and he moans some more and then it sounds like he's saying just fuck me will you, fuck me again, please fuck me, I mean it was disgusting what was coming out of his mouth, so I take a step back, just to survey the landscape, if you know what I mean, and the place was a wreck, paint all over the place and dozens of cheap, unexceptional paintings, but looks like somebody tossed them all over the room, like they didn't give a shit, I guess the guy thought he was a painter, but it was the kind of sick, twisted paintings that give art a bad rap, I mean you wouldn't want your children to see them and have to explain why somebody's penis has been cut off and shoved into a blender, that kind of thing, so I'm standing there eating the guy's pizza and he's moaning the same tired shit over and over again, and finally I see this tiny statue of a white penis, I guess it was a penis, I don't know what it was, all I know is that I pick it up and I hear myself saying, you want to get fucked, well okay then, and I shove that statue of a penis up his ass and I smash it in there pretty good, I mean I'm pretty much carving him up, and he's screaming now, you can't hear a single recognizable word come out of his mouth, and he starts shuddering some and the blood is seeping out around his crack, and then I yank that penis out and I have to take a quick step back cause the blood is just gushing, and I watched the guy for a while, and he's barely whimpering now, that kind of injury hurts at first and there's always an awful lot of blood, but you go into shock fairly quick, so there's not too much suffering, then the guy gave one more shudder and that was that, I wiped the base of the statue so there wouldn't be any prints and tossed it on the sofa, grabbed the rest of the pizza and headed out the door, I mean the guy was disgusting, what did he think I was going to do, I mean I'm usually a live and let live kind of guy, you know that Brother, but not in a situation like that, that was just too much for me.

Malachi has had enough. His brain is burning, his synapses shriveling up from the heat, his skull filling up with particles of ash. There is nothing he can do. He wonders who had tied up the painter and why, and he is struck by how fluid and fragile the world truly is, and yet nobody seems to give a fuck. He is unable to shake the image of the sad, tormented painter from his mind. Why should he be given the burden of this story at precisely this moment?

He closes his eyes and he can see the wavering ghost of a multi-colored face like the face of a drugged mascot, eyes half closed, begging for mercy and no mercy forthcoming. Waves of nausea ripple through Malachi and he realizes that, at least for the moment, God (his God, who Malachi vaguely understands to be a shadowy reflection of his own divinity) has forsaken the world. He opens his eyes and breathes in the darkness. The waves subside. He wonders how long the three voices on the rooftop will continue talking and when the door will open, but he does not yet move from the stairs. He is waiting for a sign perhaps, a message from his God that he can deliver to thirsty ears, his own ears certainly, some message of hope, and if not hope, at least compassion. There must be others who are tired of the darkness of the underbelly, who are hoping some kind of prophet will appear and lead them to paradise, or at least point the way. Malachi is almost overwhelmed by the thought that the entire universe is waiting to be forgiven. The waves return. Trembling, he wonders how long he must wait for absolution if his God does not exist (a troubling thought if he is in fact his own God). He takes a second, deep breath and then a third and the waves subside again and he sits a little while longer. The image of the tormented painter vanishes. The voices from the rooftop are no longer audible. They have sort of just floated away. Perhaps they were never truly there. Perhaps he has been hallucinating. Malachi considers briefly that his entire life has been one single hallucination. For one brief moment it is the only explanation that makes any sense.

Then the fluorescent lights from below begin to flicker. They do not stay on, but continue to flicker, again and again, illuminating the video store with brilliant flashes of light, and then the diffuse, unearthly glow from before returning.

-29-

The video store is now crawling with men in trench coats and wide-brimmed hats. They are moving up and down the aisles. Paco is nowhere in sight, but that does not mean anything. He is probably in the back pounding down a couple of cokes and a few candy bars before he takes his customary seat. But there is something off about the men roaming the aisles. They all possess the same face, a strange theatrical mask of a face with white porcelain cheeks and smartly polished black moustaches with tips that curl up slightly, and brightly painted lips, red lips, with more white porcelain where there should be teeth, and a tiny black hole in the exact center between the lips. It looks like they are about to whistle, but they don't. They move like robotic zombies, mechanically zooming up and down the aisles on rows of tiny wheels hidden by the length of their trench coats.

At first Malachi just stares at the frozen faces zooming back and forth. He can hear the droning whir of tiny motors and rotating gears. Then he hears a voice, the same mechanical voice coming out of the black hole of each machine. The voice, multiplied by the dozen or so machines in the store, is repeating the same phrase over and over again. "Everything we do follows us everywhere we go." Their tone is a very flat monotone, and yet because of the number of machines, it carries great weight.

Slowly Malachi begins making his way towards the counter where Paco should be arriving any minute. He has to stop at predictable points along the way to avoid the zooming mechanical customers. They go whizzing past without even a glance, presumably because their maker had not installed a gear so they could rotate their heads. Then Malachi stumbles into one and sends the machine flying into the shelves.

A couple of rows of adult movies fall to the floor and the machine lands on its side, its tiny wheels now exposed, spinning and spinning, the machine still repeating the same phrase over and over and over. But with the accident a change comes over the other machines. They now realize Malachi is in the store — perhaps not Malachi precisely, but someone who might knock them over — and they begin searching for him. They do not need rotating heads to survey the entire store, they can turn on a dime. They are all now spinning slowly round and round as they move up and down the aisles, searching him out. Malachi also notices that the tone of their voices has changed and now seems slightly sinister, modulated by an appetite for revenge, perhaps.

Malachi realizes he has slipped into a tedious but rather complicated hallucination. He is caught in some sort of a loop that began with the voices on the roof. The universe is playing back the same scene over and over again, and there is only one way out, at least as Malachi sees it. So he begins attacking the roving machines. Their most obvious weakness, and Malachi's salvation, is that they possess no arms, a fact which Malachi had not noticed earlier, so he simply begins pushing them over, knocking them to the floor, the sound of spinning wheels and rotating gears now echoing harmlessly throughout the video store.

By the time Malachi reaches the counter, Paco is sitting there, one eye on a new video game, the other on a security camera monitor that flashes pictures of what is happening in each aisle.

Paco smiles as Malachi approaches.

"You know you didn't have to do that," says Paco.

"Didn't have to do what?" says Malachi.

"Knock them over like that."

Malachi looks into the security camera and he can see dozens of upended machines on the floor, their wheels still spinning.

"They wouldn't hurt a fly."

Malachi isn't sure what to say after that. Paco is staring at him and he is beginning to feel uncomfortable. Malachi suddenly feels like a fly suddenly exposed to a fly swatter.

"It's okay," Paco says after a while, and then he nods

in the direction of the fallen machines. They are now back on their wheels, patrolling the aisles once again, repeating the same stock phrase.

"Sure," says Malachi.

Malachi is only vaguely troubled by the sudden resurrection of the machines. He watches them a while, first with his back to Paco, then with his eyes glued to the security camera monitor. Everything is pretty much like it was before, except every so often, at seemingly random intervals, one of the machines does a slow 360-degree spin, as if to anticipate another collision like the one with Malachi. He looks at the machines with a mixture of admiration and envy. He is impressed by their engineering. Their design seems flawless, as close to perfection as is humanly possible. He is impressed by their ability to learn from their mistakes. It is almost like the pride of a father.

"So what do you need today, Broken Bike?" says Paco.

"Just returning a few videos," says Malachi.

"The Salma de la Prada videos?"

"They're late. Sorry about that."

"Don't worry about it."

The videos are no longer stuck to Malachi's hand. He does not remember their ever having been stuck. He hands them over to Paco without comment.

"So what did I tell you," says Paco. "She's one hell of a beautiful bitch, ain't she."

Malachi turns to leave, but Paco reaches behind the counter and pulls out a gun, a shiny black revolver, and lays it on the counter. He looks around to see if anyone notices, but there is no one else with eyes to see, only the robot customers patrolling the aisles, the steady, comforting whir of gears and motors and spinning wheels.

"Hey Broken Bike," says Paco. "I want you to have this. You might need it."

"What do I need a gun for?"

"Man, who doesn't need a gun around here," says Paco, and he is grinning now.

"No, man, thanks, but a gun's too much trouble."

"Hey, no worries, man," says Paco "It's not even a real gun. It's a movie gun. A prop. It doesn't shoot anything. Not even blanks. They were going to use it in your girlfriend's movie before she quit. It was just lying around so I snagged it. Go on, take it."

Malachi looks at the gun on the counter and he can barely suppress a smile. He stuffs the movie prop gun into his black bicycle shorts and heads out the door.

-30-

Malachi walked away from the video store, his face beaming. The air was still heavy and moist from the rain, with the hint of a second storm on its way, but Malachi did not notice. He felt suddenly invincible. Even if the gun were only a movie prop, the fact that Paco had given him the gun meant that the path of his destiny was changing once again. He was no longer just a lonely Rastafarian rebel living on the edge of the edge of reality. He was someone with a future, and it did not matter what this future was going to be, any future was better than no future at all. This is what Malachi was thinking. This is why he was smiling.

He was still smiling when he reached the café. The place was packed as usual, the regular crew of Dominicans from the other side of the river and the Cubans who lived on this side. You would expect a fight to break out the moment the two groups got together, but one never did, not a real fight anyway, with knives shoved into somebody's stomach and maybe a gunshot and blood pouring out all over the place, and then the paramedics would arrive, and then the police. At worst, there were a few scuffles with someone getting his nose broke or clocked in the Adam's apple so he'd shut up so people could eat, but nothing serious ever happened at the café. Everyone checked their weapons at the door, figuratively speaking, of course, and put on their best television camera faces. (These were the very same faces they would flash to the rest of the world if they ever found themselves sitting on death row and they suddenly had one final chance to spit into the microphone of a roving television news reporter and proclaim their innocence.)

Malachi hadn't been down to the café in a few months, not since the scene with Gisela. He was hoping Señor Mendoza had forgotten all about his buffoonery, or had at least changed his mind. Wednesday nights meant all the bean soup and roasted pork sandwiches you could eat and enough beer and wine to drown the whole goddamn city.

The first thing he noticed when he got there was how quite the café was, in spite of the fact that every fucking table was full. But no one said a word, except to order another beer or another bowl of soup. Everyone was staring blankly at their food while they ate, they wouldn't even look at each other, and when they weren't eating they were smoking cigarettes or cigars and downing beers at a furious pace and then looking over at the door with deeply troubled eyes, a look of breathless agitation smeared across their faces, as if they had been flailing about in the middle of a dark, windless, wine-dark sea but now they were exhausted and it was the moment before they sank to the bottom.

Malachi had to sit all the way in the back where the counter ended so at first he couldn't see why everyone was so anxious. The smoke was pretty thick. The two rotating fans with their wide, palmetto-style blades could barely keep the smoky air circulating.

Then the door opened and someone went out and the air cleared for a moment and Malachi could see the trouble. There were two strange, obviously lunatic white men sitting at the first table when you came in. The one had crazy red hair, stringy hair like sea snakes. All he was doing was talking and waving his arms in the air. The sea snakes were writhing uncontrollably as he talked. The other one didn't say a word. He was covered in a thick black matte of hair. All you could see were eyes every now and then, and you could see murderous intent in his eyes, the kind Malachi had only ever seen in the movies, but mostly his face was mashed down into a bowl of soup and all you saw was a great heavy, sullen blackness. He knew immediately who they were. Not their names, their names didn't matter. The Velázquez brothers had sent them to tidy things up. This was his new future unfolding, this is why

Paco had given him the gun. It had been a joke. Or a warning. Malachi almost couldn't believe it, but what else could they be? The men sitting by the front door were assassins.

For a time, Malachi did nothing. The sky began to grow dark, the promise of the second storm would soon be fulfilled, but Malachi did not care. He sat there and drank a few beers and wondered what he was supposed to do and then he drank a few more. Slipping out the back was not really an option, especially if the two had seen him come in. He would rather sit there among the anxious crowd at the café. Maybe an angel would come to his aid. But if they hadn't seen him yet, then it was worth a try. But they wouldn't be very good assassins if they hadn't spotted him the moment he arrived, and he was fairly certain the Velázquez brothers hired only the best, so what should he do? Malachi did not know. He was frozen by the babble in his brain. He ordered yet another beer, but this one he drank slowly. He could feel the cool liquid cascading down his throat. He watched Señor Mendoza moving back and forth among the tables, talking with Dominicans and Cubans who had forgotten how to speak but Señor Mendoza understanding what they wanted without needing words and waving to one of the sexy *chiquitas* for another bowl of soup or beer or wine and then on to the next table.

The radio behind the counter was playing a salsa but you could barely hear it, and then a Latin pop tune came on and someone turned the radio up and Malachi breathed in the song in the hopes that it would do a better job of settling his nerves than the beers. The Latin pop tune was replaced by another salsa. Señor Mendoza was no longer monitoring the needs of the Dominicans and the Cubans. He was now standing next to the swinging kitchen door, directly behind Malachi.

Strangely, the presence of Señor Mendoza, a looming, shadowy presence arching up onto the ceiling, gave Malachi a sudden shot of courage, and he began to formulate a plan, and because Malachi was slightly drunk, his plan came tumbling out of his mouth in short, cryptic phrases, which would have sounded like the gibberish of a madman unless you were listening very carefully, in which case Malachi's logic possessed the impeccable clarity of a cloudless summer's day.

It wasn't Gisela's fault, though clearly if she had relented he would be in the clear, he hoped they left her alone, there was no reason to take her out, but these two sitting there by the window, he had no idea the Velázquez brothers would reach this point so quickly, the fucking bastards, he still couldn't quite believe these two skinny white assassins like white devils were there to put a bullet in his brain, how many bullets to do the job properly, three bullets, six bullets, one gun or two, his words ballooning now, escaping like steam, he was re-living the loop from the conversation on the roof to acting out the climax of the movie in the café, and then Malachi laughed, a sudden, unrehearsed ballooning laughter because the scene they had acted out had been a very funny scene, what had they thought, the two construction workers sitting at the bar, and the other one who came in and stared at the poster of the bullfighter, what had they been thinking when he started jerking off right there and then Gisela taking a peek and she had started laughing, and you couldn't break character like that in the middle of a scene, particularly when you were performing before a live audience, he wasn't a professional, but he knew that much, and then she was back in it, but you could tell she was playing two parts at that point, Nefertari the consort of the sun god Amun-Ra, and the laughing Gisela with the exuberant breasts who couldn't believe what her Malachi was doing and going through with it anyway, and he loved her for taking part in the scene (though he most certainly would have loved her even if she hadn't), even if she couldn't help laughing when he had started masturbating, or maybe because she started laughing, and then the tenor of Malachi's voice hardened and he stared across the café at the two assassins and there was now a deliberate darkness to his hissing words, he would take the two bastards out himself, they wouldn't get near his Gisela, not if he could do anything about it, and then he remembered his movie prop gun stuffed into his pants and he took it out, caressing it while he stared into the darkness of his imagination, his precise thoughts unable to coalesce except in a vague, dreamlike way, as if the possibility that this was a real gun was enough, and with the flicker of this possibility shimmering in his mind, Malachi exploded across the café and found himself sitting at the table with the two assassins, but once there, he had no idea what to do. You could clearly see the gun wasn't real. It looked like a piece of rubber that had been damaged in a fire. He stabbed at the air with the movie prop gun in a half-hearted attempt to look menacing. The one assassin started laughing softly, quietly, a contained sort of laughter, a suppressed laughter, but still his sea snake hair went flying all over the table. The other one barely registered any awareness beyond his soup. Then Malachi's voice took over and he heard himself hissing through his teeth.

"Tell me why I shouldn't pull the trigger," he heard himself say. Malachi knew it was a ludicrous question the moment he opened his mouth.

The one assassin seemed on the verge of busting a gut, but he was able to contain himself. "I can't think of a thing to say," he said. Then he leaned his face across the table, his head tilted, as if to get a better bead on his adversary with the rubber movie prop gun, and then his face cracked open with a smile.

Malachi's hand began to tremble.

The other one said nothing, his face mashed in his bowl, his countenance disguised.

"But what if the gun were real?" said the one, and for the first time Malachi noticed his chipped teeth. "Now that would be an interesting dilemma. What would I have said if the gun were real? That's the real question, isn't it?"

Malachi nodded stupidly. Once again he felt disconnected from events. He would just listen to the one assassin while the other one ate his soup and hope for the best.

"I suppose I would have said if you need to pull the trigger, then you need to pull the trigger."

Then he reached over and took the movie-prop gun from Malachi and inserted it into his own mouth.

He was now choking back his laughter.

"Then I would have said it doesn't make a goddamn bit of difference what you or anybody else does. We are all dancing in one goddamn eternal circle. Like angels on the head of a pin. We're all going to end up right back where we started anyway. So what the hell, let's get this goddamn fucking dance over with. That's what I would have said. Something like that. Sounds pretty goddamn existential, doesn't it? Like a fucking philosopher."

And then the one exploded in a fit of laughter, which coincided, as if on cue, with an enormous flash of lightning (for the long-awaited second storm had finally arrived) and the street outside shown with the brilliant incandescence of a second sun, and for a moment every head in the café turned to look and they thought they were looking at a washed-out photograph from years ago. Then the white glare of this photograph faded and darkness descended and with it came the rain. The atmosphere inside the café had suddenly changed. It hummed now with the happy laughter of half-drunk men. Some of the men were slapping at the beefy brown behinds of the waitresses. Or grabbing one and giving her ass a squeeze.

Malachi had been wrong about these two, he realized that now. The one with the chipped teeth ordered a round of beers and the other one slurped down the rest of his soup and came out of his fog. The beers came and they started drinking with wild abandon. Malachi shoved the movie-prop gun back into his shorts. For the first time in several months he felt completely relaxed.

-31-

The two teachers entered Malachi's life at precisely the right moment. At least this is how Malachi felt. Within days of their first meeting, he had told them of his troubles with the Velázquez brothers and how he had pinned all of his hopes on Gisela, but now he was beginning to question the wisdom of this strategy. Naturally the two teachers shared with Malachi their opinions (mostly philosophical garbage) about the kind of danger the Velázquez brothers represented (the older teacher was a sort of Trotskyite revisionist with a similar revisionist understanding of Fascism, and this perspective shaped his analysis; the younger teacher knew just enough about the gangsters of the Prohibition Era, gleaned from years of watching old black and white movies, to appreciate the dangers, both physical and social, of armed thugs who lived beyond the reach of the law), but any advice they offered Malachi on how to repair the damage that had been done by his inability to influence Gisela was either impractical (find another girl with tits as big as Gisela to take over the starring role of the movie) or uninformed (forget about the Velázquez brothers, they'll give up after a while, everyone does) or downright idiotic (challenge the Velázquez brothers to a duel with a pair of 18th century French dueling pistols made by Peniet of Paris).

To be fair, most of their conversation about the Velázquez brothers took place one night in La Mamacita's, a club up in Allapattah that looked like a bombed-out warehouse. They were all very drunk. And they could hardly hear themselves breathe, let alone talk. The air inside the club vibrated with the hazy, tinny, electric din of merengues and reggae and hip-hop and techno and Latin funk and bohemian jazzy shit, like the background static of the universe. They were sitting on tall bar stools at a small upright table in the cascading shadows of a broken light that hung from the ceiling, drinking beer and watching people dance. The greasy brightness of the bar on the other side of the club pulsed with a flurry of arms reaching for drinks (mostly green bottles of beer) and then cash exchanging hands and then thick, coarse laughter that broke through the music, and then more arms reaching, and so on.

"Who the fuck do these guys think they are?" said the one with the chipped teeth.

"It doesn't matter what they think," said the other one. "It only matters what Malachi here thinks."

Malachi wasn't listening. He was watching a group of women who had just come in, thick, heavy girls with thick, greasy hair flying about and lacey red skirts that swirled around their hips and the flash of naked brown asses as they wiggled their way to a table near the dance floor. A thin layer of filth covered the floor, a varnish with the consistency of dried oatmeal. The air reeked with stale beer, dried sweat, dried urine, the various cheap perfumes the stores at the mall were pushing. It should have been difficult to breathe, but people were breathing just fine. The girls barely had time to order drinks before they were surrounded by short, skinny men wearing yellow bandanas or orange ones and earrings and grinning teeth and dripping moustaches and switch-blades stuffed away somewhere, invisible until needed. Malachi stared at the women from the security of the shadows. Two drunken eyes blinking in the haze beneath the broken light. Malachi thought there were a lot more horse-faced women than usual. Then the voices of the two teachers plus Malachi drifted back into range.

"The way I see it these guys are every bit as Fascist as Barry Goldwater or Francisco Franco."

"Fuck Franco," Malachi heard himself say.

"Fuck Goldwater," said the younger teacher.

"You are both remarkably perceptive, my young naïve friends. But fucking them is not enough. They are just the tip of the barely visible iceberg. America in the 1960s was every bit as Fascist as Spain under Franco, maybe more so, and nothing much has changed. America is a goddamn Fascist cesspool."

"Yeah, well, maybe so, but how does that help Malachi?"

"It always helps to understand your enemy."

"I understand the Velázquez brothers very well," said Malachi. "It's a black and white fucking world with them."

"That's Fascism in a nutshell."

"Fucking Fascism," said the younger teacher.

"So what do I do?" said Malachi.

"You don't do anything," said the older teacher.

"What kind of crazy shit advice is that?"

But now the older teacher was no longer listening. He drank some of his beer. His gaze wandered away from the table and he soon found himself staring at one of the fat girls that Malachi had noticed. She was dancing with two skinny Mexicans with yellow bandanas, quite possibly out-of-work construction workers. They all seemed to know each other. The two construction workers were groping the girl while they danced. One would twist her hands around in his, holding onto her fingertips, and give her a very fancy spin, and she would twirl in the delirium of absolute joy, her skirt billowing up and the man's hands sliding up and down her body, catching her as she slowed and spreading the cheeks of her ass and pulling her close and the girl squealing with delight. Then the other one would take a turn.

"He means you need to forget about them," said the younger teacher. "And he's probably right. They'll forget about you after a while. Nobody can hold a grudge forever."

Malachi looked at the younger teacher with great compassion, his eyes softening for a moment, as if he were helping a small child across a busy street.

"Noooooo, man, the Velázquez brothers don't forget shit."

"Well maybe you can find some other girl with really big tits and convince her that the Velázquez brothers will make her an international star."

"You've seen Gisela," said Malachi.

"Of course," said the younger teacher."

Both men were now staring at the hazy, golden bubble of light that encased the bar at the other end of the club. As both men became absorbed in this bubble of light, they thought they saw Gisela. She was smiling and running and her tits were bouncing and they couldn't tell where she was, maybe out at the beach, but they didn't care. It was like watching a movie. They continued their conversation while they watched their private movie.

"Have you ever seen anyone with tits that big?"

"Hell no. I can't say that I have."

"Exactly!"

They watched Gisela's tits bouncing for a while, idiotic grins pasted on their faces. Then the image of Gisela faded.

"Hell, I don't know what you should do, Malachi. Maybe you should just challenge them to a duel."

"A duel?"

"Yeah. Like in the 18th century in Paris. A couple of antique dueling pistols with ivory plated handles. Designed by Peniet himself. Ten steps, turn and fire."

The music in the club became very loud at that point, a very noisy pop techno Latin funk bluesy sound with people screaming and shouting and jumping about, and they could no longer hear anything that was being said. For a while they tried communicating using only hand gestures and contorted expressions on their faces, like deranged Kabuki dancers, but then they gave up and drank their beers.

"It's fucking hopeless," said Malachi, grinning. "Fucking hopeless."

"What's that?"

"Fucking hopeless."

They drank beers for several hours, at least that's how it seemed in retrospect. More likely it was only several minutes. They had lost all sense of time. They had lost all perspective. Then the pop techno portion of the evening was replaced with a few slower but still rhythmic boleros.

"You ever see anything like that?" said the older teacher.

He was still focused on the dance floor and the girl in the red skirt with the two skinny Mexicans. They were now the only ones out there. The rest of those who had been dancing were lined up around the edge, half in the shadows, bodies twisted at odd angles so everyone could see what was going on. The girl was nude from the waist down, the curves of her great ass rippling with power, and she was stomping her feet like an angry bull and snorting and shaking her head and her greasy hair flying about and drops of grease splattering the air. One of the men was holding her lacey red skirt like a cape and whipping it around in the air, and then, as if to time her movements with the rhythm of the music, the girl charged and the Mexican draped the makeshift cape over her face as she went by and slapped her on the ass. The crowd of former dancers shouted "Ole, ole" and "bring it again" and "Oh yeah" and "let it out baby, let it out" and then they were cheering and whistling. They looked like they were about to explode. The two skinny Mexicans in their yellow bandanas took turns pretending to be the matador, but the girl was always the bull. After a while she was tired from charging after her skirt (and also quite drunk from the copious amounts of alcohol she had no doubt consumed) and the show was over. Actually, she sort of collapsed in the middle of the floor, but she had a happy, incurious smile plastered across an otherwise inscrutable face. (The word comatose also comes to mind.) The two Mexicans carried her off to the secluded darkness of a small hallway near the front of the club. The hallway led to the restrooms, but the lights were out. Half a dozen former dancers splintered off from the rest and followed the two Mexicans as they carried the fat girl from the dance floor, limp and glistening with sweat from the imaginary bullfight, and then they were gone. But every now and then for the next hour or so, you could vaguely hear the sounds of a girl squealing and people shouting "Ole" and then cheering and clapping and whistling, but the sound barely stood out against the music. It was more like an echo that had traveled across time. They let the image of the beefy girl being carried from the dance floor linger in their minds for a moment. Then the conversation resumed.

"It's like I was saying. Fascism everywhere you look."

"You mean the girl and the two Mexicans?"

"That's precisely what I mean."

"Don't let him draw you in, Malachi. I've been listening to this kind of garbage for as long as I've known him."

"And none the wiser, for all that."

The two teachers clinked their beer bottles together and drank. Malachi hiccupped. They were drunk enough that everything seemed like a great joke and they could barely suppress their laughter.

"He's a goddamn lunatic."

"We are all lunatics, my friends. It is an ancient religion."

A commotion broke out at the bar and the bartender took out a club and whacked a guy over the head and the guy crumpled up like a piece of aluminum and you could see a thin crack and some blood seeping out and then two body guards carried him out. Then a guy with a mop came out to clean up the bloody trail. There were a dozen or more bodyguards in the club wearing leather vests, which were quite possibly bullet-proof, and Billy clubs clipped to their sides and ponytails tied neatly. They were still chatting with the customers and smiling dumb, happy smiles, but they had taken up strategic positions around the club in case they were needed. They all had arms like granite and when they smiled you could see dozens of blank spaces where their teeth were missing. Malachi thought they all looked like younger versions of Bull when he saw them smile. They looked like paratroopers getting ready to jump.

"It's going to get rough in here pretty soon."

The two teachers nodded but it was clear that Malachi's words did not penetrate even their skin. They ordered another round of beers and then another, and the conversation changed direction several times. Then the older teacher suggested they switch to mojitos with cut limes. When the mojitos came they told the waitress to keep them coming, they were incredibly thirsty. They were at the stage when everything they drank tasted like water. After a while they were talking about women.

"Now you take young Lauterbach here," said the older teacher. "He's a fairly good looking boy with overly large hands, and if hands are any indication, he should have more pussy sniffing around than he knows what to do with."

The older teacher plucked the lime out of his empty glass and started chewing on it while he talked.

"But the size of your hands isn't the only thing that matters," said the older teacher.

Malachi's head was throbbing. He wished he could crawl under the table and go to sleep. The younger teacher seemed to be sleeping right where he was, the side of his face resting awkwardly on the table, his chin hanging over the edge, his eyes staring vacantly at the dance floor, which was empty now except for a shredded red skirt and a dozen empty beer bottles and some broken glass. The older teacher finished off the last of his lime and pushed the defruited skin into his glass.

"The trouble with Lauterbach is that he's still mooning over this young Spanish teacher named Tommie Rodriguez, a hell of a beautiful *chiquita*, beautiful brown eyes, juicy in all the right places, and she loved him as much as he loved her. But that was a lifetime ago."

Malachi stared at the empty mojito glasses on the table, at the bright green defruited skin in each. He couldn't tell how many empty glasses there were. The words of the older teacher flowed past his ears with an unsettling regularity. He understood that hidden in the spaces between the words he could decipher was a meaning that eluded him. But when the older teacher started talking about love, the meaning was unmistakably clear, the way looking up at a cloudless nighttime sky filled with stars was clear (assuming you were far enough away from the dull, electric glow of civilization). Malachi understood love to be an expansive force that stretched across the universe, so he hung on to this one word and let the others flow past, no longer caring. He wondered how deeply the younger teacher loved this woman from a lifetime ago. He wondered if they would ever see each other again. He felt sorry for the younger teacher. Then he thought about how much he loved Gisela and he knew how very lucky he was.

"Beautiful and useless," the older teacher said.

The older teacher was now engaged in a serious conversation with an imaginary friend. Or perhaps he was simply pausing at appropriate places to let Malachi or the younger teacher fill in the gaps if they once again found their voices.

"No, I don't think he had any choice. None of us have a choice when it comes to that."

". . . ."

"Precisely! After that there is only loneliness. He will suffer from loneliness until he is no longer suffering."

". . . ."

"I don't think it matters much where he is. It is not a question of geography."

". . . ."

"No, I don't think any of us have much time left."

". . . ."

"Maybe if you beat him to death with a crowbar."

". . . ."

"Yeah, well, then we're all pretty much fucked."

". . . ."

"The whole fucking world."

The last thing Malachi remembered from that night was leaving the club and the three of them walking south to the 17th Avenue drawbridge. The heat of the day had lifted and the night was clear and warm and breezy, the kind of night where you can hear dogs howling in the distance and there is an endless tide of boleros floating from window to window and the street lamps are clouded over with thousands of tiny insects, so everything looks like a memory. Malachi hadn't been home in a few months, but in an effort to reassure

Gisela that his desire to spend every waking and non-waking hour with her was not founded upon the desperation of his current circumstances, he had taken to sleeping two or three nights a week in the shadows of the great bridges that linked Allapattah to Little Havana. He felt comfortable in the shadows beneath the bridges. He did not stay beneath any one bridge for more than a few days, partly to prevent the Velázquez brothers from stumbling upon his routine, but mostly because after even a single night away, his yearning for Gisela became unbearably nostalgic. Tonight he was heading to the 17th Avenue bridge on the side closest to the yacht club. Sewell Park was on the other side. Earlier that morning he had hidden a bag with some clothes, a thin blanket and a pillow in a narrow crevice between the drawbridge tower and the underbelly of the bridge, where the bridge's hydraulic machinery was visible. A couple of times when he had slept there before, early in the morning, the man who raised and lowered the drawbridge noticed Malachi in the shadows, but he didn't squawk. He just nodded slightly, as if to say 'Go ahead, I don't mind, I might need to sleep there myself one day.' Malachi liked to stretch out on a narrow ledge next to the hydraulics, protected by the steel girders and the swirling darkness, so he could forget about the terrors of the world.

    The three men walked in silence the several miles from the club to the bridge. Words seemed unnecessary, useless, without the power to give shape to the world. Then they could see where the regular pattern of street lamps ended and the dark shadow of the bridge began and then the street lamps began again on the other side. Malachi said good night and scrambled down the embankment and then made his way along a narrow wooden walkway to the crevice beneath the steel girders. He spread out the blanket and the pillow on the narrow ledge and lay down but he could not close his eyes.

    The world seemed strangely silent, as if it were uninhabited. He looked out at the river but he could not see the other side, and he suddenly felt suspended between two worlds, between a dead or dying past and the crushing weight of an unseen future. He wondered what in the world he was going to do, what was going to happen. He imagined himself being tossed from the rooftop of a fancy hotel at the beach, landing in an empty pool and an Aqua-Clean van driving away from the scene, the driver oblivious to what was really going on, and then Malachi's broken body would be wrapped in a white tarp like a plastic shroud, a fitting emblem of a godless universe, and they would take him out and dump him in the ocean, food for the sharks, he thought, and he was on the verge of an overwhelming panic, or so he imagined, when the silence of the world was broken by a soothing, calming voice that numbed the edges of his fear.

At first he could not make out what the voice was saying. He wondered where the voice was coming from. Then he realized it was the voice of the older teacher and he smiled, but he was also confused. The two teachers must have crossed to the other side and been almost to the café by now, so there was no scientific theory that would explain why Malachi could hear the older one talking. Yet his voice was very sharp, very clear, even though at the same time it sounded a million miles away. He wondered at this minor miracle. He wondered if the angels of his destiny were closing in. Then he let the weight of his body settle into the concrete and closed his eyes. The voice of the older teacher sounded even closer than before. The teacher was telling a story, a bedtime fable.

"A cattleman once drove a herd of one thousand bulls to a modern marvel of a slaughterhouse that possessed gleaming white walls and white tiled ramps and floors. Everything was scrubbed and sparkling," he said. "And when all one thousand bulls were safely imprisoned within the polished bars of a stainless steel corral, the butcher appeared in a spotless white cloak with his great mechanized carving knives. 'Let us close ranks,' said one of the bulls, 'so we can jack up this criminal on our horns.' But the other nine-hundred ninety-nine bulls adamantly refused. 'If you please,' they said, 'how is this butcher any different from the cattleman who drove us to this place of godlike cleanliness with a cattle prod and dogs snapping at our heels?' And the one bull thought he understood their meaning and said 'You are right to ask this question, for there is no difference between the two, and when we are finished with the butcher we will then seek justice against the cattleman.' But the nine-hundred ninety-nine bulls did not understand the answer of the one bull. 'You are trying to deceive us,' they said. 'The cattleman and the butcher are not our enemy. We can see that the butcher possesses these knives only to defend himself. If we raise our horns against him, then surely he will raise his knives against us. But if we do nothing, then we can all live in peace.' And so the herd of one thousand bulls did not close ranks, and one by one they fell victim to the newly honed edge of the butcher's mechanized knives."

-32-

Malachi, a natural insomniac, lay there on the narrow ledge until the glow from the early morning sun flashed up from the surface of the river. It kind of felt like being under water the way the rippling light and shadows played against the underbelly of the bridge. But Malachi did not get down from the ledge even when twenty minutes later the bridge went up and then down for the first time that day. He was replaying the story of the bulls over and over again in his mind, mesmerized by the philosophical nature of what he had heard but unable to divine its meaning. During the short night, he had been plagued by images of bullfighters and charging bulls, their great horns thrusting at the air, and angry, mechanical butchers sharpening their knives, all of the images converging, whirling about in his brain like demonic razor blades, severing his synapses, lacerating the softly coiled, sausage-like tissue housed within his skull. He had been certain he was bleeding. As the morning drifted up from the river, he was still convinced his blood was draining away, his already pale face taking on an ethereal milky hue, as if he had died just before dawn, and then the rats had got him and were chewing on his cold white, rubber-like flesh, tearing away chunks and unclogging his arteries and then lapping up his juices.

Time took a back seat.

Then he was up and the rats became a feeling of vague discomfort, a subtle paranoia, a greening summer's mist produced by acid rainfall that he breathed in without thinking, his lungs slowly filling with the pinpricks of apprehension, and then a dull ache in his chest. Before he realized it, he had left the bridge far behind. He moved along tree-lined avenues with pastry shops and gas stations and city parks and the spires of Catholic churches winking in the sunlight. He was not sure where he was going, or even where he was, but he knew he had to keep moving. He stopped a few times to get his bearings, but nothing looked familiar, not even the street names, not even when he came upon a major intersection with city busses stopped at red lights. He wondered if somehow he had been transported to a foreign country (which most certainly would have solved his dilemma with the Velázquez brothers, but Malachi did not think of that). Once again he seemed to be drifting through the fog of a hallucination, and he knew the best thing would be to find a quiet place to sit and catch his breath and let the world re-assemble into a more familiar pattern, but he could not stop. He felt like he was trapped in a gangster movie from the 1940s and he was at the part where the detective hero was wandering through a collage of memories, trying to sort through all the clues and figure out the case. So he kept moving. The sun had become very hot and a dry wind began to hiss through the trees and it felt like the hot breath of the Velázquez brothers blowing across the back of his neck so he could not stop.

On several occasions he thought he heard footsteps, and then he would duck into the arched vestibule doorway of a corner drugstore or a hamburger joint, trembling with uncertainty, light a cigarette (he wasn't sure how the cigarette always materialized out of thin air, right on cue, but he only noted this aberration in an off-hand, ironically detached sort of way) and slide a weary eye around the outer edge, just in case, all of which would have bordered on farce had it been midnight, but it seemed strangely credible in the middle of the day. Once he even thought he saw his neighbor, the one who had been clipping her azaleas three doors down. She was still wearing the same flowery dress, if his eyes could be believed. Why she might be following him he couldn't say. But when he looked again she was gone, and where she had been standing there was only a shriveled-up tamarind tree with a piece of blue cloth or a child's kite stuck in the branches. Still, it might have been somebody, thought Malachi. All the more reason to remain alert. But no matter how many times he stopped, all he saw were the bright, wiry shadows of tree branches dancing on the sidewalks like the tentacles of crazed extraterrestrial squids.

It almost seemed that the entire planet was deserted, that the world's population had simply left the room, leaving a chaotic circus of uneaten breakfasts and lunches on counters, cars still running, waiting at traffic lights till they ran out of gas, empty elevators humming in between floors, bathtubs overflowing and the water cascading down stairwells, that sort of thing, and he had almost convinced himself that this was indeed the case when he heard a voice shout "Corinna, you wait right there!" and he spun around and there was a mother and her daughter, a child of eight or nine with a pink bow in her hair and a pink Minnie Mouse dress. The girl was holding a Minnie Mouse lunchbox. The mother was holding the girl by the shoulders, giving her some kind of earnest advice which clearly the child wished to ignore. Then a late model Chevy pulled up to the curb and they got in and the car drove away.

Malachi was aware how absurd the whole situation was, everything from imagining that his neighbor in the flowery dress was following him to thinking that everyone on the planet had mysteriously vanished, but he also sensed how dangerous and unpredictable life could be, like the trembling potential for violence that existed just beneath the surface of reality, a mythic place where at any given moment a gazillion angels were dancing on the point of a needle, a trick which Malachi always assumed was done with mirrors, an illusionist's sleight of hand, which meant in all probability only one angel could do it, if that. Then Malachi tried to picture himself stealing away with Gisela to the Caribbean and starting over, a place like Cuba before Castro, but his mind went curiously blank. He could see nothing beyond his current circumstances, and for a moment he was confused. But then he understood. He had to finish out this scene. He was playing a role like all the others, the bartender, the accountant, the news reporter, the big-time Mexican movie director. How many others were there? The Velázquez brothers were relentless villains in this movie of their revenge, and Malachi knew it would only be a matter of time before they caught up with him. He felt the soft petals of sadness opening up, and then closing, a sad, lonely flower withering beneath the hot sun. As far as he could see, and he could cover vast distances in his mind's eye, the end, a most likely gruesome end involving, perhaps, a hail of bullets, was in sight. Briefly, Malachi wondered if you could survive a hail of bullets. What were the odds?

Then his two outer eyes caught the gleam of a lithographic poster taped to the window of a corner deli. This was the crossroads moment he had been hoping for. The poster was clearly designed for tourists, but it dazzled Malachi the way a painting sometimes dazzles. At the top it said "The Entire World is Welcome at the Allapattah Heritage & Puppet Festival." Beneath the words there was a reddish orange alligator dancing in a bluish-green sky. It was a very modern looking poster that eluded any post-modern interpretation. The alligator was made up of smaller reddish blocks and orange ones and a few yellow circles and triangles all mashed together to look like an alligator. There were several other alligators dancing with the red one, but they were white and looked sort of like clouds anyway.

He wondered if the alligators had anything to do with the puppets, or if they were meant to symbolize Florida in general. He was unable to connect the alligators to the concept of "The Entire World." Then he thought perhaps the alligators might have been swimming in the sky instead of dancing, particularly the way the red one was angled upwards, as if he was about to suddenly break through the surface of some primordial bluish-green ocean, but for an unknown reason this thought bothered him, so he stuck with dancing, his first inclination. There were no other images but the alligators, which also bothered him. And so for aesthetic reasons having to do with the alligators, Malachi almost did not glance at the bottom of the poster, which contained a list of festival events and the date. Malachi's destiny, however, was determined to assert itself, which is to say that Malachi thus found himself reading the list in spite of the art critic that inhabited his brain.

The festival would take place in August. It was going to

be a very full day. There was going to be a big-head puppet parade in the afternoon, the parade of the Cabezudos, starting at the high school and heading down 18th Avenue to Duarte Park, followed by face painting and carnival rides and games and clowns for the kiddies, and music for everyone, which meant everything from Dominican rap to old-timey boleros to maybe some Latin-pop salsas, and there were going to be food vendors from all over the city, and fireworks at dusk. But this first part of the list did not appeal to Malachi in the least. It was the kind of list one might expect given the obviously flawed rendering of the alligators. But then Malachi noticed a row of glowing print in golden letters a few inches below the regular events that said "After Hours Activities" followed by "Midnight Dance Contest (Girls Only) at La Mamacita's" followed by "Special Surprise Appearance by the Internationally Acclaimed Film Star Salma de la Prada to promote her new film *The Sex Queen of the Moulin Rouge.*"

Malachi stared at the glowing gold lettering for a long time. He realized he was staring at his own salvation. If he could only speak with Salma de la Prada, explain his situation, she would surely agree to star in a film for the Velázquez brothers. All he had to do was speak with her. And show her the script. Yes, he thought, the script was the key. It was a great script. Once Salma de la Prada read the script, his troubles would be over.

-33-

The day of the Allapattah Heritage & Puppet Festival was a routine day when you consider what generally goes on at such festivals. The sky was a robin's egg blue, and there was just enough of a breeze, at least until about two in the afternoon, to make the festival goers forget about the blazing white heat of the sun. All of the events described on the poster took place. All of the kiddies had their faces painted. All of the adults drank warm beer from silver kegs which arrived at three o'clock by truck. The fireworks went off without a hitch. The only blemish on the day as far as the general public was concerned, and this would, of course, depend upon your taste in music, occurred when one of the music groups, an up and coming gay Latin-reggae band from South Beach called Crew 429, failed to show up.

It is worth noting that the members of Crew 429 had supposedly been involved in a hit and run the night before, at least the van the lead singer was driving had been identified by an anonymous caller who referred to the vehicle as "that fag fuck truck," and so they were being detained by the Miami police from 10 AM onwards, which meant that the platform stage in Duarte Park where they were supposed to perform was empty from 3:15 till 4:00. Actually, detained was the polite, politically correct word used by the newspaper columnist who covered the police beat. A better word would have been handcuffed to the radiators in a dungeon of an interrogation room for several hours while the cops sifted through the various combinations of the truth, and then, because none of the combinations rang with the epic finality they were looking for, they tossed the Latin-reggae group into an overcrowded city holding cell — after the musicians had been given their orange jumpsuits but before being assigned a specific cell block — with one vagrant wino from Homestead who had gotten lost and five hardcore Mexican construction workers who had been laid off the previous day from one of the skyscraper projects downtown, their temporary unemployment being the result of a long-standing squabble between management and the electrician's union that continued to impact the viability of several development efforts, and who had then proceeded to get drunk and then robbed a string of 7-Elevens and then were picked up speeding on the Dolphin Expressway at two in the morning, and when they learned the next day that they were sharing a cell with a group of gay musicians, in spite of the fact that they all liked Latin-reggae, and a couple of the younger ones had even heard of Crew 429, which was rising on the charts all over south Florida and had a decent shot at national exposure because their agent was working tirelessly to get them on *The Today Show*, the Mexicans immediately projected their recent workplace frustrations and their latent homophobic hatreds onto the unsuspecting musicians from South Beach and beat them all to a bloody pulp, and it was only after the group was transferred in a fleet of ambulances to Jackson Memorial later that evening (after the custodial staff of the jail had complained about the pools of blood that were interfering with their ability to mop the hallways) that the District Attorney in the case learned that the band was not really from South Beach, that South Beach was probably just promotional cover, for two of the band members lived in Coral Gables with their parents, and the lead singer (a former tax attorney who gave up his practice in the hopes of achieving musical immortality, however long that might take) was from Surfside, where he lived in a pink stucco ranch surrounded by palm trees and dolphin statuary with his wife, a jet-black cat, a Chinese Shih Tzu adorned with red bows, and two small children who went to elementary school with the nephew of a State Senator.)

For Malachi, however, the Allapattah Heritage & Puppet Festival was far from routine. Nothing worked out the way he had expected, and this was true even days before the festival took place. He had intended on going alone, but then he mentioned something about the parade and the fireworks, the words were out of his mouth before he realized what he was saying. Gisela squealed with delight, a delicate, breathy squeal, almost surreal in the way it escaped her pouty lips. She said she loved parades more than anything and how fireworks were the most romantic thing ever. Malachi wasn't sure how he was going to take Gisela to the festival and the fireworks and at the same time hunt down Salma de la Prada, so he asked the two teachers to come along and run interference, but Soledad overheard. Soledad said a festival was exactly what Señor Mendoza needed, he hadn't been feeling too well lately, a festival like this might perk him up a little bit. "Yes, a festival would be just the thing," she said. "When my Xavier was a boy of fifteen his father took him to a festival in Zaragoza. Nine days it had lasted, but Xavier has forgotten most of it, which is why I want him to go with you to the Allapattah festival, because it might jog his memory."

And then just like that Soledad had started talking about that festival when Señor Mendoza was fifteen. She said it had been very hot that year, unusually hot for October. A very hot, dry wind had come out of the south and the people thought perhaps it was a sign, but they did not yet know its meaning. The first day had been a day of speeches, with the Mayor leading off. He had been a Colonel during the war against Morocco. Then one by one a collection of old, withered generals with strings of white hair combed sideways had their turns, all of them looking out on the crowded boulevard from a wooden platform with their medals like smashed bullets shining in the hot sun. It had looked like the Mayor and the generals were melting it was so hot, and the crowd was laughing quietly at that and perhaps even hoping for such a miracle, and then the soldiers had marched past, but they didn't look at the Mayor or the generals or even the crowd, they were more concerned with the fact that their own boots seemed to be melting. They were sticking to the pavement with each heavy step. And from somewhere a military band was playing a long-winded version of *Novio de la Muerte* (a song for brothels that has become our hymn to the Legion, that's what Xavier's father had said, and then he had spat on the ground), the sounds of rusty trumpets and ancient timpani coming at them in waves. But everything had sounded very far away, as if it were all under water, or trapped in a cavern in the mountains, or perhaps up in the clouds. That's how her Xavier had once described it. Then came the tanks, half a dozen tanks like little green bulldogs with black greasy smoke trailing like banners. The crowd along the boulevard had cheered and thrown their hats into the air and small boys ran back and forth across the boulevard, daring the tanks as if they were bulls instead of motorized bulldogs and picking up the hats that had fallen. The next day the generals were gone and the temperature was back to normal, and everyone then understood the significance of the sign of the strange heat, as they came to think of it, but they kept their thoughts to themselves. (And when Soledad said that she smiled softly at Malachi, and he suddenly wondered if she were recounting her own memories.) Then she said the rest of the festival had been a wonder of dancing and singing and festival games for the children and prayers to the Virgin Mari, and there had been bullfighting for three days, and afterwards some of the younger bullfighters had roamed the streets giving impromptu demonstrations with a few stray cows that had been left to wander for the children, and on the sixth day there had been a parade of giant puppets, and on the ninth day there was an offering of flowers and fruit at the end of the procession to the cathedral. It had been the greatest festival in the history of the city of Zaragoza, which is what everyone said, and afterwards no one remembered the Mayor and the generals and how they had been melting on the platform. That is what her Xavier had told her. That is how he remembered it, when his father took him down to Zaragoza oh such a very long time ago. Then Soledad had sighed. That is why he must go to this festival of the puppets up in Allapattah, she said, so he can relive once more the life he lived as a boy, so he can remember who he once was, who he is. So there was nothing Malachi could do. Señor Mendoza was going to the festival, Soledad would not go herself, she said she had no time for festivals, but her Xavier was going, this was to be a gift to her Xavier.

The parade began at 1:30, so they arrived at 1:00, thinking they were early, but the sidewalks had been packed since noon. They had to park in an alley behind a seafood market six blocks away and walk over. The parade route went past mostly parking lots and fences, and a few bungalows from the 1930s with red roofs and red awnings and the owners sitting out in their scrubby lawns in folding chairs drinking beer and smoking cigars. Some of the yards had nicely pruned tamarind trees or lime trees out front. Vendors wandered up and down the avenue selling balloons and plastic hoops that vibrated with light when you twirled them and ice cream and cotton candy and Italian ice and tacos and cartoonish looking party masks (mostly exotic animals such as jaguars, monkeys, parrots, alligators) and miniature banners that said Allapattah. Police waved through the cross traffic at the intersections. Mariachi music filled the air.

Malachi had decided that the best vantage point was at the park, where the parade ended, but there was no room to sit or even stand. Shimmering in the early afternoon sunlight was a sea of metal and plastic folding chairs and people sitting with their faces turned slightly away from the sun, some wearing brightly colored hats, listening to radio music, reaching into coolers and pulling out bottles of beer or hard cider or wine coolers or water, small children running in between the chairs, dogs barking. It almost looked like a mirage, or how the world looks when you are suffering from a debilitating migraine. So they decided to walk up to meet the parade (they could hear the rumble of Mexican horns in the distance like a thunderstorm rolling in from the bay). Malachi took the lead, with Gisela clinging to his arm and bouncing with every step, followed by the two teachers and Señor Mendoza. At times it looked like the teachers were carrying the old man, his arms hooked around their shoulders and his legs bent up like some ancient Iberian king sitting on a throne, though his dangling feet were resting only on air.

As they walked up 18th Avenue, Malachi and the two teachers were having a passionate conversation about absolutely nothing. Gisela thought they sounded very intelligent, like professors or philosophers. It was hard to tell what Señor Mendoza thought.

The conversation while walking up 18th Avenue:
"I haven't slept in five days," said Malachi. "If that's what you mean."
"No, that isn't it at all," said the older teacher. "Sleep is a great gift. It is the greatest of pleasures."
"Except when you can't sleep," said the younger teacher.
"Or when you have better things to do," said Malachi, and a wild, hopeful look rotated across his eyeballs, like swift moving clouds, and then he buried his face in Gisela's tits for a moment and then jerked his head back, looking up through the trees at the blue sky passing by, laughing.

The two teachers were also laughing. Gisela was beaming. Señor Mendoza blinked happily, steadily, his open mouth was the memory of the sea, the smell of salt air, a cloud of seagulls sweeping past, an inarticulate longing he only half-remembered, which only a handful of others might even recognize (Soledad, Malachi perhaps, or a drunken Baptist minister from long ago) and which suddenly, strangely, miraculously, seemed on the verge of being fulfilled.

Up ahead you could see the first of the giant puppets pushing their way past the low hanging branches that arched over that particular section of the street. There were two of them, both twelve feet tall with over-sized heads, an aging prostitute with stringy blonde hair and thick droopy lips painted a bright red and bulging blue eyes, and a flamenco dancer with an exaggerated hook nose and an orange tiara with a bit of black lace hanging down to cover her eyes, and curlicue brown hair plastered to the sides of her elongated face. The puppets were weaving from one side of the street to the other, chasing after each other in tilted fashion, as if in a drunken but friendly stupor.

"But you'd climb on top of Gisela every night if you could,' said the older teacher. "We all would."

Gisela looked back, still beaming. The bouncy way she was walking seemed to become even bouncier.

"That's my baby," Gisela said, and she started nibbling on Malachi's ear and he winced.

"Pain or pleasure," said the younger teacher. "Sometimes you can hardly tell them apart."

"Ah, yes," said the older teacher. "The road to eternal damnation."

"But it is true."

They stopped talking for a while.

A Mariachi band was marching behind the prostitute and the dancer. The musicians were wearing white sombreros and white sequin-lined jumpsuits with black jackets and black boots, like eager waiters in a fancy hotel but with trumpets and guitars. They were following the path of the weaving puppets but stopping every time they saw a pretty girl so they could perform. They surrounded Gisela and the others with their gleaming gold trumpets and their gleaming gold-capped teeth and their polished guitars and sang to her an ancient love song that only Señor Mendoza seemed to recognize, and then Gisela gave the one closest to her a kiss and waved at the others and they went running after the puppets. No one remembered what they had been talking about before, so they started talking about beer.

"Aren't we heading in the wrong direction for the beer?" said the younger teacher.

"Man, there's beer everywhere you look," said Malachi.

And it was true, but it was all private beer, green bottles

of *El Presidente*, gold and brown and black bottles of *Alhambra Negra*, the red bottles of *Alhambra Mezquita*, a kaleidoscope of colored glass. But it seemed unlikely the men who drank from those myriad bottles would give up their beer without a fight (and a fight in this neighborhood usually meant guns, with knives being reserved for cutting rings from fat fingers once the issue was no longer in doubt).

"Why don't we head back to the park?"

"Man, it too crowded."

"And some of us are feeling too lazy."

"But that's where the beer is."

"Man, the beer won't be there until later."

"Okay. Sure. That's where the beer will be."

"So relax, man. Anyway, there won't be any good Spanish beer with that truck, so it just as well."

"No. You're probably right. But I'm thinking quantity, not quality. That truck has just what I'm looking for."

"Ah, you mean it is loaded with silver kegs."

"That's exactly what I mean. Enough beer to drown your sorrows."

"When the truck arrives."

"Man, forget about them kegs. What you need is a good Spanish beer. A beer that's full of flavor. You won't find a good Spanish beer on that truck.

"Why not baby? What's wrong with Spanish beer?"

"Nothing babe. It because we all living in America."

"But baby, you can buy good Spanish beer in any grocery store. We go all the time."

"Yeah, sure babe. But it's too much money for festivals. They give you Coors and shit for festivals."

"Ooohhhh."

"Malachi, I didn't realize you were such a connoisseur."

"What's he mean, baby?"

"A connoisseur, in this case, my voluptuous young *chiquita*, is an expert who knows which among the many vagrant beer brands that litter our grocery store shelves we should drink and which we should forgo. His palette is an exceptionally well-tuned instrument."

"His what?"

"His tongue, my sweet young thing, his tongue."

"Ooohhh, yeeesss, that's my baby."

Gisela started tonguing Malachi's ear and giggling.

"You mean he's an expert when it comes to drinking beer? We're all experts when it comes to that."

"Ah, but only in the most obvious sense, my young friend. Malachi's abilities extend far beyond the world of beer."

The two teachers watched Gisela and Malachi for a moment. Her tongue was making a second pass at the dangling lobe of his right ear, an incredible feat of timing and dexterity given they did not break stride. Malachi buried his face once again in her tits.

"Far beyond, my young friend."

The conversation drifted into an explanation of the differences between the smoky sweet earthy tastes of the dark Alhambras, the true Spanish beers, compared to the paler versions they served in overpriced resorts in the Caribbean. Then they debated whether they should turn back and head to the park or keep walking. The younger teacher reminded them about the beer truck. He said he wanted to head back right then to be sure he was in line when the truck arrived. The older teacher decided he wanted wine instead of beer and voted for turning east on 35th street, there was a liquor store on 12th Avenue near the metro station. Gisela also voted for wine. Señor Mendoza had no opinion. He had been walking on his own for the last several blocks, a half step behind the two teachers. In all probability, he didn't even realize a conversation was taking place. He pulled out a small flask and drank from that, smiling happily at the two teachers every now and then and looking vaguely in the direction of the street. Malachi carefully noted every viewpoint (both expressed and unexpressed) and then said he wanted to see a bit more of the parade, and since the rest were not yet adamant in their thirst, they kept walking. But they were not walking as fast nor covering as much ground as they had been before. The earlier breeze had vanished and now the sun had become very hot. The air itself was bleeding with the heat, molecule by molecule dripping to the ground. Blue jays cried out in agony, their razor-like cries slicing through the air like radiation. Young men on both sides of the street began pouring bottled water over their heads and down their backs and encouraging the girls they knew (who were already wearing only bikinis) to strip to their waists, or at least give them a taste every once in a while, the heat was excruciating so they might as well make the most of it. And on top of the problem of the heat, which whitewashed the landscape and made for lazy walking, there was now also the problem of large gaps appearing between parts of the parade, since the police were having difficulty managing the flow of the cross-traffic. The whole world had suddenly become a fabulous and exalted dream, a fading, faded, somnolent black-and-white photograph that had begun to yellow, a memory of falling water, hypnotic, fragmented, eternal.

It was during one of these monochromatic lulls that a voice from the other side of the street called out.

"Oye Broken Bike," the voice said, and a sun-burnt shadow waved with great energy. Malachi did not recognize the voice but he waved back anyway.

Then another voice called out, "Oye Broken Bike, where you been?"

Malachi was struck by two anomalies, one, he was unable to pinpoint the location of the second voice, and two, the second voice was also unfamiliar. For one person to call out his name, shouting out a hello like a warning but without a care in the world, after Malachi had been months in seclusion, well, maybe that was mere coincidence. But a second voice overlapping the first, that seemed to Malachi slightly suspicious. Okay, more than slightly. Okay, it was downright sinister, the scent of it.

"What's the matter, baby?" Gisela said.

Malachi did not hear the question, nor did he react to the tone that lay beneath the question, the gentle, playful tone of a boisterous, untroubled lover (for surely there could be nothing seriously wrong in such a carnivalesque atmosphere). But Malachi heard nothing, even though Gisela's mouth was only inches away, poised, ready to nibble on his ear some more. His ears were at that moment engulfed in a crisis of indecision spurred on by a chorus of inner voices giving opinions on a range of topics from the wisdom of the creator in imbuing his creations with the instinct for self-preservation, to the contradictory sometimes ludicrous even self-defeating He-man urge to protect the weak (in this case Gisela) from certain death, to the numbing comfort that a case of beer might provide at two in the afternoon, to the irremediable danger of drowning in a sea of lacunal thinking. The hairs on the back of his neck were vibrating so intensely that he thought perhaps a rare earthquake had hit Miami or was about to hit or they were still in the throes of the disaster but time had frozen, as people say often happens during such disasters, which seemed to Malachi a plausible explanation as to why the white and gray stucco houses that lined the street and the apartment towers by the park had not yet crumbled into dust.

Malachi was ready to slide into the abyss. But then he remembered the lesson of the Greeks. Whatever was going to happen was going to happen. If he tried to alter his course mid-stream he would only cause more calamity for himself, as was the case with Oedipus, and the end would be the same. So there was nothing to worry about. His strategy would remain the same, it had to, and at this point he clamped down on the remaining critics that lived inside his brain, for they wanted him to consider the possibility that by remaining true to his original plan he was actually altering the course he was supposed to take, but he refused to be drawn into that level of abstract and ultimately meaningless discourse and from that point forward he did not waver in his conviction, he would find Salma de la Prada, if she was not part of the parade itself (presumably, which is to say fluttering feverishly along the sun-gilded edges of Malachi's imagination, she was languishing in an unfrozen and thoroughly seductive state of undress on a float somewhere up ahead in an effort to promote her new movie), then certainly later, at La Mamacita's, and then he would show her the script and that would be that. Salma de la Prada was still his salvation, no matter what the voices in his head were saying.

"Baby, come on baby, do you want something?"

The voices inside Malachi's head quieted down. (Gisela always had that effect.) The color of the landscape returned. Even the heat seemed less bewildering. Gisela repeated her question, staring up at his muteness. An ice cream vendor had pulled over to the side of the street and the two teachers and

Señor Mendoza were getting Rocket Pops. Malachi said he didn't want anything and then he and Gisela started walking again. Señor Mendoza tried to talk the guy into three for the price of two, but the guy wouldn't budge. They caught up to Malachi and Gisela several minutes later, their Rocket Pops already beginning to drip, and by then the police had let through the next wave of the parade. They could see the shadowy charisma of three giant puppets bobbing a block away.

"What are they supposed to be?" said Gisela.

Malachi peered into the sun-blurry glare of the next block.

"Two matadors chasing a nun," said Malachi.

"Or perhaps she is leading them on," said the older teacher. "Hoping they will follow."

Everyone laughed.

The matador puppets wore crazed, triangular black hats and looked out at the world with droopy black eyes and droopy black moustaches and wide, piano teeth smiles, and they wore royal blue jackets with polished black buttons winking in the sunlight like the eyes of dazed rats. They seemed to be suffering from a radical form of hypomania. The nun wore a white habit that towered majestically above her head like a glowing apocalyptic cloud (and which, when the puppet was hanging in storage, had served as a roosting perch for incontinent warehouse pigeons, in fact, upon closer examination it was quite apparent that the habit was not as pristine as it had first appeared, bearing the streaked, unremovable stains of many generations of pigeons). The nun had the same brown curlicue hair plastered to the side of her face and the same hook nose and elongated features that distinguished the flamenco dancer. The two might have been sisters. All three puppets ran from one side of the street to the other in the same drunken, tilted fashion as the previous puppets.

Then there was a second Mariachi band, but this one was interested only in young, unattached men, and after them there was a high school marching band from Osseo, Minnesota. The band had come down primarily for a band festival in Orlando, but their band director had grown up in Allapattah and knew the festival organizers, who were eager to have a group from Minnesota, for now they felt justified in inviting the entire world to come and enjoy their festival, an invitation which had been a hallmark of their festival promotion campaign, but which they feared had left them open to charges of false advertising from their critics (which was a group of three social agency women with thirty-seven collective years' experience working for the Housing Authority who kept asking why the entire world would bother with Allapattah, what use was there in pretending, though precisely why this possible pretense bothered them they did not say; but with the inclusion of the Minnesota band the organizers felt thoroughly, even heroically vindicated in the presence of their critics and thereafter referred to the Minnesotans as a shining example of the reach of their promotional arm, as it were, and after that the festival organizers all but forgot that the Housing Authority women even existed.)

The Minnesota high-schoolers, in an effort to express their solidarity with the plight of the people of Allapattah (for they were from the Mid-West, not counting the director, and considered Miami a third-world country, a unit in their eleventh grade history textbook), wore uniforms with a decidedly "Spanish" look specifically designed for the festival, which is to say they wore tall visored hats with gold braiding on the sides and gold medallions in the middle and dark blue brocaded jackets with red lapels and gold buttons like capped teeth and neatly pressed blue pants, a lighter blue than the jackets. They looked something like soldiers in the Mexican National Army under Santa Anna, which very much pleased the festival organizers for the reasons already mentioned.

After the band from Osseo there was a small funeral wagon, a plain black color with maroon trim and a narrow seat for the driver and a wider one for funeral guests (though no guests were present) and iron-rimmed wagon wheels. The wagon was pulled by a mule, which was following a feedbag attached to a bar that hung just out of reach. Every so often the driver of the wagon pulled the feedbag close enough for the mule to grab a mouthful and then he pushed it away and laughed a strange, greedy laughter that swirled above his head for a while like a geyser and then the laughter faded and there was only the sound of the mule's hooves on the pavement.

There was also a narrow black box in the wagon with a modern reproduction of a 19th century Mexican flag draped over top. Presumably the box was a coffin, but there was no sign hanging from the sides of the wagon to indicate who or what was supposed to be inside the box, but perhaps no sign was necessary, for the wagon seemed at least spiritually aligned with the band that had preceded it, and so metaphorically it was clear, at least to Malachi and a few others in the crowd, that the box contained the remains of Santa Anna's infamous leg, which was a casualty of a war that began because five soldiers stole a few croissants from a bakery in Mexico City, and which was later buried, in spite of the widespread belief that Santa Anna had lost his mind, with full military honors in 1838 (or 1839, depending upon your sources).

After the wagon, there were several late model convertibles displaying local tomato queens or orange princesses (along with advertising appropriate for the sponsors of said royalty) and then a couple of ambulances with the EMTs waving happily, relieved, perhaps, that they were not on duty until later that evening and sneaking sips of beer from bottles they kept between their legs.

Then there were a few more high school bands, and then the last of the giant puppets, a lecherous old red-eyed bishop wearing a crooked miter, it might even have been perched on his elongated head in sideways fashion, or even backwards, and he was holding up a tarnished crucifix in one hand as he weaved his way back and forth across the street. One could imagine he was chasing after the nun that had taken up with the matadors, for he seemed to be weeping tears of an inconsolable sadness, though whether he was sad because he had he truly loved the nun and she had rejected him after an unsatisfactory performance or because he had not yet taken her to bed was unclear. A magnificent black bull with gleaming white horns and bulging black eyes followed the inconsolable bishop. The bull was not weeping tears, indeed, his eyes seemed to be glistening with what could only be described as dark, incendiary rage (though blind fury would have served just as well), and one presumed that his rage was actually directed at the vanished matadors as symbols of the ritualized slaughter of countless innocent victims over countless defeated centuries and that he (the bull) was only chasing after the bishop because there was no one else so close to his horns and his horns had been recently sharpened and needed to be used.

After the puppets there was a third Mariachi band, which seemed interested only in playing music for small children under the age of five, and they sang in a language that no one but the children recognized, which suggested, among other interpretations, that they were singing in the language now used by the angelic hosts and originally used only by God himself, a claim which sounded suspiciously like an argument once advanced by a French abbot named Diharce De Bidassouet in the 19th century in his *History of the Catabrians*, who claimed that the language of heaven was Euskera, the language of the Basques, and who was later ridiculed by those who believed that God communicated telepathically so He had no need for a spoken language.

Then there were several elaborately designed but immediately forgettable floats, except for one, and this one received a great deal of attention because no one was quite clear about what it was depicting. It seemed at first blush to be merely a confused representation of an ancient fable from Iberia, but then after the first blush had deepened into something resembling a drunken stupor there came a second blush, and it suddenly seemed less a single fable than a series of fables mashed together, as is the case with all of the world's dominant religions, though some might argue that the whimsical, random sense of chaos generated by simple folktales and a belief in magic (which was clearly present in the artistic tone of the float in question) is no match for the sublimely ridiculous, which hovers above the great religions like a cloud of radio static, but of course Malachi was not concerned with any theological debate about the artist's' intentions, for he had already moved to the second blush stage, his lips quivering as he studied each scene: there was a giant moon near the back of the float with a light bulb that was supposed to make it glow but the light bulb didn't work, and printed below the moon were the words "guardian of death," and the lips of the moon were pursed, as if it were whistling; and staring up at the moon, but at the front end of the float, was a young girl with long golden hair and a golden comb in her hand, and she seemed to be listening to whatever it was the moon was whistling; and in between the girl and the moon were dozens of painted scenes, tiny miniatures that could only be glimpsed as the float rolled past, a labyrinth of images that were virtually undecipherable if you were standing along the sidewalks or on the edges of the lawns or in the middle of the parking lots, scenes of sea snakes swimming in stormy seas and flaming trees uprooted by crazed peasants and white clouds and rainbows painted into green skies and a flock of birds, pelicans or cockatoos by the look of them, flying up from the desiccated remnants of a cornfield, as if they had been startled out of a winter's nap (though why pelicans or cockatoos should have been taking a nap in a winter cornfield was a mystery), and there was a strange woman with long golden, flowing hair (like the girl, but older) riding across the green sky in a chariot drawn by four white horses with golden plumes, and another strange woman with golden hair (possibly the sister of the first one, but more likely the result of an artist who could only draw one kind of woman) riding a magnificently imagined white ram into a mountain pool; and in between the pictures (or paintings or miniature dioramas) there were all sorts of woodland creatures mixed in with demonic animal genies with horns and pitchforks and deformed feet, though in truth it was sometimes difficult to tell these two groups apart, and after the float of the whistling moon, which was probably the best name one could give such a float, Malachi found himself listening (or perhaps he was only half listening at this point) to the music of several more high-school marching bands (this particular parade was nothing if not a musical extravaganza, though each new band seemed little more than an echo of the previous ones), and then he paid homage to a few more tomato queens and orange princesses (he quickly realized that the orange princesses outnumbered the tomato queens by a two-to-one margin, and he wondered about the stunning discrepancy in the numbers for a while, for the orange crop the last few years had been quite poor).

It was at this point that Malachi started laughing, a low, murmuring kind of laughter that had nothing to do with tomatoes or oranges or strange woman with flowing golden hair. It was the kind of laughter that some would call lunatic, but which was really just a unique blend of relief, happiness, and incredulity, for there, bringing up the rear of the parade, he saw a lavish sequence of floats depicting scenes from *The Sex Queen of the Moulin Rouge,* and on the very last of these, languishing on a red velvet sofa beneath the blazing white heat of the sun, just as Malachi had imagined, though perhaps not quite so clearly, was the ravishing, beguiling (and practically naked) Salma de la Prada herself.

-34-

There is an ancient Iberian proverb (with ancient being a relative term and Iberian not altogether accurate) that says that the longer one dreams about something in the future, the more difficult it is to react decisively when that future suddenly begins to unfold. The same could also be said for those who dream with great intensity. It is like two sides of the same coin.

Malachi thought he was prepared for his dream to unfold. He had brought along the now dog-eared copy of the Velázquez brothers' movie script (it was back in the pocket of his safari vest), and he was armed with the movie prop gun, which was still safely stuffed down the front of his black bicycle shorts, resulting in an enormous, superhuman bulge that didn't bother him in the least.

All of which is to say that the moment Malachi saw Salma de la Prada languishing on that red velvet sofa on the very last float of the Allapattah Heritage & Puppet Festival parade, his understanding of what to do next deserted him (an understanding, it is worth noting, that some would call courage, and that Nietzsche would have defined as the will to power, or in this case the lack of that will, a concept which makes the most appearances in his book *Beyond Good and Evil*, and which that bastard Adler later turned into a commercialized pop-culture cliché referenced in dozens of poorly written, useless books on how to strengthen your self-esteem after divorce or how to parlay good grades in middle tier colleges into extravagant careers on Wall Street or in the Foreign Service or when to select a red wine with fish and in what company or if it's usually better to leave it to the sommelier because that is, after all, what he gets paid to do). So Malachi's courage deserted him (fled is more like it), but not in the overly noisy, vainglorious manner of, say, a stampeding herd of zebras (if zebras running from lions can in any way be considered vainglorious), but in a gentle, muted, stealthy fashion, as if fearing discovery, the way water seeps through limestone, a slow, inexorable draining of energy.

But while Malachi stood cemented to the sidewalk, a barnacle now in every meaning of the word, pandemonium broke out all around him. Indeed, one could say without the slightest hint of exaggeration that the sighting of Salma de la Prada ushered in an improbable sequence of events (which one could consider as an example of destiny regardless of whether or not God and his angels knew anything about it) that resembled more than anything else the mad-capped slapstick of a Marx Brothers' movie (*A Night at the Opera* comes to mind). Or perhaps what happened next had a slightly more sinister tone. Or perhaps a mixture of the two. In any event, there was a great deal of chaos.

As if reading from cue cards, the crowd along both sides of the street swerved closer to *The Sex Queen of the Moulin Rouge* floats, creating a bottleneck which forced the first of the floats to come shuddering to a halt. The crowd was so close they could touch the outer cloth fringe which blew in the breeze that had suddenly reasserted itself.

The bodyguards who accompanied the floats were lounging along the edges in the same languid manner as Salma de la Prada, chatting happily with each other in German (they were all employed by a movie star security company headquartered, for poorly conceived strategic reasons, in Freiburg, Germany) or talking on their cell phones to lonely girlfriends or even lonelier ex-girlfriends heading at that very moment to evening shifts in cheap restaurants or adult movie houses in Düsseldorf or on their way home from small boutiques on Kronenstraße in Saarbrücken where they sold second-hand clothes or perfumes or designer shoes to the busloads of Italian and Portuguese tourists that came by way of Luxembourg every Saturday. But as the crowd surged forward, the bodyguards quickly deployed themselves, sensing a vague threat to the safety of their movie star queen.

There were two groups of bodyguards. The first, an outer ring, was comprised of twenty or thirty bulging ex-soccer players, probably midfielders all born in Freiburg, but with black hair and biceps like boulders or decorative cornice pieces in the Gothic style or perhaps slightly deflated leather soccer balls from the 1930s, and this outer ring pushed back against the surging crowd, who had probably just wanted to catch a glimpse of Salma de la Prada's obvious nakedness — she was wearing only a bright red thong and a pair of red sandals edged with fake red poodle fur — or else they had been carried along unwittingly by those with voyeuristic intent; but the German ex-soccer players were not about to take any chances, especially in a pseudo Latin-American neighborhood riddled with pockets of Dominican and Cuban immigrants (the black haired Germans, who presumably lived in the thriving, efficient, eco-friendly, newly refurbished working class neighborhoods of either Reiselfield or Vauban, viewed the immigrant populations in every country except Germany as unrepentant and profligate exiles). And so they (the outer ring) brandished an up till then unseen assortment of batons, clubs, Billy clubs, crowbars, small sections of rusty pipe, cudgels with ornately carved ivory handles, golf clubs, the slightly curved leg of a Biedermeier period console table from Berlin, a few baseball bats, even an antique Alpine walking stick one of the bodyguards had stumbled upon while vacationing in the Otz Valley, warning the surging crowd (which immediately stopped surging) with vigorous shakes and unexpected balletic gestures and possibly polite (hopefully) but mostly inscrutable smiles.

The inner ring was made up of ten crackerjack blond-haired behemoths who had relocated to Freiburg from the Baltic coast near Lübeck, all of them former Olympic swimmers dressed in Speedos, flip-flops, and tight-fitting Spandex t-shirts with the word FÜKKENRÜKEN in fluorescent blue lettering written across their chests and then a graphic of one stick figure swimming desperately after another stick figure and little wavy lines to represent the water, and then the slogan *"Gehen Sie ficken einen Schwimmer."* They (the inner ring) stared out at the swerving, surging, and then partially subdued crowd from behind amber-tinted sunglasses, forming a tight bubble around their queen, as tight as possible without blocking her view of her adoring public. They had obviously been instructed never to block her view.

One of them, presumably the head-honcho (all the others called him Herr Konrad), was reading a dog-eared copy of *Biedermann und die Brandstifter*, a play written in 1958, which his father had given him when he entered the Gymnasium near Sharbeutz hoping that one day he might become a lawyer or an advertising man or perhaps a poet or at least a well-respected journalist, all of which he gave up when he realized he did not possess the talent for verbal ambiguity and the creative re-imagining of events those professions required and so focused instead on a career in security; the book was the only thing that remained of his days at the Gymnasium, and he thought it was a thinly disguised philosophical reflection on the relationship between honest men (*Biedermann*) and arsonists (*die Brandstifter*) in a post-apocalyptic society, not unlike Ray Bradbury's Farenheit 451, but it was (is) really a satiric exploration of the nature of Fascism in Nazi Germany.

Life is so strange. It was hard not to think of the Nazis when you stared at the German bodyguards, even though there was no doubt whatsoever that a movie star security company from Germany would never employ anyone even remotely connected with the Nazis.

The head honcho bodyguard was quite happy to let his subordinates handle whatever came their way, and in truth, the remaining bodyguards of this inner circle were quite capable. They glanced at Salma de la Prada now and then to make sure she was safely seated in the middle of her red velvet sofa, her naked body reflected in their sunglasses, a miniature version repeated eighteen times like a digital echo, squirming and smiling and waving and blowing kisses with puckered lips and laughing soundlessly and then receding, a tiny dot in the center of each plastic lens, and then vanishing as the bodyguards turned their attention to the crowd once again, like falling into a black hole.

Had the bodyguards not been wearing these sunglasses, which were designed specifically to filter out unwanted UV light as well as eliminate the blinding flashes that accompany a gun battle, their grim, impassive staring faces would have suggested a great inconsolable melancholy, or at least a temporary resignation, in the way that serial killers or storm troopers or criminal circus clowns suddenly deprived of breakfast are temporarily resigned. Clutching what appeared to be Uzis, they gave the distinct impression that they would willingly, eagerly, even joyfully, mow down anyone who came on board the floats uninvited.

Actually, this impression of unrestrained (heroic?) violence was more like a scent that emanated from the dilated pores of their exposed skin — mostly the pinkish-beige skin of their rippling, swimmer's legs (where the skin was already starting to peel from the merciless sun), but also the dry, cracked skin on the backs of their necks and the taut, bullet-proof skin along the bottom two-thirds of their bulging, improbable arms — the scent drifting unseen on the resurgent breeze, the way pollen drifts, or nettles, or mace, or the microscopic spores of a virulent disease.

No one could later recall the scenes the floats were trying to depict.

No one took any pictures of the floats, which suggests that the chaos of the parade occurred in the days before cell phones came equipped with cameras, or, alternatively (or alternately, depending upon your point of view, whether you live within the boundaries of time and space or outside those boundaries, what some would call the sphere of the imagination and others would call eternity), that in the absurd (but also surreal) anxiety of the moment, everyone armed with a camera/cell phone, or even a plain old camera for that matter, simply forgot that public disturbances of any kind had become an opportunity for the swelling ranks of unpaid photojournalists everywhere.

No one took any pictures.

Besides, the people who were closest could not even see. The scent from the inner ring of bodyguards had gotten into their eyes and their eyes were stinging, and some even thought their eyeballs were melting, and they were all rubbing their eyes and blinking back tears, but all they could see was a black circle with fire burning along the outer edge, the glowing corona of all their accumulated fears, their paranoias, their manias, their unbidden bouts of madness, their tucked away sense of perpetual loathing, whatever they might be feeling guilty about. It was like staring into the abyss of the collective unconscious. What some would call the collective soul. What others would call Sheol, and others Hades, both neutral holding cell type places where the souls of the recently departed await (hopefully) some sort of judgment before ascending (their hope, as opposed to descending) to Nirvana or paradise or Abraham's bosom, which leads one to imagine a sort of giant amusement park with couples taking boat rides through dark tunnels with appropriate romantic background music and trying their luck at skill games like Jacob's Ladder and devouring tons of cheap lemonade and ice-cream and clouds of cotton candy, and no matter what they eat they are always twenty-five years old and reflect picture-perfect health, without even the fear of tooth decay, because their bodies (and teeth) are now incorruptible, and, depending upon who you talk to, even unbelievers can get into this amusement park, assuming, of course, that they recant their unbelief, and who wouldn't recant given the alternative, which, according to some, is a place of general wickedness, like Gehenna (which is not to be confused with a hip tattoo parlor whose owners picked the name from a list of mythological places), where apparently there is no indoor plumbing and everyone sits around in their own watery, muddy filth and the stench is overpowering, and yet it is also a very dry place, which is something of a paradox, where the rain turns to black ash as it falls and gets into your lungs and breathing becomes very difficult; or if you were terribly evil (which from Dante's perspective meant you had rebelled against some kind of ultimate authority, which sort of makes Dante a pre-Fascist; then again, maybe everyone is a Fascist at heart, or would be, if they were the ones in positions of authority) then descending would mean a place of eternal torment and damnation like, for example, the Lake of Fire, which might be a great sea of fire where fire flows and drips and falls from the sky like rain or water or molten lead, a place where everyone is suffering from a great, burning, unquenchable thirst — which certain progressive theologians have argued is simply a thirst for the presence of God which can now never be slaked, but which others have taken quite literally, which may explain why the Egyptians and some rebellious Vikings and a few overly ambitious Polynesians and many, many others throughout the centuries packed their canoes or their symbolic canoes (sarcophagi) or their rafts or their seagoing ships with all sorts of provisions, including (presumably) jars of water, for the journey into (or through? or beyond?) the afterlife, because you can never be sure where you will end up but you certainly want to be prepared if you end up in a place where the souls of the damned and all sorts of fallen angels, their bodies blackened and charred from an eternity of overpowering heat, float about, writhing in agony, or at least shame.

Happily, not everyone went blind.

Señor Mendoza thought he smelled the sweet smell of gardenias from his boyhood (or perhaps it was from Soledad's girlhood), and breathing in deeply this heady aroma he stepped fearlessly, even brazenly, towards the line of floats, towards the last float in particular, unconcerned about the amber-tinted bubble of danger represented by the inner ring of bodyguards (who were at that very moment shifting over from single shot mode to automatic) or the possibility of intransigent, punitory blindness, or perhaps he was just unaware. The younger teacher stepped after him, trying to pull him back.

Later, people described hearing a short burst of popping sounds that reminded them of the mechanical whirr of dozens of motorcycles roaring past, and then several abrupt clicks, the echo lingering, and then dissolving. Those who were still trying to catch a glimpse of the naked Salma de la Prada, which is to say those who had not been overpowered (and then blinded) by the scent of violence emanating from the bodyguards, later said they saw flashes of light as bright as solar flares and white smoke curling up into the air, and some said they could smell burning rubber, and others said it was a burnt diesel smell, and some said it smelled vaguely like Linseed oil, and others thought it was coffee beans roasting, or maybe peanuts.

Some heard voices jabbering in German. Or maybe it was a German-sounding laughter (haughty? robust? stoic? efficient?).

A few at the back of the crowd looked up, following the paths of what they assumed were bullets, and saw tiny black holes appearing at random in the blue sky and the sky shuddering and a sludgy, black liquid falling to the earth like muddy drops of rain.

People started to run.

People started to run as if they were ants scattering before the blackness of a coming storm.

People started to run as if a siren had sounded and the skies were suddenly and mysteriously black with airplanes from the Second World War and the breeze (which had now become an enormous wind, a night terror shaking the dust of fallen stars from its wings) was the sound of falling bombs.

The older teacher and Gisela ran off in search of wine, the older teacher making obscene remarks having nothing to do with the parade or the unmoving line of Moulin Rouge floats or the possibility that the bodyguards were firing their Uzis at the sky just for fun, and Gisela giggling in response to everything he said.

Three members of the inner ring, thirty-three-and-a-third percent of the field of towheaded warriors, leapt off the last float and pushed their way through the retreating crowd in the direction of Señor Mendoza and the younger teacher.

Small clouds of white Uzi smoke hovered all around, the bright sunlight streaming in through the clouds but then changing direction, becoming a thousand points of beaming, refracted sunlight, a soft, hazy, silent explosion.

Even those who were not blind found it difficult to see.

Some passed out on the ground, perhaps from gulping in too much smoke, or perhaps they suffered from an underlying and heretofore unknown heart condition, or perhaps because they thought the end of the world, a topic that had received a lot of press of late, was now becoming a reality.

Then the smoke began to clear.

To Malachi it looked like the world was now under water. The floats had started moving again, and the bodyguards were once again lounging about on the edges of the floats and chatting lazily in German and laughing even when nothing funny had been said, but everything was happening slowly, with the deliberate, exaggerated, rounded movements and twisted facial expressions of slow-motion, underwater cinematography.

Señor Mendoza and the younger teacher were now sitting next to Salma de la Prada on the red velvet sofa. Salma de la Prada was whispering into Señor Mendoza's ear and laughing softly, or perhaps cooing, her hands placed casually on his leg, and his face was glowing with the ecstasy that the words of Salma de la Prada promised. The younger teacher was staring at the German bodyguards who were surveying a once again well-behaved crowd.

Malachi took a single step, as if to follow the float, as if he had suddenly remembered he wanted to speak with Salma de la Prada, but then he collided with the owner of an unseen voice who was calling out his name with increasing volume.

"*Hola*, Broken Bike, *hola*, Broken Bike, Broken Bike!"

It was as if the voice was trying to wake him up.

"Where are you going in such a hurry, Broken Bike?"

Malachi stared at the unrecognizable face. He had no idea how to respond.

"*Hola*, Broken Bike, what's the matter with you?"

There was a short silence.

"Broken Bike?"

And then Malachi recognized the voice, and thus the face. Both belonged to his neighbor three doors down. But Malachi still did not know what to say. He was not even certain if saying something was required.

"It is still the same with you, eh, Broken Bike. Always you are disappearing into the darkness to watch a picture show. Never looking out at the world. Never noticing what is real. What is right in front of you. Hah! And now your movie star is right there in front of you and you do nothing. Hah! Your sex queen goddess and you forget your tongue. Oh, Broken Bike, it is very funny. I am sorry but it is very funny." The woman began to laugh, a series of short staccato bursts like exploding suns, and Malachi noticed she was wearing the same flowery dress she wore when pruning her azaleas, but he did not think this strange. "You are like all young men," she said, after the laughter had subsided. "You do not know what to do, what to say. Life is gibberish to your ears, an epic giglamesh, a sweet, musical *glíglico* that you do not understand. Such a pity. It is a wonder the army of your sex queen movie star did not feel sorry for you and put you out of your misery."

Then the woman's tone changed, somewhat abruptly, but Malachi did not think this was strange either. He was sort of expecting it. "But there are many more dangers to consider, Broken Bike," she said, and her pupils narrowed to the point of disappearing, leaving only two flinty, colorless discs, like the eyes of a blind person. "But you already know this." She took his arm and led him away from the noise of the parade route and the faint smell of a gun battle, and he went without complaint, without a sound, not because he had given up or had nothing better to do or because he knew she was right, all of them good reasons. Malachi went with her because he suddenly realized that God works in mysterious ways. "You can speak with your sex queen movie star later," she said. "But not now. Now there are too many eyes watching, too many ears listening."

They were headed for a dive that was once the talk of the town, she said, it used to be called La Campana, it was very fancy, but now it is nothing, a sleepy ghost next to an auto parts store and junkyard on one side and a fenced-in parking lot on the other. It was just a few blocks away, she told Malachi, and he had not known about it before (a surprising revelation), and when they got there it seemed to be less than nothing, an abandoned shadow of a three-story building that may or may not have once gleamed like a palace in the sunlight, but it was now clearly less than nothing with its boarded up windows and vaguely pink stucco crumbling in places and the perimeter littered with broken glass and empty beer cans and clouds of graffiti sprayed here and there, wherever the graffiti artists could reach, slogans and curses and derogatory epithets and soulful laments and declarations of eternal love written in bright greens and dusty blues and swirling, dazzling blacks and deep, bloody reds. A rusted neon sign like an old movie house marquee was loosely bolted to the corner on the parking lot side. The neon sign hadn't worked in years and looked like it might come crashing down with the next strong gust of wind.

-35-

The crumbling structure that used to be La Campana:
Malachi follows his neighbor from three doors down without question. He follows her up a set of crumbling stairs. She stops a moment to stare at a small tarnished brass bell fixed to the exterior. So he stops. He hears her mumble something under her breath, almost like cursing, and then she pushes her way through a rotting, mahogany door that is hanging by a single hinge. He follows her through the door. She stops again, as if she has lost her bearings. Her head turns this way and that, but there is very little light. All Malachi is able to make out are the gray shadows of a set of stairs that end in absolute darkness, and on the tiled floor, perhaps because it is illuminated by a narrow wedge of afternoon sunlight, he notices dozens of tiny black scuff marks or burn marks. He wonders what kind of fire would cause such markings. Then he notices that his neighbor is also staring at the burn marks. Perhaps she, too, is wondering what had caused them. Or perhaps she is remembering. Then she starts whispering, or someone starts whispering. '*Pedir la luna,*' the whispering voice says. The words are filled with a haunting sense of great sadness. Then Malachi follows his neighbor from three doors down towards a Spanish-style archway with the paint peeling. The archway marks the entrance to what was once an elegant bar.

Malachi does not know how much time has passed since they left the parade. They are now sitting at a small café table in the once elegant bar. But it is a strange place. It is just a single narrow room, like a waiting area in a railway station from the 1940s. You can see a bare, pale patch behind the counter where there had once been a mirror. You can see other tables here and there. You can see where the padded booths that once lined the wall have been ripped out. You can see the bare, light patches where they were. Like tombstones in a cemetery, Malachi thinks. The smell of death is everywhere. He wonders what kind of place La Campana had been in its glory days. It is hard to guess. For one thing, there is not much light. Just the gloomy, diffuse dimness of being indoors on a bright sunny day and the soft, far-away orange glow of two glass globes fixed to the ceiling. For another thing, the bar is the only part of this gigantic, dilapidated pink stucco behemoth that he has seen.

  The bar is empty except for the two of them and a lonely fat man of a bartender who spends all of his time sitting at a table in the middle of the bar watching a television (cartoons) perched precariously on a small diagonal shelf in the corner above an ancient relic of a cash register. The cord from the television drops down into the abyss behind the register. Next to the register there are several more glass shelves that end abruptly where the bare, pale patch begins. The shelves are empty except for a couple of bottles of Suisse La Bleue and a single bottle of 1691 Clos de Griffier Vieux Cognac. The bottle of cognac is bone dry. It was polished off years ago. Yes, Malachi thinks, it must have been a very elegant bar indeed, although it could also have been a café or a two-star (one-star?) restaurant or even a private club. With the windows boarded up and the lack of good interior lighting it is difficult to make a good guess. Malachi suddenly feels as if he has been sitting in this bar for centuries. The sounds from the festival have hidden themselves away like mice. Malachi sighs, his open mouth like a clock ticking, begins to form a word but then the word dissolves. The clock of his open mouth is still ticking.

  The woman says her name is Isidora. It is a good thing she says this, for Malachi was beginning to wonder. Nothing exists unless it has a name. Someone said that once. His grandfather, perhaps, although he doesn't ever remember meeting his grandfather, or a nun he did meet on a bus going to the zoo, or a German tourist who stopped him just outside the Armani store at the airport mall (Malachi was scouting talent) to ask in broken English where the taxis were. So there she is, Isidora, an ancient Spanish name which must mean something beyond the mere fact of granting his neighbor corporeal existence, Malachi is certain of this (as much as one can be certain of anything, even death), he is on the verge of remembering, it is on the tip of his tongue, but no, he has lost it. Then the woman, Isidora, whom Malachi has known previously only as his neighbor from three doors down, the woman in the flowery dress he has noticed on occasion, however incidentally, out in her front yard with pruning shears pruning her azaleas, disappears through a black curtain near the back of the bar (or café or restaurant or private gentlemen's club).

Isidora's departure is followed by an excruciatingly lengthy period of absolute silence. Even the bartender's cartoon characters have become mute. Malachi suddenly realizes that the floor is tilted at roughly a forty-five-degree angle, which would seem to defy the laws of physics, at least in south Florida, and for the briefest of moments Malachi wonders about this, but he concludes, quickly and without any additional inner commentary, that the universe, reality, if you will, at this particular juncture of time and space, is itself tilted, simple as that. Then the general noise of the universe reasserts itself. Malachi imagines that he hears the sound of someone tiptoeing so as not to attract any unwarranted attention. To Malachi each tiny footstep pricks his brain as if dozens of tiny suspension feeders, most likely goose barnacles, have cemented themselves to his skull (the weakest part along the sphenoparietal suture) and are in the process of cracking it open. Then Malachi hears the sound of a door opening and closing. The barnacles pause in their busy work. The clock is no longer ticking. A fog of confusion spreads out across his shoulders and then filters into his lungs, like a great chill. Then Malachi orders a beer and the fat man disengages himself from his cartoons (it is an awkward moment) and brings Malachi a green bottle without a label and then re-enters the world of his cartoons. Malachi drinks from the green bottle while he is waiting for Isidora to return. The pale liquid inside the bottle doesn't taste like beer at all. After a while the fat man leaves through the same black curtain as Isidora, but he leaves the cartoons on. After a while Malachi forgets he is waiting and becomes absorbed in the cartoons.

Malachi found himself watching a very strange cartoon indeed. He did not catch the title. It was a silent cartoon, except for a little background music (symphonic, from the 1950s) and occasional sound effects (squeaky, balloon sounds and bizarre moaning sounds and cars whizzing by and a crash and a strange ethereal buzzing sound and the sounds of war, buildings falling to the ground, explosions, that sort of thing). Malachi assumed it was a French cartoon. It opened with a woman standing on a partially deflated leather ball or a squishy but surprisingly durable balloon, but she wasn't directly on top, she was sort of leaning out at an angle, like a figure stuck on top of a cake, only it was a ball (or a balloon) so she couldn't help listing to one side, and then you could see that there were hundreds of balls or squishy balloons each with a woman sticking out from the curvature, a subtle commentary perhaps on the theory of multiple universes or the ethics of cloning or perhaps even a critique of Fascism. Yes, Malachi was certain it was a French cartoon. At the twenty second mark you could see a row of something behind each solitary woman, like a tiny forest or a mountain range, but then the camera zoomed in on one of the balls (balloons) and you could see on the other side of the woman a town spread out against the sky like the old mining towns in Colorado in the 1870s. The opening sequence took forty seconds. Then you could see a farmer from the old town (where else could he have come from?), but he was a very poor farmer, or perhaps still a novice, which seemed odd given how old he looked, but nothing he planted seemed to grow, and he tried everything he could think of to make his plants grow, but his ideas were flawed, like supporting the leafy appendages of his plants with sticks (what kind of plants were these anyway?), or hammering nails into the leaves and hanging a giant magnet above the garden to attract growth, this didn't make a whole lot of sense to Malachi, and because nothing worked, the farmer started weeping, copious tears, a flood of tears, and that was the magic formula, the tears. At the four-minute mark the farmer's plants all of a sudden began to grow, and they became super-sized plants, the kind that would win prizes (maybe not the Grand Prize, but certainly a host of Blue Ribbons) at any county fair, and the farmer was quite pleased with himself and he was humming and he did a little happy dance and the background music sounded jovial the way it does on a carousel, but also kind of sad, like an old Edith Piaf song. But at the five minute mark the tone of the music changed to something more sinister to call attention to the fact that the farmer's tears had also caused the snails, which no one had noticed up till that point in the cartoon, to grow as large as tanks, most of them, and some even larger, and then the snails began to attack the town, devouring everything in their path and smashing cars and the townspeople were getting squished, and then at the six minute mark the giant snails were all of a sudden zooming down city streets, knocking down skyscrapers, like they were alien spacecraft intent on conquering the Earth, and it seemed to Malachi that the animator had lost control of his cartoon at that point, as if he had been working for hours and hours and needed a break so he decided to watch *War of the Worlds* (the 1953 black-and-white movie version starring Gene Barry and Ann Robinson) and when he returned to his animator's desk he had forgotten where his story was going so he filled in the gaps with images from the movie. That was the gist of the cartoon, as far as Malachi could tell.

The cartoon was eleven minutes long.

At the seven-minute mark the giant snails raided a brothel and carried off some of the girls and apparently ate them.

At the eight-minute mark someone pushed their way through the rotting mahogany door out front and the interior of the bar was suddenly illuminated by a blast of sunlight that made it difficult to see what was going on in the cartoon, and then the diffuse gloominess of the bar returned. A young man about twenty-five came in and sat down next to Malachi, but he didn't say a word. Malachi wasn't sure what he had missed.

At the nine-minute mark the snails had apparently won the war, but just as in the H. G. Wells story, their victory was short-lived. They collapsed moments after the last of the people had run off into the mountains to hide. Dozens of snails were lying in heaps, and then time speeded up and their giant snail flesh rotted away and their shells crumbled.

Malachi wondered if maybe Salvador Dali was the animator.

At the ten-minute mark Malachi heard the side door open and close and then the shuffling of heavy feet, and then a couple of figures sat down at the counter, but Malachi couldn't see who they were.

At the ten minute, thirty seconds mark the camera zoomed in once again on the farmer, who was busy trying to get another group of plants to grow. He seemed to have forgotten about the effect of his tears on the first group. Or maybe he had learned his lesson with the snails. Malachi wasn't sure. The meaning of the cartoon kept shifting. It looked like the farmer was now living in the desert. Or maybe he had been in the desert the whole time. Perhaps that was the source of his difficulty.

At the eleven-minute mark the credits began rolling and the young man sitting next to Malachi pushed his chair back from the table as if he needed some extra room to breathe. The young man (twenty-five? thirty?) was wearing a silvery-colored designer jump suit (it kind of looked like an astronaut's suit), Reebok sneakers and a pair of Porsche Design sunglasses. He was very thin, thin shoulders, a thin face, thin lips, the features of a mannequin, and his hair was slicked back, a wet look, but not greasy, as if he had just emerged from a swimming pool. But his most striking feature was his tan. He was overly tanned, he seemed to glow even in the dim light of La Campana, as if he moved only and always beneath the light of a tanning bed. Grinning at Malachi as if they were old friends, as if they had been watching cartoons together since they were children, he started talking in a very loud voice. At first Malachi thought he was talking about the cartoon, but the relationship between what the young man was saying and the cartoon was tenuous at best.

"That's the way to kill some time," he said.

Malachi stared at him.

"You know what I mean?"

Malachi said that he did. He heard grumbling from the two shadowy figures sitting at the counter by the black curtain, perhaps they were bothered by the suddenly loud voice of the young man, but the grumbling was a fairly vague sound, like it had been traveling for miles under water to get there. Malachi still couldn't see who they were. The young man smiled wearily, oblivious to the grumbling.

"Don't get me wrong," the young man said. "I don't mind the time it took to get here. That's part of my job. But you think he'd have the courtesy to pick me up at the airport. I don't even know the name of his hotel."

"Man, what are you talking about?"

"You mean who."

"Okay, who?"

"Manny."

"Manny?"

"Manuelo."

"Man, I still don't know what you're talking about."

"Manuelo. Juliano Manuelo Marquez. The movie director. I called him yesterday and said I was coming out. MGM wanted to know if he was interested in doing a reprise of his masterpiece, *The Old Guitarist*. But he didn't answer. But he never answers, he says phones are a fucking nuisance, an invasion of his privacy, a plot by the government, or some fucking shit like that, but MGM wanted an answer pronto, you don't mess around with those boys, so I said of course he's interested, and they asked when they could set up a preliminary meeting to hash things out, and I said how about Tuesday, Manny always likes to start a new project on a Tuesday, and they said fine, and that's when I called and left a message, said I was coming out. Do you know what it costs to get a last-minute flight out of Mexico City? Fuck. I don't even know what he's doing here."

The grumbling from the shadowy figures at the counter grew suddenly louder. For a split second Malachi thought he heard the dusty snorting of two bulls pawing at the ground, but then the sound faded, barely registering a blip in his upper consciousness.

"Who the fuck is Juliano Manuelo Marquez?" Malachi said.

But the young man's voice had already trailed off. A *Road Runner* cartoon had come on and he had started watching. Malachi wasn't interested in any more cartoons. Instead, he watched the young man for a while, but then it was like he was watching a cartoon anyway. He had the oddest sensation that he was watching himself. But then he realized he was looking at his own photographic negative, a facsimile likeness punched out from the inside, a caricature. The young man was absorbed in the *Road Runner* cartoon, or perhaps by the cartoon, thought Malachi, as if he had been swallowed whole, and as he was thinking this peculiar thought it suddenly seemed that he (the young man) was actually suspended in the pale, yellowish shimmering light beaming out from the television, and for a moment Malachi lost sight of him, as if he (the young man) had dissolved, his molecules mixing with the molecules of the pale, yellowish television light, as if the world of the cartoon and the world of the bar were merging, a re-ordering of reality at the subatomic level. Malachi was convinced that if he turned to the cartoon he would see the young man (and thus his own photographic negative) wandering about the strangely undusty cartoon world of a cartoon Arizona in search of an effective means for ending the life of the Road Runner, assuming the young man was the Wiley Coyote character — but then what was Malachi? Was he the Road Runner? And who were Wiley Coyote and the Road Runner anyway? When you got right down to brass tacks. When you got down to the bare essentials. Were they another pair of photographic negatives running circles around each other in a never-ending loop? And what if the young man was the one trying to escape the Coyote's wily clutches, assuming Malachi and the young man had reversed roles, leaving the Coyote (Malachi) to fall with dizzying speed over the edge of a cliff with several tons of TNT strapped to his back and land several miles below in a gigantic white poof of smoke.

  Malachi gave a short uncomprehending laugh, a silent inner laugh that disturbed no one, and gave up on the inner complexities of this odd comparison. He suddenly felt like he had known the young man for years, and then he wondered exactly how old the young man was, for upon closer inspection he appeared much older than twenty-five, closer to thirty-five, or even forty. What Malachi had assumed were characteristics of youth (thinness, a darkly glowing tan) seemed now like they had been painted on. The image of a mannequin overpowered every other image, even the cartoon one.

"Juliano Manuelo Marquez is the greatest movie director of our time," said the ageless mannequin man, as if there had never been a lull in the conversation. "He is the greatest movie director who ever lived."

Malachi finished his beer.

"Sure," Malachi said. "It sounds like a famous name."

"Or one of the greatest, you would have to give him that. In the top one hundred at the very least."

"Sure."

"There's no telling how far up the ladder he would have gone if he had been born in Los Angeles, say, and not San Pedrito, a nothing of a village in the middle of nowhere Mexico."

"Uhh hunh."

Malachi sat looking at the empty beer bottle. He allowed the words of the ageless mannequin man to flow through him, an incessant flow, without worrying too much if they made any sense. He said "Uhh hunh" at appropriate intervals to keep the conversation moving. Or sometimes he said nothing at all and just stared into space, nodding slightly, reflexively.

"To be honest, I was just making up that shit about San Pedrito."

". . . ."

"He didn't grow up in San Pedrito. No. I think he actually spent his formative years in San Diego, if you want to know the truth. I think his family moved back to wherever they were from when he was nine or ten. Maybe they got deported."

"Uhh hunh."

"Hell, I don't even know where San Pedrito is. But it was some place like that. In the middle of nowhere."

". . . ."

"He's got to be in his sixties by now. That's getting up there. And he's made something like sixty films too. Sixty films and he's in his sixties. That's got to be a record if you ask me."

"Uhh hunh."

"Pretty god damn amazing. MGM wants him to a do a reprise of his masterpiece, *The Old Guitarist*. They think it's got real potential."

Then the ageless mannequin man noticed the empty beer bottle on the table and grinned at Malachi. The precise attitude conveyed by this grin was difficult to determine.

"Say, where's the bartender?"

Malachi shrugged.

"Hey, anyone know where the bartender is?"

The ageless mannequin man had lifted his voice to a decibel level usually associated with rude, noisy shouting at football games in an attempt to reach the ears of the two shadowy figures still sitting in the shadows at the counter. They grumbled something, but it was unclear just what they said, or even if they were aware they had been asked a question.

"Thanks!"

Malachi thought he heard a tone of sarcasm or even thinly veiled contempt in the voice of the ageless mannequin man, and he turned his attention to the two shadowy figures at the counter to see if they had also noticed, but he still couldn't make out their faces. He assumed this was because of the way they were sitting and the absence of any direct light, and yet he was also struck by the impression that they were shrouded in an unnatural, perhaps sinister, but certainly mischievous darkness that seemed to project outwards, and he wondered about this. The darkness seemed almost alive, a glowing picture of health. By contrast, the light in La Campana, what little light there was, was a dead or dying thing, it was riddled with holes (bullet holes?), as if it were the victim of a horrendous, unspeakable crime. You could see stretch marks of shadow where the light had retreated. Spider veins of darkness now covered the walls. And as Malachi sat there in what could only be a waiting room for death (this was both his first and second thought), he suddenly felt that he was standing in two worlds at the same time. He could taste the stench of rotting flesh, but also the saltwater flood of a woman having an orgasm and the champagne bubbles of weddings.

It was almost like he had stepped through a portal into another time (a more elegant time, perhaps) but had only made it halfway through, and so he was trapped in the fluid, twilight, shape-shifting darkness of the in-between, which, as Malachi himself wryly observed, obscured the past and the present as well as the future. He wasn't sure how to extricate himself, but then he wasn't sure he was supposed to. He tried to zero in on the eyes of the shadowy figures, as if their eyes held the key to both their identities and Malachi's fate (which some might say was strangely prophetic even as it seemed tragically absurd), but their eyeballs danced around in a crazy, gyrating fashion like the glinting wings of beetles bathed in early morning starlight.

The two men (men?) had not ceased their grumbling since they sat down, though the volume increased or decreased with great variability, as if they were arguing over baseball scores or what to eat for dinner or why their wives had left them or how long before they could retire. Malachi assumed they were men, as opposed to unusually masculine women with tattoos of lightning bolts or laughing skulls on thick, fleshy arms, based on the hunched-over, guarded way they sat, as if they were trading uncut diamonds for heroin or cocaine while they guzzled beer, and also the general odor of sweat and urine and horse breath that enveloped them like a cloud.

Malachi wondered if the two men were struggling with the darkness as he was. He could not help wondering. The longer he sat there trying to sift through his thoughts, to make sense of what was happening, to understand the nature of this darkness which seemed both physical and temporal (and perhaps even spiritual, a billion soulless bodies on the edge of oblivion, gasping for breath like fish drowning in the muck of a newly evaporated sea), the deeper and more unyielding the darkness became. Then he heard one of the men laugh, and then the other, and he recognized the timbre of their laughter, or he thought he did, or he was beginning to, but then he was distracted by the ageless mannequin man, who was trying to explain in greater detail why he had come to Miami from Mexico City.

"So I had no idea where he had gone, and no clue how to find him either, and then Beatrice, she's sort of a secretarial assistant, she wants to be an actress but she has no talent for acting, unless you consider big tits a talent, and Manny doesn't care about big tits but he felt sorry for her so he gave her a job filing bank statements and scheduling lunches and limos and going shopping. Anyway, Beatrice said Manny was on some sort of a scouting trip, and wherever he went he was getting paid, there was a boatload of money pouring into the account, and we looked it up and she was absolutely right. In the last few months an outfit called La Campana Enterprises paid Manny over two-hundred thousand dollars. That's a hell of a lot of dough for a scouting trip, but that's beside the point. But then they stopped paying him. I called the number but it was disconnected, but I didn't know about the address, so I came to Miami. You know the address for this place doesn't exist. Not anymore. 25½ La Campana Boulevard. There is no La Campana Boulevard. And certainly no 25½. I only found this place by accident. A drunk at the Metro station remembered a fancy club from the seventies called La Campana, and he was fairly precise about how to get here for an old drunk, but it sort of felt like I was wandering about in a dream. I mean it feels like I haven't slept in a week. And now that I'm here, it still feels like a dream."

Laughing a hollow, unconvincing laugh, the ageless, mannequin man glanced up from the empty bottle and the table to the empty bar. "I sure could use a drink," he said. "I don't even care what. The last few days have been hell."

The grumbling of the two shadowy men at the counter intensified, as if neither man was willing to concede an inch in their debate over baseball scores or dinner menus or the logic or illogic of their ex-wives or the chances that they would have a sufficient income for their golden years. The shadowy cloud of their concealment seemed now to glow, as if it had become embossed with a lacquer finish.

Then the back door opened and closed and Malachi heard the sound of quick but heavy footsteps and then the fat bartender re-emerged. He stopped for a moment, as if he were uncertain that the world was a solid, physical place. He looked over at Malachi and the ageless mannequin man, and then at the glowing shadow, and the grumbling became even louder, and then the ageless mannequin man saw the bartender, and relieved that now he could order something to drink, and also perhaps bleary-eyed from lack of sleep, lurched in the direction of the bar just as the two shadowy men were making a beeline towards Malachi, who was still sitting at the table. But the ageless mannequin man wasn't looking where he was going or how fast the two shadowy figures were moving through the gloom, and in his oblivious state he was shouting at the bartender about how many beers he wanted to drink and the fat bartender not saying anything, just blinking stupidly in the dingy dim light, and then the three of them, the ageless mannequin man and the two men from the shadows collided and everyone fell to the floor and a couple of tables were knocked over and a few chairs went flying. Malachi did not wait around to see what happened after that.

-36-

That so many threads of meaning had converged in the dingy dimness of La Campana seemed to Malachi proof of the existence of God. He wondered that his neighbor, Isidora, had chosen that exact spot to escape the prying eyes and listening ears that she said were lingering along the parade route. (He never once considered her complicity.) He wondered that the ageless mannequin man had arrived precisely when he did. He wondered that the television programming team at Channel 39 (the network that was beaming out the cartoons on a Saturday afternoon) had selected the cartoons that they did and what profound meaning lay buried in the dust of the dead snails or was illuminated by the spectacular failures of Wiley Coyote. He wondered at his own clumsiness at failing to recognize Bull and Horse, and then at his own agility in escaping the dingy dimness of La Campana at the most opportune moment. All of this suggested to Malachi the hand of God, or if not God, then at least a well-designed facsimile of God, a photographic negative, perhaps, better suited to the incomprehensible vagaries of life beneath a middle-aged sun, the random nature of existence in a world bombarded daily by gamma rays and x-rays and the exhaust fumes of alien spacecraft, which some said was simply the jet-fuel smell of unanswered prayers, and everywhere, even along the cleanest, whitest beaches of Florida or Puerto Rico or elsewhere in the Caribbean, you were breathing in unseen clouds of cosmic dust from the Dark Horse nebula (also known as the Great Dark Horse nebula or the Pipe nebula), a mere 650 light years away, containing, among other elements, trace amounts of ammonia, formaldehyde, and even nitrous oxide.

    Malachi smiled at his good fortune. He had a few hours to kill so he killed them. He wandered through a labyrinth of alleyways until he crossed 12th Avenue and went into the metro station. It was after five and he didn't know when the next train was coming, but he didn't care, he wasn't going anywhere. He just wanted to sit on one of the green benches facing the northbound side and look out at the red rooftops of the apartment complex directly below and think about what he was going to say to Salma de la Prada.

    For Malachi, the metro station platform was a place where he could let his mind wander freely without the fear of interruption. Sitting on any one of the green benches on the platform he was both a part of the bustle of humanity and detached from it at the same time. Nobody bothered him. Sometimes he faced the southbound side after the sun had set so he could see the distant lights of the airplanes landing and taking off at Miami International. But on this particular afternoon there were still a few hours of daylight left. He took out the Velázquez brothers' script and began leafing through the pages. There was no one else on the platform. The traffic on the streets below seemed like a distant memory.

    Then quite without realizing it, Malachi slipped into a dream. He found himself wandering through the airport mall and it was in the middle of the day but all the stores were closed. There was a sign in each window that said closed for renovations. Malachi stopped in front of the Armani store. At first he was only looking at his reflection and wondering where everyone had gone, but then he looked at the mannequins in the window and he saw they were all in various stages of undress. Some were missing arms or legs or even heads, as if the sales associates had been in a tremendous almost blind hurry to change their clothes and didn't care about the damage they might cause by yanking off useless limbs by accident, and who cared if a few heads popped off as well. Then Malachi noticed that every mannequin that still possessed a head possessed the same exact face, and he was not surprised in the least that they were all the face of the ageless mannequin man he had met earlier that afternoon at La Campana. He stared at the sad, thin-lipped smile as if he were reminiscing about time spent with a long-lost childhood friend. He wondered what the little fellow was doing, if he had found Juliano Manuelo Marquez, or if he was still watching cartoons. Then all at once the mannequins (those who still possessed heads) in the Armani window and in the windows of the other stores opened their mouths like bullet holes and began to scream, a horrendous, thin-lipped scream that caused the air to vibrate, and then crack, and then there was a tear in the fabric of reality and Malachi saw layer after layer of subatomic particles flaking away like soot where the crack had appeared. Soon Malachi was wading through an ocean of soot. One by one the screaming mannequins were consumed by this ocean. First their legs disappeared, and then their arms, their shoulders, and lastly their heads, but the screams of the now drowned (buried?) mannequins were somehow as loud as ever. It sounded like the screech of metal tires on metal rails.

It was at that point that Malachi realized he was dreaming and woke up. A train heading north was pulling away from the station. The sun had already set and the sky was a swirling purplish light because of the glow of the city, and beyond the glow he could see the faint glimmer of a few stars. He shoved the Velázquez brothers' script back into his vest pocket and headed for the street.

The voices inside his head were all chattering away, each with a different strategy for presenting Salma de la Prada with the script, each warning him against the sudden paralysis that had gripped him at the parade, each with a different opinion of how the evening ahead would go. But all of them agreed that Salma de la Prada was most certainly at La Mamacita's by now. Or if she wasn't she would arrive there shortly.

The scene at La Mamacita's:
Malachi is at the door of the club almost before he realizes it. He is lost in thought. Perhaps he is thinking about

what he is going to say when he first meets Salma de la Prada. Perhaps not. Who can say what he is thinking? And then he is at the door. The whole building is dark, even the windows are mysteriously blacked out (though perhaps they have always been blacked out), which gives the impression of a bombed-out building in London during World War Two (or it could just as well be a bombed-out building in Berlin or Dresden or Lübeck or Hamburg or Cologne), or, conversely, an air raid shelter. Perhaps it is inaccurate to say this shell of a warehouse gives the impression of a bombed-out building. Perhaps it is more accurate to say that it gives the impression of a washed-out photograph of a bombed-out building in one of the cities already noted, although certainly the cities of Rotterdam and Warsaw and Wieluń and Frampol could be added to the list, and many others as well, Guernica, for example, which gave the Nazis a chance to test the effectiveness of terror bombing in somebody else's war, or Marseilles, which nobody remembers, but not Nagasaki or Hiroshima, that was a different kind of bombing altogether, a different level of destruction.

Malachi pushes his way through the door and the impression of a bombed-out building is replaced with an impression of absolute oblivion, as if a small but still terrifying black hole has swallowed up the interior of La Mamacita's and is gathering up the courage to venture outside. He wonders what has happened. He is no longer standing on the edge of the abyss, he thinks, he has already descended. He notices a ringing in his ears, as if a winged night terror is calling out his name. The ringing grows louder. He can feel the spider vein tentacles of dozens of unseen creatures pricking his skin. Dozens of tiny puncture wounds appear as if from tiny teeth, and before his body can respond with even a flinch, the owners of these teeth, which seem directed by some kind of superhuman intelligence, plunge in through the dozens of tiny, open wounds and race through his bloodstream, surrounding his vital organs with the icy cold embalming fluid of the universe. This is what it feels like, the dizzying sensation that usually accompanies the end of one's life, of any life, of all life.

But Malachi is not dead yet.

He embraces the darkness and the unseen creatures and then the darkness settles. His pulse rate returns to normal, and so does the rate of his breathing, though he had not realized either was elevated. The unseen creatures crawl back underneath their rocks. Then he thinks he sees a glimmer of something in the distance (he is not sure how far away, he is not even sure he is still standing just inside the door at La Mamacita's). He thinks he sees a line of reddish-golden light slicing through the darkness, like an aerial photograph of a busy highway at night with the blur of red taillights and golden headlights sweeping back towards the horizon. He stares at the reddish-golden light until he is certain it is not a figment of his imagination. Then he walks towards it, pushing out at the darkness in front of him and then sweeping back on either side with his hands in a swimming motion, cautiously, as if he is concerned about spider webs or the stray branches of unseen trees.

As he gets closer he hears the faint clatter of masculine laughter and the clinking of full beer bottles and near-full and empty and then the sound of glass breaking as the empties are hurled against a wall, and then the click of automatic weapons, and then more laughter and more bottle clinking and the cycle repeats.

Then a voice calls out to him, asks him what he wants. Malachi is sideswiped with sudden clarity. He realizes that the reddish-golden line of light is the bar at La Mamacita's, a row of humming, buzzing stained glass lamps (a bright cherry red) hanging from the ceiling. Standing at the bar are half a dozen bouncers wearing their leather bullet-proof vests and Billy clubs clipped to their sides, as usual, and heavy black boots with the laces neatly tied and their long black hair pulled back in precise, ponytail fashion.

Malachi is struck by their well-groomed appearance, their bouncer costumes are spotless, even pristine, and they all seem happy and untroubled, as if the evening has not yet taken its toll on their attitudes, as if they are pacifist by nature and only do what they have to do to keep the peace.

The half-dozen happy, untroubled bouncers from La Mamacita's are happily entertaining half-a-dozen blonde-haired German behemoths from the inner circle of Salma de la Prada's unflappable security force. They are also happy, untroubled, chatting away in German and then in perfect English with a few garbled words in Spanish and then back to German, still wearing their amber-tinted sunglasses and their Speedos and their flip-flops and their tight-fitting Spandex t-shirts with the word FÜKKENRÜKEN in fluorescent blue lettering, and Uzis strapped to their backs or leaning up against the counter or on top but within easy reach.

All of the German bodyguards are drunk. They are almost slap-happy they are so drunk. And yet they are as immaculate in their appearance as the half-dozen bouncers, as if they (the bodyguards) had only moments ago picked up their costumes from the dry cleaners and slipped them on. Malachi is staring up at the six bouncers and the six bodyguards, almost straining the muscles in his neck, for they are all half a foot taller than Malachi, at least. The head honcho, Herr Konrad, who appears decidedly older than the rest, is having an animated conversation with two of the younger ones. He is waving his dog-eared copy of *Biedermann und die Brandstifter* in their faces and pointing out passages and having them take turns reading.

Then the voice from before calls out again, and Malachi is wondering where exactly the voice is coming from, and because he cannot tell, he holds up his own dog-eared document, the Velázquez brothers' movie script, for everyone to see, and says he's there to deliver this script to Miss de la Prada. The voice relaxes, as if it has been expecting someone to come along with a script, as if Malachi is no different than any of the messenger boys delivering scripts on a daily basis, as many as ten different messengers with scripts every day. The voice tells Malachi to have a seat at one of the tables, it may be a while, Miss de la Prada is entertaining guests in the VIP Suite, and then the rest of the bouncers and the bodyguards break into happy boisterous laughter, and then one of the Germans, a hulking brute almost seven feet tall who is sitting on top of the bar at the far end, says they (the producers) should put him in one of Miss de la Prada's movies, he's plenty big enough, and then one of the other Germans laughs and says, but not where it counts, and then everyone is ribbing the big lummox, but he's too drunk to care. The rest of the evening unfolds with the precision of an award-winning film. Or at least a box office smash. If you can imagine the scene as part of a movie, you can imagine it done in a jerky, 1940s newsreel-footage style.

"THE HAIL OF BULLETS SCENE AT LA MAMACITA'S"

INT. LA MAMACITA'S — EARLY EVENING (SORT OF A MONTAGE, OR A SERIES OF SHOTS, BUT NOT QUITE)

WIDE ANGLE VIEW OF THE BAR.

WE SEE the **BOUNCERS** from **LA MAMACITA'S** and the **GERMAN BODYGUARDS** standing at the bar, chatting, guzzling beer, laughing. The red stained glass lamps hanging above the bar provide the only light, which extends the length of the bar and perhaps five feet out away from the bar. The rest of **LA MAMACITA'S** is bathed in absolute darkness.

WE HEAR a mix of German and Spanish and English being spoken.

THE CAMERA ZOOMS IN ON MALACHI, who is sitting at a small table half in the light, half in the shadow. **MALACHI** is leafing through the pages of **THE VELÁQUEZ BROTHERS' MOVIE SCRIPT**, but he has to lean out away from the table, holding the **SCRIPT** up in the air to catch a few scraps of the reddish-golden light, so he can see.

WE HEAR the sound of a **DOOR OPENING**, followed immediately by the sound of a second **DOOR OPENING**.

AT THE SAME TIME, THE CAMERA PULLS BACK AND WE SEE the **DOOR** to the **VIP SUITE** opening suddenly and the interior of **LA MAMACITA'S** is immediately bathed in a brilliant **GOLDEN LIGHT**, presumably from a single golden chandelier hanging directly over the great king bed in the **VIP SUITE**, which is past the far end of the bar and then up a set of three carpeted steps (red shag carpeting that has seen better days) and then through a pair of padded oak doors, which means you can't see either the bed or the chandelier from the bar, or at least not easily.

THE CAMERA SHIFTS to the other end of the bar and **WE SEE** the **FRONT DOOR** opening and two heads emerging. As the two heads emerge, the **GOLDEN LIGHT** from the **VIP SUITE** fills the entire room and we see **BULL** and **HORSE** standing at the entrance, blinking in the sudden glare of the **GOLDEN LIGHT**, with surprised looks on their faces.

THE CAMERA SHIFTS IMMEDIATELY BACK to the **DOOR** to the **VIP SUITE** and WE **SEE SALMA DE LA PRADA** moving down the steps and then heading towards the bar. She is flanked by four more **GERMAN BEHEMOUTHS** with **UZIS** strapped to their backs. Trailing **SALMA DE LA PRADA** are **XAVIER MENDOZA** — an old café owner who was picked from the crowd during the **PARADE** for an afternoon of unrestrained pleasure (he was picked because he reminded **SALMA DE LA PRADA** of an old uncle she hadn't seen in years, or perhaps an old boyfriend, or maybe the town where she grew up, or maybe there was no particular reason, maybe it was just a random occurrence, as so many things are) — and **THE YOUNG TEACHER**, who had been trying to restrain **XAVIER** when the **BODYGUARDS** plucked them both out of the crowd, and who had later been invited to participate in the activities in the great king bed, but who had declined (though he did watch), claiming a previous and still unresolved romantic attachment to a young Spanish teacher named **TOMMIE RODRIGUEZ**.

THE CAMERA PULLS BACK AND WE SEE a mix of **BOUNCERS** and **BODYGUARDS** looking in the direction of **SALMA DE LA PRADA** and a mix looking in the direction of **BULL** and **HORSE**.

MALACHI sees **SALMA DE LA PRADA** and stands up, turning slightly, holding the **SCRIPT** in the air. **SALMA DE LA PRADA** smiles at **MALACHI**.

EVERYONE looks at the **SCRIPT** in **MALACHI'S HAND**.

THE YOUNG TEACHER waves at **MALACHI**.

> **YOUNG TEACHER**
> Hola, Malachi. Your salvation awaits!

BULL and **HORSE** are distracted by **THE YOUNG TEACHER'S** greeting. **HORSE** looks in the direction of **THE YOUNG TEACHER'S** voice and sees **SALMA DE LA PRADA**. **BULL** hears the name **MALACHI** but suddenly realizes that **BROKEN BIKE** and **MALACHI** are the same person (who can ever truly understand how the brain works at the subconscious level). The expression on his face resembles religious conviction.

> **HORSE**
> Oye, ñoo! esa heba esta buena pa comersela con ropa y todo!
> (Which means "Oye, fuck! That hottie is good enough to eat with her clothes on and everything!" and which is sort of an odd thing to say since **SALMA DE LA PRADA** is already practically naked, wearing only her bright red thong and her red poodle fur sandals.)

AT THE SAME TIME, BULL sees **MALACHI** and **PULLS** a **GUN**.

> **BULL**
> (walking towards **MALACHI**)
> Ladrón (Thief)! Traidor (Traitor)!
> Me cago en la leche que mamaste, cabróncete de mierda.
>
> (Which means "I shit in the milk you suckled from your mother's

breast you shitty/fucking little bastard.")

MALACHI turns towards the sound of **BULL'S VOICE**, tosses his **SCRIPT** in the air with an overly emotive, theatrical flourish and the **SCRIPT** becomes fifty single sheets of paper whirling about, fluttering, falling to the floor, and in that same moment, instinctively, which is to say without taking a look at the room of bodyguards and bouncers with guns, **MALACHI** pulls out his own **RUBBER MOVIE PROP GUN**, as if the mere appearance of the toy will stop **BULL** in his tracks.

AT THE SAME TIME, SEVEN OF THE TEN GERMAN BODYGUARDS whip out their **UZIS**, all in a single fluid motion.

AT THE SAME TIME, WE HEAR WAGNER'S *RIDE OF THE VALKYRIES* as performed by the American Symphony Orchestra for Edison Records in 1921.

TWO OF THE GERMAN BODYGUARDS turn, shielding SALMA DE LA PRADA, and whisk her back to the safety of the **VIP SUITE**. Her curvy, heart-shaped ass is glistening with sweat as she departs through the air.

AT THE SAME TIME, the **REMAINING GERMAN BODYGUARD** (the one that is seven feet tall) seizes **MALACHI** from behind, disabling him with a double bear-hug karate chop, confiscating the **MOVIE PROP GUN** as he sends **MALACHI** to the floor.

AT THE SAME TIME, THE BOUNCERS dive for cover behind the **BAR** and pull out **CONCEALED HANDGUNS** they weren't supposed to carry so they can return fire as warranted.
AT THE SAME TIME, BULL, still advancing, **FIRES** at **MALACHI** but misses, thanks to the zeal of **THE ONE REMAINING BODYGUARD.**

AT THE SAME TIME, THE YOUNG TEACHER grabs

XAVIER in a sort of tackling motion, which sends both men to the relative safety of the floor. Or perhaps **XAVIER** was in a panic because he suddenly couldn't breathe so he grabbed **THE YOUNG TEACHER** and then fell backwards, pulling him down. Sometimes it is difficult to determine cause and effect.

THE MUSIC OF WAGNER RISES and **FALLS** as appropriate.

The **LIGHT** from the **VIP SUITE** vanishes, as **SALMA DE LA PRADA** is now safely behind closed doors.

AT THE SAME TIME, HORSE pulls out his own **GUN** and begins firing randomly in a misguided attempt to help out his brother.

AT THE SAME TIME, THE SEVEN BODYGUARDS with **UZIS** and the **BOUNCERS** with their **GUNS** open fire on **BULL** and **HORSE**.

WE SEE a **BLINDING FLASH** from the **HAIL OF BULLETS** flying about, which is to say that no one can see anything for a few moments. Actually, **THE EIGHT REMAINING GERMAN BODYGUARDS** can see just fine, as they are wearing their **AMBER-TINTED SUNGLASSES**.

AS THE FLASH OF LIGHT SUBSIDES, WE CAN SEE a photographic negative imprint in the air where **BULL** and **HORSE** had been standing. The imprint is riddled with bullet holes. Then the photographic negative imprint fades and **WE SEE** the lifeless, bullet-ridden bodies of **BULL** and **HORSE** stretched out on the floor.

THE CAMAERA PULLS BACK AND WE SEE the **BOUNCERS** and the **BODYGUARDS** engaged in various activities: some are checking to see if everyone else is all right, some are examining the damage done to the bar, some are sweeping up broken glass since several shelves of glassware were destroyed during the gun battle as well as the mirror behind the bar, the red glass lamps hanging above the bar, and various beer bottles (some full, half-empty, and some empty).

AT THE SAME TIME, someone has turned on the entrance lights, three dim yellow bulbs ensconced in the ceiling above the threshold which provide a smoky glow, just enough to see by.

THE MUSIC OF WAGNER FADES.

AT THE SAME TIME, TWO BODYGUARDS are checking the bodies of **BULL** and **HORSE**. They are chatting with a **THIRD BODYGUARD**, who is still clutching his **UZI** and surveying the battlefield to make sure there is no further threat. **THE THIRD BODYGUARD** possesses the air of one who is in command.

> **THE THIRD BODYGUARD**
> Sind Sie tot?
> (Translation: Are they dead?)

> **ONE OF THE TWO BODYGUARDS**
> Ja, Herr Konrad, Sie sind tot.
> (Translation: Yes, Mr. Konrad,
> they are dead.)

> **THE THIRD BODYGUARD**
> So wüst und schön
> (Translation: So desolate and
> beautiful.)

> **ONE OF THE TWO BODYGUARDS**
> (to the corpses)
> Was ist das für eine Art?
> (Translation: What kind of way is
> that to behave?)

> **THE THIRD BODYGUARD**
> Drum geht die Welt in den Eimer
> (Translation: That's why the

world is going to pot.)

ONE OF THE TWO BODYGUARDS
(still to the corpses)
Was stellen Sie sich eigentlich vor?
(Translation: Who do you think you are?)

THE THIRD BODYGUARD
So wie zwei Schwimmer ringend sich umklammern, Erdrückend ihre Kunst, eingefroren in Tod.
(Translation: These two swimmers wrestling, an oppressive art, frozen in death.)

ONE OF THE TWO BODYGUARDS
Wie Schweine egwürgte.
(Translation: Like strangled pigs.)

WE SEE THE TWO BODYGUARDS rifling through the pockets of **BULL** and **HORSE**, removing anything that could identify the bodies, bagging various items for disposal, pocketing valuables. They are working with great speed and efficiency.

THE THIRD BODYGUARD is still surveying the battle scene, but mostly he is looking at the shredded-by-gunfire remnants of the front door. He can see the deep purplish glow of the evening through the shredded door. He now possesses an air of calm detachment.

THE THIRD BODYGUARD
Das ist Amerika.
(Translation: This is America.)

ONE OF THE TWO BODYGUARDS
Ja, das ist Amerika.
(Translation: Yes, this is America.)

THE THIRD BODYGUARD
  (To the corpses)
  Wir sind immer die Guten,
  diejenigen, die helfen. Wo führt
  das noch hin, wenn keiner mehr
  dem andern glaubt? Ich sag
  immer: Wo führt das noch hin,
  Kinder! Jeder hält den andern
  für einen Brandstifter, nichts als
  Mißtrauen in der Welt. Oder hab
  ich nicht recht?
  (Translation: We are always the
  good ones, the ones who help.
  Where will it all end if we stop
  believing one another? That's
  what I say, where will it all end,
  eh? Everybody thinking the other
  bloke is an arsonist. Nothing but
  mutual suspicion in the world.
  Am I right?)

ONE OF THE TWO BODYGUARDS
  (to the other one)
  Es ist mir alles Wurst.
  (Translation: It's all sausage to
  me.)

THE TWO BODYGUARDS finish rifling through the pockets of **BULL** and **HORSE** and stand up and join **THE THIRD BODYGUARD**, who is still surveying the scene, still with an air of calm detachment. **WE SEE** the scene vaguely reflected in their **AMBER-TINTED SUNGLASSES**.

THE CAMERA PULLS BACK AND WE SEE the hustle and bustle of a great deal of activity.

THE BODYGUARDS OF THE OUTER CIRCLE have arrived and are busy restoring the interior of **LA MAMACITA'S** to the precise condition it was in prior to the gun battle, almost as if they are a stage crew, more sweeping, scrubbing down the floor, repairing the bullet holes in the walls and in the bar, replacing the mirror behind the bar, hanging new red glass hanging lamps above the bar.

AT THE SAME TIME, WE SEE MALACHI in somewhat of a daze on the floor in front of the table where he had been sitting. The pages of the **MOVIE SCRIPT** are scattered all over the floor. **MALACHI'S** arm is clearly broken. It is dangling in places where it should not dangle.
THE BODYGUARD who broke **MALACHI'S** arm is squatting beside him, checking his vital signs and talking in a soothing voice. **WE HEAR THEIR VOICES,** or at least **WE HEAR THE VOICE OF THE BODYGUARD**, but it sounds very far away.

>**THE BODYGUARD BESIDE MALACHI**
>(in English)
>I am sorry my little messenger boy.
>How was I to know it was a toy gun?

>**MALACHI**
>(some inarticulate groaning, a few grimaces)

>**THE BODYGUARD BESIDE MALACHI**
>(smiling, still in English)
>You sit tight my little messenger boy, an ambulance is on the way.

AND THEN WE SEE THE YOUNG TEACHER helping **XAVIER** to a sitting position and **TWO DIFFERENT BODYGUARDS** checking his vital signs with medical equipment from a small black bag. **XAVIER** is still breathing with difficulty and **THE YOUNG TEACHER** is concerned, but **THE TWO DIFFERENT BODYGUARDS** tell him that the old man will be all right. Their voices also sound very far away, like they are underwater.

>**THE TWO DIFFERENT BODYGUARDS**
>He will be fine. Do not worry.
>Whatever it was has passed. Just

a little too much excitement. How old is he?

AND THEN THE CAMERA SWINGS BACK TO THE THIRD BODYGUARD. He is watching the **OUTER CIRCLE OF BODYGUARDS**, who are still engrossed in their restoration work, but close to finishing now.

AT THE SAME TIME, a couple of the **OUTER CIRCLE BODYGUARDS** appear with two body bags and soon the bodies of **BULL** and **HORSE** are bagged and the bags are zipped. **THE TWO OUTER CIRCLE BODYGUARDS** scrub the floor to get rid of the blood and then they carry the bodies away, out through the open jagged-seeming hole where the front door had been. **THE THIRD BODYGUARD** looks again at the hole. It is almost like looking through a doorway to another world, or perhaps a window, the kind of window they have at many a coastal aquarium so people can look in on the fish. For a moment he thinks he can see bubbles rising, as if he is looking through a small window into the abyss of a gigantic aquarium.

Then **TWO COMPLETELY DIFFERENT OUTER CIRCLE BODYGUARDS**, not the ones who took away the bodies, two different ones, remove the remnants of the old shredded door and put a new one in its place. A few other **BODYGUARDS** are painting the newly repaired walls. **AS THE WORK PROGRESSES, WE HEAR THE VOICES** of **THE THIRD BODYGUARD** and the **TWO BODYGUARDS** who had pilfered the bodies of **BULL** and **HORSE**. They are continuing their conversation from before. Their voices sound very close, though we cannot see the men talking.

> **ONE OF THE TWO BODYGUARDS (O. S.)**
> Euresgleichen ist immer so
> ideologisch, immer so ernst, bis
> es reicht zum Verrat —'s ist keine
> rechte Freude dabei.
>
> (A loose translation: It's a shame

these Americans don't care about
private property. Look at them
just sitting there, drinking. Isn't
this their bar?)

THE THIRD BODYGUARD (O. S.)
Das ist gar nicht natürlich.
Heutzutage. Im Zirkus, wo ich
gerungen hab, zum Beispiel - und
drum, sehn Sie, ist er dann auch
niedergebrannt, der ganze Zirkus!
- unser Direktor zum Beispiel, der
hat gesagt: Sie können mir, Sepp! -
Ich heiße doch Josef... Sie können
mir! hat er gesagt: Wozu soll ich
ein Gewissen haben? Wörtlich.
Was ich brauche, um mit meinen
Bestien fertlgzuwerden, das ist
'ne Peitsche. Wörtlich! So einer
war das. Gewissen! hat er gelacht:
Wenn einer ein Gewissen hat, so
Ist es meistens ein schlechtes...
(Translation: They probably have
insurance.)

WE HEAR ALL THREE BODYGUARDS LAUGH.

THE CAMERA PULLS BACK AND WE CAN SEE the men laughing, and a moment later **WE SEE** that the restoration work is complete. **THE THIRD BODYGUARD** waves his hand in the air, whipping it around in a strange figure eight pattern, and then all of **THE GERMAN BODYGUARDS** head for the door. They are all now **CHATTING** amicably in **GERMAN**, laughing and telling jokes.

AT THE SAME TIME, SALMA DE LA PRADA goes floating past, **TWO BODYGUARDS** on either side. She is wearing a small chiffon robe to cover her nakedness and a wide-brimmed hat and sunglasses so you cannot see her eyes or the expression on her face, like Greta Garbo.

THE TWO BODYGUARDS who pilfered the bodies of **BULL** and **HORSE** are walking a step ahead of **THE THIRD BODYGUARD**.

> **ONE OF THE TWO BODYGUARDS**
> (to the other one)
> Was macht denn die Holzwoole?
> (Translation: How are you getting on with your Woodshaving?

THE TWO BODYGUARDS LAUGH.

> **THE THIRD BODYGUARD**
> Was ist der Witz daran?
> (Translation: What's so funny?)

> **ONE OF THE TWO BODYGUARDS**
> Ich sagte ihm: Was macht denn die Holzwoole?
> (Translation: I said to him: How are you getting on with your Woodshaving?)

ALL THREE BODYGUARDS ARE LAUGHING as they head out the door.

THE BODYGUARD BESIDE MALACHI puts a blanket around **MALACHI'S** shoulders. It is not clear where he got the blanket. Perhaps from one of the **OUTER CIRCLE BODYGUARDS**. **MALACHI** is still on the floor.

> **THE BODYGUARD BESIDE MALACHI**
> I have to leave you now, my little messenger boy. Try to be careful with your toy gun. I will no longer be here to watch over you.

THE BODYGUARD BESIDE MALACHI laughs gently and lays the **RUBBER MOVIE PROP GUN** in **MALACHI'S** lap and lumbers off to join the others.

WE SEE MALACHI is beginning to shiver, presumably from shock, hence the blanket. It looks like he may pass out at any moment. He hopes the ambulance will get there soon.

WE ALSO SEE that **XAVIER** is in a very bad way, still breathing heavily, his eyelids are fluttering erratically, his eyeballs rotating in similarly erratic fashion, back and forth and up and down, as if he is trying desperately to identify a familiar face. **THE YOUNG TEACHER** is watching over **XAVIER** until help arrives. They are both still on the floor.

THE BOUNCERS begin to leave, one by one.

WE CAN HEAR A SIREN in the distance, presumably the **AMBULANCE.**

FADE OUT — THE END

The story continues in *The Mad Patagonian: Part Two: Into the Abyss and Back Again*

Printed in Great Britain
by Amazon